THE YOUNG SHALL INHERIT

Aerolan Saga: Book I

By

Larry W Crow and Jennifer L Ricks

Aerolan Saga: The Young Shall Inherit

Copyright: 2001, CrowsToes, USA

Printed in the USA.

Cover Template by: CreateSpace Cover Creator
Interior Map by: Larry W. Crow

First Printing
9 8 7 6 5 4 3 2 1 0

ISBN10: 0-9744042-3-3
ISBN13: 978-0-9744042-3-3

And our thanks:

Larry Crow:

To my loving wife, Penny – who has supported me all these years and encouraged me to finish what I started.
And to my co-author for her diligence, patience and intelligent input throughout the whole wonderful process.

Jennifer Ricks:

To my family and friends who have offered encouragement and support for this work.

Aerolan A World in Turmoil

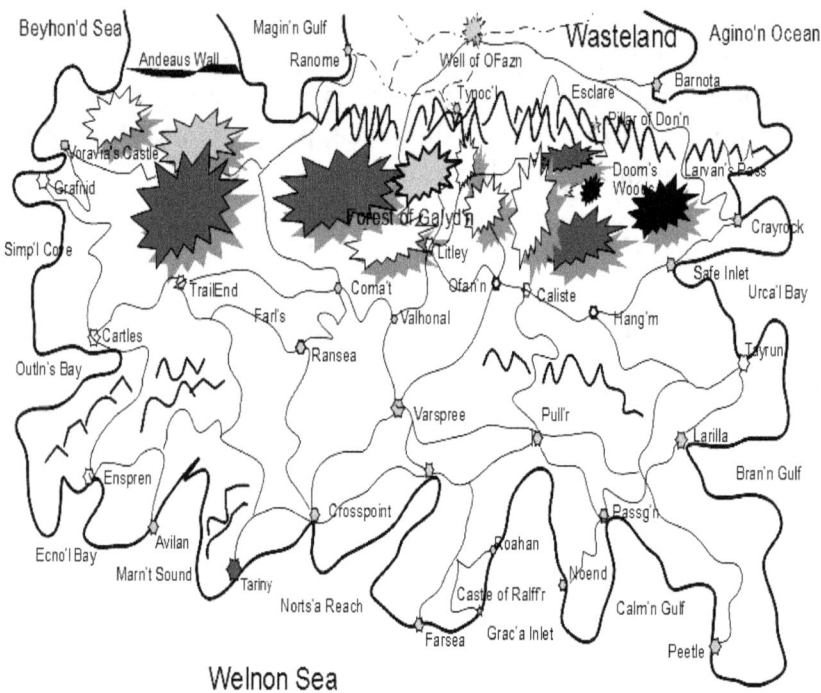

Table Of Contents

Prologue	6	Resting Place	128
Death Unadorned	14	Together	146
Again	17	Decisions	156
Summons	19	Parting	163
Haughty	.22	Evil Waits	173
Tribulation	.24	Destiny	176
Perchance Hope	26	Concerns	203
Impetuous	28	Pursuit	212
Pride	30	Treachery	216
Imperium	.31	Confrontation	
Anisah	.34	With Evil	221
Gathering	.49	Unrelenting	229
Geth'n	.52	Allies	240
Rebuff	.61	Discovery	254
Obstinacy	.65	Search For	
Discord	.70	A Friend	263
Garv'n	.72	Solace	283
Travail	.82	Guardian Reborn	288
Rab'k	.97	Hidden Forever	291
Sojourn	106	Borny'a	307
Deception	114	Captured	314
Voravia	122	Revelation	318
		First Battle	322
Next Installment	334	The Authors	335

PROLOGUE

The intent and not the deed
Is in our power; and, therefore, who dares greatly,
Does greatly.

Arsan'h – Book of Aerolan VII

For those of you who would know the truth, I, Kalbr'an of the Al-Es-
fer'n, have come to tell these tales of a time after we created Aerolan and
after the creation of mankind.

We all shall look nearer, first to a world men named Narhtrae and to a
time when there was a greater need for these men to combat the darkness.

If you are a pilgrim on this journey, then you should know what has
gone before. Of great universal magic, mystical wisdom freeing life for this
world and others; of great tragedies transpiring, by and to the gods and
man; of a need for these things about which I tell you now; and of the
days to come.

Let us then begin.

I will tell you of the Al-Esfer'n, rediscovered and reborn on Narhtrae,
who bring yet another great change in the lives of man, and how they lost
their home and regained another.

And too, of the Om-Esfer'n, who would destroy it all.

May this tale bring you fear, but hope; it must, inevitably, bring you wis-
dom . . .

The world Varkan glowed softly in the light of all three
moons floating above. This had always been -- since the creation. The moons seemed always present, at least one hung silently in the heavens each night.

The people of this beautiful world discovered the value in a
beneficent life; their passing through this time and in this place
was filled with contentment.

Today, there was no living thing for the moons to shine upon.

Today, the air moved softly through the great trees covering the surface, but there was no sound -- only quiet, a vacuum. Nothing stirred, it was mortal life ended.

Time no longer mattered.

In this First Age, when the Al-Esfer'n were populating planets with living beings, Baalsa'n, an Om-Esfer'n, raised objections to the creation of mortal beings. He began to interfere with the projects of the others. He became more vehement in his disapproval with each new world settled.

Then he began to destroy; he conquered. He raged and began to enfold himself in the convictions he had the power to overcome what the others were doing. He became enraptured with evil, banded with others of his ilk, gathered a great force -- a mixture of other diabolical Om-Esfer'n and ogreish mortal beings from many of the planets.

With magic and his huge force of malcontents, Baalsa'n easily overcame the unsuspecting mortal inhabitants and crushed any resistance the Al-Esfer'n were able to conjure to defeat his evil. He wreaked a terrible and gruesome devastation on the inhabitants, and, on the Al-Esfer'n, when he could find them.

With this terrible host, he swept clean all of the planets standing in his path.

The attacks surprised the Al-Esfer'n, many of them had taken residence on each of the planets to teach; they were overwhelmed by this horrific force. Most lost their existence.

The Al-Esfer'n gathered to stop Baalsa'n and there were great battles fought. Some won, some lost. In the end, Baalsa'n was the victor.

In the destruction of this life the Al-Esfer'n had given to the worlds and destruction of all they hoped to achieve, there was now only a void - a terrible consequence of Baalsa'n's evil.

Varkan was the last of all known creations to fall.

By a grievous error, these things came about; there had never been a consideration in the plans of the Al-Esfer'n for such evil as they encountered, especially from one of their own.

Baalsa'n was not only a disappointment, but a deadly one. He was conducting a witch hunt for the living. His forces swarmed through towns and villages, seeking those Al-Esfer'n who still lived.

In Taymal'n, a seaport of the Southern Ocean, a small troop of armed soldiers trotted through the streets near the center of the demolished city. Their feet crunched the shards of pottery, glass objects and other household items thrown from the homes destroyed along the way.

These troops moved almost silently and without caution, searching for survivors, not expecting resistance.

One group seemed especially successful in their pursuit.

Rounding a corner, they came upon a barricade of sorts. Piled high were timbers and furniture from some of the homes. Twined through the upper reach-es were electrified wires, small flashes leaped from these, sparking as a slight breeze moved the wires enough to make contact.

The leader of the squad held up her hand and the rest slowed to a stop, dodged into the shadows, glaring into the dark, look-ing at every window in the buildings still erect, waiting for an at-tack.

None came.

There were whispers near the leader. She stepped out, holding her hand aloft and then suddenly dropped it. A thump from the firing of a small launcher jarred the ground; the missile flew over the barrier and exploded violently beyond.

A building creaked as it leaned more precariously, eased over with increasing momentum and, as portions broke away, crashed to the empty street below.

The officer once again raised her hand and gave a spinning motion.

Four of the squad leaped up, charging the barricade. Grunting and swearing as they ran across the haphazard surface, weapons swinging loosely from one hand while the other grabbed for obstacles to help them climb toward the top, they began to scale the barrier. Reaching the top, they squatted, looked over care-fully and could see no activity.

They looked down at the officer. She held up two fingers and moved them forward. Two of the men rose quickly and took one step toward the top.

Just as they rose to move across, two rapid, low-powered shots rang out from behind the troops and the two men on the barricade dropped.

Before any of the others could turn to find the source, Areb'l had shifted his weapon into a high yield setting, spun around and fired at a building behind them, completely ripping a window and one corner from the building. The remains crashed downward smashing into other buildings, raising a cloud of dust as it struck.

"Sniper!" he shouted, ducking back into the shadows on the other side of the street. High intensity rapid fire assaulted the buildings near where his round first struck the building. Masonry flew every direction; the building was being demolished by the onslaught.

Quickly, the officer ran into the moonlight, held her hand high and rapidly pulled it down. The firing stopped.

She motioned for Areb'l. He, dodging carefully from shadow to shadow, leaped and rolled behind a battered divan with her.

"What did you see?" she asked him, bending closer to whisper.

"There was a small arms flash, where I first shot," he answered, pointing to the area, "I saw someone, or something, jump back into the shadows and run back into the building".

"Good work," she looked into his eyes, noting the strength in them,"take Luro'm and search. We're going to stay and clear this away and continue on to the harbor. Meet us there".

"Yes Sir," Areb'l nodded, "we'll get this bastard. C'mon, Lur." He waved to Luro'm to follow him.

He jumped, running toward the area of his assault; the other soldier close behind, dodging from one piece of rubble to another. They ran to the entrance to the alley below where Areb'l had fired.

After they ran down the alley a short distance, leaping over obstacles while keeping their weapons at ready, Areb'l held his hand up.

They stopped, catching their breath, while they listened for any sounds. Just beyond was a low wall, perhaps intended to separate two living areas. They approached slowly, crouching until they reached it.

"What now?" whispered Luro'm.

"We have to go over and keep searching, but Leanna won't be happy if we're not at the harbor soon. I'll go first. Wait five seconds, then follow," Areb'l answered.

Areb'l placed his weapon across his back, reached up, grabbed the edge of the wall, and pulled himself up and over.

"All clear?" Luro'm whispered.

No answer. He stood a moment, waiting his five seconds then he too climbed up the wall and dropped into a crouch on the other side.

There was no sign of Areb'l.

Where is he?

There was no activity, it was deadly quiet. Luro'm peered into the dark but could see nothing.

Suddenly a flash of light caused him to straighten, his eyes blinking with the pain. A hand, with a whistling murmur, chopped Luro'm in his throat with a powerful stroke. He dropped his weapon, his eyes widened, he reached for his throat. Blood began to burble from his mouth. Slowly he tilted and fell forward on his face, still holding his neck. He was dead before he hit.

Areb'l look around to determine if anyone else was near. Deciding there wasn't, he looked down at the young man lying in death and shook his head.

"Sadness is all war brings," he murmured, turned and ran along the street a few sections before turning into a smaller alley. Traveling along it for some distance, crossing streets cautiously as he went, he came to a street crossing he recognized.

On the far side and about half a section to his right, was a small tower standing silently next to the rumble of the building formerly attached. At the base of the tower was a door, somewhat akimbo but still clinging to the frame.

He looked both ways, moved around the corner into the shadows of the street, slid along the opposite wall until he was directly across from the tower.

He darted across and stood against the wall next to the hanging door. Behind the door was a makeshift panel covering the opening.

Areb'l reached his free hand behind the door, still watching the street with caution, and slammed his fist against the panel. He paused for a few seconds then lightly knocked on the panel three times, then repeated the sequence.

He waited a moment, held himself against the wall, prepared to run into the shadows if something unexpected happened. But the panel slowly eased away from the doorway and left an opening through which he stepped.

The panel was replaced quietly, but quickly. A small light illuminated the chamber.

There were about twenty people gathered; their eyes filled with certain fear. They were hiding from the holocaust outside, trembling and desolate. His sud-den arrival surprised and frightened them.

Kalbr'an stepped forward and clasped Areb'l in an embrace that spoke of a long friendship.

"You made it," Kalbr'an, eased out through anxious lips. "Thank you for this."

"I could not have done otherwise. This is an atrocity. I never wished to participate in anything like this. I've come to help if I can." Areb'l answered, looking deeply into his friend's eyes.

Kalbr'an turned back to the others in the room.

"This is Areb'l. A good man who has helped us through many of our early troubles," he glanced around, noticing many of the faces beginning to soften, the fear leaving them.

They suddenly broke the silence, asking questions about outside, all trying to speak at once. Their faces filled with expressions of mourning. Confusion raced about the room.

Kalbr'an raised his hand.

"I apologize for the surprise and know a soldier's entry here was the last thing you expected. But Areb'l has given me his word he will help us — and there is the one thing we've been discussing here I believe we must decide."

"Areb'l is the only one here who can survive this horrible and malicious attack – because he is human and a member of Baalsa'n's forces".

More voices were raised. "How can we know him to be trustworthy?" one young woman asked. Others mumbled their agreement.

11

Areb'l looking quizzically at Kalbr'an, obviously as curious as the questioners around the room.

Kalbr'an spoke softly, "I can only state I believe Areb'l to be sincere; I assume he doesn't lie and I have never known him to do so. He has pledged to me he will fulfill my request. He only asks, when the time comes, he too will be allow to rest on another world.

But we are trapped here without hope and must relinquish our spirits for now. We must attempt to place ourselves in a position at some future date to resist this brutality, to fight back – but we're too weak now."

"I have chosen Areb'l to be the Guardian of the Ahar'n and of our lives".

Kalbr'an waited for another outburst, but there was none. Most knew now what was planned, others still wondered.

"We must release our spirit to the Ahar'n."

Many in the room gasped, some began to weep.

"We must do this and escape – or all will be lost. I was informed by the last message from Tarnasia Baalsa'n's forces have destroyed every other world on which we have worked so hard."

Kalbr'an had searched for and managed to save the Ahar'n during his escape. The object of creation used by the Al-Esfer'n to form and build Varkan and other worlds was safe, for the present.

The Ahar'n revealed no form; its shape flowed within its constraints; colors changed and flashed; a swirling internal mist continually moved across its face, but faded when viewed closely.

It seemed to have no substance, but its magic glinted as it turned. It seemed to have no consistency but resisted destruction by any means known to all Esfer'n.

When first created, it was encased within a small cage formed from an impregnable metal, only allowing a glint of light from the stone; a small chain looped through the clasp. The amulet hung loosely as Kalbr'an held it aloft for all to see.

They looked about themselves, and at each of those standing near them, as though questioning the reasons for this drastic measure, but, in the end, they decided.

They would allow the Ahar'n to absorb their spirits — each one of them knowing they might not survive, but they knew they could not stay on Varkan.

It proceeded. Areb'l watching, in awe, as each spirit vanished from the darkened room into to object Kalbr'an held.

So, Kalbr'an lowered the object to a small, dilapidated table in the center of the room. Each of the Al-Esfer'n entered it, some quickly, some with hesitation.

Kalbr'an was the last. "Until we meet again. Take care." He floated away.

Areb'l raised the Ahar'n tenderly, lowered the small chain over his head, and concealed it beneath his armor. He waited solemnly and felt its power envelop him, bringing him joy in what he had promised and a strength he had never felt before.

A few moments later, he opened the casement panel throwing it aside, knocked the door from its hinges, and stepped back into the street.

He looked briefly at the moons overhead, then turned his gaze toward the waterfront and trotted toward it to rejoin his unit.

In the moonlight, a change in his appearance, he wasn't aware of, revealed itself — a long white streak though his hair glimmered as he ran. No one ever asked him why.

Officer Leanna, noticing when he returned, asked about Luro'm. Areb'l explained they had met a group of Al-Esfer'n who they eradicated, but Luro'm had not survived. She only nodded and dismissed him.

For hundreds of years, he hid in plain sight, pretending to be a member of Baalsa'n's forces. He followed the masses each day, helping those he could. And waited.

Few Al-Esfer'n survived Varkan.

DEATH UNADORNED

The air lay heavily upon her, pressing her breath from her. She only sensed the candles glowing; the dark curtains hanging limply along the black walls.

There were only two others in the small parlor; only those she did not fear had come; her mother was ill at home.

But, she could taste the air; this foreboding place. She only wanted to go away; she wanted this to not be true.

There was death here, deep unforgiving death. She couldn't draw a breath, she couldn't see clearly. She felt as though she was barely clinging to life; she felt she was dying.

Anisah was weeping bitterly. An older woman sat next to her – Mistress Elspeth. Anisah sagged and placed her face in the old woman's lap and cried. She couldn't stop.

Her father was dead. And she couldn't save him. He was dead and there was nothing she could do.

She stopped crying suddenly, raised her head while tears ran down her face, and looked around the dismal room. The candles wavered slightly in a sudden gentle breathe.

She stood. Around her the air hushed, soft, gentle, warm. The room held its breath. She reached out to touch the softness, but it pulled away from her.

She looked at her father lying so still. Raising her hand to reach for him, she saw his eyes open. He held her with his eyes.

"Don't be afraid, my daughter. You will discover much about yourself over the years; you will be much more than you are now. Take solace in that and do not weep for me.

Care for your mother; she needs your support before you need to leave. Don't cry. And be not too sad I'm gone," the her father spoke to her softly.

"I'll try, Father. I will try. But where am I going?"

She felt heavy, weighted, not believing, not wanting him to go away again. Her thoughts raced in confusion. Then slowly her father's eyes closed, the glow faded.

14

She came back to her surroundings; her head still lay on the woman's lap, but she wasn't crying anymore.

Old Bas stood, backed into the shadows, watching her with soft eyes of sorrow. Mistress Elspeth, holding her, wept, wiping her eyes with the edge of her old apron, wanting to help

But nothing, nor anyone, could help. Anisah felt lost in a vapid dream, grayness washing over her. She tried to stand, wavered a moment, and reached toward her father. She felt death swallowing her.

She moaned.

The ground begin to tremble; the room shuddered as the tremor passed beneath. Pictures hanging along the walls, articles on shelves, began to fall or fly about the room. Some glass shattered on the floor.

The room began to glow.

Mistress Elspeth slid from her chair in sudden fear and kneeled, covering her head with her shawl. Old Bas, surprised but not alarmed, only watched.

A shallow light began to swirl at the center of the room, a material thing. Its whirlpool swallowed more articles, ripping them from every direction.

Anisah stood abruptly, arms out by her side, eyes closed, her head back. Her bright hair flying about her; everything began to move with the vortex.

Just as suddenly as it had begun, it all stopped; items released, fell crashing.

The blackness overwhelmed her as she slumped to the floor.

Old Bas stepped from the shadows, his face concerned. He ran to Anisah and held her close for a moment, looking down into her young face. He marveled at her strength; at her raw power.

I've never seen such power before in one so young. I must keep this to myself. This is not a thing to be revealed — to anyone.

He looked down at Mistress Elspeth still on her knees, bowing and covering her head, whimpering softly.

He glanced once at the coffin, smiled.

You performed well as a surrogate, Hanf'r, the child is strong. Fare ye well.

Old Bas lifted Anisah and carrying her, stood and walked out the exit to his wagon. He spoke softly to her, "I just need to take you to your mother now; she'll be worried about you. You both need to rest. I'll watch over you for a while before I leave."

He looked about, feeling somewhat exposed and wondered how he might keep that promise undiscovered.

Mistress Elspeth ran past him, tottering along at what speed she could gain, not looking back.

AGAIN

The desert lay silent, its surface an inferno. The sky was dark and cloudless. Nothing stirred.

If anything was alive in the waste, it was unlikely it would survive for long. No creatures roamed this plain, except in haste; it was lifeless and threatening.

The air was dead.

From somewhere, a high keening sound shrilled at the open space. It increased in volume, each moment more piercing.

Above the beaten desert, dust began swirling upward, forming a great funnel, growing until it stood from sky to earth. The baked soil tore from the land, lifted and flew into the winds.

The swirl expanded, its girth soon stretching as far as one could see. Blackness flowed into the cyclone, blotting the moon. The desert became darker, dense with the impenetrable dense mass of dust and debris drawn into the storm.

To the south of the desert, a great mountain range stood, blocking the storm from the southern regions. Across the face of the mountains, escarpments slowly disintegrated under the ferocity of the wind lashing against them. Massive stone fragments hurled outward and into the vortex, whipped away into dust.

The wind devoured the mountains' vaulted face.

A magnificent and ornate mosaic etched deeply into the cliff face began to show, ancient beyond the known history of Aerolan.

Great sculptured heroes of ancient wars holding aloft beautifully wrought gables spread across the face of the bared wall. Chiseled in the ebony marble beneath the surface, the bold venue seemed blasted from the cliff.

On the face were two massive doors, many times taller than any man. One opened slowly against the storm's onslaught.

From the face of Esclar'e, a massive and bold mountain rising into the clouds above, a sudden glow invaded this miasma. A single beam sliced through the blackness of the crushing darkness, flaring against the whirling stream of the cyclone, rippling with the change in the texture of the immense funnel.

A man, a specter, floated into view; his face hidden beneath a black hood. He glowed with an aura as he moved across the great plateau, unaffected by the wind. The swirling cyclone seemed to wrap away from him, to avoid him as though he was death.

He stood tall, strong. His long white hair did not move as he traveled across the prominence. His robe, black with a wide golden band circling the neck and slashing diagonally across the front of the robe to the hem, hung loosely though not touching the ground beneath.

He stopped at the edge of the precipice, glared out at the darkness with eyes that seemed endlessly deep, raised his arm and held it aloft for only a brief moment.

From the black crystal in his hand, a slashing light struck across the land and into the skies above. A tearing sound, ripping the air, inundated the land with thunder echoing across the prairie. The ground drummed in a low rumble.

Suddenly, the ferocity of the storm abated; it stumbled. Slowly it vanished, drawn into a crease in the sky. With a groaning anguish, its life force eroded and extinguished.

It had served its one purpose.

Turning he watched the sun just moving above the horizon. Light spread across the flat expanse, brightening the skies.

Within moments, the heat baked the land more than before; any moisture gathered in the night was parched from the air.

He turned and walked into the mountain.

SUMMONS

A few days passed. All was quiet.

The great door of the mountain once again opened and the wizard again walked toward to the escarpment high above the desert floor.

Baalsa'n raised his hand, extending it in a great sweeping motion. The surface of the land seemed to fold, to bend to some demand to do so.

He willed a view of Barnota, the seaport on the distant eastern shoreline of the Wasteland, and it rose before him.

Looking nearer, he saw a man walking along the dock through the morning fog. He watched him amble along the boardwalk, carrying his belongings stuffed into the duffel thrown over his shoulder. He trudged along under the weight.

Quickly he engulfed the man with a great flash of light, streaming around and blinding him. Surprised, the man stumbled, almost falling. He dropped his burden and raised his hands to shield his eyes from the light erupting around him.

"Mano'n!" a voice thundered.

"Baalsa'n?" Mano'n asked hesitantly. He tried to peer into the light, but he knew who called his name.

"In deed," Baalsa'n answered. A soft rumbling, but demanding, voice rolled from the brightness, "You must come to Esclar'e. We must begin. Now."

As suddenly as it had appeared, the light vanished.

Mano'n staggered from the release. He shook his head to clear his vision. He looked around to determine if anyone else saw, but the dock was empty.

From all around came the sounds of the sea; horns hauntingly blaring their purpose into the night; birds gathered here and there along the dock noisily waiting for the sun.

The air was of the water, moist and salty; the sky was leaden with moisture. Out beyond the edge, the first light glinted off the water, smooth with no breeze to ruffle it, moving in the

19

rhythms of the slow progress of the tide.

With a grimace, he looked out over the water and shook his head, a haunting look in his eyes; something was unfinished inside him.

He shrugged his shoulders to relax his tension, turned, picked up his duffel and hurriedly walked away; the fog folding behind his passing.

Meanwhile, Baalsa'n turned his attention to other concerns; he assumed his orders would be obeyed.

****

Baalsa'n sought and found a young girl in the fishing village of Ranome on the opposite coast of the Wasteland. He decided he wouldn't speak to her as he had Mano'n, but, instead, have her brought to him.

His thoughts then recalled those who would come to him at his call.

Below where he stood, a village lay nestled against the mountains; by his design, it was protected from the tempest.

The tented city spread out some distance across the desert surrounding the small oasis in its center. People were stirring, gathering their belongings after the storm. Baalsa'n looked for one man, Rena'x, and found him.

"Rena'x, my friend. You must come to Esclar'e. Quickly."

Rena'x, an older, wiser man than the first, turned slowly to face the light inundating his tent. He had waited many years for this day. He smiled and bowed his head slightly in agreement.

"You must bring the boy." Baalsa'n added, "His duties will be assigned. Be here on the morrow. We must prepare for what is to come."

The light vanished.

Rena'x, with an expression of sadness appearing on his face, looked slowly around his home and knew his own time with his son was soon to end.

He was long in bringing the boy to young manhood, and it troubled him the boy was probably going to leave him. Rena'x felt lonelier knowing that.

After all these years, he wasn't certain he wanted the changes he knew were to take place.

He, the Protector of the Black Crystal, had hopes of passing the tasks to the boy, Rab'k, but had no idea what Baalsa'n planned for the boy, or himself.

He walked to the entrance to look out. Rab'k was practicing his forms with Prox'm, the blade master. He learned quickly. As young as he was, his skills exceeded most of the other swordsmen in the village.

He already stood as tall and was stronger than other men in the enclave. He seemed to take delight in learning each skill. Through Rena'x teachings, he had formed an extreme hatred for the peoples of the southern regions.

Rena'x taught Rab'k, from the first moments of understanding, it would be necessary for the *Sandr'n* to ravage those lands, destroy everything and everyone, so it might be possessed for a greater day.

Rab'k took these teachings to heart and, during his combat practices, had often shown a penchant for violence.

Rena'x was pleased with the boy's progress.

Now he had to prepare the young man for a new life; a life destined to be revealed in this meeting with the master, Baalsa'n.

Rena'x would do what he must, but he no longer had the desire.

HAUGHTY

Enough!

Voravia was angry and expressing it violently.

This was the worst day of her life, dragged from her home by these brutes and forced to come to this forsaken place.

Not without a fight, she thought smugly.

How could these people just come and kidnap her and not expect her to fight? She had her own reasons for turning the one guard to a stone statue; he had annoyed her.

She was bound and dragged kicking, forced to come.

And now, standing in a room in the castle in the mountain, she was told to remove her clothing.

She looked about, glaring, frowning fiercely.

A large and brawny, her desert red skin and hair stringing wildly out from her head, shouted at her, pointing her finger at a pile of clothing laying across one of the beds.

"Get dressed in one of those and be quick about it,". the crazy woman yelled at her.

Voravia glared and stuck out her tongue when the woman turned her back. But she realized the futility of her aggression, shrugged her shoulders and walked to the bed to look down at the long gowns.

She chose one and held it up in front of her, admiring the lines, the deep blue colors.

She quickly removed her old clothing and slipped the dress over her head; it slithered around her body, caressing it, and formed itself to fit snugly.

She stood defiantly, wanting to tear the dress from her body though she knew the servant woman wouldn't allow it.

She turned, admiring herself in a large mirror placed just so one might have the opportunity to do so.

This dress is beautiful. Well, Voravia, where else could you find a dress like this? Certainly not in the desert!

She, determining there must be a unique reason why the sol-

22

diers had taken so much trouble to grab only her from all the females living in her village, began to wonder what might come next.

Marte, the matron of deliberate intent and assigned to be her watchdog, told her there was to be a gathering and it would be important in the lives of the people and her. Marte didn't know, however, why Voravia was brought to the palace.

At least, Voravia saw it as a palace. She could remember no talk of this place before and one could be certain such a place would have been talked about among the people; it was as though it came into existence over night.

They made me walk up that stupid hill!

She almost grunted with disgust.

I haven't worked that hard since I was a child.

She fluffed her hair on one side, peering into the mirror again.

Maybe I'm here because of what I did to the filthy Yetr'y a fortnight ago.

She giggled to herself.

He deserved it, the stupid ox.

Yetr'y had tried to persuade Voravia to come with him into the desert one evening and was being more forceful than she was willing to allow.

She, without trying and without knowing how, turned the man into a sand column.

A rather nice one overlooking the sea at least.

She smiled to herself.

I suspect I'll never know how I did it, but it had to be me -- I was the only other living thing around and I was mad at him, the fool, for what he was trying to do. And, I did it again with the soldier.

"Hm-m-m," she sighed, "wonder how?"

TRIBULATION

The wind blew roughly across the scraggly plain, dry grass whipped about, dust swirling up until it touched the clouds and brushed them with powder, painting them in translucent yellows. The tints contrasted with the open sky above and made the clouds seem painted on a canvas of shallow blue.

The sun bore down relentlessly on it all.

A man, standing solemnly in his black robes, stood on the sheer cliff overlooking the prairie, the wind blowing around him.

Dust blew across the plateau but his robe never fluttered. There was no sign, in his stance, the wind blew at all.

But even he squinted from the glare of the desert sand and held his hand above his brow, trying to see across the vastness.

Darker clouds roiled above and behind him, tossed out of the translucence into a presence that seemed evil.

They boiled and tumbled quietly, but with a ferocity that made them seem alive.

The clouds charged at the mountains and bolted across into the lands to the south, punching with difficulty through the high passes.

Mano'n watched for a while, but couldn't tell whether the clouds actually made it across. He felt certain some did.

Darkness should sweep across the south, destroy it and all people there one day. He hesitated a moment.

Maybe there were some exceptions.

From his lofty perch on the edge of the sheer cliff, he looked out over the land searching for something living out beyond where he stood. Except for the tent village far below, he could see no way anything could be alive anywhere in the broad reach of this desert.

The oppressive heat didn't affect him significantly. But there were others, he knew, wandering out there, trying to find some safety from the inferno.

Along the coast, small clusters of people tried to survive; small villages squatted in coves and canyons opened to the sea , enough to have fjords which ebbed and flowed continuously.

Salt water was better than no water and these nomads had learned how to distill the precious fluid.

The hate keeps them alive. The hate and the promises.

The mountains rumbled behind him. He turned and looked at the bluff towering upward toward the peaks.

The face of the cliff was sheer, black and glistening in the sun. It didn't reflect the light or the intense heat, but seemed rather to absorb it.

Carved into this edifice was a cavern, only showing itself by the gaping dark hole which seemed out of place in this wasteland.

Those he could see entering the darkness disappeared quickly into the black. Others leaving the gaping entrance stopped suddenly, as they exited, holding their hands, or something in their hands, over their eyes to shield against the sudden brightness.

Above the entrance stood an immense wall with ornate carvings, some large enough for him to see from where he stood, but most were small -- a display of stories and fables.

Tales were carved in runes; tales of the passage of time in this place and of the ruination of this blighted land during the First Age of Imitation -- the time when the Al-Esfer'n walked the planet before Baalsa'n came to alter what they had done.

Mano'n turned back and looked across the prairie again, a grimace on his face.

We have much to do. Much to do before they discover we are near again.

Abruptly, he turned and walked quickly toward the wall of legends.

As he burst into the shadows, the people working there bowed to him as he passed by.

Mano'n paid them little heed. His thoughts were preparing him for his meeting with Baalsa'n, and he needed to make certain there were no mistakes, especially today.

PERCHANCE HOPE

The men in the boats pulled with all their strength on the nets boiling with fish. Two young boys tried to help and pulled with the older men; their young arms ached with the effort.

The nets were so full; some portion of the catch was lost with each passing moment. Between the two vessels, the fish flailed above the water, leaping and crashing back to the surface.

Waves crashed over everyone, almost washing them into the sea.

They all struggled to land the catch; larger than any they had ever seen. The village needed this; it was too long since there was sufficient food. Peetle was dying and could no longer exist without this catch.

The boys strained with the men, pulling, pulling.

Suddenly, a quietness fell over all. No sounds from the sea; no squawking of birds flying above trying to steal fish, their flight halted in mid-air, waves hung suspended above the surface, clouds like slits in the blue, cascades of emerald sheen hung in the air.

The world had stopped.

The boys could see and feel the change. They looked at each other; they didn't understand.

Suddenly, the tallest stood and began to pull, with unexpected strength. The nets began to rise, pulling the boats together. The other, smaller boy, held forth his hands and the violence of the fish ceased.

The churning mass of life stilled completely.

As the net reached the top of the water, the quiet was shattered. There was confusion, fish leaped once more and pulled to free themselves. But it was too late, the catch was saved.

The older men were unaware of that moment, unaware of anything except their salvation. They shouted encouragement to each other, laughing and shouting for joy as they pulled the massive catch on board their vessels, tightly surrounding the closing net.

The boys glanced at each other briefly, almost embarrassed to look. They still didn't understand, but were happy the day was better for all.

IMPETUOUS

Rab'k, strongly built and walking with strides of one recognizing his new strengths, paced around a grand room not far from the hall where the meetings were to be held.

"But, Father, why am I here? What have I done?" the boy was brusque. He was frightened, but Rena'x wasn't going to reveal what he knew.

"You've done nothing wrong, Rab'k. This is to be a special day for you, one that will be noted in the great epistles of this Age. You're a part of what will come to be the history of this world. The moment has finally arrived when you'll be rewarded for all your hard work," the older man answered, lounging comfortably on one of the divans.

Rena'x sat and watched his son being young and impetuous, as he should be.

Maybe this is the last time I will see him at all. Maybe.

"But I don't want to be rewarded for anything. I want to ride through the mountains and slay the infidels who do nothing to deserve the land they possess," he flung himself around to face his father.

"I want to tear it away from them and bring our people to a land of blessing to rest from this misery. I want to do that instead of prancing about foolishly before this being, this one who isn't from our land!"

Rena'x jumped up, crossed the room and slapped Rab'k across his face with a violence that would have flattened a lesser man.

The boy's head snapped aside, but sprang back instantly; his hand reached for his sword instinctively, but he stopped before he withdrew the blade, though his hand lingered on the grip.

"You. You will not speak of this one in that manner. Without him, our people would not have been. I've known him for long years and I'll never let him be spoken little of, by anyone!" Rena'x's face drew close to the boy's.

Rab'k glared at the older man but turned and walked away. His face was crimson from the blow, but he would never ad-mit there was any pain.

"But, Father, I don't see the need for this," he turned to face Rena'x again.

"There are reasons, old reasons. We'll be told today what must be done and when we must do them to right the wrongs about which I have spoken before.

We cannot and must not slack from our duty to fight for these things, and this one, this Om-Esfer'n, will be the one to whom we must and will turn to when the day of reckoning comes for the offenders," Rena'x spoke slowly and deliberately. "We cannot but follow his wisdom and his will in these things".

Rab'k began to pace again. He threw one of the ornate chairs across the room, shattering it against the cavern walls. The sound of impact echoed through the chamber. All was quiet again except for the boy's boots striking the floor.

"Rab'k. Come, sit and talk for a moment," Rena'x implored and held his hand out, gesturing toward another sofa, "Come and I'll tell you the history of this thing."

PRIDE

Mano'n hurried to his chambers, wondering what he would be doing in the near future. He felt certain Baalsa'n planned to prescribe the next steps in the conflict that was to come. Mano'n hoped he would be able to provide a great deal to that effort.

He heard, through the palace rumors, there were others. *Strange what one could learn by listening to the hum of voices in a great beehive such as this.*

Many of the desert people had migrated to this place in only a short time, but then what else would they consider in their miserable lives as more important then what was happening here.

This place had only just come to these high plains, and so quickly, was mystery enough for most. But if they knew how it came to be, there would be widespread fear and distrust.

Not the emotions Baalsa'n wants the people to feel right now.

Mano'n knew he would have to give audience soon so he dressed in his finest robes. The one he admired the most was black with a single wide band of gold running down his right side to the floor. Not elegant, but tasteful.

It should do.

A clanging reverberated through the great halls of the cavern.

The time had come. There would be much discovered today; much about what the future bore for these people and for the chosen.

And for myself and those others, it begins.

He turned and walked from his chamber, into the hall and out toward the throne room.

IMPERIUM

Voravia heard the clangor of the gong and the noise of people rushing down the hallways; she wasn't aware of why there was such confusion, or why the offensive clanging continued, but she wanted it stopped.

Marte burst into the room without knocking.

Voravia turned to look at the woman, her eyes snapping in anger.

"Get up, you lazy! The time's come for you to be ready and headed toward the throne room," Marte shouted.

Voravia, ignoring the old hag, was lounging on one of the sofas, luxuriated in the presence of so much wealth and plenty.

There could be no better place on this world.

Water everywhere, in bowls, jars, with flowers protruding from vases filled with it. Food, of all varieties, in other containers scattered around the room, so anyone could just walk by and take what seemed to be the most delicious at the moment. Clothing, beautiful things, lay everywhere.

Voravia never dreamed such a place could exist and here she was.

Marte was an unnecessary nuisance. Voravia, her bright copper hair tossing across her shoulders, only glanced and scowled at the woman.

Marte, however, was more than concerned her charge wasn't ready for this moment.

"I told you you must be ready when the time came. You are being summoned. Get up off your behind and do it now! Do you think I'm willing to get into trouble because of your insolence?" Marte was yelling at the top of her lungs now.

Voravia's anger began to well up inside her; she felt she should dispose of this woman, and now. It all seemed strange, but exhilarating at the same time.

As she stared at the woman, there was no sound coming from the woman's mouth though Voravia could see it moving.

There was only the quiet she always enjoyed at these moments when she was about to extend herself once again, just to deal with yet another worrisome thing.

Just as she was starting to concentrate on what she was going to do, staring at the woman who now stood over her, the door to the chamber opened.

"Come! Now!" a soldier, maybe an officer, shouted at Marte, stood holding the door open, ready to leave immediately.

"Yes, I know, but I can't get this fool girl to move," Marte ,showing her frustration, paced back and forth nervously.

Voravia, losing her focus on her attempt to rid herself of the woman, stood slowly and walked to the wardrobe nearest the mirror.

"I'll be ready in a moment, if you'll leave," Voravia was as insolent as she could be.

I never wanted to come to this place. Let them wait.

"You will get dressed now and will come with me, or I will drag you to the throne room as you are. You have two counts to comply. Now, do it! One! . . ," the guard shouted back at her.

Marte stood back, her arms folded below her huge breasts, grinning at Voravia. She wanted the man's threat to humiliate Voravia, her eyes gleamed with delight.

Voravia sulking, chose one of the gowns she liked most, started to remove the blue one she had tried first, turned and looked at the guard.

He wasn't moving, only glaring at her.

She dropped her clothing to the floor without looking to see if the man was shocked, reached and chose a black gown with silver slashing across the bodice from her left shoulder and down to the right hem.

She raised it over her head and slid into it. She was pleased when the gown nestled into place and conformed to her body shape as though it was made for her.

There are no fastenings. She was fascinated.

She turned to look at Marte and, more importantly, at the guard, but he had turned to look down the hall and when he looked back into the room, the expression on his face was the same as before.

32

Men! I should like to turn them all to suskrit and throw them back into the sea!

She stomped to the door. Marte, in tow, pushed the man aside and stepped in behind her.

Once in the hall, Voravia had no idea what she was supposed to do. She stopped confused, looking both up and down the great hallway.

Overhead, the light glittered through dusty air in the highest eaves, too high to see any detail.

"Walk this way," prompted the officer, turned and walked down the long corridor. Voravia noticed he had an officer's insignia.

She smirked at Marte, spun on her heels and walked, mocking the man marching stiffly along in front of her, barely suppressing her giggle.

ANISAH

When time has brought together an instance of weary hope with an opportunity yet thought of, a release caresses the soul and becomes faith in one's self.

To accomplish what must be done, and go beyond, becomes a dream - a possible vision requiring strength to endure but promises more than the pain to achieve.

Strength of the soul, not of the body.

Before those stories we humble ourselves in obeisance to the simple glory in each success. This then is yet another tale of one of these young adventurers.

Let us not tarry then . . .

Anisah sighed deeply as she trudged along. She was just returning from Mistress Brand's, their nearest neighbor, where she was sent by Brae'x to fetch some eggs. It wasn't even dawn, but it was already too warm and she had to finish her other chores soon.

"Stupid hens, so scared of the fox they can't even lay eggs," she grumbled, deliberately kicking dust up from the road, "might as well just roast them all and be done with them".

She was so engrossed in her dark mood she didn't hear the cart coming behind her.

"Well, Good morning to you, young wool gatherer. You best watch where you're goin' there, or you'll get run over. For sure."

Anisah jumped when the man spoke, almost spilling all the precious eggs; one of them tumbled out before she could catch it, breaking.

She turned and saw who it was and quickly regained her composure. Old Bas, the tinker, was driving his wagon directly behind her and she hadn't noticed.

"Goodness, sir. You scared me half to death. I'm surprised I only broke one of these," Anisah said, holding the basket so he could see.

"Well, didn't mean to, you know. You just had your head in the clouds, is all. Would ya like a ride the rest of the way home? I'll be going right by your place on me way to town," the old man smiled at her and patted the seat.

"Oh, thank you so much. My feet are hurting," Anisah answered. She reached and gave Bas the basket of eggs, gathered her skirts and scrambled up beside him.

He gave her the basket. She held it on her lap and rode in silence for a while. The sun glimmered on the horizon. She could feel the softness of the early sunrise and thought how beautiful everything looked in the morning light. From this higher perch, it didn't feel so hot.

Light mists floated through the great willows near the creek; a rooster crowed on the next farm; morning doves were cooing; it all seemed so peaceful.

They arrived at her cottage too quickly. Smoke was rising from the chimney. Anisah knew she needed to get the eggs into her mother soon. She handed her basket to Old Bas and jumped down.

"Your mother be needing any pots fixed, or any pins or needles for her stitching, or the like, while I'm here?" Old Bas asked, carefully handing her the basket of eggs.

"I don't know but let me take these to her and I'll ask.

I'll be right back to let you know," she answered as she started to turn to run into the house.

He bent over, reaching to give her the basket, and a crystal on a thong fell out of his shirt, swinging from his neck.

"What a beautiful crystal," she stopped and drew in her breath at the sight, her eyes opening wide, "I think I have one that looks just like it. Same color and everything."

She pulled her necklace from inside her dress to show him. "My mother told me my father gave it to me when I was born. Where did you get yours?"

He sat up, looked down at his chest where the crystal lay glittering darkly in the new sunlight and smiled, "Don't know really. I think I traded for it some years ago, somewheres up north. I had an old mare that just tagged along tied behind me wagon. I kinda thought this thing was pretty," he held it up showing it more clearly, "and they needed the horse. So here it is," he chuckled.

"I suppose I'd sell it if I needed the money, but ain't had that problem yet. You're right though, except for the cording, the two could be twins," he observed.

His cord was green like hers, but her crystal was held to the cord by leather thongs, his seemed to be set in a golden cage. Each stone was jagged across one end as though it might have been snapped from some other source, but both, though black, were dazzling in the light.

"Tis odd we have them and so much alike," he added, dropping the stone back into his shirt.

Anisah also returned hers to its place against her skin. Neither cared to talk about the necklaces anymore, both looked away.

It was as though the incident never occurred.

"Thank you so very much for the ride, but I'd better get these eggs inside before I get into trouble. If you'll wait, I'll ask my mother about the pots and stuff." She ran for the back door just as her mother came to peer out, looking for her.

"Mother, Old Bas is outside. He wants to know if he can do any fixin' while he's here?" Anisah asked, quickly thrusting the basket of eggs at her mother. She wanted to leave the house before Brae'x decided to send her on another errand.

"Slow down, Anisah. I don't need any mending done, but I do need some sewin' things — needles, pins and thread," her mother answered, sitting the eggs down on the table.

She walked to the fireplace and bent down to stoke the wood, raised up and walked to a chest sitting under the window. It was often piled high with coats and other winter stuff, but with spring coming, the coats were all stored.

She raised the top of the chest, reached deeply into it, and brought out a small purse and removed a few coins. "Just a dozen pins and two spools of black thread, dear," she added as she handed Anisah the money, "and come right back because you need to go to the spring to get some water and bring in more firewood from the shed."

Anisah barely heard the last about the chores, but what she heard made her frown as she ran back to the road where Old Bas sat waiting.

"My girl needs a family of her own to settle her down. Something else that needs tendin' to," her mother muttered, shaking her head and brushing aside the hair that falling into her face. She reached and began stirring the soup again.

"We need a dozen pins and some black thread," Anisah told Old Bas, catching her breath. She had run all the way back.

He reached behind the seat, rummaged around for a moment, and pulled out the packet of pins and a bobbin of thread. He handed them down to her and took the coins, straightened on the seat, and reached for the reins. "I thank you, my dear. May you keep yourself in good health," he said, looking over his shoulder at her. He flipped the straps once and the oxen begin to pull the wagon away.

"And the same to you, sir. Thank you again for the ride," she shouted, waved, watching the old man and his cart for awhile, turned and walked back to the cottage.

Something happened to her as she walked back into the house. Something new and strange; she didn't understand it, but she sensed a power within her.

Her crystal stood on end with its point against her chest and when she put her arm down from waving, it pricked her and she jumped. "That's strange, almost magical," she said, as she shook the cord and the gem fell back into its usual place. She looked down the road again, but Old Bas was out of sight.

"Anisah, honey, I need you to go get water for coffee. You know your father will be down in a moment and he needs his morning coffee to get started off for work," her mother smiled and told her as she walked back into the kitchen.

"He's not my father!" Anisah spat out as she stomped out the door, slamming it behind her. "And won't ever be!"

Anisah savagely kicked the wooden bucket down the gently sloping hill and screamed at it. Her hair flared at the effort, and sparkled golden orange in the glint of sunlight peeking through the trees.

The bucket rolled toward the small stream running through the forest behind the cottage, bumping along as it banged against rocks and trees, finally coming to rest against the cooling shed spanning the creek.

She had to vent her anger in some way, kicking the bucket provided a certain satisfaction. Her green eyes flickered with amusement. It wasn't the first time she taken her anger out on the bucket, and she always wished it was Brae'x's head.

She pointed at the bucket and shouted, "I could kill you, Brae'x Habberns. Why do you treat me this way? I've done nothing to you?" She stood trembling, turned toward the forest, and screamed with all her might, collapsing on the damp ground and sobbing because she couldn't stop.

"Father, why did you leave me? What am I going to do?" she talked between her knees to the ground, holding her head in her hands. She lingered there for some time.

Soon she quieted, stood up and walked to the bucket. She wanted to kick it again, but she had to go back.

She hated him.

Of all the men in Caliste, her mother decided to marry him. He was a pompous, self-important fool. He was always telling her mother, Callex, and her what to do and when.

She didn't need to be told to get water. She was doing that since she was old enough to walk, for as long as she could re-member, before her father had died.

She stopped, bitterly remembering that day. She stood, for a moment, and cried softly before continuing down the hill.

It now seemed so long ago. It was an early spring, the air still cool in the mornings. She was up all night with Mistress Elspeth, the village healer, watching over her father.

Although Mistress Elspeth wasn't a real healer, only an old woman who knew more about herb lore than any-one else in the village, she had helped many and was one of those special people for Anisah.

Anisah's mother collapsed in exhaustion a few hours before daylight, having stayed awake by her husband's bedside for days.

She didn't respond when Anisah tried to wake her.

It became clear her father was gravely ill; seizures wracked his body. Anisah decided her mother needed the rest, and nothing could be done anyway, so she let her sleep.

Mistress Elspeth did all she could but it wasn't enough. Just after dawn, when the world was just awakening, Anisah's father had breathed softly, a sigh, and died. Anisah remembered how horribly empty she felt looking down at his calmed face.

"Hey girl, did you forget where the house is? We need water for breakfast, not supper. Now get up here," shouted Brae'x.

Angry her private moment was interrupted, Anisah looked up the hill and frowned. Ignoring Brae'x, she sat for a moment more, then stood, picked up the bucket

and trudged further down the hill still thinking about her father and Mistress Elspeth on the last morning.

Perhaps if they had known more about herbs and how to use them, her father would have lived and she wouldn't be carrying water up to help cook breakfast for a man she couldn't stand. The way he bullied her family, as well as everyone else he came in contact with, was unbearable.

There must be some way out of here, she thought.

Suddenly, she felt something odd happening on her chest, something was changing her crystal. It lay warmer against her skin. She pulled it out quickly and it began to glow. Surprised, she jumped up almost breaking the line that held it.

She began to sense the gem, something tugged at her heart and her thoughts. She wanted to lash out at something, at anything, just to feel this power was suddenly surging inside her.

She never felt anything like this before.

"Oh, the gods are trembling," she moaned aloud, not realizing she spoke.

Across the creek from her, the trees began to sway, the water in the creek stopped flowing, and the grass began to whip about with the wind.

Anisah felt nothing. She held her long slender hands in front of her and gazed at them. She peered through them and focused on a large boulder lodged halfway into the ground in the field beyond the thicket.

She wanted to smash it; she needed something to release the tension building inside her. Suddenly the boulder moved.

The boulder shuddered once, then pitched into the sky, traveled almost beyond her sight and plopped down, falling heavily onto the ground again, dust and grass kicking up where it landed.

The moment of exhilaration passed. She could only stand and stare as the dust settled. She couldn't believe what happened.

The crystal, hanging at her front, was dark and cool again. She absently placed it back inside her dress. She searched about her in disbelief, stunned; she couldn't even blink her eyes.

What have I done? How can this be? What did I do? She quivered with excitement.

She sat down heavily to recover, still trembling. She looked at the boulder in the distance, at the hole where it was. She shook her head slowly, trying to think.

Was that magic? She placed her hand on the crystal beneath her blouse. *What is this stone?*

Suddenly she gasped. Old Bas has one just like it.

Do they fit together at the jagged edges? If this stone gave me such strength, if the two were joined, would that mean even greater power?

She sat thinking for a while longer, trying to put together possibilities.

Each of these stones must be serving some purpose. Together Old Bas's and mine probably could create a force beyond imagining.

She couldn't imagine the power, unbelievable power, for the bearer. She turned, looked back at the house on top of the rise above the creek, and grinned with an evil sneer.

She turned and picked up the bucket now filled with water though she didn't know how, and started walking toward the house with slow deliberation. She glared at the house from under her brow as she walked.

Abruptly, she frowned and the glaze left her eyes.

What am I doing? What am I thinking? I'm not like this.

She shook her head from side to side, trying to break the aching inside, not knowing what to do.

Stopping in the yard in front of the house, she turned around and around, trying to hold, to see, to find something concrete to bring her back to her old world.

"Don't make me have to come out and get water, or you'll be sorry," Brae'x's voice invaded her thoughts again.

That does it! I hate this man.

She walked to the door and slammed the bucket down in the entryway. The water splashed about, spilling over. She leaned over, dipped her hand into the water, straightened and pushed her wet hands through her autumn colored hair.

Jerking the bucket aloft defiantly, she kicked the door back, actually hurting her toes a bit, and pushed her way into the room.

She walked to the hearth and, once again, slammed the bucket down. More water splashed out and spilled over onto the floor.

Anisah stomped away, her slender frame tense with anger. Her skin flushed, the freckles showing through her lightly tanned face. Her eyes were red from crying, sunken and tired. She rubbed the back of her hand across her small nose and sniffed. Her mouth quivered and made the corners of her lips turn down.

"What're you snifflin' about now? You need to get control of this girl, Callex, 'fore I have to," Brae'x growled over his empty cup.

Anisah went immediately to the cupboard without saying anything, almost snatched the wooden plates and cups out, and began to set the table.

When she finished, she went to the end of the eating area, plopped down on a stool, hiked her dress up to form a pocket, grabbed a pail of potatoes and began to peel them for dinner.

She amused herself by fantasizing each potato was Brae'x's head and she was stripping the flesh from his face with each stroke. She took great pleasure in this little farce and, by the time she finished, she felt much better.

After they ate breakfast and Anisah cleaned all the dishes, there was little for her to do but go outside. She didn't want to be near Brae'x for fear he might actually want to talk to her, and her mother never seemed to want to spend time with her anymore.

Anisah passed the time wandering in the small thicket near the creek and dreaming about being free.

Why is my life so miserable? What have I done to deserve this awful life? And, what is this stone hanging from my neck? Where did my father get such a thing? Does Old Bas know what he possesses?

The thoughts raged through her head. She fell to the ground and cried until her eyes hurt.

At last, she grew tired. It was late and she missed sup-per again, but she didn't care. She avoided Brae'x who always ate first. Then he would sit around drinking until he passed out in the chair.

She returned, crept up to her bedroom, lay on the bed, and fell asleep exhausted wondering what had happened today. She reached and clasped the crystal tightly and dreamed.

She's awake. Maybe. No.

She knows she's dreaming, but it seems so real. She isn't in her bed; she's walking on a long, empty road.

It's cold and wet; the sky is emptying rain. She can hardly see more than two steps ahead; the road is full of water. She stops, afraid to take another step, and stands shivering, listening.

Someone is calling her name; she knows the voice, but where is he? She can't recall the face; she knows and can't remember. She shakes her head trying to make the voice go away. She wants to lie down and wake up; she wants out of this misery.

"You'll have to wait. I need to rest. Leave me. Go away," she cries out. Instantly, the voice is gone. She raises her head, listening.

Why did it stop?

Suddenly, lightning streaks through the darkness, crashing into a tree not far from her.

She jumps to her feet; she can't see. She reaches out with her hands, feeling for anything. Falling to her knees, she touches the grass, the rocks, anything solid. The thunderclap comes and seems to break open the world, deafening her.

Am I going to die?

Suddenly, the rain stops. The sky opens, sunlight almost overwhelming her. She throws her arm over her eyes, bowing over her knees, trying to hide.

The water. It's gone.

She opens her eyes and can't believe what lies before her.

She's kneeling in a meadow. It's nightfall, dark and clear; stars stand out against a vague mistiness that softens their light. A small stream meanders slowly across the field. It is unbelievably peaceful. She sits on a small patch of lush grass for a moment; her breathing softens slowly.

The voice speaks again, **"No, you are very much alive. But we are here. Here to save your world, but we cannot do it with-out your help?"**

"Yes. Yes. What do you want? What have I done?" She hears other voices join the first, then more. She ventures a peek then, holding her hands in front to shade the glare from the light.

Before her, images of men and women appear, ethereal in form, luminescent, glorious. Her eyes open wide in wonder; she rises slowly to her feet and stands in amazement.

The beings hold out their arms to her and beckon her to sit on a small stool that suddenly appears at the edge of a stream. Willowy trees suddenly appear to shade the chair. It's a small sanctuary. She sits slowly, amazed by what is happening.

"Anisah, we have come to you for help. We cannot succeed without you, for it has been forbidden. Only you can do what we cannot."

They seemed to all speak with one voice.

How can this be; how can I help these beautiful beings? "

But what can I do? What can I possibly do?" she trembles, her voice quavering.

"The Ahar'n, the light of good must be found," *they answer in accord,* **"without its return, this world will be destroyed. Look."**

Anisah turns. The land whirls, dizzying her. Other images flow into her view. She sees a great room, a cavern, a light flashes an unbearable brilliance, she has to cover her eyes.

Shortly, she senses the light has dimmed and she is moving. She looks

*over her arms and sees the farms and meadows flowing beneath her, moun-
tains come rushing toward her. She soars up and up, the mountains fly
away below.*

*Abruptly, she pauses, hovering in the air, and can see clearly into a small
cave where two men sit eating and talking. Somehow, something about the
two men seems familiar, seems right.*

*Her flight continues and takes her over the mountains. The land is bar-
ren now; intense heat blasts upward toward her. The clouds seem to rip
themselves apart, seem to be attacking the mountains to rise over them. Below, tented villages are scattered across an open desert, a great plain, only
the green of scattered oases providing a change from the drab, dusty land.*

*The light flashes in her eyes again, and fades slowly. No longer over the
barren land, she is looking down on two young men walking along a great
road, chatting.*

*Another flash and she's standing in a street in a small town, its street
bustling with activity. A woman walks from one of the buildings as she
watches. Anisah catches her breath. The woman seems to be her, only
older.*

*Is that me? Where am I? What am I doing? Why am I so much older?
She wants to ask why; she wants to know what this all means.*

She's suddenly back in the sanctuary. The faces are visible again.

*"Who are you? You must tell me what you want from me?" she im-
plores them, "Please. I don't understand. I can't help if you won't tell me
what you want."*

**"We cannot reveal more, this is all we can show you
about what will be. You have seen what you need to. You
will understand, you must. You have a power you do not
know, you and the others you will meet. You will know
them when the time arrives. Search your heart and, in that,
you will learn what is to be done,"**

*Speaking as the one voice , their statements cause the words to buzz in
her head.*

**"For you and your world, you must think about what you
have seen in this moment. All is in jeopardy; all is lost unless you can find the answer,"**

*Then the voices become softer, murmuring and fade into silence. The im-
ages float away as though smoke, disappearing.*

She woke with a start, sat up in her bed, stared wildly around her room. She stopped and closed her eyes again. Her hand fiercely clasped the crystal at her chest, her heart beating wildly.

She looked around again. Her bedroom was the same. She exhaled forcefully, realizing she was holding her breath. Her clothing was drenched.

What is happening to my life? Who were they? What can I do? Those places, those people, could be anywhere. Where do I start? Why was I older and where was I? What will my heart lead me to. How can I trust that when I'm so miserable with my life now? Does Old Bas have these horrible dreams?

"I'll ask him the next time I see him," she muttered.

She lay down and, despite tossing and turning, drifted back to sleep with fantasies of places and things drifting lightly through her dreams. She knew she searched for the beings, but they were gone. She cried softly, tears blurring her eyes. She drifted into sleep exhausted.

When she woke again, it was late. She knew immediately she was in trouble. Brae'x would be talking about how lazy she was to her mother. Changing clothes quickly, she ran out into the kitchen, still buttoning her dress front.

"It's about time," Brae'x mumbled over the top of his stupid coffee cup, "Plan to sleep all day? We need to find you a good husband to straighten you out. Your mother and me don't seem to be able to do much with you anymore. You've gotten pretty uppity of late."

"Sit down, eat your supper!" She jumped when he shouted, quickly sat down and began to eat. She turned to look, but her mother was looking away, not wanting to be involved.

She turned back to look directly at Brae'x. *I think you should be more careful, Brae'x. Yes, I believe you walk on dangerous ground.*

She glared at the man. Her eyes glinted.

Brae'x was staring at her, his brow bunched in a self-satisfied look, the one in power.

But slowly, his eyes began to wander away from hers. His face smoothed and he began to busy himself with his plate, shoving the food about as though preparing it to eat. She smirked at him and felt a certain pleasure knowing he had just become a little afraid of her.

She was seventeen now and considered old enough to marry. She had escaped that fate so far but she knew Brae'x wanted her out of the house. He talked about how a girl her age should be married by now and how he would have to do something about her impending spinsterhood unless he could find her a man.

"Maybe marry her off to Old Bas, the tinker, when he comes through the village next time," he said. Old Bas was about eighty with wisps of white hair, small spindly arms and legs, and a great beer belly that hung over his trousers -- he looked as if he were carrying twins.

Anisah knew Brae'x was needling her and she didn't care what he said; the hardest part for her was her mother laughing at his stupid jokes.

She rose from the table and left for her room. Tears came to her eyes as she thought again about how things would be if her father were still alive. If only there was one more herb to try, if they had only known.

Known what? They tried everything Mistress Elspeth knew. She slumped on her bed dejectedly.

Suddenly she sat up as an old memory crept from the back of her thoughts like a mole stealing from its hole. Hadn't Old Bas, old and rickety though he was, once mentioned a school for healers somewhere in the   south?

She remembered he told her it was in a city near the southern coast. Tariny was the name she remembered. Old Bas also told her of sailing ships and the exotic people found there.

Oh, how glorious if it was true. There she could learn those things that would have saved her father. It was too late for that, but not for the opportunity to help others.

How will I tell Mother what I want to do? She asked herself. Schools cost money and they had so very little, certainly not enough for anything so frivolous as an education.

"Oh blast! Why can't I go?" she muttered. There wasn't anything to stop her except herself.

"Just get up and go. Once I find the school mayhap I could find a way to obtain money, or shelter -- cooking, cleaning, sewing or any of the other five hundred things I am forced to do every blessed day anyway."

And now she used those skills for nothing more than the privilege of staying in her own home with her mother and her brothers and sisters.

She decided, at that moment, this was the best time. She had to leave and now, while it still seemed a good idea.

Anisah slid quietly out of her bed, to avoid waking the children sleeping with her.

Quiet as kitten paws on new fallen snow, she dressed in an old brown woolen pair of trousers she wore whenever she had to clean the muck from the horse stalls and all of the other unpleasant chores.

Over the trousers, she put on a dark blue tunic that had been her father's, a bit large but tied with a piece of rope from the shed, it would be fine.

She took her largest kerchief and spread it on the floor. On it she placed her only skirt of gray nubbin wool, her tunic of soft brown wool and flax blend wove with her own hands.

Another skill I can bargain with.

She pulled on her boots and laced them loosely. From over the fireplace she took a small chunk of bread, a few dried apples and figs, and a small bit of cheese. She placed these in her kerchief, carried the bundle and leaned it on the wall next to the door.

She gathered a few more items. Along with her tin cup from the table, a bit of twine and a fishing hook she stole from Brae'x's tackle box -- something no one was allowed to touch -- she gathered things as she thought of each need and bundled all these together to carry on her
back.

Carefully, so the old hinges wouldn't creak, Anisah lifted the lid on her mother's oak chest in the corner near the door and took out the short leather scabbard that held her father's hunting knife. She slid the blade, gleaming in the moonlight coming through the window, from the soft leather and looked at it for a moment, tears forming in her eyes.

Sliding the knife back into the scabbard, she set it down beside the handkerchiefs she bound together loosely to form a sling.

She suddenly felt the warmth under her top; the crystal her mother had only recently given her with no explanation. She asked her mother where the amulet came from and her mother only answered, "From your father."

Now she reached down and pressed it to her chest gently, and a tear rolled slowly down her cheek.

Shaking her head to stop from crying, she put her arm through the loop of the sling and seated it behind her shoulder.

Picking up the knife, she opened the door. Inch by inch she pulled it aside. Once the hinges groaned softly and she froze. Not hearing sounds of anyone moving in the house, she pushed the door open wide enough to slip through.

Once outside, she closed the door gently. She turned once to look back through the window of the tiny house, the only home she had ever known and saw her brothers and sisters tumbled about on their two beds. Her eyes began to water again.

She quickly wiped the tears flowing, despite her effort to be brave, and scurried down the path leading to the road out of town.

She didn't look back until she knew she couldn't see the house, stopped for a moment peering through the dark to catch just a glimpse, turned and ran farther down the road.

"Good riddance," Brae'x mumbled. He was standing in the dark looking out the window as the young girl ran down the path; he smiled to himself. "Just as long as she doesn't show her face around here any more."

In front of the tavern down the road a short distance, Old Bas watched the girl, nodded approval, turned toward the door and entered.

GATHERING

There were five of them, waiting for something to happen without knowing what to expect. They were taken to a huge anteroom.

Three of them, who knew they must go before Baalsa'n, paced in their own way. No one spoke to the others.

Everyone, except Rena'x and Marte, was dressed in black. Rena'x wore light beige, a wrap around his head, garb fitting a desert life; he thought Rab'k's choice was a bit odd but said nothing to the boy about it. Marte wore the drab blue uniform of the servants.

The three in black were bold contrast to the room itself.

They milled about. Rena'x talked in low tones to Rab'k. Marte muttered instructions to Voravia who ignored her completely. None of those in black spoke to each other. Each took furtive glances to form a mental picture and questioned why the others were there.

The great room still seemed empty.

Rena'x had taken a seat on one of the velvet-cushioned couches; he felt relaxed but knew Rab'k wasn't. The boy paced incessantly, scowling at those who happened to walk into his path. Marte busied herself brushing at Voravia's hair or, smoothing down her gown, as though it needed it.

Voravia watched the boy pacing.

Stupid boy, why is he so nervous?

She looked out from under her brow, frowning.

What is this all about any way? Should I be concerned too?

She glanced at the other man who walked more casually. Tall and handsome, he seemed to be one of the gods. He occasionally looked in her direction, but there seemed to be no intent to actually take notice of her; he was just waiting. The older man was obviously escorting the younger man.

Voravia rose, moved across the room, and sat down on another plush sofa just to stop Marte's incessant jabbering and picking at her.

Rab'k glared at everyone.

I can't believe I have to go through this. Who are these people?

He frowned and shook his head, walking even more ardently across the floor, his boots thumping loudly. He didn't want to be here; he was afraid of what was going to happen and he was angry for being afraid.

Mano'n stopped walking about and sat on one of the low benches, waiting.

This is preposterous. What can Baalsa'n be doing? Why hasn't he called us?

No sooner was that thought completed than the heavily gilded door to the chamber swung open and an officer stepped briefly into the room.

"The master will see each of you now," he announced and paused for a reaction. Only the boy jerked around to look at him with those piercing eyes. The officer actually expected more reaction from the rest, but casually dismissed his curiosity.

"Rab'k," he summoned, nodding when the boy turned to face him. Rab'k's face was drawn and pale, "Please come with me." He motioned for the young man to follow him.

Rena'x rose from the couch when Rab'k was called and started to walk toward the door with him. The officer looked at him with no expression at all.

"I'm sorry, sir, but my orders were to bring only the boy," the soldier told him. Rena'x was stunned though no one else could know.

Rab'k obeyed, walked to the door looking back at Rena'x with a puzzled look on his face, turned and walked out of the room. The officer shut the door behind.

The others glanced at each other trying to avoid notice.

Rena'x fought side by side with Baalsa'n during the Varkanian wars; he was the Keeper of the Crystal, an object he always wore beneath his tunic.

Why have I been slighted? Rena'x turned away from the door as it slowly closed, a certain sadness obvious on his face.

Mano'n stood shocked. He knew who he was going to see,

knew mostly what was going to be said and yet this young boy was taken first.

This doesn't make sense. Why the boy first? Who is this boy?

He turned back, looked at Rena'x a moment, then slumped to another couch near the door.

Voravia watched as the two men left. She noticed those remaining seemed to be troubled by the first choice. She found that amusing.

Men are such idiots.

She looked around the room, totally disinterested in the proceedings. She couldn't believe the wealth so obvious in this room; even the ceilings had gold-edged filigree around each of the sectional panels. She gaped, her head drawn back to look at the ceiling.

She was oblivious to what was, or wasn't, going to happen.

She stood to stretch her legs, and the two men rose from their seats.

Well, at least, these two seem to be gentlemen.

She smiled at them, turned and walked toward the rear of the room to look more closely at the two huge vases sitting on pedestals beneath the largest mirror she had ever seen in her life.

She realized she was gawking as she followed the inlaid gold streaming upward to the ceiling. She reached out to touch one of the strains when she heard a noise of the door opening and jumped in surprise.

GETH'N

Geth'n, arise for there is much to be done and it is to you these tasks have come.

Geth'n sat up suddenly on his cot, gasping, shocked from his sleep. He looked around his room in dismay. Jumping up, he stumbled from his bed.

He walked to a window, opened it and looked out, leaning forward to look in all directions. He saw no one. He shook his head trying to clear his thoughts. There were no sounds outside his cottage.

He didn't understand. Someone called him. There was some great urgency; the voice seemed all too clear.

What was that about? Non, I had to be dreaming -- it doesn't make sense.

Now he felt uneasy, a dark foreboding crept into his thought; he shivered from the cold running through him. His clothing was drenched, but that wasn't the cause of this sudden iciness he felt. Shaking his head, hair flying, he pulled back into his room.

Lately, he often dreamed about a darkness sweeping across the land, destroying everything in its path. It was difficult for him to imagine what these dreams meant, if anything.

He had heard nothing of dark evil, or destruction to any part of the land. There were no rumors, nor tales, of any of this happening anywhere.

Only one thing. A great storm, maybe the greatest ever, had destroyed an entire fleet returning from Habeinland to Tariny, sweeping it all into the depths without a trace. No one was there to witness the sinking, but the fleet had not returned and there was no doubt the storm was more destructive than thought possible.

He and Pet'r, his lifelong friend, were attending the university in Larilla, just north of their home, Peetle.

Peetle was a quiet and sleepy village where fishermen and their families struggled to live comfortably. The boys wanted a bit more from life than this though they had labored hard for their families while growing into young men.

Pet'r, who lately seemed aimless and held a vague look in his eyes, had long wondered about the desolate wasteland north of the great mountains and, being a fisherman's son, the monstrous, storming sea on its shores.

Geth'n, a brilliant young man, was always more curious about the dark lands of the west and the stories of strange things that happened to men who wandered too closely.

He believed in the magical realms of wizardry and sorcery. He felt certain these things existed, but everyone in Peetle scoffed at him, except Pet'r.

What brought all of these variables into this world? Geth'n often wondered. *Isn't there strong evidence magic is in the world? Isn't obvious this effected the dramatic changes documented in much we read?*

He felt magic and mystery entwined; he thought Narhtrae a great land of the commonplace but with intrigues accepted as natural.

In his talks with Pet'r late at night, he questioned. *Am I the first to notice a pattern in some of these things? Were there others who wondered too?*

Now, Geth'n felt an overwhelming desire, a need to know more about these mysterious things. He realized he was pursuing something only intimated in what he had read thus far.

But often he ran across passages about a talisman purported to hold the souls of the gods buried deep within it; and of another which held demonic souls of the creatures of a darker world.

He became obsessed with knowing more about both. He couldn't erase the constant ramblings of his thoughts, especially his dreams. It began to show in his studies.

"Pet'r, I've got to do something about this. I can't sleep. I'm not able to concentrate on what I should. I can't get rid of these dreams I'm having. No, they're nightmares. Nothing makes sense." Geth'n talked earnestly to his friend one night, desperation in his tone and in his face, slapping another of the great books closed.

Pet'r looked at his friend askance, "I think you should go and discover more. And the only place I know you can do that would be Tariny -- the great university there," he said, gazing at the ceiling of the old building. "There are no guarantees you'll find the answers, but you've exhausted these." He laid his hand on one of the ancient volumes on the table.

"Pet'r, you're right. Would you consider going with me? You have an interest too," Geth'n asked, not actually expecting Pet'r to agree. "Maybe it's asking too much of our friendship, but I really need you to go with me if I'm to do this."

"Geth'n, you're like my brother. And you've not been very agreeable lately. You just seem anxious about everything I'd assumed your search has something to do with that. But,I have to admit feeling a longing to go somewhere, just for the adventure. If for no other reason than discovering great fun, let's take a sabbatical and go in search of your lost secrets," Pet'r answered slowly, looking off toward the ceiling of the library again, "You're right; we two fishermen need to swim upstream for a while and experience more than can be found here."

"What? Are you agreeing with me?" Geth'n questioned in amazement. "Aren't you concerned about losing our chance to get what we've always worked for?" Geth'n, remembering how often Pet'r was the calming factor whenever they talked about their future, was surprised by the answer.

Pet'r shrugged his shoulders and grinned at his friend. "No, not really,"

Pet'r looked directly at Geth'n now. "We've worked hard. We know what we must discover. Possibly I'm not as troubled as you are by my quest, but I believe there might be some force beyond us, beyond you particularly, causing our anxiety."

"I believe some of this magic you talk about so much is becoming a part of us -- what we are and will be." He sat up and stretched his arms above his head. "Besides, we can always come back and finish this."

Geth'n had wanted to broach the subject for some time now, but he hesitated to do so. He knew he was going to pursue this dream, this nightmare, to find some answers but he hadn't expected his friend to relent so easily. Geth'n would've never insisted. Pet'r couldn't have given him a greater gift.

"Ah well, what is a better teacher than real life?" Pet'r laughed. "You know, my father always says that whenever he's questioning me about why I had to come to Larilla to school. I can imagine what he's going to say about this grand idea."

They both laughed aloud. A number of the others in the library turned to look at them with frowns of disapproval. One hissed at them and only caused them to laugh louder.

"I believe we must do this, my friend," Geth'n said softly to Pet'r. "It is time we embarked on a real adventure, as you said, and see what the world holds for us and determine if our world is in some sort of danger."

"Then let's get some rest," Pet'r said calmly. "I believe an adventure does indeed await us and we shouldn't be too tired." They laughed again.

Geth'n closed the great book in front of him slowly, placed his hand gently on the old cover, smiled and turned away.

Leaving the library, they went home, occasionally bursting into laughter again as they strolled along. They weren't in any hurry now.

Later that night, as he lay in the dark thinking about their journey, Geth'n felt a certain sense of relief. He still couldn't quite understand the strength of resolve he had in this quest.

The sad thing, and this troubled him, was there might not be any answers anywhere to the puzzles he had discovered in the ancient books of the small library in Larilla.

There was no direct answers about an object called the Ahar'n, only implications and a name for it. Geth'n had not discussed this part of his search with his friend; he didn't know why but there seemed to be something making him hold back that part of what he sensed.

He couldn't explain this concentration on one element because he didn't understand why he was driven to do so.

He arrived at home and, being so intensely immersed in thought, went straight to his sleeping quarters and lay down to think. But he could feel himself drifting away as soon as he lay down.

He is standing, looking out over a broad plain, mountains jut starkly from the earth beyond. The ground is shrouded with a gray blanket of snow, or dust. He can't tell which.

Here and there a sickly tree begs, branches outstretched toward the sky, a plea for life. There is thick, but shapeless, cover over the sky, moving slowly, slipping silently through the mountain peaks; there is an odd sameness in everything he can see.

Above him, the clouds, barely discernible in light shades of gray, flow gently but swiftly above him. There are no colors, he realizes. Everything is shaded in white, gray and black.

He begins to walk sluggishly toward the mountains he can see, in the distance where two ranges meet with a pass between. He feels he needs to reach the pass to escape. But, he can't tell whether he is moving or not.

He can see trees creeping, strangely, away from him. If he turns toward any of the small patches near him, they seem to move obliquely from him as though avoiding him.

The skies never change though they shift so the clouds are always flowing toward him.

He trudges on at a slow pace, not able to walk any faster. Looking through the mists flowing around him, he notices a small black patch breaking the surface ahead. He turns toward it and the whole scene spins in the opposite direction as though pivoting with his movement.

He stops and slowly moves his body back and forth, then stops when he feels he has the patch just ahead of him. He continues walking, trying to maintain a straight line.

As he nears the patch, he realizes there is a hole in the blanket and walks to it. Stopping, he looks down and notes someone, or something, has fallen from above, striking the ground and breaking through into a strange space below. The texture of the void in the opening is fluid, like the sky, and seems to always be flowing.

The ragged edge of the opening shows the impact and he decides the object was, in fact, human, but he sees no other sign of what it might be. Suddenly a face appears and an arm reaches toward the surface from below. The apparition floats away but returns again. He can't see who it is though he senses he should know.

He wants to help. He looks around him slowly. Every direction he turns he causes the landscape to spin about him in the opposite direction; it is dizzying to move. He can see no trace anyone has passed through the land; he sees no trace he has either.

That last bit of information puzzles him.

Turning back, he is surprised by the presence of Pet'r. He wasn't there a moment ago. Pet'r is standing without moving, looking into the gap in the surface.

Then Geth'n notices a young woman standing a short distance away. She is holding her hand out to him; her face implores him to see her, but she doesn't come nearer.

"Welcome, young Geth'n. Is this not a beautiful place?" A voice speaks softly; a sinister, but mellow, voice which seems to come from everywhere. "Do you not think so -- and this could be Aerolan, could it not? Ah, beautiful Aerolan." Strong, deep laughter rumbles across the empty land; it seems to flow over him but passes on. He almost falls forward into the abyss below the hole but rights himself somehow.

Standing and staring at the opening, he decides he must help, bends slowly and reaches his hand toward the broken surface. His hand disappears as he pushes it into the liquid to his wrist. The image from the other side reaches for his hand, but can't touch it.

Suddenly and mysteriously, there is a touch. A shudder passes through his body and he jerks his hand back quickly, looking at it and frowning.

There was no harm done, but his hand looks strangely different than it had; it seems withered or weakened somehow. He looks around again at the featureless terrain; he notices his companions have disappeared. He dizzily looks around in all directions but the others have truly gone.

Standing slowly upright, he looks for something else to put into the liquid. Not far from him lays a branch from one of the trees; he turns -- this time with his eyes closed — opens them, walks to and picks up the limb, closes his eyes, turns, reopens his eyes and walks back to the hole.

The image in the opening occasionally becomes more visible and then fades, as though the person below is leaping to reach the hole.

He begins to lower the branch into the hole slowly. The image disappears, as does the end of the branch. Nothing is happening.

Why doesn't the person take the branch? How did anybody else get here? Did he or she fall from the sky? What is the meaning here? I should be able to . . .

The branch suddenly is pulled violently into the fluid. He can't release it quickly enough. He feels himself being dragged toward the opening, yet he can't let go. He sees his hands, grasping the branch firmly, meet the surface and disappear. All his movement, his falling, his mouth opening to cry out seem extended in time. He wants to reach out and stop his fall, but he can't.

His face approaches the surface. As he reaches it, he tries to crane his head backward to avoid the entrance, but he feels himself plunging through and beyond . . .

Geth'n, screaming, slammed to the floor of his bedroom; he was falling in his dream. He quickly jumped up but stumbled backward and sat heavily to the floor.

Scrambling up again, he turned quickly to look around his room. He couldn't believe it; he was safe, but exhausted. He stumbled to his bed and fell across it, staring at the floor.

His hand hurt; he looked at it and something seemed wrong. He flexed it and it seemed to work correctly. He tried to pick up one of the books lying beside his bed, and it slid through his fingers. His hand was weaker. He looked at it again, turning it slowly and shook his head.

Why am I dreaming about such horrible things?

He rolled on his back, his eyes darting about the room looking for something wrong, something to explain what he had just experienced. It surely was a dream, an incredible nightmare.

But what about my hand? What is happening to me?

He sat up and stood beside the bed, turned and walked to the window. Darkness had fallen again. He was asleep all day -- and nothing was readied for the journey tomorrow.

I'll probably not get any more sleep tonight either. I leave tomorrow and I'm not ready. I'm not certain I can get ready.

He lay down again, rolling onto his back. A feeling of dread flowed over him, yet he also felt a need for haste. At this moment, he had his first doubts about his decision. He wasn't certain what he was doing, or what he needed to do. Something in the dream was a message.

From whom? Why?

Suddenly agitated, he began to rush around his room collecting his clothing and other gear. Tonight, I'll just refuse to sleep and dream again. I have to be ready by morning.

The night wore on. Geth'n placed everything in his pack, then removed it all. He chose some other items, discarded some and repacked. He would sit for a moment then redo everything. But as he worked, he pondered the wonder of his dream and decided there was a message.

A message of doom he felt he could not ignore.

Maybe it is destined for me to take this journey, maybe it should be.

He felt comforted by the admission. He calmed himself and packed the final time, certain he had chosen the correct items. Each item was uniquely what he felt he needed.

By dawn he had changed, Geth'n was in no great rush to depart nor was he concerned about his dreams; his journey was beginning at last.

He felt his mission was a good one, or certainly, the right one. He felt tired, but much calmer now. He had made his decision.

He knew he had justified this journey with vague explanations before last night. His friends, and particularly his parents, expressed their concerns with worried glances at him, but he knew now he had to go.

The dreams made that need real.

He also knew his life, and the answers to what he would do with it, lay ahead, not here in Peetle or in Larilla. He couldn't answer what the journey would bring, only that it had to be taken.

He and Pet'r left in the early afternoon and, though they were not aware, an old peddler watched as the two boys walked away from the village and disappeared over the first rise.

The old man then turned away and climbed slowly into his cart, flipped the reins at his oxen, and began to travel slowly toward Peetle. He looked over his shoulder in the direction the boys had taken.

"You shall rue the day you left this simple land, young Geth'n. You shall rue the day," he chuckled to himself, his eyes glowing momentarily.

He turned, flicked the reins again and rode away slowly, the cart swinging from side to side on the rough road, pots and pans clanking.

REBUFF

Rab'k walked down the corridor with growing apprehension as he and the officer approached a massive door standing partially open. He sensed he was probably going into the room behind it and was, despite his efforts to ignore his feelings, troubled by what he was about to face.

What trials will be presented? Am I worthy?

Thoughts not at all like those only a short time before.

He and the officer arrived, he could feel his tension grip him; he stopped before turning, not looking into the great hall he knew was there.

"Are you coming, sir?" the officer had stopped, turned and looked back at Rab'k, "You must follow me. Baalsa'n does not like to be kept waiting."

Rab'k looked up quickly and nodded. With great effort, he faced the door and stepped through.

Rab'k hadn't walked into the room very far when he stopped. He couldn't believe the immensity and the mystery; the lights were dim and he was not able to see how far the room extended in any direction.

He had never seen such a place, not even the great corridors, through which he just passed through, compared. He stood and tried to absorb all of it.

"Rab'k! Come to me!" a voice, seemingly from a great distance, boomed across at him.

Rab'k had some difficulty finding the source.

Softly, a dim light began to glow to his left revealing a man sitting on a throne. The man sat straight; he was dressed in a long black robe with a longer coat draped over his shoulders, dropping in folds to the floor below. Rab'k could not see the face, but the glow around the man pervaded the area.

Rab'k turned briefly and noticed the officer had departed.

The boy walked slowly toward the dais. He looked around to

see more of this cavernous room, but he could barely perceive anything with the dark shadows. He still couldn't make out the features of the man sitting on the throne.

"Come," a softer voice implored.

Baalsa'n motioned with his hand, beckoning to the boy. Rab'k could only see a large man, strongly built, silver hair sweeping down and across his shoulders, dressed simply in the black robe.

"We have much to talk about," the voice continued. He walked toward it.

Rab'k felt drawn by a force holding his soul.

Baalsa'n raised his hand with the palm toward Rab'k. "That is close enough," he spoke from out of the light, "I wanted to tell you what you must do to help destroy the heathens to the south. I understand, from talking to Rena'x, you are anxious to get started."

"Yes," Rab'k choked, trying to talk, "Yes, sir. I've been trained for that. I am eager to bring destruction on them. I don't understand why I'm here today. Rena'x, my father, should be here, not me."

"All in good time. My friend, Rena'x, has his own mission to perform. He has never failed me. Do you believe you can achieve the same?" the voice raised in volume slightly with the question. Rab'k noticed the change, but gave no outward sign.

I need to be cautious. I must answer correctly, or all is lost.

"I've not been tested, sir. But I do feel Rena'x has taught me well, and I think I've learned from the experience. My father has no peer." Rab'k answered, as he thought he ought.

"You're first impression, the one about being cautious, is wisdom I seek," Baalsa'n said, "You must be as strong as your father. You will be subjected to much until the time for the change is upon us. At first though, you will have to be willing to live among those you hate."

"But, I thought . . ." Rab'k interjected. There was only a blur of movement from Baalsa'n.

Suddenly, Rab'k's throat constricted, he couldn't breathe. He grabbed at his neck trying to release the pressure. Then it was gone. He gasped for breath.

"I'll not tolerate any insolence. Take that as a lesson. You must control your tongue; there is no room in what I have planned for making errors in judgment. You will be watched; you will restrict your anger and learn about your enemy. Any people can rise up against their masters if they are incited to anger by the willfulness of those masters.

We will not bring our justice to these people if you are not cautious. That is the most important lesson you can learn from this visit," Baalsa'n leaned forward, placed one hand on his knee, and spoke with malevolent intensity.

He is not to be toyed with. Rab'k learned during those moments. *Here is a man, a god, who must be feared.*

"You will go into the southern region. You must go to the city of Tariny and attend the university. You must learn all you can about these people, their customs, and their lives; become a captain of commerce; attach yourself to men of wealth and power. From this, we can discover much.

More importantly, there is the Ahar'n, a talisman, the antipathy of the Crystal Rena'x protects. It was hidden many centuries ago on this world. You must do everything in your power to find it, or its whereabouts, and report those findings to Rena'x immediately.

This one command, above all, is the most important of all I tell you today. This Ahar'n could prevent our victory if it is discovered by anyone else. Be cautious, as you acted earlier, but it is imperative the Ahar'n be found." Baalsa'n sat back suddenly, as though signifying the completion of his instructions and quietly watched Rab'k.

Yes, sir," Rab'k spoke in a low tone, disquieted by the experience of a moment ago and by the instructions he had just received, "When should I leave, sir?"

"Immediately. See to it," Baalsa'n waved him away, as he rose from his throne, turned and walked away, disappearing from Rab'k's sight.

Be cautious? Find the Ahar'n?

Rab'k could only shake his head. After a moment, he turned back toward the door through which he had entered. He pushed it open, walked through.

The officer was waiting for him outside the door. He turned and they walked slowly down the long corridor.

Rab'k had nothing to say.

OBSTINACY

"Voravia. I believe it is your turn," a voice announced. She jumped at the voice and looked around at the door, the officer stood there motioning for her to follow.

The young man had returned with him and was talking to the older man in low tones. He was shaking his head, but the older man talked and motioned with his hands apparently responding to the boy's questions.

She glanced at the young man as she walked past and observed an angry boy, maybe violently so.

She arrived at the chamber quickly. The officer said nothing to her and she no longer was in a gay mood. He led her to the center of the room, turned and walked away.

She could see a raised platform where a small throne sat. She was alone, or so she thought. It was difficult to see anything because the light was so low.

"Welcome, my dear," a voice spoke gently. She jumped again in her nervousness; she knew her palms were wet. She wiped them quickly on her gown, trying to hide her action, and looked up to see a man sitting on the throne.

She was stunned by his presence and curtsied to him as best she could. She never had an opportunity to show respect for someone before and certainly not in such a grand place.

"I understand you have a special talent," the man stated. His voice was so mellow she began to feel more comfortable and not so vulnerable. She wrinkled her brow at the statement, not understanding what he was talking about.

"Probably learned from your mother," he added.

What does this man know about my mother?

"I don't understand, your highness. What special talent? Do you know my mother?" Voravia asked with a great deal more bravado than she felt.

"Your mother and I had a rather special relationship at one

time," the man answered, "possibly she mentioned me. I am Baalsa'n."

Voravia's eyes rounded with surprise. She remembered her mother telling her of the man who was her father; a father who left them behind when he went off to war. That man's name was Baalsa'n. She had never known him. This surely couldn't be him.

"But, sir. That cannot be. He was killed in a war in some distant place. We never heard from him again. The name is a coincidence; you can't be that man," she was speaking in earnest now, walking slowly toward the man. He held up his hand and she stopped.

"But I am. I'm happy to see she spoke of me," he offered.

"I believe you wouldn't have liked what she said,"

Voravia spoke forcefully, "We led a hard life, a terribly hard life. Barely surviving the land and the life we lived. Our customs are cruel to a widowed woman with a child. You left us when we needed you. You are a blackhearted and evil man!" She was shouting at him now.

"Yes, I suppose I am," he agreed, chuckling at her ferocity, "but you did survive and now you are here. Welcome, daughter."

"I am not your daughter. I refuse to admit it. How could you do leave us?" she yelled back at him, stomping about in her anger, glaring at him. For some reason, she was afraid to approach any closer.

"I had other priorities," Baalsa'n stated, simply, without emotion. "I had many things to do to gain this power," He waved his hand as though pointing out the obvious. " I intend to keep it. And you will provide more advantages with your power and will support me in what I now must begin. You will be rewarded for the effort and intensity you show."

"What are you talking about? I'm not helping you; I'm going to leave now," Voravia shouted again, turned back around and walked toward the exit.

Suddenly she rose into the air, rotating so she was upside down, looking down at the black marbled floor below. She tried vainly to keep her gown from falling.

"You are impetuous," he laughed lightly, "You must teach me a bit of this strength you have. Believe me, I would be an apt and attentive student," he laughed again.

Voravia opened her mouth to disagree, but willed herself to fall. She reached out with her hands and, as she did, she righted herself and sank slowly to her feet in front of, but no closer to, Baalsa'n.

She gave him a haughty glare; her arms clasped below her breasts in defiance.

"Ah, there. I knew you could be a malleable student yourself," Baalsa'n spoke, shifting in his seat.

Voravia stood and stared at the man who claimed to be her father.

"You see, you just saved yourself from a serious 'accident' by stopping your fall. It seems you know a number of 'interesting' things. But, time is short. I would love to chat with you more but I have much to do."

"Leaving again." Voravia could not contain herself, "Seems fitting."

Baalsa'n stood. He stepped toward her. She backed away, wanting to escape, but couldn't move. He rushed closer as though to attack her.

She could see his face, handsome but fiercely strong, a will so strong, it would never be broken. She backed away, hoping not to fall.

"Enough! Silence!" Baalsa'n voice rumbled as he stopped, glaring at her. She clamped her hands to her ears, "I will not tolerate anymore!"

Voravia cringed from the voice and the man. Baalsa'n turned and walked back to the throne. She backed away slowly, thinking again she might escape.

"You would be ill advised to try to escape, my daughter," he spoke as he spun about to sit again, "and there is nowhere you can go without my permission. I must tell you that you will serve me. It's your purpose in my plan whether you like it or not."

Daughter! Not likely or accepted

She stood glaring at him. She could think of nothing else to do; she didn't want to talk or listen.

She wanted to turn this man to stone as she had the other, but nothing worked -- she had tried. So she waited to hear what he had to say.

"Even should you attempt to deny what I have told you, it is true. There is a purpose and now there is you with the power necessary for you to contribute," Baalsa'n spoke softly but insistently.

He gave her more instructions about how, when and where she was to go, why she had to be there and what she had to do after her arrival.

She couldn't believe what she was hearing.

Go to the South? Claim an ancient castle? Build an army that would follow their leader into hell? How can I do these things; I know nothing of these things. I know nothing. I'm a simple girl from the wasteland

She began to cry softly, tears slowly flowing down her cheeks.

"It will not be as bad as you may think now, but whatever you think, you must do these things," he added, "there is much to be learned where you are going."

"Below this castle to which I send you, there are great manuscripts buried, prepared through the ages and placed there as men lost interest in their 'gods'," he chuckled. "There is knowledge to be gained by their reading. Particularly about an object called the Ahar'n hidden on this planet since its rebirth.

It's imperative we know the whereabouts of this amulet. You must research the writings and discover where it is. I, and the rest, will await your discoveries with interest."

"Why me? I have no diligence with resolving problems; I can't work like that. Isn't there someone else?" Voravia implored, knowing as she spoke the die was cast.

She realized she would have to go. She knew immediately and now she felt compelled to go. And didn't know why.

She stopped crying, her mood changed dramatically. She held her head higher, her brilliant hair flared out about her face, which now showed a hardness that wasn't there before.

Her face, beautiful as it was, wouldn't delight the young men again; there was too much danger evident in the green eyes glistening with anger. Too dangerous.

"I will leave at dawn. I'm eager to serve you, Father," she spoke sullenly, "and I will search diligently." She paused and glowered at Baalsa'n.

Hate was a part of what they were to each other.

"The two men. The younger one and the handsome one. They are your brothers," he added, looking toward a distant part of the room she couldn't see, but she didn't look away nor did she react to what he said about the others.

"They too have their separate tasks and when the time comes, they will come to you for guidance. That is my decision. It will be done," he stopped talking abruptly, "You may leave now."

Without looking either left or right, Voravia turned toward the door and walked out without speaking again.

<u>DISCORD</u>

The door of the sitting room opened again. The young woman walked into the chamber, glancing at Mano'n briefly and smirked. She paused, said nothing, then walked deliberately out the entry door and disappeared. The older woman jumped up and followed.

"Mano'n, if you please?" the officer looked at Mano'n as he rose, turned and walked away. Mano'n followed him to the chamber.

"Welcome, my son," Baalsa'n offered, a light smile on his face, "Please make yourself comfortable." He pointed toward a small divan nearby.

"We have a problem, you and I. You have known for some time what needs to be done. Yet you have dallied a bit too much and tarried too long for my liking. Do you have an explanation?"

Mano'n walked to the couch and sat, crossed his legs and tried to relax.

He was here before.

"Have you revealed your fatherly affection to the other two, Sir?" he asked, ignoring the question proffered. He fiddled with a small crevice in the workings of the arm of the couch.

He didn't look up to see the reaction; he knew Baalsa'n had no emotional tie to any of them and he only wanted to goad him.

"I see you haven't given up your flippant ways either; strangely, your sister. and the boy, have much the same tendencies. I find this very curious, must be the nature of humans to feel the need to be more arrogant than they can afford. Particularly with me. I've little patience for it."

Baalsa'n spoke evenly, but now Mano'n knew he should keep his face averted. Baalsa'n demanded and expected obedience.

"Without wasting more time with you, I expect you to return to the tasks I assigned you before. This time you will be more diligent or suffer the consequences.

Your daughter, how is she developing? Have you begun to teach her as yet? Or were you running away to avoid your responsibility to her and me?" Baalsa'n turned in his seat, his arm resting on the arm of the chair for support and spoke quickly and harshly, glaring at Mano'n.

"I d-don't know; I've been away," Mano'n was stammering now. He was more concerned than he thought he would be.

He hoped, on his way here and before, Baalsa'n wouldn't pass too severe a sentence for his future. He wanted to be a part of what was to come, but didn't wish to expend too much effort.

"Then return to your duty! You, of the three, should know what you must do. Now, return and accomplish what must be done. I will not tolerate this lack of effort any longer!" Baalsa'n stood abruptly and shouted, angrier than Mano'n remembered seeing him before.

"Yes, I'll do so, sir," Mano'n could think of nothing else to say. He sat looking at the floor, both feet down now, his hands on his knees, hoping this would come to an ending gracefully.

"Then get out of my sight! I expect reports showing you've accomplished something, right or wrong," Baalsa'n' voice rumbled with his decree.

There would be a harsh sentence to experience, if the decree was not followed. Mano'n was aware of too many things that might happen to him if he failed.

In silence, he rose and without looking at Baalsa'n, left the room.

GARV'N

For generations, men dealt with each other through fair barter, but there were some wished to control more.

There were those who gathered together materials in isolation from need; who felt using the means of other men was reasonable and even a service extended in generosity.

They stored away in great houses more foods than any one man could use in order to sell back to those without, only a portion of what they produced. And these men rose to power.

These men created wealth -- wealth that costs the many more than they could afford.

In the end, there were only a few men who held, in a vice grip, all that was produced by the work of others. These wanted only the wealth; the manipulation and control of this wealth filled their souls with excitement.

These men were held in awe. They were not only infected with their own greed, but they soon only wanted to possess in order to control. Of these men, and of one man, a man who did not fit this mold but wished only to relieve the injustice, we now learn . . .

Garv'n Anspar sat at the table in his huge study, skimming over pages in several books scattered around him. The books were ancient and in several stages of wear and deterioration.

All of his wealth gave Garv'n free time to pursue the study of magical arts; a study he had become fascinated with in the last few years.

These led him to the discovery of something that could be just what he needed to satisfy some longing he did not yet understand. He searched continually for a mystery -- one seemingly beyond comprehension.

He had recently acquired a small dusty diary, part of it was written in an ancient tongue. He gleaned, from the parts he could read, there was some source of power lost before recorded time.

72

An object, the Ahar'n, was the source of more power than any man knew.

Garv'n had no use for power except it helped him retain his wealth, but he knew this Ahar'n could be dangerous in the wrong hands. He also knew if there was any chance a power so strong could be discovered, the man who could ,and would do so, was Rab'k Monthen.

Abruptly, he paused and began to mumble to himself about one of the pages in the smallest book. He pushed his head near the page, his long gray hair falling about his face, squinted and then raised his head, pushing his glasses back onto his nose.

What a pity. Whoever wrote this could have had better handwriting.

"Stupid. Why write something if you wanted no one else to read it?" he grumbled about the scribe's carelessness. He read further, mumbling even more.

Suddenly he sensed movement behind him. He looked, glancing over his glasses, and realizing his surroundings had changed dramatically. He almost dropped the manual in his surprise.

He is no longer in his library but in the mountains to the north. Looking up, he sees the sky swirling with dark clouds racing through the passes.

He turns slowly, looking about him and trying to decide where he is. But all he discovers is he doesn't know where he is.

He feels endangered and runs to a small grove of trees to hide. He isn't certain what he's afraid of, but he senses this place is enchanted in some way.

How did I get here? The book? The statement I just read?

He glances down at the book, which he still holds.

What is this place? Why did that particular passage bring me here?

Suddenly a great light flashes, blinding him. He shuts his eyes and when he opens them again, he isn't alone.

A man stands before him shimmering., as though a ghost.

Garv'n. How curious.

Strange you have come. You have somehow discovered an immense secret, a vital one to mankind.

You were not expected, but you are here and must be told some of the secret. We implore you to use this information to help prevent a disastrous ending for this world.

Garv'n realizes there are no sounds other than the wind blowing through the trees. The other man's thoughts are being transmitted into his mind. He shakes his head from side to side to clear it, but to no avail.

The other man looks at him with an amused expression.

I see you do not believe. Why have you taken the time to study this small epistle, unless you anticipated such as this happening? How curious you disbelieve.

Garv'n opens his mouth, but finds he can't speak.

Am I too only allowed to think of what I should say?

So, you can accept some things.

The other's thought came to him quietly.

At least, you are an honest man. But we can not tarry, time is important. Let me reveal those things you need to know before this moment is ended.

The incantation you spoke was no more than a signal intended to propel you to this spot in time, it will not last much longer. Soon you will return to where you were before.

How do you know my name?

Because you have told me.

I am Yenist'n of the Al-Esfer'n. You have just read some of my scripts. The Al-Esfer'n did and do exist, but that is not so important now. Let me tell you of things important and dangerous we hope you will help deter.

I must elaborate on some of your history. Ages ago, we came and brought life to this planet. But we knew it was a life that eventually would be disrupted by an enormous power from beyond this world.

We have tried many times before this and have always fallen to this great scourge that devours all living things. We have decided to fight back this time and thus the warning you are now entrusted with.

We hope you will go forth and bring our message to

74

mankind, in anyway you are able, so the battles and wars to come shall not be lost.

But what can I do?

Garv'n is astonished by what he is hearing and how he is sensing it.

I'm not a man of war. I've no such influence with men of my world. I have only been trying to be a scholar of sorts and came to by by your small volume by chance.

That is understood. As I said, you are a surprise. But, you can do many things, I believe. A man of your public image and standing in this world can influence many. But the major request we have is you find the Ahar'n and protect it.

We cannot express any greater need than this. There are others who will serve by their might and their power, but you, if you are able, can preserve what we, the Al-Esfer'n, can provide at the day of a final battle.

We know the time is coming and we are preparing those others for that eventuality. You can find this Ahar'n. It is the source of power that will win the day at Erxmag'dn, the day of reckoning.

Without it, there is danger of failure.

We ask, we implore you, to accept this search and hold it dear to your heart. Aerolan must have this Ahar'n, and this world must have it.

In your hands, we place this task and the gods, you only vaguely remember, will be with you.

And a warning now before you return to your home.

Beware of Rab'k, he is evil and will try to destroy you for this Ahar'n. He serves the Evil One and will show no mercy if he knows you might know a way to find it.

The man's image began to waver; the background of the mountain and trees began to fade.

"But how will I know where to look?" Garv'n shouted at the image.

The book will tell you, be diligent.

The other disappeared from view, or actually the view simply disappeared. Garv'n, staggering from the sudden change, reached for a chair to steady himself.

He was desperately clutching the small manual in his hand, so tightly his arm ached. He relaxed, looked around and realized he was back in his library.

It took him a moment to recover but he knew no matter how badly written the small book was it held immense significance.

He recognized he needed to discover the single bit of information he sought after all these days of reading.

He now knew this would be one of the most important things he would ever achieve in his lifetime.

He walked slowly to a nearby chair, sat down again and opened the book to a page at random.

At that moment, the book began to glow, radiating light into the room. And shimmering in that light, balanced in the air, was a vision of a place in the mountains to the west and near the sea.

As he watched, the apparition grew larger, revealing more of that country and he realized the Ahar'n must be hidden in the caves of that region.

Voravia's land? How could that be?

The light winked out. Garv'n sat stunned for a moment, but slowly leaned back in his chair and made the decision to make the effort to do what was asked of him.

Pushing away from the table, he stood and walked across the inlaid floor of his enormous study, his long robe whistling with crispness of its fine materials.

Walking to a window where great curtains draped in certain magnificence, he pushed one aside and glanced out at his wife and their children playing in the garden.

Beyond, the sea glistened in the late afternoon, sparkling into an eternal sky beyond.

Truly a beautiful place.

He turned back, letting the curtain fall back into place, and looked around his study.

Like everything Garv'n owned the floor was beautiful but overdone. More like a tapestry than a floor, there was a picture of a forest scene, inlaid in the wood, containing pieces of many different fine woods delicately carved into shapes of exotic flora and fauna.

The room glistened as the candle flickered; the fine metals in the ornate carvings and gilded paintings hanging all about the room glittered in the low light.

Owning fine things mattered very much to Garv'n. This mansion was but one of his homes. He also owned several hunting lodges and smaller seaside castles. All of these were filled with only the best.

Garv'n was born into a very poor family; he, his mother and siblings often went hungry, but the gods blessed him with a sharp mind and he learned quickly.

Begging was his first job and, observing the crowds, saw the pickpockets and cut purses among them and took note.

As soon as his mother allowed him to leave her sight, he began bringing home more money than she had ever dreamed. He knew those few coins were nothing compared to what the merchants made.

He saw fine homes of these men in Tariny, saw the ships loaded and bound for other ports. He watched as exotic goods arrived from abroad. There were silks and spices. More ships arrived each day laden with fine woods, furniture and thousands of crates filled with crystal and other finery. This was where the money was, this was what he wanted.

At the age of ten, Garv'n was out knocking at the doors of the fancy homes in town asking for any odd job. They all gave him a bit of change for sweeping the walks or polishing the doorknockers.

Everyday he would make the same rounds, finally began to acquire small tasks from several, and the servants of these houses began to trust him.

He was soon being sent on errands to the butchers, bakers and other shops. On certain nights, when there were parties, he brought special confections from the sweets and pastry shops.

His rewards were the special tips and other goods, freely given to him. These he took home to his mother.

One day, after running deliveries for some time, one of the merchants, Lord Farss, noticed him as he ran up to complete one of the deliveries.

"Who is that youngster?" he asked his butler, after the boy scampered away.

"Just a boy from the village, sire. He frequently performs odd jobs or carries messages for us. He does no harm and I can actually trust him with the money. Brings all the change back and usually gets a bargain to boot. I've asked at several shops about the prices they've given him and he's been honest every time," the butler answered.

"Well then, perhaps we should find him a more permanent position. Good honest help is difficult to find," Lord Farss said, and then instructed the butler. "Have him to come to my library when he has finished."

The next day, Garv'n was offered the position of scullery boy. He accepted eagerly, although he knew what hard, dirty work it was., because he saw it as a way to be near wealth.

Happily for him, this was only the beginning. His duties and responsibility increased as he became older and as Lord Farss's staff realized what an intelligent lad he was.

Lord Farss took a special interest in Garv'n and began to teach him aspects of handling the assets of large institutions and the finer points of making deals at the markets.

Garv'n eventually became Lord Farss's personal assistant and frequently dealt with financial arrangements when his employer was busy elsewhere.

When his mentor died, Garv'n was not surprised he had inherited a bit of money for his years of service and loyalty. With this tidy sum, he began to build his own business.

He was now taking care of his family, building them a better home outside the slums, providing them with better clothing and food. He and his family would not want for anything ever again.

At first, Garv'n's dealings were small, but he was shrewd and usually made the better of any business affair, reaping a greater profit each time. He built a reputation as a man to be reckoned with at the auction block.

He began to buy ships and one by one he built his own fleet. He hired servants, bought land and properties all about, aided by his loyal assistant, Rab'k Monthen.

He met Rab'k Monthen through mutual friends at the gentleman's club. The boy had just completed his training at the university in Tariny and was beginning to make a name for himself as a strong, though somewhat ruthless, businessman.

Garv'n liked the young man when he finally met him and took the boy under his wing, as his mentor had done for him.

Since then, they both were quite happy with the arrangement, making good their decisions at the markets and earning great sums of money in the bargain. In a very short time, they became the controlling forces in all trade areas. Garv'n became a very wealthy man with nothing much to do with his money, except make more.

Unfortunately he was going to begin losing money if things continued as they were. Droughts in the South had ruined crops of fine smoking tobacco and a strange disease in the northern regions wiped out whole herds of cattle. Storms in the sea of Cegros delayed several of his silk shipments. His failure to deliver was making his clients extremely unhappy.

Garv'n's concern with protecting his wealth, along with his faltering interest in business, brought him to the decision Rab'k should become the manager of his great estate.

Quickly, the problems were resolved and everything became orderly again. Garv'n had no idea how Rab'k managed to accomplish such a feat but he was happy with the results and felt a certain trust in Rab'k's ability to protect his financial interests.

Garv'n turned to other interests.

He trusted Rab'k in business, but he was uncertain he could trust him as a man. He heard a few stories from his servants that made him uneasy about his partner.

There was a need to attend to that problem first.

Garv'n strode to the massive door and rapped three times.

Instantly a servant appeared; he obviously was standing on the other side of the door.

"Bring Serl'n to me," he ordered. The servant disappeared down the vast hallway, echoes of his footsteps resonated from the walls.

Garv'n left the door ajar, returned to his desk and laid the book down on some old transcript casings. Then he sat and composed a short message informing Rab'k. He wished him to attend to the some problems in Safe Inlet; there were extreme problems needing attention and he wanted Rab'k to do so without delay.

Garv'n thought he was being extremely clever sending Rab'k in the opposite direction from the one he himself must follow to try to discover this Ahar'n.

The Ahar'n, as he determined from his study of the old writings, lay somewhere in the great northwestern mountains. He felt the hiding place of what appeared to be this most important object lay within Voravia's lands.

After a moment, there was a rap at the door. "Enter," Garv'n commanded.

"You wished to see me, your Lordship?" Serl'n asked, as he entered the room. Serl'n was Garv'n's favorite and most trusted servant; it was he alone who would correctly handle this special mission. He stood by while Garv'n finished what he was writing.

Serl'n had overheard his lordship reading aloud many times before while he waited for one of these deliveries. The room didn't look any different to him than the last time he had seen it, with one exception.

One of the scrolls, lying in its leather sleeve at the edge of the large table, seemed different. Its case seemed to glow along with the small book lying against it.

Serl'n couldn't be certain, but felt these were unusual documents. There must be some magic in them.

Are they of this Ahar'n about which Garv'n rants all the time? Has he indeed found the keys? It must be true!

He tried, with difficulty, to conceal his surprise.

"Yes, I need you to take a message to Rab'k immediately. You will leave within the hour," Garv'n interrupted Serl'n's reverie. He looked quickly back at Garv'n who was holding the note toward him.

"Yes, my Lord, as you say," Serl'n said and bowed as he took the note, "I can leave in just a few moments."

"Good, go with speed. The message is vital," Garv'n spoke softly, but looked strongly into Serl'n's eyes suddenly felt a sense of uncertainty. It surprised him and he watched as the other man walked out into the hallway, wondering. He shook his head; it was nothing.

There was a great need for haste. Garv'n felt his instructions would be carried out without delay.

Serl'n was a good man.

TRAVAIL

Innocence often brings a false sense of security for those who have not experienced the many vagaries of mankind. A certain naive look at the world leaves these individuals open to trials of fear and pain.

Strangely these are often the ones who survive, for they do not know to fight until they are fully ensnared. The hope for such as these is that those who are evil often create their own downfall and the innocent escape.

Our young heroine will soon learn her journey -- the real journey -- has many goals. Many more than she could have imagined . . .

Anisah stumped along the road to Varspree. No one had ridden by, in a long while, and she felt terribly alone and afraid. She had never been farther than the village from her home and family and she missed being there.

Hearing the sound of horses, she stepped to the side of the road. The horses slowed and stopped.

"So, my beauty, where are you off to today?" A man spoke to her from one of the horses. She turned and saw a fat, repulsive man, missing more teeth than he still had, sitting on an old horse smiling at her with a grizzled face. "Wouldn't you like to have a little ride with me?"

"No, sire. I'm fine walking." She responded, turned away and began to walk along the road again.

"One as pretty as you needs an escort, I think," he persisted, walking his horse beside her. She refused to look up or talk to the man.

Suddenly she was rising in the air, her clothing pulled upward at her neck and strangling her. She struggled to break free, but the man was too strong for her. He plopped her down on the saddle in front of him and trotted off. The other men roared with laughing approval.

Anisah couldn't believe this was happening; she had just started her new life and now this. She tried to remain still and stop her trembling, shrinking away from the man's touch as much as possible. She wasn't able to succeed with her resistance and as her anger grew she became quieter, ignoring the violations, planning an escape.

"You should keep Old Sumt'r's bed warm tonight," he laughed loudly, squeezing the girl even tighter to his foul and sweaty body. Anisah held back the tears that wanted to flow.

How could this be happening. I've done nothing wrong.

The party rode most of the morning in relative quiet. The men were all gruff and dirty and smelly.

The sun was just reaching its highest point when one of the younger men yelled at the others. "Hey, I'm gettin' hungry. We've been ridin' since before sunup and we didn't have a mornin' meal."

"You're so right, Garr'k, I could do with a bite of somethin' myself," replied Sumt'r. "Let's top that ridge ahead and we'll find a spot to stop. This lovely lass can make herself useful," he added, pinching Anisah on the bottom through her dress.

"You can cook, can't you dearie? Girl like you should be married by now. Were you running away from some husband who made you cook, clean and do other wifely duties, is that what you're doin'?" he breathed into her ear, hugging her tightly.

He was being particularly offensive now and Anisah was beginning to worry he might start something she didn't want to happen. She jerked out of his grasp.

"I can cook," she replied haughtily, "what do you have that's fit to eat?"

"Well, you do have a bit of life in you, huh?" he laughed, "I was beginning to wonder."

He stopped crushing her, kicked his horse into a trot and quickly reached the top of the rise and reined in his horse.

"Okay, men, I can see a clearing just ahead, check to see if there's water nearby. We'll set up camp and do a little huntin' for our supper."

In a short time, they found a small stream well hidden from the road. Sumt'r began shouting orders.

"Garr'k, you and Ald'n gather some wood and make a fire.

Rar's and Legg't, see what you can find for the stew pot. Red and Kar'n, see to the horses and make sure you hobble 'em good."

He swung from his horse and lifted Anisah down. "You lassie, will get the water," he said, pointing to the stream, "and be sure you boil the water good. Don't need any bad water."

From a pack on the mule he was leading, he pulled two battered pots and handed one to her. "Come along now; They'll have the fire going in no time," he added. He pushed her toward the stream with the pot he still held.

Anisah flung her hand out to knock the pot away and started walking silently ahead of Sumt'r toward the stream.

Her heart was beating fiercely but she began to form a plan for an escape and Sumt'r himself had presented it to her. She could certainly cook and she knew just what she wanted to prepare for these gentlemen. She grinned and looked away from Sumt'r so he couldn't see it.

She searched for herbs along the stream's bank, looking for just the right ones. The herb, aldock, grew almost everywhere; she noticed it bunched beside the road during the long ride today. She assumed these particular men had no idea what the herb did or how it was used.

Aldock, used sparingly in many prepared dishes provided an interesting spicy flavor, but applied too liberally would cause severe stomach cramps, nausea and other intestinal difficulties. Mistress Elspeth warned her about those problems years earlier.

Anisah found a small patch of the herb and, fortunately, in the same patch was mixed with a gentler green. She could gather both and not be noticed at all. She stood and spoke to Sumt'r who was watching her closely.

"Do you have any seasonings for the pot? Stew's no good without the proper herbs. I could collect some, if you like, like wild onions and drayslip root from this patch of greenery here by the bank," she suggested, pointing around the general area near the aldock. She could tell the thought of a good meal was making Sumt'r's mouth water.

"That sounds just fine, I'll sit here while you get what you need. Just make sure I can see ya." he said and sat, leaning against the trunk of a broad oak tree, and watched her closely.

Anisah actually gathered other wild herbs besides the aldock. She always gathered in this way. Each herb provided a special potion for healing, aches and pains, or for sleeping, any she picked might come in handy later.

Anisah never expected this whole affair to happen. She chastised herself for her blunder.

It's my own stupid fault, I should have known better. I should have known there are people who might want to harm me along the road.

She pondered her problem.

There seemed no doubt what these men, particularly Old Sumt'r, planned for her, and, if that wasn't enough, she also assumed they would kill her afterward.

Well, if my idea works, I shouldn't have to concern myself with my fate at the hands of these men. They are probably going to be very sick and very busy.

She was strangely amused, despite her dangerous circumstance.

I probably can just walk away without any problem.

"All right, time to head back to the camp," Sumt'r growled abruptly, "the fire should be hot by now and we need to get this water on and the greens cooked for when the boys get back from their hunt."

"You'll need to carry both buckets, my hands are full," she told him, holding the greens she had picked in a small fold in her skirt with both hands. She didn't want to take the risk Sumt'r knew about aldock.

Sumt'r picked up both buckets, growled something about lazy women, started away toward the clearing, suddenly stopped and looked back at Anisah.

"You get in front of me, just like I said, so I can keep an eye on ya," he spoke sharply. Anisah lengthened her stride until she was marching along in front of him.

They reached the clearing just after several of the hunters arrived. They were preparing some of the game for the fire.

"Got us a couple of fat hares," Rar's shouted, holding the

skinned animal aloft.

"And some quail," Legg't boasted, laughing with his success and holding the plucked birds for everyone to see.

"Just shut up and finish cleaning the rest of the game! The water's gonna be hot in a few minutes and I'm gettin' hungry," Sumt'r yelled at his men. They jumped up and scurried around trying to rush their efforts.

Anisah was sorting the herbs.

"Could I please borrow a knife or possibly one of you would like to chop these greens?" she asked sweetly, trying to be careful not to antagonize or make a mistake in what she was doing.

Red wiped the small hunting knife he was using to skin the hares on his pants' leg, looked over at Sumt'r to make certain it was all right.

Sumt'r nodded his approval.

"Aye, give it to her. I ain't chopping no vegetables," he sneered.

Red handed the knife to her, handle first

"Thank you," Anisah said and smiled up at Red as she kneeled next to the fire. He looked at her and grinned sheepishly, turned and walked back to the others, joining in the chorus of jokes, tall tales and stories they were shouting out.

They were being strangely boisterous, particularly since any passersby could probably have heard them, for no apparent reason. Once they all turned to look at her, Rar's slapped Red on the back then they all laughed, poking one another like little boys.

I can imagine why they are acting so stupidly but I'll see how that turns out for them.

She quickly cut the herbs, adding them to the pot. When she was through with the general preparation, she cleaned the aldock

The men again laughed loudly again and, when she looked, she noticed they were still glancing over at her and laughing even harder.

Maybe just a bit more of my favorite item in this. Maybe just a bit more for you fine gentlemen.

There were only a few opportunities for Anisah to take some of the stew out for herself before she added the aldock. There was one coinciding with another round of laughter from Sumt'r henchmen.

"I don't have a bowl," she said loudly, "may I get my cup from my bag?"

Sumt'r turned and stared at her a moment before waving his hand toward their bags now laying on the ground at the edge of the camp. She cautiously walked to her pack, searched around for her cup and drew it out, showing it to Sumt'r.

"I's watching for any of yore tricks," he said, calmly, grinning at her. "Tricks can come later."

She walked back to the fireside, took some of the stew out into her cup, then put a generous portion of the aldock into the pot, dusted her hands and stirred the mixture until all the greens were mixed thoroughly.

Soon the men brought over the game they had cleaned. She added the hares to the pot, stirring them into the brew, choosing to save the quail for herself for later.

Yes, a brew. That just describes this concoction.

The men lay about under the trees, laughing and joking while passing around a wineskin. Anisah occasionally stirred the pots, silently watching the men. She smiled each time someone looked toward her.

Might as well make them feel comfortable. Can't run.

The men were slightly intoxicated by the time the stew was cooked enough for Anisah to know the aldock was mixed in well.

"Stew's ready, if you care," Anisah announced.

The men jumped up, staggering, pulling their bowls from their packs and rushing to be first. Pushing and shoving, they jostled for position at the pots. Sumt'r spooned himself a generous portion, much to Anisah's delight.

Sumt'r stood and walked near her.

"Eat up, we have a long way to go before dark," he growled at her and began to eat his stew.

The men gulped their meals quickly, asked for more, and finished the second portion quickly, handing their dirty bowls to Anisah to clean.

"Red, take her down to the stream and watch her while she washes those. Fill the water skins while you're there," Sumt'r commanded, tossing the water skins to Red. "We need to move to a safer place for the night."

The others began putting out the fire and saddling their horses. It took Anisah and Red only a few minutes to do their chores. After they returned, everyone mounted their horses. Sumt'r grabbed Anisah roughly and jammed her in front of him again.

The ride was the same as the day before, the men talking and joking crudely, laughing the most at those about loose women, when Kar'n suddenly doubled over clutching his stomach, almost falling from his horse.

"By all the Gods, I'm dyin'," he cried out, feebly pulling back the reins to stop his horse, weaving in the saddle with his head resting on the horse's neck.

"Stop tryin' to trick us, twar'n't no arrows comin' through here," Garr'k laughed, looking about in case he was wrong.

"Ain't no arrows, you dope, it's comin' from inside like a rabbit's trying to scratch out of my gut," Kar'n groaned, falling from his saddle to the ground, rolling in obvious pain.

"That's what ya get for being so greedy," Sumt'r roared with laughter at Kar'n squirming in the dirt.

Suddenly, his face contorted in pain and he doubled over grabbing at his stomach. "You scoundrel, whatever you got, I got it too. What were you doing back in Aleria," Sumt'r groaned, slowly slid from behind Anisah to the ground.

She held on tightly to prevent being dragged from the horse.

Legg't suddenly fell from his horse, shouting and cursing, holding his stomach. The other three men also jumped to the ground, clutching themselves, crying out, and desperate to get away from the pain. Two of them tried to run into the bushes – neither made it in time.

Anisah sat, eyes wide, watching the men writhe on the ground. She had never used aldock in larger doses before and was amazed at what was happening.

"Look at her. She's not suffering. Witch, witch, you put a curse on us. We're all gonna die," Legg't shouted, twisting his face, pointing his finger at her, "We shoulda taken you and killed you when we had a chance."

Anisah, alarmed at the accusation, jammed her heels into the horse's flank and it bolted forward, almost pitching her off backwards.

As the horse broke into a full gallop, she desperately grabbed the mane flying in front of her, held on tightly and closed her eyes.

She had never ridden a horse before and was too frightened to look at first. After a moment she realized she hadn't fallen off, so she decided it was a good time to learn how to stay on and more importantly, how to guide the animal.

She opened her eyes and saw the reins flapping against her leg. Building up her courage, she let go of the mane with one hand, reaching desperately for the reins flailing just out of her reach.

Finally, the reins flew around near her. She lurched to the side and grabbed them, pulling them into her other hand, but still holding desperately to the mane. Only then did she look up to see where she was going.

The road ahead turned sharply to her left and she began to worry the horse wasn't going to make the turn because he was going so fast, or he was going to run into the woods where the branches were low enough to knock her from the saddle.

She quickly sat up straight, yanked back on the reins as hard as she could, holding her hands close to her face with the effort, leaning as far back as she could, her fear of falling overwhelming her.

The animal twisted its head to the right but kept running, but he began to run more slowly. She pulled her left rein harder.

"Whoa, horse, whoa! Please stop! Please!" she began yelling at the animal. The horse eyed her wildly; it yanked its head forward almost pulling her off its back, running even harder now.

"Oh, please stop, please stop," Anisah was crying and pulling back on the reins with all her strength.

Suddenly, the horse stopped, stiffening its forelegs and jamming its hoofs into the dirt road, skidding to a stop. Anisah quickly grabbed the pommel of the saddle and was somehow able to stay on the animal though she smashed her face into the horse's neck as she pitched forward.

The horse stood panting heavily tossing its head, and blowing foam everywhere. Anisah glared at the animal for just a moment, stopped rubbing her nose, reached forward and hit the horse as hard as she could on its neck.

"You stupid horse, where do you think you're goin'," she screamed at it, still crying but happier now the horse had stopped running.

They stood in the road for a while trying to recover when Anisah heard yelling, back toward the direction she had come.

She turned to look and could see the men trying to crawl to their horses, attempting to mount them. Unfortunately for them, standing was almost impossible since every attempt to stand straight sent searing pains through them, and they flopped back to the ground holding their midriffs with both arms.

Anisah thought she should leave before they were able to get back on their horses. She gently bumped the horse with her heels this time and it began to trot down the road in the direction they were running earlier.

As she rounded the turn, she could here Sumt'r cursing and screaming at her, "You witch, I'll find you and we'll see who wins the next fight."

She then decided she should go a little faster, bumped the horse with heels and started a slow trot which bounced her about at first. But she soon caught the rhythm and the ride began to be more fun. She suspected the effect of the aldock would soon be wearing off and there was plenty of reason to put as much distance between herself and Sumt'r's band as she could.

After an hour, Anisah pulled the horse up. She looked around to make certain she was safe and slid to the ground, holding the horse's mane.

She, and the horse, just stood for a few minutes trying to regain their breaths. She looked around, trying to decide what to do and spotted a likely hiding place. Taking the reins, she led the horse off the road and into the woods.

When she was comfortable with her distance from the road, she stopped to watch and listen for any movement beyond her shelter. Satisfied all was quiet, she led the horse further into the trees and found the same stream that flowed by the campsite the previous night.

Here the banks were sandier and less steep. She led the horse to the water and it began to drink eagerly. She moved upstream a couple of paces and bathed her face in the cool, clear stream.

She sat for a while waiting to see if she was being followed, letting her face drip-dry. The breeze blew softly through the trees overhead and she began to relax some.

I'd love to shed these dusty, foul smelling clothes and splash in this beautiful sparkling water. But I believe that wouldn't be too smart today.

She looked at the stream, particularly at one small pool beckoning her. She shook the thought away. She had no idea where Sumt'r's gang was. And no way of knowing how quickly they would recover, nor how far behind they were if they were following her -- which she assumed was going to happen and decided she needed to leave. She breathed a great sigh at having to leave without her bath, grabbed the horse's reins and led him slowly toward the road, stopping to listen occasionally as a precaution.

When she reached the edge of the trees, she cautiously peered out through the leaves making certain there was no one about, and guided the horse back to the edge of the road.

But being exposed made her feel uncomfortable.

I wonder whether I should stay in these trees longer. I believe I will for a few more miles. So, I start in the morning. So much for big plans.

She took the horse back inside the forest, tried to mount but found it impossible because the horse kept moving away from her. She finally discovered she could pull hard on the right rein when she stepped up in the stirrup the horse moved toward her rather than away, and she was able to mount him finally.

Once again, she sat quietly listening for any sounds, heard none and slowly walked the animal through the trees, keeping the road in sight as she dodged branches and moved around other debris in their way.

After an hour or so passed, she turned the horse out through a clear spot in the trees, looked up and down the road, seeing nothing she moved out, crossed to the middle of the road through a rocky patch, to cover their tracks.

She trotted the horse slowly down the road, occasionally looking over her shoulder to see if the men were behind her. The next few hours passed without incident. She saw no one for the remainder of the day. She lost most of her jitters and, toward the end, began to enjoy the trip.

It was becoming dark and she was getting a bit hungry. She decided she should make a camp, found a likely area, veered off the road again choosing a rocky patch of ground, got off the horse and led him into the woods looking for the stream again.

She soon found it and looking around she noticed the woods were particularly thick here.

The thicker the better. Maybe no one will see a small fire if I'm careful.

She watered the horse, tied him to a small tree with a line long enough for him to feed in the grass near the bank and built the smallest of fires.

Retrieving the pot from Sumt'r's bag, still on the horse, she boiled some water and cooked some of the greens she had saved in her bag from the previous day. She then wrapped the two quail she had hidden in some wet leaves and dropped them into the coals and waited. The leaves smoldered and smoke rose, but it was becoming dark and she felt no one could see.

Well, this was an exciting two days. I'm not as certain as I was this trip to Tariny is what I should be doing. Maybe I need to just go home.

The night closed softly around her, She was very tired, not having slept well the last two nights. She gazed through the branches over her head, up at the stars and the two moons overhead, and felt comforted by how peaceful the place was.

"And maybe I don't," she spoke softly, pulled one of the quail out of the coals and chewed it slowly and ate some greens, "going back would be a big mistake. After all, if I can survive what happened these last two days, I probably can handle whatever lays ahead."

Suddenly she stopped talking thinking she heard some rustling in the woods across the stream. She waited for more movement.

Then she relaxed and shook her head.

"I'm just too jumpy, everything's fine. I just need to rest," she talked aloud again, finished her small meal.

Carefully dousing the fire with water from the stream, she walked around in the area looking for a place to sleep.

Maybe I can bathe in the morning. These clothes are impossible.

She soon found a soft spot near a great tree, pulled her clothing around her and fell asleep quickly. She dreamed about a day when she helped others with her skills.

You will have many other adventures, young Anisah, but do not be afraid, for you will succeed in what you wish. Find two young men from Peetle, they will help you complete your journey. There will be other deeds you must perform before you can become a healer. And healer you will be, but more. The day approaches when you will help save your world.

She awoke the next morning with a start, looking around her frantically, and then realized she had only been dreaming.

She lay back on her bed of dirty clothes, looked up through the trees, and was thankful she had survived her ordeal of the day before. The horse stood patiently at the end of the rope she had used to tie him to a tree.

I've got to get up and get on my way. Sumt'r and his gang may have passed last night, but they may be behind me yet.

She stood, walked to the horse and took her packs from the back of the saddle. She left the packs on the poor animal overnight because she was afraid she wouldn't be able to get them back on if she had to leave in a hurry.

Leaning back comfortably against her tree, she dug the last of her bread and cheese out of her pack. Opening Sumt'r's larger bag, she found an old weathered tunic and some baggy pants; an old cloak covered with patches; the pots she used to cook her concoction of poison vegetables; a mug; utensils; a bowl; a rather large knife and a small leather bag.

She pulled out the leather bag and opened it.

Oh, happy days, it has a bit of money in it — gold, semi-silvers and coppers. Sumt'r must have taken this from some poor soul and simply thrown it into the bag without thinking.

She finished the last bit of her bread and cheese, got up, threw everything back into the pack and tossed these over the horse's back, except the coin bag. She tucked it into a hidden pocket of her dress.

She untied the horse, grabbed the saddle horn, placed her foot in the stirrup, and mounted the horse without effort and realized, with satisfaction, she was getting much better at relating to the animal.

As she prepared to leave, she suddenly heard voices nearby, froze and jerked back on the reins. The horse grunted and backed noisily into the small clearing.

Did they hear that?

"Cursed witch! Harlot! Blasted Slut!" shouted several voices, all of them much too familiar. Sumt'r and his men caught her, but they were passing by on the road, making much too much noise and didn't notice her sitting just inside the tree line. She held her breath and watched them through the limbs of the trees. She leaned over, wrapped her arms about its neck patting the animal softly.

"Sh-h." She whispered, "Please don't make any noise."

None of the gang looked in her direction as they trotted past. She held the horse tightly, hoping it would not whinny to the other animals.

Her heart was pounding, her eyes closed, she was trembling so violently she was afraid the men could hear it.

Time seemed to stop; there was nothing she could do but wait. There was nothing in her world, but her heart pounding in her ears and the voices of the men passing by on the road.

After what seemed like hours, the voices faded. Sitting slowly upright, she got off the horse again. Holding the reins, she walked quietly to the edge of the trees, looked in each direction and decided to move slowly toward the road. She saw nothing in either direction and sighed a breath of relief.

Well, this is as good a place to camp as any. At least for tonight.

She couldn't bring herself to actually walk onto the road. Shaking her head, she turned about and lead the horse back into the trees. She wanted to give Sumt'r a very long lead.

Once safely behind the trees, she patted the animal on the nose. "Seems we stay for the night," she muttered.

Retying the horse to another trees near another grassy spot, she removed the packs from its back and actually discovered how to take the saddle off.

She remade her camp and took the old cloak from Sumt'r's bag to give her added warmth. She was afraid to make another fire and the cloak would keep her warm enough.

She walked into the woods to find something to eat. She quickly found some berries, took them back to the creek to clean, sat and munched them slowly, wondering what lay ahead.

The rest of the day passed without incident. She took the bath she needed, washed some of her clothes and Sumt'r's old cloak.

They dried while she sat in the sun, with her own cloak wrapped around her, peeking through the leaves just in case she had unwanted guests.

She decided to wait until dark to start her journey again. Her days were much more adventurous than she wanted and the tension had exhausted her. She lay quietly for a while and actually dozed a bit. But each time she woke she did so with a start — still apprehensive.

After her clothes dried, she put them on, spread Sumt'r's old cloak under the tree, wrapped her own cloak around her, rolled into a ball to keep herself warm, and quickly fell asleep.

As the first rays of light blinked through the trees, Anisah opened her eyes, looked around, and was amazed she slept so soundly. She thought she would be awake all night.

But she felt much better after the rest and was ready to go.

She packed everything again, placing the bundles back on the horse. She washed her face in the stream, pulled the reins over and mounted the horse easily, walked him through the edge of the forest, looked both ways, and slowly approached the road.

On the road, she again looked behind her, kicked the horse, heading for Varspree, hoping to reach the town by evening. She soon had the horse trotting at a good pace.

She rode all day, often walking the horse, stopping only to grab a bite to eat from the herbs she spotted on the side of the road, or to water the horse and get a drink herself.

She began to see more people as she traveled; most of them paid little attention to her passing. Occasionally, a child would wave at her and she would return it.

The variety of people began to change from those who lived in the farm areas to city people whose descriptions were indescribable in most cases. Most were on foot or horseback, some in carts and buggies, all looking dusty and tired.

Probably like I do. Tomorrow, there will be new life to begin.

She was so tired she wasn't certain whether she thought that, or it just appeared in her thoughts as though someone had spoken to her.

She closed her eyes as the horse walked toward the lights she could see in the distance.

Not much longer now, maybe I can be at peace in this place.

RAB'K

A sense of foreboding came into the world. Each day crept into the next with the air stale, hot and windless. There were no great wars, as yet, to busy the people.

There were only some who would be more than they could be. These began to wonder and to wander away from the peaceful past when no man felt he had enemies. As there was often before, there will always be ambition controlling some men's souls.

Because of a few of these men, there will always be danger. We now tell more of this tale . . .

"Halic, Master." Mal'm, so frightened he was shaking, spoke as softly as he could, but to no avail.

"What do you want?" Rab'k growled. He turned to look over his shoulder at the servant. Rab'k smiled inwardly, his eyes almost relaxing.

"What is so important you felt it necessary to interrupt me?" he spoke with deliberation, punching out each word.

Rab'k was a huge man, standing some three kalghs high, with massive shoulders and arms.

He had the appearance of a man who would as soon smash your head as talk to you. It was known he had murdered many with his bare hands; he seemed to take pleasure in the act itself.

No one knew where he came from. Many rumored he was from across the mountains and was of those rough and terrible people who lived in the wasteland. But no one knew -- and no one asked.

His current servants, those who remained, quaked at the thought of being in his presence. They often ran and hid whenever they heard him striding through the hallways of the castle.

They all knew to stay as far away from this mysterious chamber Mal'm had quietly entered Rab'k's study. Often they refused to go to the great gate to allow entry to the many messengers and noblemen who were constantly visiting Lord Rab'k, for fear they would have to go to the chamber. Mal'm was the unfortunate one today.

"I-I-I'm s-s-sorry, Master." Mal'm couldn't make his tongue work correctly. He began to back toward the door.

"Wait, I haven't dismissed you!" Rab'k shouted. "What is so important? Answer me!"

"Master, there's a messenger at the door," Mal'm answered, trembling with fright. "He says he has news from his lordship, Lord Garv'n."

"Lord, indeed," Rab'k muttered to himself.

He, feeling a certain pleasure in stretching his power even if only in reprimand, stood, turned and shouted at the frightened servant.

"I've told all of you not to come into this chamber unless I call. Do not fail to remember that or you shall pay the consequences. But for now, show him in!"

Mal'm stood so transfixed he hesitated.

What are you waiting for?" Rab'k roared.

"Yes, yes. I understand, sire." Mal'm, without looking, was reaching behind to find the door, ran into it, stumbled forward but hastily ran around, through the opening and down the hall.

Rab'k could hear him running for some distance. He chuckled and there was a brief twisted grin on his face which disappeared almost immediately.

Rab'k's private chamber was impressive. He was proud of this room. He had collected some remarkably valuable treasures throughout the years attending Garv'n's small empire. Most of them hung on the walls surrounding him so he could admire them.

Trophies of hunts in the mountains; some of the mightiest animals in the land died to provide him with amusement.

Some of these items had dark pasts, pasts only Rab'k could remember. Most of the others who witnessed the taking of the prize were no longer among the living.

Some interesting reminders.

At one end was an enormous fireplace providing warmth to the room. The servants didn't need to actually come into the room to attend the fire. A trap door opened at the rear of the hearth through which logs could be passed and placed on the fire without entering the study.

The ceilings of the room were high and arched into the darkness above, only flickers of the dim firelight touched at the beams forming the vaulting supports. The floors were worn and polished by many hours of pacing.

The walls were overlaid with a fine fabric taken from some sea traders with whom Rab'k had engaged in a small confrontation. The doors into the chamber were massive, reaching twice as high as Rab'k's reach.

Looking out through great windows made of a rare material allowing an almost clear view, one could see the low hills, the village of Roahan and, further out, the sea crashing against the shoreline.

Rab'k had received the castle from Garv'n for some task seemingly difficult for Garv'n, but actually had presented no great problem for Rab'k.

He vaguely remembered his instructions to "ask" the previous tenants to leave because of some debt owed Garv'n; and he always felt his particular method of requesting something was very efficient and cleared the air entirely. Besides he rarely had further disputes -- dead men don't argue, or talk too much.

He generally, and quickly, reported the problem resolved.

Rab'k had no interest in the castle itself other than it provided an excellent fortress, if ever there was a need. He rarely walked into the inner chambers except rest, or sleep; he left those areas to his servants.

He usually arrived from one of his journeys and went straight from the stables to this chamber. He spent hours studying new ways to enhance his employer's wealth and further his own ends as well.

Wealth itself meant little to him. He was wealthy in his youth. The power to rule men and their lives; the sense of control he felt whenever he cast some wretch into a prison or physically threw them from their homes or, better yet, simply disposed of them, provided his pleasure.

As he gazed out toward the cliffs and the water beyond, he realized he needed to become more cautious with the old fool, Garv'n. Power was an attractive element in the old man's soul, too. Garv'n still currently possessed the real power and his influence spread wide and far. Until the center of power shifted completely, Rab'k thought it wise to humor Garv'n a bit longer.

A knock came at the door. Rab'k, with a scowl, rose and crossed the room to address this fool messenger from Garv'n.

"Master Rab'k, I greet you and bring information from Lord Garv'n," the messenger spoke, glancing over his shoulders as he entered the room.

Serl'n always felt a need for caution whenever he came into this room.

"I also have other information you might find interesting," he said smiling.

He was one of those men who always had a larcenous look about him, like a weasel; instinctively others knew he couldn't be trusted. Yet he generally placed himself into those positions providing a way to come to the notice of his superiors. He took advantage of this effort and now was a confidant of Lord Garv'n. He was always the opportunist.

Today he felt he came with a particularly juicy tidbit of news for Lord Rab'k and was very pleased with himself.

"What is this news?" Rab'k spoke gruffly. "I haven't the time for one of Lord Garv'n's errands. I have enough to do taking care of his business arrangements," he told the man. Rab'k, of course, was using some of those irritating errands to make a few of his own discoveries.

"Master Garv'n has found something, a magical thing," Serl'n spoke quietly, looking about furtively. "He has found the key to what he has been seeking for all these years."

"What are you talking about?" Rab'k whispered with forced effort, almost a growl. He pressed his face close to Serl'n's. "What did that fool find I should know about? What key? Key to what?"

Serl'n recovered enough to know he needed to speak quickly -- this man wasn't patient and would kill him.

"What?" Rab'k whirled and seized the man by the neck.

"He has discovered something. I saw signs of his secret when I was called to his chamber," Serl'n coughed, "He believes he has discovered within the ancient writings, some great magical power. I thought you would want to know."

His eyes were now flicking from side to side looking for an escape. His fear was evident in his face, pale from his ordeal. He was almost frantic. Rab'k squeezed ever tighter.

Serl'n's eyes were bulging, his pallor becoming an odd shade of blue, his chest heaved to force another breath. He beat at the great arm holding him off the floor.

Rab'k suddenly released his hold and the servant fell to the floor, gasping, trying to squirm away from this madman. Rab'k reached down and yanked Serl'n back to his feet. Serl'n swayed and seemed ready to collapse, but Rab'k held him easily.

Rab'k eyed the servant, released the man's neck and stood, waiting.

"Garv'n would not have sent you to tell me that," he spoke quietly, menacingly. "Why did he send you?"

"He wanted me to tell you he needed you to investigate a stirring on the eastern coast. There's a trading captain who is not reporting his shipments accurately." Serl'n was regaining his breath, but his demeanor showed obvious fear.

"Hmm, maybe that's just a way to divert my attention," Rab'k muttered, stroking his chin thoughtfully. "Now, what about this key. What do you want to tell me?"

Serl'n previously considered the possibility there would be a reward for this new information, but now realized his life was in the balance. He knew he had to speak honestly, as coldly honest as he could be, for the first time ever.

"Master Garv'n has been searching for years in his library looking for a clue to the presence of a powerful amulet," he spoke slowly, intently watching the man who stood glaring at him.

"He purchased every ancient text he could and has poured

over every page in each. He has been looking for some ultimate power. He has mumbled about the Al-Esfer'n and a magical 'Ahar'n' on several other occasions when I was called before him."

"The Ahar'n is just a fable," Rab'k spoke softly, surprising Serl'n.

"Maybe that's true, but Master Garv'n believes it's real," Serl'n said. He was recovering from his ordeal, but there was no hesitation -- he still spoke the truth.

"What is he doing about it?" Rab'k asked, turning away from the servant. "I wonder why he wants me to go south?" He felt he already knew. His assumption was Garv'n's discovery revealed the Ahar'n was in the northern regions somewhere.

Baalsa'n mentioned this Ahar'n many years ago when he forced Rab'k to leave his homeland and come to this place. Baalsa'n commanded him to place the discovery of the Ahar'n as his highest priority.

Rab'k, though he had followed leads slim more than once, was never able to learn anything concrete about the legends, or stories, about the Ahar'n. He heard those legends all his life; his people particularly seemed to think the legends were fact.

"Was he going to send you on any missions?" he asked Serl'n.

"No, my Lord. He only ordered me to come here," Serl'n answered.

"Then he suspects me. He knows, or has guessed, my own intentions to take his wealth," Rab'k grumbled.

"Have you been in his presence when he spoke of this Ahar'n?" he turned back to Serl'n and asked.

"No, sire. He rarely allows anyone into his library. I came in for the message to obtain the missive to you and overheard him reading a chant from one of his ancient books.

"I believe he read a passage: 'There are masses of stone near masses of water under which there lies the great Ahar'n. Therein lies the power of the gods but only one man can be the Guardian'." Serl'n offered.

Then Lord Garv'n shouted, "'I believe I've found it, but I must be wary of Rab'k.' Sorry, my Lord, but that is what he said and I assumed it might be important to you," Serl'n almost whimpered, holding his arms over his head as he spoke the last.

Rab'k, no longer concerned about the servant, whirled about and walked to his table of maps.

"There are only a few bodies of water other than the seas -- I can't believe the stone is below the surface or why would it be known in the myths?" Rab'k talked aloud, without regard for the servant.

"There is Lutyromma Lach in Ertyula; Sunprotyu in Quiter. My god, Hurtelanx in the central plains of the northern regions. Hurtelanx. What a foreboding place that is," he spoke slowly, re-membering.

"Do you think the stone might be there, Master?" Serl'n asked.

Rab'k spun around and eyed the servant, still standing where Rab'k left him.

I shouldn't have allowed this man to hear me.

"I think there is nothing to guide anyone anywhere based on such a vague phrase. I think Garv'n has simply lost his mind," Rab'k answered quickly.

"But sire, he certainly had the look of a man who believed he had found an answer," Serl'n spoke, regaining his confidence. "I thought the information might be valuable to you -- since you were mentioned."

"Yes, yes, you might be right," Rab'k, answered, thinking now of how to dispose of this nuisance, "As a curiosity, who did he assign the duty of searching?"

"I think it is Vil'n; he would normally be his choice, sire. Garv'n trusts him completely." Serl'n was now certain he had re-gained his status with this violent man; his composure was re-turning. He replied more casually with each statement. "Should we follow him and discover what his mission is?"

"That's a good idea. Yes, *we* should follow him to see where he leads us," Rab'k answered casually, his brow wrinkled with thought.

Rab'k knew Garv'n suspected him of having ambitious inten-tions, but more importantly, this might be an opportunity to

103

find what he was searching for himself.

There now seemed to be a prize that would give him more power than he could have ever imagine.

"We'll start first thing in the morning. Perhaps you should return to Garv'n's castle before you are missed. And here, take this, a reward for your good service."

He reached into a small vault and pulled out a pouch of precious stones, handing it to the servant.

"Thank you, my lord. I hope I haven't offended you in any way," Serl'n said, bowing his head, trying to hide the smug look on his face. "I will return home as soon as I retrieve my horse."

Serl'n turned about and started toward the door, not looking back.

Rab'k deftly threw the blade he had also taken from the vault, striking the servant at the base of his neck. Serl'n never knew why he was suddenly lying on the floor. He turned to look up at Rab'k and saw more malice in that moment than during his entire life.

He died wondering why.

"Send for Jond'r," Rab'k shouted to the guard standing outside the chamber. "I have killed a thief in my chambers."

He pulled the bag of stones from Serl'n's clutched hand, placing them in the messenger bag on the servant's back and was pretending to remove them when Jond'r arrived.

"What happened, sire?" Jond'r asked, standing at attention above the body.

"I caught this thief stealing these jewels," Rab'k answered, pulling the stones from the bag. "Take him and throw him over the cliff; the sea will welcome him."

"As you say, sire. Is there anything else?" Jond'r asked, not looking to the left or right.

Jond'r was a strong man, but he didn't trust this master. He didn't want to create a problem for himself.

"Yes, have my horse saddled and ready a squad of riders. They will travel to the north tonight," Rab'k answered. "Better yet. I will go with you now and proceed to the stables. I'll meet you there. Be sure you have someone take care of this mess before you go and send a message to Lord Garv'n about his man servant's treachery."

"Yes, sire. It will be done," Jond'r answered, saluting as he backed toward the door.

Rab'k waited for Jond'r to leave then turned to look through the window at the sea beyond.

I have learned many things today. Rena'x will be proud of me. Soon, I will bring this power to my people.

As he pulled the door open to leave, he looked around the chamber and felt pleased things were going so well.

Rab'k didn't notice as he pulled the door shut the trap door in the hearth slowly closing after his departure.

SOJOURN

As you read of this time in history, remember there is some evil in man by blood, or by inclination, which cannot be ignored nor pushed aside easily.

Evil takes its substance from the very soul of its victims. It feeds on the vitality of those souls to gain strength to destroy others.

No man is immune to the voracious appetites occurring when he succumbs to this great consuming force. No man who avoids the enticement is without danger from those who would practice the religion of evil. No man should submit to either.

These are reasons for a cause; reasons and justifications for destruction if the final victim is that of evil; fighting against these evils is how man becomes a hero to his people.

Yet evil seems to lurk, waiting patiently for weaknesses, delving and feeling the tremors of a willingness to accept. There are gods who would encourage this path, needing a complete destruction to satisfy their needs.

It is of man and of gods I speak . . .

Geth'n and Pet'r journey had only been unpleasant so far.

They hadn't traveled far from Larilla when thieves attacked them. They were each tied to a small tree and guarded while several of the brigands ripped through their belongings.

The robbers were bitterly angry. They only found food, clothing and nothing else of value. Now they were growling in their irritation, tossing the clothes in their frustration, and stamping about glaring at their captives.

Pet'r was busily working to break free, twisting his wrists and using his innate strength. He finally loosened the bindings and released himself. He concealed his freedom from their guard, but nudged Geth'n and revealed one of his hands.

"When they come closer, I will tackle their leader and force him to let us go," Pet'r whispered.

"No, you shouldn't. You might get hurt," Geth'n answered softly, but the guard heard them mumbling.

"Shut up, you two!" he grunted at them but quickly turned his attention back to the other men.

They were grumbling even more now, holding up the clothing, shaking them, and violently tossing them about on the ground. Some were shoving the cheese and bread Geth'n had so carefully packed into their mouths, swilling down the wine, and kicking the clothing and knapsacks in their anger.

"Pet'r, can you loosen my hands?" Geth'n asked.

"I can't without revealing I'm loose. I have to do this alone, but I have a plan," Pet'r whispered.

"I thought I told you to be quiet?" the guard looked around growling at them.

What happened next was as great a surprise to Geth'n as to their captors. The guard unfortunately was to suffer the consequences of being the first to know.

Pet'r broke the last of his bonds with a great surge and grabbing the guard by his shirt and the seat of his pants, threw him through the air toward the largest group.

The guard's flying body hit and bowled most of them over into a great mass of tangled bodies, clothing, food, drink and dust. The men howled their rage, cursing, and flinging each other aside while scrambling to their feet.

The leader of the group and two of his men were standing aside in a small huddle talking about how to dispose of the young men without anyone discovering their bodies.

Before they could turn to determine what was happening, Pet'r was upon them.

Those years of toiling at the nets with his father were to provide Pet'r with more power than was needed to dispatch these fools, but there was something else in his actions, a fluid motion which seemed to prepare his body for the next movement before the move was needed.

He tossed another man into the others causing them to stumble and fall into the great pile of confusion already on the ground; then he grabbed the leader's sword away with one hand and raised the man off the ground with the other, holding him aloft.

Pet'r stood there without effort. The leader's feet kicked loosely in the air, wriggling about trying to get free.

"You fools, kill him!" the leader shouted at his men. They were still trying to disentangle themselves from each other, but a few broke free and rushed to help.

"Wait!" Pet'r spoke with a certain chill in his voice. "I will not hesitate." He held the sword to the leader's throat. Already a small stream of blood oozed down from the edge of the blade pressed into the skin.

The men stopped suddenly. The others were still extracting themselves from the tangle and approaching, but they too waited.

"He is bluffing! Get him, you idiots," the leader shouted more violently at his men.

What happened next was so remarkable Geth'n couldn't remember many details later.

But Pet'r dropped the leader to the ground, deftly slicing the sword through the air and down the side of the man's face, stopping just short of his shoulder.

Then he turned the sword outward and sliced along the top through the man's outstretched hand, grabbed him by his neck and again lofted him above the ground. All this carried out smoothly, effortlessly.

"My God, he has killed me!" the leader screamed, his pain real enough for him to believe he was dying. He held his arm out and could see he was missing fingers from his hand.

"He is chopping me to pieces! Stop him!"

The men however realized this young man was not ordinary; they hesitated. The leader's ear lay on the ground with his fingers. Possibly he didn't know his ear was cut away because of the shock. But they could see it.

The blood was gushing down the side of the leader's head and saturating his clothing, but he only screamed about his lost fingers as he stared at his hand in disbelief.

"How will I be able to live without my hand?" he moaned. Then he noticed his men looking at the ground and he saw the ear. "I am dying. Help me," he moaned, crying now.

"Stop. I will let you all go if you leave now," Pet'r said, glowering at the other men and waving the sword at them, while still holding the man in the air.

The men had never seen anyone with such strength and, though there were more of them, no one was going to be the first to face this man.

They had yet another surprise in store for them. Geth'n had broken his bonds and circled around behind the men unnoticed.

As the men turned to run, he flattened several before they could start, dumping them to the ground unconscious. He too was bringing his own strength to the gathering.

The others ran away, scuffling along as fast as they could through the dust and out into the open country. The men Geth'n attacked lay as they had fallen.

"You should be more cautious about those you attack," Pet'r spoke to the leader, staring into the man's eyes intensely. "Someone might create a problem you can't handle."

The leader looked at Pet'r while holding his violated hand to the side of his head trying to stop the bleeding. He was only able to cry.

"Go. Don't look back," Pet'r said, as he dropped the man in the dust beside the men who still lay unconscious.

The leader wobbled to his feet, and still moaning in his pain, stumbled slowly away to follow his men, still running as fast as they could.

"Well, Pet'r. You seem to be a little upset," Geth'n said, walking over to his friend.

Pet'r was trying to clean the mess from his hands and waving the sword about as he did.

"Would you like to put the sword down now?" Geth'n added, holding his hand up to ward off injury.

Pet'r, realizing he still had the sword in his hand, raised his arm and threw the sword as far as he could into the prairie opposite the direction the thieves took.

"I'm not now, but I certainly was. I don't know what happened actually, can you tell me?" Pet'r asked, looking at his old friend with a puzzled look on his face.

"I think you wouldn't believe it if I told you, but you did get us out of this mess," Geth'n answered. "But we still have to gather our things." He waved his arm around, gesturing at their scattered clothing and food.

"We should probably get out of here quickly. I doubt if our friends will stay frightened for very long." He looked at Pet'r again, noticing the iciness in his eyes had faded. Geth'n scrutinized his friend.

Curious, Pet'r is not a violent man. How could what I just saw have happened?

They gathered their clothes quickly, jamming them haphazardly into their knapsacks, but most of the food was ruined and all the wine spilled.

Geth'n gave one of the men, who was trying to regain consciousness, a solid whack on the head with his knapsack. The man slumped back to the ground.

"It appears you could use a good walk to calm you down, my friend," Pet'r laughed, placing his hand on Geth'n's shoulder for a moment.

Geth'n laughed heartily, threw his knapsack over his shoulder, stood back and gestured with a wave of his hand in the direction they were traveling before being attacked.

"After you, my famed warrior," Geth'n said, still laughing about the whole affair.

"Someday I'll have to tell a tale about this young student who fought off the evil bandits, but let's not tarry too long. We should wait until we can savor the adventure of our little battle in more pleasant surroundings," he laughed again, shaking his head.

They turned and walked away, actually feeling somewhat high-spirited because of their brief experience with danger.

Playfully, like young boys on a lark, Geth'n jokingly poked at Pet'r's side, skipping away, as they walked northward along their route to Varspree.

****

Rab'k watched the small battle from a distance. He and his men had just ridden over a rise when they saw the thieves' encampment and were proceeding with caution.

Suddenly, one of the young men, tall and sinewy, broke free of his bonds and tossed his guard some twenty feet through the air. With hair flying in the wind, the boy threw himself toward the leader of the group.

Several of Rab'k's men were expressing their admiration for such a demonstration of power with a few comments. Jond'r, and then Rab'k, stared back at them. The men stopped talking and sat silently again.

Rab'k, turning back to watch the boys below, couldn't refrain from admiring the feat himself.

The young man then demonstrated remarkable abilities with the sword he snatched from the leader's scabbard and showed no qualms about using it on the man he now held in the air. He obviously was threatening the man's life.

The gang members stopped with indecision and felt the attack of the other young man who had also broken free. It was soon over.

Some of the thieves scurried across the prairie; the leader limped away in another direction. Several still lay unconscious on the ground.

Rab'k pointed his finger at the leader and one of his men galloped off in pursuit. No command was given but the leader of the robber band was not to remember this day.

"Come," Rab'k commanded, watching while the boys gathered their things and walked away from the scene and up the road. His group trotted down to the encampment, stopping as they searched the grounds for anything of importance. Finding nothing, they woke the thieves lying unconscious.

"Who were those two boys?" Rab'k asked, glaring at the three men cowering before him.

"We don't know, sire. They were just boys we grabbed because we thought they might have money, but they had none. Our leader was going to kill them, but something terrible happened and we don't remember now," one of them spoke, trembling.

"Kill them," Rab'k commanded, not looking back as he rode off in the direction the boys had taken.

His men remounted after they dispatched the robbers and quickly returned to the original group following Rab'k.

A short time later, Rab'k and his men caught the young men. Geth'n and Pet'r scrambled off the road when they heard the troop approaching, moved away to a safe distance and turned to face these new attackers.

Rab'k halted his men on the road and looking over at the boys. "Where are you going?" he shouted, sitting tall on his horse.

"We are simple travelers going to Tariny," Geth'n answered. He realized Pet'r quickly reverted to the warrior he was only a short time ago; his stance was taut and menacing.

Geth'n also understood these men should not be taken lightly and a bit of talk might preserve the day. "We don't want any trouble, sire," he added.

"And I intend you none. Perhaps you would like to travel with us, we are headed to Varspree ourselves," Rab'k proposed, liking the boys for their bravery in the face of overwhelming odds. His supplication was strangely truthful.

"Thank you, sire. We actually would prefer to walk," Geth'n responded, relaxing somewhat. He felt he and Pet'r were in no immediate danger from this man.

"We are on a pilgrimage and one is supposed to suffer a bit from such a journey, as we understand."

Rab'k laughed. "You boys seem to be able to take care of your 'suffering' very well," he added, motioning with his hand back toward the small battleground. Several of his troop chuckled. Rab'k's man who chased down the leader of the bandits rode up, reined in, and handed the leader's sword belt to Rab'k.

"Have it your way. I believe you should have no more trouble from those men. A safe journey to you." Raising his hand, Rab'k tossed the bandit leader's money pouch at Geth'n's feet, turned his horse and galloped away over the next rise with his men in pursuit.

Geth'n watched as they left then turned to his friend whose

eyes were still glazed.

"Pet'r! Pet'r! Wake up." Geth'n held Pet'r's arm. Pet'r shook his head and stared blankly at Geth'n.

"What happened? Where are those men?" Pet'r was confused and seemed to find it difficult to remember what had occurred.

"They've gone," Geth'n said slowly, realizing his friend had shown again this new and strange personality. "I believe we should be more aware and stay hidden, at least at night, for the remainder of our trip. There is too much danger about and we might not be so fortunate again."

He frowned looking again up the road where the small troop had disappeared, wondering about the man in black who had just shown them a respectful kindness.

Who could that have been?

He reached over, picked the pouch up and placed it deep in the folds of his robe.

"We probably are going to need this now," he added, looking around to see if any more danger was riding their way.

He saw no one.

Satisfied, he took Pet'r's arm, pulled him back to the road, turned toward Varspree.

"Let's continue our journey, my friend."

DECEPTION

One moment passes in relation to all other moments when a change occurs in the thoughts of one person, a discovery of something new and exciting. Mankind usually benefits by this simple action.

There are, however, those who only seek to proceed along a path both destructive and onerous.

If a person desires to be more wicked than others then often such a person will digress toward absolute evil with no concern for any but self, at the huge cost to others, and this change becomes the norm rather than the exception.

Power, in itself, can be one of those imaginary processes which draws a man, or woman, to serve it. As though one becomes godlike through achieving the control over other men's' wills, evil is a goal unto itself.

Gods do not need to consider the ramifications of power, nor its counterpart, greed; but many mortals are victims of the overwhelming desires that can come from such worship. Let us observe such a person as this, in our tale . . .

Rab'k and his men set a fast pace; he knew they needed to travel at all possible speed to intercept Garv'n's men. Garv'n's troop would have left Tariny before the messenger arrived at his door, therefore must be beyond Varspree by now. He pushed his men to travel throughout the night, resting only once just before dawn.

Afterward, they pressed onward for the rest of the day on the road. And by evening they reached a place easily guarded and set up an encampment.

Jond'r, selecting several of his men and placing them on first watch at the perimeter, walked through the camp inspecting the grounds carefully for anything unusual.

When he felt satisfied all was well, he returned to the main campfire. Rab'k was sitting there looking at the sun setting.

"Your men are doing an excellent job." Rab'k reached and

pushed a log further into the fire. Jond'r had learned silence was the better course of action whenever around Rab'k. He witnessed too many harsh results for interrupting and he didn't need to bring that on himself.

"Yes, sire. I chose these men from the many who came our way. These are the best; they work hard and obey commands," Jond'r answered, not wanting to engage in conversation for very long. He needed rest after the hard day's ride.

"We're going to need good men and will find out soon enough how well you have chosen," Rab'k replied, not looking at Jond'r. He knew he was putting pressure on the captain. He wanted to see if there would be any reaction.

"Yes, sire," Jond'r said. He recognized the prodding and adhered to his decision to say as little as possible. Jond'r was assigned to Rab'k's staff by Garv'n and warned Rab'k was ruthless, but a good man when a task needed to be completed.

Jond'r now knew why Rab'k was so successful. He simply eliminated competition. Jond'r didn't trust Rab'k but planned to make the other man trust him.

He had no idea what Rab'k's goals were, but he felt they could lead to no good.

"Do you understand what we are doing?" Rab'k asked, disturbing the Jond'r's reverie, "What we are after?"

He looked at Jond'r across the campfire with dark piercing eyes, not looking away when one of the guards walked up and stood at attention just at the edge of the firelight.

"Yes, Ar'n, what do you need?" Jond'r asked, breaking his gaze from Rab'k's. "Is there something afoot?"

"No, Captain, you asked me to report when the perimeter was covered," the soldier answered, still looking at no one, "The men are deployed and alert."

"Thank you, Ar'n, you will set watch for every four hours, rotating the men. You're dismissed," Jond'r replied, watching as the man turned and strode away.

He turned back and noticed Rab'k wasn't aware of the soldier, but was again looking at the horizon.

A curious man. And dangerous.

115

"We must catch Garv'n's men, those going north," Rab'k spoke, after a long pause. The sudden statement surprised Jond'r.

"They've possession of something vitally important to me. They possess the knowledge of good and evil."

Jond'r sat in amazement. He was troubled.

What could this man mean? What is this man planning?

"Sire?" he asked, his curiosity overpowering his resistance to talking with Rab'k.

"Good and evil. Garv'n has discovered the whereabouts of the Ahar'n, I believe," Rab'k spoke in low tones, once again gazing at Jond'r as though there was some great secret between them.

"But, sire, isn't that an old wife's tale," Jond'r asked, now engrossed in this great mystery Rab'k had created, "The Ahar'n, I mean. I thought myths and fairy tales would mean nothing to you."

"What!" Rab'k snapped, his attention bearing down on Jond'r, "I don't accept idiotic tales! This goes beyond mystification. There is always some truth to the myths; my people have long been led by the gods and have spoken of the Ahar'n many times. This is truth. If indeed Garv'n has discovered where it is hidden, I must get to it first."

Jond'r was quiet, not wanting to disturb Rab'k again.

His people

"We are going to find the Ahar'n," Rab'k spoke softly, more to the sky than to Jond'r. "It should be found for my people."

Jond'r wasn't certain what Rab'k meant by "my people". He generally didn't listen to gossip and had little reason to investigate Rab'k's background.

He trusted Garv'n, a good man if a bit greedy, and Garv'n had told him Rab'k was ruthless but loyal.

At this moment though, Jond'r was wondering how good a judge of men Garv'n really was.

"We should ride at dawn," Rab'k said, "have the men mounted and ready to move quickly." He rose, looked at the two moons above, and strode away toward his tent.

116

Jond'r, watching the man walk away, shook his head and wondered what was going to happen the next few days; he felt certain it was not going to be pleasant.

He still didn't understand, but then it was his lot to lead men and obey, not puzzle over mysteries that didn't involve him.

****

Rab'k lay in his tent, remembering the great steppes of his youth. He remembered his own disappointment after Baalsa'n's decision he should go to the South and attend the university at Tariny.

He thought about the promises given him. The promise he would become leader of the tribe when the elders and the gods felt he was ready.

He had wanted to stay in his beloved land but he had to obey. He had gone to the university and learned little except how pathetic most of the people of the South were.

But, as Baalsa'n had suggested, being diligent in his studies and excelling without effort had led him to certain peoples' attention, some of them very important in this culture.

Most were men of money, owning vast lands, properties, and commercial endeavors. These men were always looking for strong people to attend to their affairs.

Rab'k could still remember the first time he met Garv'n. The man wasn't a very impressive man, but he was a man of great business cunning and in control of all around him.

Garv'n liked Rab'k's willfulness he noticed during one of the early discussions and offered to place him in charge of Garv'n's empire as caretaker.

Garv'n was looking for someone to take the care of the daily dealings with others. He wanted to pursue other interests and felt he needed someone to ensure him his empire would stay in tact and flourish. He asked Rab'k if he would take those tasks.

Rab'k accepted. This decision was an opportunity that pleased him. He, by proxy, was given control over all within his grasp. He often worked in the guise of a man of means; traveling with

117

the ships to other lands; though discovering those cultures and beliefs took some of his time which he thought a waste. He had rare opportunities to meet with Garv'n.

Riding about the land and making "business deals" became his specialty - he never failed. His contempt for these people allowed him to have no awareness of wrongdoing.

Only on those occasions when he traveled with the ships to his homeland was he different, wanting to roam the harbors. He was friendly with those he met, talking in the languages of his youth. Only then did he feel at home and comfortable. Getting back on the ship and leaving only made him more bitter each time.

Tonight though, Rab'k lay awake amazed this opportunity had fallen into his lap unexpectedly

The Ahar'n. With that I can return to my home as a hero.

He tossed about for a while unable to sleep because of the excitement of what lay before him. He made plans to achieve these ends he wanted, knowing success was easy if the plan was carried out methodically. Baalsa'n would be pleased.

The morning came softly but soon men were noisily breaking the camp. Rab'k and Jond'r sat on their horses silently watching the proceedings.

As soon as they were ready, Rab'k turned his horse away. He and the group left the camp behind and rode toward Varspree at a fast pace while the wagons lumbered along behind.

Rab'k had business in Varspree he needed to complete so he wanted to go there while the rest proceeded northward. He knew there would be ample time to catch the wagons later. When they arrived at the fork for the road to Valhonal, he halted the procession.

"Take the men and wagons and hold them just before your reach Coma't. I have some business in Varspree and I will return later this evening. Find a campsite at dusk and you should be easy to catch," he commanded.

Spinning his horse about, he rode toward Varspree. The troop and wagons turned northward and traveled slowly along the Valhonal road.

Rab'k had no time to wait. His was an urgent mission. He intended to discover certain information in town. He assumed Garv'n's men would be visiting there and possibly provide him with information he could use.

He arrived after a few hours riding. He slowed when he reached the outskirts and rode quietly down a back street on the north of the city. He rode deliberately to a certain bar, the Queen's Ransom, and walked his horse slowly behind the building.

He stopped, sitting in the dark and listening. His eyes glinting in the moonlight, he watched for any activity. After a while he grinned, stepped down from his horse, letting the reins drop to the ground. The horse would wait.

Entering the bar through the rear door, he took a seat near the back of the room. Wrapping his long robe about himself to conceal the black uniform he always wore. He waited for some event to lead him to a source who could tell him what he needed to know.

Several men milled about drinking their ale, talking loudly and picking at the women who hung on them, trying to encourage a little business. The air was smoky and smelled of the ale spilled about as the drunks talked and jostled each other.

Rab'k was looking for certain men in the crowd and they weren't here as yet, so he waited patiently. One of the barmaids started toward him, but he shook his head at her without speaking and she left him alone.

Suddenly the door opened with a flourish and several men in uniform came bursting into the room, pushing others aside as they strode to the bar and ordered drinks.

"Barkeep, we need ale. We must ride hard tomorrow," one of the men commanded, "We need a little brew and some women tonight before we ride into the dark mountains."

Rab'k knew these men; their uniforms revealed what he had hoped would be true. They were Garv'n's; they had obviously been riding slowly trying to draw no attention on the road.

Now, of course, the fools were announcing their intentions to everyone else in this hovel.

Rab'k waited.

As the evening wore on, Garv'n's men began staggering out of the bar. Rab'k sat until the last man had departed, got up and left the room out the rear entrance, circling through the back alleys until he arrived at a back street hotel where he knew these men were going.

He stood and waited for them in the alley beside the building they would have to pass. He watched them teeter by. Having counted their numbers in the bar, he knew how many there were, reached out and snatched the last straggler into the alley with him.

"Whats do you thinks yous doing?" the soldier asked, slurring his words, "I'm one of Garv'n's soldiers and you hadj better be careful." Rab'k smacked him across the face viciously then waited as the soldier began to cry.

"I need to know who has the map," Rab'k spoke low and harshly, holding the man face close to his own and growling directly into the man's ear.

"What maph?" The soldier was having difficulty concentrating, but he had already begun to shake in fear. "I don't know noshing about no map." Rab'k slapped him again.

"Wait, wait," the soldier begged. "Sergeant Vil'n has the papers the Garv'n gives him."

"I'm not an idiot, boy. The sergeant wouldn't have them on his person," Rab'k growled at the man.

"I . . . I don't know," the soldier answered, beginning to sober now, "I don't know."

Rab'k reached down and took the man's knife from his belt, raised the man's hand above his head, and held the knife to his forefinger. "What did you say," Rab'k was placing emphasis on each word, "tell me now or you lose this finger."

The soldier knew now there would be no mercy from this man. "By the gods, I don't know," he stammered out, trying not to cry now though just barely able to stand.

Rab'k sliced off the finger about halfway from the top and caught the tip as it fell. The soldier tried to scream, but couldn't because Rab'k held his throat in his massive hand.

Rab'k moved to the side and, for the first time, the soldier recognized who his assailant was.

"You worthless idiot, tell me who has the map," Rab'k had exhausted his patience, tightening his grip on the soldier's neck, "and maybe I'll let you live."

The soldier nodded his head, grasping desperately at the Rab'k's wrist. Rab'k let him go and he dropped to the ground.

The soldier lay gasping for breath, but Rab'k was impatient. "Tell me, who has the papers," he snapped at the man, his voice low but containing violence, "tell me now."

The soldier could make sounds for he was crying again. "My lord, Rab'k, I have done nothing wrong," he sobbed, not knowing what to do.

"You will tell me who carries the pouch," Rab'k was emphatic, grabbing the man by his clothing, standing him upright, "now!"

"It is Farn's. Sergeant Vil'n's second. He has the papers," the soldier answered, sighing.

"What room is he in?" Rab'k spat this out, irritated with this stupid game.

"Top floor. Next to the Sergeant's," the boy mumbled. Rab'k sneered at him, turned his hand only slightly. The boy died in the next instant, his neck snapped. He fell softly to the ground, not knowing he had died.

Rab'k looked at the dead man. "Fool," he said, turned and walked from the alley.

As he turned the corner, he almost ran into an old beggar who was stumping along the street moaning, "Alms for the poor. Alms for the poor."

Rab'k grinned and dropped the soldier's severed finger into the beggar's cup and walked into the night.

VORAVIA

Perhaps there are those who toil for evil, perhaps these are no more than slaves to their own desires whether evil or not.

For the opportunity to advance that inner wish, these search but stay hidden from others in the belief there will be no notice of what they do. Of what is ill gotten because of what they sacrifice.

And of the compounded pain of their actions for the ambition to achieve something not yet attained.

We must observe and pity . . .

"Mord, get in here, you wretched waste of flesh!" Voravia shouted, her voice echoing through the caverns. "Do it now!"

Throwing back the covers, she rose from her bed, stomped to the washstand and splashed her face with its freezing water. She dried her face on the towel hanging on the edge of the stand and looked into the mirror.

The startling green of her eyes stared back at her; they were harshly red-rimmed with deep purple shadows beneath. Her skin was paler than she remembered with a revolting translucency. She snapped her gaze from the mirror.

Pausing only a moment, she reached down into the water again and splashed the cool liquid over her face. Her long tresses of red and gold fell over her face as she continued to refresh her face.

Maybe I can wash some color back into it with the cold.

She looked again into the mirror. Her small face, the lips so pinched they were almost invisible, her disheveled hair falling loosely about, irritated her and she became angry.

What sort of idiot are you? What can be so important you have to sit in these damned caverns to find some unknown answer?

She snatched up another towel her servants had brought earlier and scrubbed her face with it. She stopped and, peering over the towel, saw the small twisted face of her servant peeking

122

around the edge of the door.

"Where have you been? Never mind. I don't care. Go down into the lower caverns and spread out all of the oldest scrolls you can find. NOW!" she shouted at the little man.

The door slammed loudly as he pulled it closed. He ran away to do her bidding.

She turned back to the mirror over the washstand, looking at her face. The dreams were robbing her of sleep.

The strongest of the dreams revealed places and people she had never seen, nor known, standing around a huge table in a crystalline cavern.

Above the table a revolving object floated, flashing great bursts of light outside to reveal those parts of the cave previously hiding in the darkness.

Exploding worlds were cracking apart and rejoined, becoming something different yet staying the same -- destruction and rebirth.

What she saw was not upsetting her, she thought it thrilling to dream such a grand display, but she was restless through the night because of the dreams. Exhausted when she awoke, she felt she was there as part of the experience.

Where were they? Who were they? Was the dream about the past or the future?

"Why am I dreaming these things?" she asked herself aloud. "Maybe I've a stronger imagination than I thought."

She had a certain uneasy feeling however someone was inside her thoughts revealing these things, possessing her dreams to bring her a message of some sort.

But who?

She pondered, looking back at the mirror.

Who? Baalsa'n? Probably?

She slammed her hand on the washstand, splashing some of the water over. Absentmindedly, she wiped it away with the towel she held.

Voravia was more than a little upset by this whole affair. Normally she shunned all contact with other people in this land, with one exception. Her few servants, over which she placed tight controls, were totally dependent upon her.

It was not to her advantage to be starting a new project at this stage in her life; she was enjoying herself quite nicely before these stupid dreams began and she wanted to return to her old life.

Many years before, as a child, she had heard tales of powerful people who created and destroyed worlds using magical objects of power. Even then, as young as she was, she thought such tales ridiculous and scoffed at the elders who told them.

Her people were nomads, moving at a whim of nature or a leader, traveling constantly and scavenging from the land until it lay desecrated, stopping only when they found yet another place to destroy.

She thought with strange introspection but wasn't aware of the difference.

Perhaps a reason I prefer the caves. They are barren, cold and violated as everything I've seen throughout my life.

The caves were indeed imposing. The violence that created the caverns was evident from the great creases folded from the strain of building mountains at the beginning of creation.

When she came to this castle, many years before, she felt as though she had come home despite a realization there was never any peace in her life nor had she ever had a permanent home.

Perhaps the scrolls would give her some answers. She discovered them, hundreds and maybe thousands, far below the level where she made her home. Though she had looked through a great many of them after their discovery, she eventually lost interest.

She saw nothing of importance in them. They were filled with mostly ramblings of a historical nature revealing tales of various lands, peoples, other places and things for which she had no concern or saw how she could benefit from knowing about.

"These dreams. I can't dismiss the idea those scrolls have a bearing on the meaning of the dreams," she mumbled, looking once again at her distraught visage in the mirror and frowning.

"Perhaps those old tales held a certain bit of truth in them and the scrolls, the oldest of them at least, might offer a clue to this magical Ahar'n I dream about and the verification of the tales. Gods, I hope so!"

Voravia didn't care so much about things as she did about simply being left alone. She had always hated people. Even as a small child, she would kick and scream if someone dared to pick her up. Maybe the reason these dreams were so disturbing.

It was as though someone wanted to contact her and was trying to do it directly through her own mind. She certainly didn't like the intrusion. She didn't want people coming anywhere near her forest and lands, let alone directly intruding into her thoughts.

Voravia , shaking her head, stomped off to the pantry to break fast. She rummaged through a few sacks and jars, taking out bits of dried fruit, bread and honey, poured a dipper full of water from the barrel, and sat down at a rickety little table.

She spat out an apricot pit and got up from the table.

Well, even if there's nothing in the stupid scrolls about this blasted Ahar'n, there, at least, might be a spell to ward off these dreams.

She rose, leaving the table for the servants to clear, and made her way down the back steps to the caverns below.

****

Baalsa'n, observing, was pleased with his daughter.

Certainly, long ago when choosing the women he sired there was no selectivity involved. He captured young women from the "broods" of the other Guardians, roughly serving his own needs to have offspring, casting them aside once the children were conceived.

He placed each in a wandering band of castoffs for which he did nothing. He, however, like those of the other Om-Esfer'n, had long ago lost his ability to command firsthand these peoples created by the "gods", as these foul creatures called the Al-Esfer'n.

His efforts to disturb and destroy what had come from the others were not as easily accomplished as he had hope.

However this one, this whelp grown into a woman, could be

the key to a greater success than before. Even more than he had during the Varkanian wars when he defeated the weakened forces of Kalbr'an.

Now only a force of equal strength could sway him from his aim to destroy this ridiculous new experiment of the others, destroying this world and any others throughout the universe , would give him great pleasure.

But he needed the Ahar'n destroyed so he might strengthen himself beyond the measure of all other Esfer'n. This was always his resolve but it required him to use these puppets -- a difficulty that did not please him at all.

Another also watched Voravia.

She held the fate of this world and perhaps others by what she could do and might do. There had to be an alternative to avoid the disaster she held in her soul.

Her heritage was a known, requiring extreme caution. Willing the changes to happen through other brave people was now the only way the Al-Esfer'n had to accomplish their ends.

New leaders and warriors were needed and must be chosen soon. The Al-Esfer'n must do something soon.

****

Voravia was sick of looking at scrolls.

Fortunately, she was right about them containing the information she sought. She poured over the crumbling pages for days, having her meals brought down to her, yet hardly eating at all because she was so absorbed with some new discoveries.

She would awake sometimes, her hair tumbled over the ancient pages, and realize she had fallen asleep while reading.

The tales she heard in childhood about magical objects of power were written in these dusty, abandoned scrolls. The scrolls, she discovered as she read on, actually were stories of the lives of the ancient and powerful peoples who controlled the Ahar'n, the fanciful and most important object of magic mentioned.

"Mord. Kesk!" she shouted.

She, long ago, discovered it was always the best way to get the attention of these slovenly beasts she had to deal with every minute. Her creations but too stupid to learn anything.

The two misshapen servants, never daring to venture too far away for fear Voravia might call for them, peered around the archway and quickly shuffled to her and fell on their faces in the dust.

"Get up, you fools! Take these scrolls and carry them to my study," she scowled and pointed her long hand at four or five large scrolls she had chosen to study more carefully.

The creatures scurried about gathering, bumping into one another and raising a terrible dust cloud in their haste to obey, then turned to look at Voravia once more before bolting up the great stairs leading to the floors above.

Why do I find every living thing I've tried to nurture just hangs around me like some stupid creature?

Voravia, with an obvious disdain for these beings, rolled her eyes, then closed them a moment. She shook her head, rose slowly from her chair, looked around the chamber she quietly vowed she would never enter again, turned and began the long slow trek upward.

She reached her landing and crossed the great chamber and headed up another long staircase to her own quarters. She could hear the two servants chattering ahead of her, sometimes raising their voices as they squabbled with each other.

Finally, Voravia reached the top and stiffened at the sound of new voices in her study. She recognized the voices. Two of her guard were yelling and arguing with Mord and Kesk.

Voravia walked deliberately through the entrance to her quarters, slamming the door against the wall, and the four small beings fell silent.

RESTING PLACE

There are no matters of the heart overlooked in this tale. There may be those who are the best of what another desires.

This union of thought has often brought those together who might never have known what happiness could be.

This need may not be one of a romantic nature but more, a sense of being a part of something larger or greater than oneself. The union with these others will naturally form with no need to bring attention to what becomes obvious.

Our young travelers were to have each their own adventures along their way but would only come together because they each are of a blend of peoples who had more need to know than to attend to their private affairs.

These were drawn together across a great gulf of time and place simply because it should happen. Let us see how the journey progresses . . .

Varspree was a centrally located town, much visited by the surrounding countryside, but being on the intersection of several byways it was obvious its possibilities were unlimited.

However, the unusual seemed the rule rather than the exception.

Topping a rise, Anisah's eyes grew wide as the town spread out below. Varspree was not really very large, just a conglomerate of buildings, inns, pubs, shops, shacks, and a few finer homes on the edge of the hill where she sat.

It was, however, the largest place she had ever seen and she couldn't believe such a place could exist.

Shaking herself from her reverie, she walked the horse down the hill and into the hubbub of the streets. Horses, carts, wagons, people walking across the streets at random made her uneasy.

Sumt'r could be anywhere and, in the confusion, she could not distinguish individuals. Everyone smelled badly, dressed extravagantly, and bumped their ways along the avenue.

128

She arrived at dusk and now darkness was beginning to envelop the town. Anisah knew she shouldn't be out on the streets.

She was again feeling she should have never left home; she could turn around and ride back the way she came and none of this would matter. But she remembered Brae'x, her stepfather, and knew to return was impossible.

Suddenly a low, lewd voice growled from her side near her stirrup

"Eh, lassie, got something to keep a fella warm, have ye?"

Anisah stiffened and instinctively kicked the horse, sending him into a loping gallop. The horse was dodging obstacles in its way, knocking people into the dust, upsetting carts. Anisah had to cling to its mane to save her life.

She spotted an alley ahead and yanked violently on the reins. The animal slowed enough to turn into the opening and headed for an open stable door near the end of the alley. Anisah was pulling back on the reins as hard as she could, hurting her arms with the effort. They burst through the opening together.

The horse, realizing he had gone as far as he could without running into a wall, slammed his hooves into the dust and slid to a stop. Anisah, thrown from her mount and over his head, landed in a pile of hay in a stall.

"Hey! Ow! What do ya think yore doin'?" a muffled voice yelped from the hay.

Anisah, still in shock from her ride through the streets and just realizing what had happened to her, tried to scramble backwards but tumbled head over heels down the hay pile.

She landed with a grunt and lay groaning in the dust in the stall, sputtering from the dirt in her nose and mouth.

Looking up, she could see a dark head poking up from the hay, the straw jutting out in all directions from its hair.

"Who're you and why'd you come crashin' into my life ?" demanded the boy from under the head of straw. He stood up, brushing the hay away, staring down at her. She sat where she was; her hands propped behind her to hold her up out of the hay, and blinked.

"You should take care where you fall asleep," she said finally, with certain haughtiness obvious in her voice.

"I wasn't sleepin'. I was hiding!" he grunted back.

"Hiding?"

"Yes, hiding. I'm bone tired. Mistress Farlen's got me scrub-bin' pots, doin' wash, just a plain ole servin' maid stuff -- and I still gotta keep this stable clean." he added, plopping down on the hay and sliding down to sit in front of Anisah.

"Damn Esme, the stupid cow, hope she gets herself drowned."

"Esme? Who's Esme?" Anisah interjected.

"Oh sure, Esme! She's one of the serving girls, ran off with a sailor a fortnight ago. Now I'm doin' her job and mine," he spouted, looking at Anisah hatefully. "Ya still haven't told me who you are and what you're doin' in this stable."

"I don't know what I'm doing here. Actually, my horse threw me in here," she told him, realizing this situation might be an opportunity she needed desperately. "Maybe I can help you though."

"How?" the boy looked impatiently at this foolish girl. He had had about enough of foolish girls for one life.

"Maybe Mistress Farlen would give me the serving maid job. I'm new here, need a job and a place to sleep," she said, waving at her horse who stood at the end of the stable blowing his breath in gasps, "and a place for my horse"

"Well, I don't know whether she'd hire you lookin' like you do. Where you been sleeping? In a tree?" he laughed. "But maybe we can figure out a way to get you a job. It sure would help me a lot.

"Let's see what we can do 'bout the way you look. You look like a wood sprite and methinks your lovely gown could use a bit of washin'."

"You'd look quite a sight yourself if you'd been nabbed by a gang of thieves," Anisah snarled back at him. "I've escaped from them, spent the night in the woods, rode a horse all day. I'm hungry and tired. I should have never left home!"

Anisah began sobbing, covered her face with her hands and sank wearily back into the hay; her defiance totally spent.

130

"Now, now, lassie, don't ye cry. You girls are always a' cryin'. My sisters cry all the time for no good reason I can see. Come on now. Don't cry. Look, I'll feed your horse and get 'im some water. Then we'll get you all cleaned up. I'm sure Mistress Farlen'll have ya. Please, just stop your cryin'," the boy babbled on. His concern showed on his face, as he paced back and forth, trying anything to distract Anisah.

"Do you think she will give me the job?" Anisah snuffled, wiping her tears away on her dirty dress, smearing her face.

"Yes, yes. She surely needs someone to do the sewing at least and she'll probably have you seeing to the rooms as well; those were Esme's jobs. But let's get you cleaned up first. I'll get some water so you can wash up and we'll get those leaves out of your hair. Just brush your dress off for now, and don't worry. Everything'll be fine," the boy said as he jumped up and ran out the barn door, "Stay here, I'll be back with the water."

Anisah stood up and looked down at her dress. The boy was right; she looked a mess. Dust and dirt everywhere and a tear in the hem of her dress, but who could blame her.

Sighing deeply, she sat down and began to try to beat some of the worst of the grime from her clothing. She was making some progress.

At least, I was wearing dark clothes.

Shortly the boy came back through the door, carrying a bucket.

"Here's the water, just like I promised," he said, smilingly like a bonrago, "and I got a comb from Mercy, she'll want it back, but I figured it would be easier than using yer fingers since ya got such long hair." he held out the comb.

"Thank you," Anisah said, taking it and placing it next to the bucket. She walked over to where the horse was standing quietly munching hay, retrieved her pack and dug inside to find her kerchief.

"Could you see to my horse, please? I'm sure he's awfully tired and thirsty," she asked, smiling at the horse with his nose in the hay, "but then, he seems to be taking care of the eating part himself," she added, laughing.

"Sure, I'll get him some oats and more water, then I'll get the saddle off and he'll be fine. Where'd ya get him?" asked the boy.

"Stole him from the cursed son of a whore who tried to have his way with me. Might teach him to pick on someone his own size," she said with more bravado than she felt.

She plunged her face and arms into the water and begun rubbing at them to get as much dirt as possible off with no soap available. Wetting the edge of the kerchief, she wiped her face and neck then she swabbed at her arms.

While she was washing herself, Col'n attended her horse. He removed the saddle, fed and watered the animal, and brushed him so his coat was shiny and gleamed in the lamplight.

"Well, how's that. Col'n?" she said, turning so he could see her. She held her arms out and turned slowly. She asked his name while he watched her cleaning. She liked it, a good name.

"Well, better. But yer hair is a mess," he suggested, grimacing a little as though there might be no way to resolve some problems.

"We'll see!" she snapped, and laughing she grabbed up the comb and began pulling it through her tangled mop. After a few struggling strokes and some pulled hair, she stopped.

"This might take a little longer than I thought and I might need some help since I can't see behind me. I'll, at least, need to know when I have brushed all the leaves and twigs out." She yanked at her hair a few more times.

"I might as well just cut it off," she sighed. Then she pulled a part of the snarled mess over her shoulders and began to comb in earnest. But she was so tired the effort seemed too much.

"Won't you be getting into trouble soon. Someone must be looking for you by now." Anisah asked, as she dragged the comb through another clump of hair.

"No, no one will come around for a while. Besides, I'm supposed to be muckin' out here in the stables, tossin' hay, and seein' to the horses, so I ain't gonna be missed," he answered, turning to look at her, noticing what a terrible time she was having reaching all of her hair.

"Here, let me help ya," he suggested, putting the curry comb

132

down beside her and began picking some of the large pieces of trash out as she dragged the comb through yet another section.

"You was really kidnapped?" he asked after a bit.

"It was a nightmare come true," she answered, pausing and giving a great sigh as she remembered. "But it's turning out just fine now. I even have my own horse." She dropped her arms to her side for a moment.

"I think I was pretty clever, if you ask me," she added, laughing again and returning to her task. She told him her story of adventure while they worked.

"Well," she said, giving her hair a final pat, "what do you think?" She turned slowly so he could see the transformation.

"Much better," Col'n replied, nodding his head, "Decent enough to meet Miz Farlen anyhow. Though she'll want to be givin' ya a thorough washing up once she sees ya. Best I get back or they will be lookin' for me," he added. She picked up the lantern and they started for the barn door.

"Come on, now's as good a time as any to meet her, if she likes ya, she'll be wantin' to' feed you a solid meal anyway."

"Thank you so much for all your help," Anisah said as she handed back the lantern and the comb, "I was at the end of my wits until I ran into you," she said laughing. Col'n looked at her strangely then he too began to laugh.

"Don't thank me too much just yet, wait'll you see what happens inside," he said over his shoulder as he led the way.

They crossed a small garden, went up and through a back door Anisah noticed earlier. She paid particular attention to how neat everything was and how well repaired.

They stepped into a huge kitchen, bustling with activity after the dinner just completed in the dining hall.

A girl, in swirling skirts, crashed through a door opposite them, her arms loaded with plates and utensils from the tables. Anisah caught a glimpse of her as the girl passed, hair was hanging loosely about her face. She was flushed from her efforts.

She spotted them and shouted, "Here now, Col'n, when I lent ya my comb, I'd no idea you'd be half the night, playing ladies'

133

man to some trollop. I got my hands full here, get out there and make yourself useful, boy."

"Please, it wasn't his fault," Anisah interjected

"I've no time for yer explanation, girl." the girl spoke sharply as she slammed the dishes she was carrying into a huge tub of soapy water, sending suds flying in all directions. "Col'n knows what his job is and when its supper time he's supposed to be done with his outside stuff so he can help in here."

She turned to the large table spread with food, filled several plates, balanced them perfectly along her arm, grabbed some clean hand towels with the other hand, and turned to go back through the door again.

Anisah stood stunned by the brash attacks of this fiery lady.

"If you'd like to make it up to me for stealing my help, you could grab some more plates and follow me, otherwise be off with ya' and out of my way. I'll thank ya to be courtin' on someone else's time," she hurled the last over her shoulder as she banged through the door, almost hitting Col'n who was on his way in with a load of dirty dishes.

Anisah snapped out of her shock. This whirling dervish must be Mercy.

Anisah ran and began grabbing dishes, balancing them as she saw Mercy do, pushed her hip into the door and out into the dining room. She spotted Mercy's red kerchief bobbing through the crowd of tables, chairs and people eating.

Working her way across the room, dodging swaying patrons, flailing arms, dancers, having her bottom pinched. She did squeal when that happened and jumped.

But it occurred more than once and she wasn't able to retaliate because her hands were so full. She tripped over several obstacles but still managed to make her way to where Mercy was standing by a table.

"Well now, here ya are, thought ya might have gotten yourself lost," Mercy's eyes twinkled with mischief as she grabbed the plates from Anisah's arm and practically threw them on the table as though they were playing cards.

"Now, go get some of those wine pitchers," she pointed to

134

the bar on the front side of the room. "They need another round here. Be quick about it. When yer done, get back to the kitchen and mind ya don't come back out here with empty hands!"

Anisah scurried toward the bar, dodging the same problems she had crossing the room the first time. She was beginning to think she might be getting better when she finally reached the bar.

A little bald man behind the bar was yelling and taking orders from everyone within a few feet, pouring ale and wine into great pitchers as fast as he could.

"Please, sir," she shouted, above the noise in the room, "I'm to get a pitcher of wine for that table there," she pointed in the direction of the table across the room.

"Who are you, girl. You're not any of our help, unless my wife has hired you without tellin' me," he shouted back at her.

"No, sir, you're wife hasn't met me. Col'n was helping me, and he was late to help with supper. So Mercy, she told me I had to help to make up the difference," she yelled back.

A drunk staggered against the bar almost knocking Anisah off her feet, but she stood her ground, grabbed his shoulder and twisted him around and back out into the crowd.

"Well, if yer helpin' Mercy, go ahead and we'll sort it all out later. Mind you'll not be servin' anybody not payin'," he grinned at her and returned to filling the great pitchers.

Anisah pushed her way back through the crowd.

I'm definitely getting the hang of this.

She deftly dodged a hand headed for one of her breasts and arrived back at the table without too much damaged to her person. She poured wine all around the table and headed back toward the kitchen, placing the pitcher on a table where a cluster of empty ones sat.

Banging through the kitchen door, she saw Col'n scrubbing dishes in one large tub, dunking them in another one, and stacking them as fast as he could.

A large woman suddenly burst through another door into the kitchen, scaring Anisah so much she jumped backwards almost

135

falling into one of the tables of food.

"Here now, who might you be, what're ya doin' in my kitchen, young lady?" Mistress Farlen spoke with authority, marching straight to her as she talked.

She was a large, round woman, her face, her hands, and even her hair, tied tightly in a bun, evoked a certain roundness. She wore a simple blue woolen dress with a white cotton full apron, brown woolen stockings and sturdy brown leather shoes.

Col'n tried to intercede. "Mistress Farlen, m'am, I found this girl in the stable all cryin' and afraid, she'd escaped from a bunch of thieves and looked a sight. She doesn't have anywhere to go and needs a place to stay and some money so I thought Esme's runnin' off like she did. Well, maybe you could use a servin' girl and she's already been helpin' Mercy . . ."

He finished with a great gasp as he tried to catch his breath after his long speech.

Mistress Farlen glared down at him, "Such wild stories, Col'n. Your stories will be the end of you yet."

"No, m'am, he's telling the truth. He brought me water so I could wash some and wanted me to meet you, but I took so much time he was late for supper. So Mercy said I should help her to make up for the trouble I caused, so I just started helping. But you don't owe me anything for what I've done and I - I can be on my way," Anisah offered.

The woman waited for Anisah to finish, looked at Col'n again and back at her. Anisah had a sinking feeling this wasn't going to work out as well as she hoped. Mistress Farlen's stare now concentrated on her.

"I don't know about these stories of thieves and such and don't have time right now for the listening. But seeing as how you're willin' to work, you may as well get back out there and do what ya can to help. I'm short-handed, so if ya do a decent job there might be a place for ya. We'll see how ya do, show ya how to do some other things as ya go along."

She turned back to Col'n who stood watching, water dripping on the floor from his wet hands, "And you, mister, can get back to scrubbin' dishes instead of standin' there gawkin'". Col'n jumped as though hit and busily began to grind away on the dishes as Mrs. Farlen turned away from both of them to talk to the cook.

As Mistress Farlen rushed off, Col'n turned slightly and smiled at Anisah. She grinned back at him, got busy loading up another group of plates, and slamming her bottom against the door again and pushed her way back into the dining room.

It was late when Anisah and Mercy finally finished and the bedlam in the dining hall was reduced to a small murmur. They gathered all the empty plates and dishes, washed all the pitchers and mugs, put up the chairs, banked up the fire in the great hearth at the end of the great room, and turned the lanterns down low for those still sitting at the tables talking.

"You didn't do too bad a job," Mercy admitted, nodding her head, as they were completing the clean-up job, "And I gotta apologize. I'm sorry for callin' ya a trollop."

"That's all right, you were angry. I'm just glad you let me help," Anisah replied wearily.

"Is it like this every night?" she asked.

"Well, lass, I didn't let you help, I couldna have finished without you, or Col'n, takin' at least part of the load, especially since Esme ran off. But yes, every night except Sundays, and not just nights either, we serve all day. Mistress Farlen is a good woman though. I get a nice bed, hot meals and a bit of money for me troubles," Mercy talked, as she placed more dishes on the shelves.

She was fairly young, older than Anisah, but not much. She always seemed flushed and flurried as she worked, but she was a big girl and Anisah knew Mercy probably could handle most any problem she came across. Anisah worked hard. When she was at home, Brae'x saw to that, but this was different, very different. She wasn't certain she could endure it.

Mistress Farlen came back into the kitchen, where the girls were sitting while they talked.

"Well, lass, you're still here, that's a pretty good sign. You did a passable job tonight, and I do need the help. So if you'd like the job, I'll give you what Esme got in pay. You can always make a little out there from some of the more generous gentlemen in that herd," she laughed. Her smile was pleasant and she seemed much less harsh than before.

Anisah relaxed a little and knew she liked Mistress Farlen now she had a chance to actually talk to her quietly, "Do ya think ya might like to work for me then."

"Oh, yes m'am, I certainly would love to have the job," Anisah blurted out, knowing this was an unbelievably fortunate circumstance for her. She almost cried, but sniffled and smiled at Mistress Farlen, "Thank you ever so much."

"Well, now we have a different problem," Mistress Farlen added, the frown back on her face, then she smiled again, "first thing we need to do with ya is give ya a decent bath, a little food, and then to bed with ya."

"Oh, Mistress Farlen, thank you so much, I can think of nothing better. Lord knows I need the bath and I'm starving. I think I last ate a couple of days ago, but I can't really remember. Things have been movin' so fast. But, thank you again," Anisah poured out, her happiness, her hunger and her weariness, making her a little giddy.

"Come on then, child. Let's get some of the grime offa ya. Col'n, ya go get some water for the tub and put it on the fire, and stoke the fire up a bit while you're there, put some more wood on it." She turned and startled the boy who was quietly stacking dishes, and wiping the counters and tables while he listened, but he jumped and grabbed a pail and started to dash out the back door.

"I've a pack of clothes out in the barn," Anisah offered helpfully.

"Take a lantern, boy, and while you're out there get the girl's pack from the stable," Mistress Farlen yelled after the boy,

"Mercy honey, ya go ahead upstairs and make up the other bed in your room; if you will, child; I know ya must be beat down and I thank you, as you know. But you can help, then come back down and get yourself some supper," she spoke gently to Mercy.

Mercy nodded and went up the stairs. Col'n ran out the door, stumbling through it. He returned shortly, poured water into a big kettle hanging from its irons in the fireplace, added a couple of logs to the fire, swung the kettle over, turned and walked back out through the door with his lantern.

Mistress Farlen wandered around the room slowly, hanging some things, putting away others, while the water in the kettle was heating. Anisah stood where she was, too exhausted to move, watching the woman tidy the place.

"Come here now, lass, ya get into this tub and relax a little," Mistress Farlen was talking as she pulled the kettle away from the fire, dipped into it with one of the buckets. She poured the boiling water into a tub setting near the hearth on the side away from the staircase. Mistress Farlen turned to Anisah, "Now do you have a name, child?"

"Yes, m'am, I'm Anisah," Anisah moved slowly toward the tub, yawning as she went. She was just about to remove her clothes when Col'n came back in with her pack.

"Wonderful. Thank ya, Col'n," Mistress Farlen said to the boy, "but I believe we need two more buckets of water, if ya will, lad." Col'n grabbed two more buckets and flew out the door, thankful he wasn't in trouble.

Anisah removed her clothes after the boy left. She almost had to tear them off; they had gotten so crusty. She slid slowly into the tub letting the water engulf her as she sank into it.

Mercy returned bringing a sliver of soap from upstairs. She handed it to Anisah, who, as drowsy as she was, had enough awareness to reach and take it.

"Thought ya might be a'needin' this. Took a chunk off the big roll in the pantry," Mercy added, as she backed away smiling at this little girl almost drowning herself.

"Oh, thank you, Mercy, that's very nice of you," Anisah spoke in low tones, wondering if she was going to be able to stay awake.

She began to lather her body and even dunked her hair and began scrubbing it, when Col'n burst back into the room.

Anisah, surprised, trying to slide quickly back under the water, went completely under but rose as quickly, spewing and sputtering, soap trailing down her face. She wiped her eyes with her hands but that only made matters worse. Mercy grabbed a towel nearby and helped Anisah wipe her face.

"Sit down, boy, and quit your gawkin'" Mistress Farlen spoke to Col'n who had stopped just inside the door, standing and holding the buckets of water without moving, "put your buckets down over here, and get yourself some food. You too, Mercy." She pointed to where she wanted the buckets, and turned back to Anisah.

The boy stumbled over, put the buckets down and went to get some food but ran into a table, still staring at Anisah who lowered herself back under the water. Mercy just shook her head and followed him, grinning and mumbling about how foolish boys were.

"Now, Anisah, tell me some of these stories Col'n was blathering about," Mistress Farlen sat down beside the tub and watched the girl finish her bath.

Mr. Farlen came blasting through the door at that moment, returning from the cellar where he had retrieved more wine kegs and ale for tomorrow's business.

Anisah ducked back under the water again but not quite as much as before, amazed at the sudden increase in traffic, particularly male traffic, since she had climbed into the bath.

This whole affair was like an open parlor; she wasn't accustomed to so much activity when she took a bath. But Mr. Farlen didn't even glance her way but barged into the dining room with his load, too busy to worry about her.

Once again, Anisah recounted her tale of adventure bringing it to the point where she walked into the kitchen. Col'n left to go to bed while she was talking.

"Ya lived an exciting life, Anisah. I'm not so sure there ain't just a bit more danger than I want to expose myself to. Right now I'm tired and goin' to bed. I'll see ya at breakfast," Mercy said as she stood up, stretched, and went up the stairs.

"My goodness, lass, that's quite a tale. Can't believe a little girl like you could have managed all that," Mistress Farlen said shaking her head.

Anisah had, while she was finishing her story, stepped out of the tub and dried herself. She put some of her clothes on from her pack, not exactly clean but not as dirty as what she had just taken off, sat and ate a bit of the food though she was surprised she wasn't as hungry as she had thought, and felt totally exhausted.

Anisah found it hard just remembering her travels.

And all I wanted to do was go to Tariny and study herbal curing. This was not what I expected either.

"So off to bed with ya, girl. Mercy's probably left the lantern on for you. Just go to the top of the stairs and turn left, the room's about five doors down."

Anisah nodded her head drowsily, climbed the steps and following Mistress Farlen's directions, found the room and her new bed, blew out the candle Mercy had left burning for her, fell into bed and was asleep instantly.

Mr. Farlen had returned during Anisah's story and was sitting on a bench listening. He rose and walked toward the hearth to knock out his pipe; his wife paused a moment listening to him before heading up the stairs.

"I wonder where she really comes from; we'll probably never know. It don't really matter to me as long as she does her job and doesn't steal from us. Her story is certainly hard to believe. Seems the gods are protecting her. Well, time to stop this day and get some rest. I need it, it's been a long one," he said to his wife as she disappeared around a corner, banked the dying coals in the fireplace, and followed her up the stairs.

He was very cynical about some of the people his wife had had working for her; several had stolen a night's till and run away.

I work hard and don't need to worry about some tramp taking what's mine.

Anisah was watching a young girl sitting on a small rock in the middle of a field of flowers. Other children surrounded the girl. Many were run-

141

ning about, shouting, laughing; some were sitting around near the rock the girl sat on.

As she watched, Anisah realized all of the children had some physical defect, some had clubbed feet, others had facial deformities, some were blind, some seemed deaf, and others had no control over the muscles in their bodies. She felt cold at the realization, her heart ached and she couldn't breathe freely.

These poor children! Why do they seem so happy? She wondered as she watched the girl rise from the rock and began to walk among the children. She was dressed in a shimmering blue robe and turned to each child and gently caressed each one's face as she moved.

Anisah felt her heart would stop; she felt only numbness and her thoughts whirled. Then the girl turned and looked at her and she knew why.

The girl from the rock was her, a bit older; she was watching herself. The other reached into the folds of the robe and drew forth a small clear ball, wrapped in a net of gleaming metal, a gossamer bubble.

The sun's glow shimmered and sparkled as its light passed through it. She turned the ball slowly in her hand and let it drop from her hand. It hung suspended reflecting the sun as if through clear diamonds; everything viewed from the other side of the globe was magnified.

The sky somehow seemed much bluer reflected in the misty jewel. The children oohed and aahed as the orb began to spin faster and faster, rising over their heads.

Suddenly, the orb became incandescent, burst into a shower of tiny diamonds, floating softly down like a gentle snow, onto the heads of each child. The tiny flickers seemed to expand and flow like crystal liquid over the children's bodies touching them gently where the injuries were more pronounced.

The children began to cry out with joy and amazement, touching themselves as the essence flowed over them like slow rivulets of clear silver.

One small boy cried out and began to leap about, "I can see! I can see!" All around other children began to cry out in amazement. "My feet! My feet, I can stand! Look at me!" And another, "Ooh! Too loud." she moaned as she covered her ears.

All the children seemed to be cured of what had affected them; they danced about, perfect children who were rescued from their own hell.

Anisah, of the vision, walked to the last little girl and picked her up,

142

smoothing her hair, and rocking her softly.

The orb floated back to Anisah and hung in the air. She reached and cradled it in her hand, slipping it back into her robe.

Anisah sat up in bed gasping, looking around her in the darkness. "What's the matter?" Mercy asked sleepily, rolling in her bed and fumbling about in the dark with her cover.

"Nothing. Please, nothing. Please go back to sleep. I was just having a nightmare," Anisah answered, "Don't get up, it's all right. Go back to sleep." She heard Mercy lay down.

Anisah slid back under her own covers, disturbed but yet intrigued. *What kind of magical healing was this? She had never seen, or heard of, such a thing. How lovely it was. A magic bubble spread its healing powers over all. But why was I the person who possessed the orb?*

She drifted back to sleep, wondering.

Anisah awoke the next morning to Mercy's voice shaking her and calling her name, "Get up, Anisah, we'll be late if we don't get a move on. We've got to get downstairs to freshen the fire, heat up the stove, get the milk and eggs, and help Col'n get water for washin' the dishes."

Anisah jumped up but sank back to the edge of the bed. The cold crept into her feet from the floor and helped clear her head. She made her way to a washstand she saw by the window, splashed her face with its icy water. Giving a short gasp at the cold, she turned to find Mercy almost dressed.

She grabbed her skirt from where she had tossed it on the end of the bed and pulled it over her head, trying to button it, her hands were numb from the cold. She retrieved her boots and sitting on the bed, tugged them on, jumped up and ran down the hall after Mercy.

The morning was a rush of chores and orders. Mistress Farlen kept several cows and chickens for herself, so she wouldn't have to deal with the 'thieves in the market.

"And they call themselves farmers, probably all stolen goods in this town," she huffed.

143

The girls were starving by the time they had a chance to sit and eat. "How'd you girls sleep last night?" Mistress Farlen asked Anisah.

"Oh, quite well. Thank you," replied Anisah. Mercy gave her an odd look from under her brow but said nothing as she returned to her food.

"After breakfast, we'll get your clothes washed before the first drunks begin to arrive. It won't take long and I have my own to do anyway. Mercy'll help. Col'n will too when he's finished with his stable chores.

Col'n, you'll need to get us some more water and start it heating over the fire, bring enough so's we have plenty of rinsin' water." "More important than you know, the rinsin' water," she nodded toward Anisah, "makes things fresher smelling."

They all jumped, began gathering the clothes, separating them, and scurrying about, like Mistress Farlen's chickens. They wanted to try to get them washed and rinsed so they could hang them to dry.

Anisah and Mercy finished this chore just in time to start serving dinner. Mercy taught Anisah about the costs of the food and the drinks, and more about how to properly serve a table instead of flinging the food at the guest.

She also pointed out there was a special dining room where the more refined guests ate and, grinning as she mentioned it, where the best tips were. Luckily, Anisah knew how to add and subtract money, learned when she had helped her father at the village market.

Later, the two girls cleaned all the rooms, emptying chamber pots, and bringing in fresh pails of water to clean the washbowls, while most of the guests were out wandering around the town.

Soon, the evening arrivals flowed through the doors in a continuous line, calling for food and drink, and more food, and more ale, round after round, endlessly.

Finally, things began to slow down and, as the last of the diners staggered out the front door or up to their rooms, the girls were able to walk into the kitchen.

There they grabbed a crust of bread with some cheese before starting the cleaning of all the dishes; mopped the floors of the dining hall; wiped all the tables clean; and stacked the chairs for the night.

As usual, Col'n was performing the dish washing chores, but helped occasionally by carrying an especially large load of dishes for the girls.

At the end of this second day and Anisah's first full day of work, she staggered into the kitchen with a last load of plates and collapsed into a chair. Mr. Menden and his guest were just finishing their wine and beginning to disperse to go to their rooms.

"I'll finish the dishes if you'll mop," offered Mercy, sitting with her arms draped in her lap, too exhausted to move.

"I don't know which is worse, but it doesn't really matter. All I want is to be done and go to bed." Anisah replied.

She went to the far corner of the kitchen, opened the door to the closet under the stairs and pulled out the mop and tub. Pouring water from one of the buckets into the tub, she pushed the mop into the water; splashed it onto the floor and began to mop near the rear entrance.

She scattered a few flakes of soap she shaved from the cake near the sink and methodically scrubbed the old floors, pushing the mop in small circles. She felt she was working through the process while sleeping on her feet.

Once, she pulled back the door to throw dirty water out into the yard and paused so long the door swung shut and smacked across her bottom. She yelped, kicked the door and slumped back to her task.

She was mopping in the corner of the dining hall near the bar when the door on the other side of the room opened and she heard a man's voice.

She whirled about with the mop held out in front of her as if it were a shield.

TOGETHER

Often great deeds occur after the sun has fallen below the horizon; lives and nations saved, or destroyed, in the secret of the night. The sense of stealth and wonder encompass the hearts of those who choose to be night wanderers.

And there are places where those gather when they want to be in the company of others of their ilk.

These young people, wishing to face adventures in their lives, will caress the feel of the night to gather their hearts in a sudden rush of surprise and emotion.

They can fulfill promises of what they are to be when they wander into and out of the dark and have only superficial wounds to show for the exposure -- and thus they become more than they were.

That is how some become more than others.

Our story here will show how our young adventuring students are progressing in their journey.

They have not yet entered their night; they are only just beginning . . .

"Pet'r, do we have something to eat besides that rotten cheese we begged for in Pull'r," Geth'n asked, his face wrinkling with disgust at the thought of eating any more garbage.

"No. In fact, we're almost out of water," Pet'r answered. He smiled looking at his friend's face screwed into such a shape. "I think though we should be arriving in Varspree by this evening. I'm sure we can get good food, drink and a bed. I believe we need them after this journey. We know, at least, we need some water."

"We'll find something along the way. Certainly in those hills ahead there should be a cottage where we might get more supplies," Geth'n responded.

He was in great spirits; it was a long while since he felt so good. Pet'r, concerned about his friend in those last days before they left Larilla, noticed the change and thought Geth'n's new attitude much better.

"Actually, I think Varspree is just beyond that rise. We should be there within the hour or so," Pet'r insisted.

They had walked quietly for most of the day, each lost in his thoughts. Though not speaking about it, they both were experiencing a certain agitation and their dreams were adventurous. They couldn't imagine how such dreams were coming to them -- some were violent, some were pleasant, some dressed in grandeur, and others shocking.

Geth'n had another voice speak to him in a dream. This time he told Pet'r what the voice said. The messages amazed them both.

"There is much to be done. You must get to Varspree as quickly as possible. There you must find a young girl with flaming hair who will be of greater help to you than you will soon discover. You must find this girl and make her your friend; it is vital."

Pet'r did ask, "Flaming hair? What does that mean?

Geth'n shrugged his shoulders, "It's a dream. How should I know what it means?"

So they entered the city puzzled about what was to come.

Varspree wasn't very impressive, low rolling hills and a low valley with a broad street running through the center. It wasn't a city really but more like a large town.

The streets that extended outward from the center of the main street were all a pleasantly shady even in the daylight because of the overhanging roofs that seemed fashionable here. The town's claim to fame were the great cattle pens and slaughterhouses, spreading out to the west in long lines of fence rows. The moaning of cattle in the heat of the day, and the accompanying odors that hung in the air were particularly odorous.

Pet'r looked over the town and into the distance.

"It doesn't seem much like Larilla, so much larger, but at least there is a road here leading to where we want to go," he sighed, "and there isn't much here to make anyone want to linger."

"The only question we have about whether or not we linger

very long has more to do with finding this girl than how far we go in the next few hours. I gather from the dreams and voices we both have experienced we should start our search quickly," Geth'n added.

"Sure," Pet'r added, "and whatever happened to our real reason for taking this trip?"

"Real reason?" Geth'n asked, "what real reason? I was going to Tariny to the great library to search for answers. Answers about those things that either were troubling me or were making you wonder what was in the northern countries. I believe we have to admit now -- assuming that our dreams are not just indigestion -- the answers are coming to us."

He slapped his friend gently on the back and started down the hill. "Come on, we have to find a place to sleep and there certainly seems to be a lot of fine places here."

"You've got to be kidding. Right?" Pet'r looked at his friend walking away. "This place is a dump -- and stinks to boot. I say we camp out here, look for this strange girl tomorrow, and hit the road early."

" believe we don't have that option," Geth'n yelled over his shoulder, pointing at the skies to the north.

Pet'r looked and saw only a great dust cloud and at its base the faces of the herd being driven directly toward them.

"Great! So we try to find this girl tonight," he shouted down the hill at his retreating friend.

Throwing up his hands, he ran after Geth'n.

"What do we do -- knock at every door?" Pet'r shouted as they ran.

"I believe we will be informed," Geth'n said to himself more than to his friend. "Besides I have more than one problem."

Pet'r caught his friend. "What is your other problem?"

"You, my wild-eyed friend," Geth'n laughed, "and I hope you contain yourself in this innocent place."

They both laughed, trotted along slowly, entering the town with a great deal of curiosity.

Several sets of eyes watched them as they sauntered down the main street. The town was notoriously riotous. The boys were

148

unaware but the local clientele of the many taverns were in town with the cattle drives and felt obliged to allow their playfulness to wander into the wild side -- uninhibited frolicking and violence.

There was also a group there that intended to take advantage of the poor fools who might tarry just a bit too long in one place. The worst and foulest of all these wanderers who entered the town gathered here simply to steal what they wanted, or worse.

Varspree was indeed a frontier town and was for centuries. There was little change in its appearance, manner, and generally offensive atmosphere since its founding.

The town had not grown very large because of the lack of interest. The residents were setting no example for others, so it remained as large as the need required. A business could change hands frequently often because the previous owner lost it gambling, lost it in a fight, or simply died at the hands of the new owner.

There was some competition between the taverns for customers, but there were usually enough taverns to provide a night on the town every night without conflict -- so an uneasy peace held the whole together.

The two young travelers finally noticed what seemed to be one of the cleaner lodging houses, contrasting with its neighbors strangely enough, near the center of the long avenue.

They walked into the lodge and the change from the outside surprised them. Fine elegant woods were used for the door and window frames. The floors were polished and glowed. There was pleasant aroma as they entered. The boys were a bit puzzled how such a place could exist.

At that moment, their questions were answered. From one of the hallways stepped a man, tall and distinguished, a man of money, with a young woman holding his arm. They were laughing as they exited the building, looking only briefly toward the two ragged young men.

The young men, looked at each other knowingly, walked into the room staring about the room as though looking for

149

someone.

One of them noticed Anisah, standing with the mop held out, staring at them, and walked over slowly and asked her a question.

"Excuse me, Miss," Geth'n wandered up to her, "are any rooms available?"

She jumped back, flaming red hair flaring out, her eyes steeling as she raised the mop in front of her, looking as though she would easily swat Geth'n with it.

He extended his arms in front of him, raising his hands in an appeal.

"Wait, wait! I meant you no harm. We just need a room," he added, pointing casually toward Pet'r who was standing behind Geth'n and grinning at his friend's new embarrassment.

Anisah realizing she was staring like an idiot and he was only asking her question about the lodgings, shook her head a bit

"I'm sorry, sir. I don't handle the arrangements. I mean, I don't handle the lodging rentals," she answered, "Mistress Farlen can help you."

"Well, thank you very much. I'm sorry if I frightened you." he apologized, smiling and nodding his head at her.

At that moment, Mistress Farlen came from the kitchen through a curtained doorway across the room, noticed the young men and walked over to them with a big smile.

"May I help you?" she asked, noting their rough dress but simple manner and seemed to be relieved they weren't ruffians from the street.

"Hopefully," Geth'n said. "We've just arrived after a rather long journey from Larilla and wondered whether you might have lodging here for a few days." He looked at Pet'r with a wrinkled brow, showing his concern, and looked back imploringly at Mistress Farlen.

She talked to them about rooms and rates, drawing them back toward the front of the hotel and the registry desk.

"Hm, maybe. If you don't mind a rather small room -- for the both of you -- I believe that you can stay in the loft. Otherwise I'm afraid we're full."

"We've been sleeping on the ground for the last few weeks, the loft would be a blessing. May we take a bath somewhere?" he asked, only half believing the last was possible.

"Yes, there is a public room on the fourth floor just below you. You can bathe there and possible freshen your clothing a bit," Mistress Farlen added, looking at their clothes and general appearance with some amusing disdain.

Anisah stood for a moment after they drew away. She look down and realized she was still holding the mop in front of herself, quickly lowered her arms.

Something important just occurred. I don't understand what.

As they left the room, Pet'r looked back at her, wrinkled his brow as though puzzled by something. Then he smiled, nodded his head, turned and followed the others out of the hall.

Somehow these two seemed familiar, though Anisah couldn't remember ever meeting them. There was something about them, something she couldn't explain.

I can finish this in the morning.

She put her mop back into the tub. She walked through the door and out into the hallway, stopping just inside the great lobby, and watched the young men as they made their request for a room.

Mrs. Farlen had completed her little speech and had offered the boys a section of the loft and was about to take them when she saw Anisah standing at the dining hall door.

Pet'r was listening, but he had noticed Anisah lingering and was watching her. She was diligently scrubbing the floor, but seemed to more intent on gazing out the window and day-dreaming. He thought she was certainly and curiously interesting, but he couldn't quite place his finger on why.

"Geth'n, we couldn't ask for better. How much?" Pet'r suddenly spoke up.

"Two farspen," Mistress Farlen answered. Turning to look at Pet'r, she smiled and noticed his attention was diverted, "and possibly I could get Anisah to help with your luggage, or show you to your room?"

Pet'r realizing she was speaking to him, reddened with embarrassment.

"I don't think that will be necessary," he blurted out, "we are traveling lightly and will just take care of ourselves. Right, Geth'n?"

"Yes. And thank you, Mistress Farlen," Geth'n answered. "We greatly appreciate what you are doing for us."

He looked at his friend and then turned slightly to glance at the young lady who accosted him earlier.

". . . find the young girl with flaming hair."

Geth'n looked back at Pet'r who too was looking at him, and they nodded to each other without saying a word.

"Come on, Pet'r," Geth'n said, "let's get some rest, we may be very busy tomorrow." He turned and began walking in the direction he thought Mistress Farlen indicated to get to the room, motioning for Pet'r to follow.

"No. Wait, Sirs," a young voice came from the other side of the room, "you need to go through the next door to your left." It was the red haired young woman.

She seemingly felt no embarrassment at her own boldness and certainly no longer appeared to be angry.

"Perhaps I could show you the way?"

"Ah . . ." Geth'n began.

"Yes, please, if you would," Pet'r answered her.

Mistress Farlen raised her eyebrows at Anisah's actions, but decided to let the girl do as she seemed to want.

"Anisah, would you please take these gentlemen to the loft in the east hall?"

She gestured to Anisah to come nearer. She also gave her a stern look indicating surprise Anisah was there at all.

"Yes, m'am," she said and just stood there for a moment. She was frozen to the spot. But, with a small jerk of her head, she turned and walked toward another exit into the hallway.

She only nodded at the young men and led them down the long corridor, turned to the left, leading them toward the east wing, not looking back to see whether they were following. But, she knew they were.

Finally she turned back to the right, stopped, and pointed at the ladder that disappeared into the ceiling.

"This is your room. The bath area is just down that way and down the stairs," she suggested, again pointing down the hallway extended to their left, "it's four doors down on the left."

She turned, smiling as she did, and walked down the hallway and stopped, looking back.

"I hope you have a restful night."

"Thank you for your help," Pet'r spoke up, smiling back at her.

Standing there, she gathered the courage to look at their faces and gazed into what she thought had to be the deepest and most haunting eyes she had ever seen. And both looked back at her, their eyes strong but almost gentle, and smiled, thanking her.

She curtsied, turned and walked back down the hall. As she turned into the connecting hallway, she stopped and looked back at them again, thinking she should, needed to, say something. She couldn't and walked away.

"Do you think that's her -- the red-haired girl?" Geth'n asked, watching his friend intently.

"Well, she certainly has that -- and there's something else I can't quite decide about this whole business," Pet'r answered, "why are things happening so rapidly. Why are these answers coming to us so randomly, or is there a pattern here?"

"I think the last is true," his friend answered. "I believe we have been and are being led along some preordained path, but I have no idea why. Come, let's get some sleep and, maybe on the morrow, we can decide what is coming to pass." He turned back to the ladder and climbed into the loft.

Pet'r looked down the hall again, nodded his head in agreement, and followed his friend upward.

Looking around the corner again, Anisah watched the two young men climbing into the loft. She knew it was going to be necessary to learn more about them. There was something that drew her to them as though some hidden need existed to do so.

How could I? What can I say that won't make me seem just another stupid girl, asking stupid questions?

As she turned away, she noticed the taller one still watching her and he smiled again.

What is happening to me? What is this strange feeling?

She walked quickly to the lobby, turned into the dining hall; the mop still sat in the bucket.

How strange, this feeling. Who are these men? She stopped and stood staring at the mop.

She suddenly turned toward the kitchen, went through, and started up the stairs to her room.

"Where are you goin'. Have ya finished . . .?" Mercy started, watching as Anisah walked by her and left the room without responding. "What could be wrong with that girl?" she mumbled, shook her head and went back to work.

Anisah, though only a few moments before was dragging herself through all her movements, ran down the hall to her room, her heart beating madly. She jumped on her bed and stared out the window, watching as the moon rose over the plains, the light shining through the window, brightening her room.

The moonlight light washed over her, cleansing her, and she couldn't believe the great joy she felt. She had no idea why she felt this way at this moment, but she believed now she understood what happiness might be. The troubles experienced over the last few months seemed to disappear from her thoughts. She could feel something more important than all she had ever experienced was going to take place and nothing was going to be the same again. Yet, she still could not comprehend why she was having this overpowering sense of well-being.

She wanted desperately to go to Tariny but she was afraid to leave the lodge. If she left the safety of the hotel she was concerned about the awful men outside in the streets causing problems she didn't need and she still worried Sumt'r might find her.

Her trip and eventual position here at the lodge was part of a hard fought battle -- she had few fond memories of that effort.

She lay in bed for a long while and soon nodded off to sleep but not before deciding she would find a way to talk to these two, maybe tomorrow.

My god, this is wonderful; I hope this dream never ends.

Across the street, a beggar looked at the lodge with an approving smile. Nodding his head under his great robe, he began to amble down the street. "Alms for the poor. Please alms for the poor. I am a poor beggar and would be grateful for your gift," he pleaded into the night.

A loud clank sounded from his cup he actually was disregarding. "Bless you and thank you," he shouted at the back of the stranger.

Looking into the cup, he saw a finger recently severed from some misbegotten soul's hand, turned to look at the black stranger departing and frowned , but looked around again at the lodging where the three young adventurers were resting.

"The time is upon us, my young friends," he spoke softly, "be wary."

Bowing his head even more, a small smile came to his face just before it disappeared again into the darkness under the hood.

"Alms for the poor. Alms for the poor."

He walked down the street and evaporated into the night.

DECISIONS

Now a tale of the perils of the unknown, a tale of courage and bravery, of innocent endeavor for right, and of a brave man, braver than his years should allow.

I feel no remorse as I, Kalbr'an, do admit to being the hand behind the will.

That desire had greater strength than I too could have imagined, a secret reserve that came from the depths of the soul of one young woman who would be not only a leader, but also a warrior for right. So let us tell this tale and you shall see . . .

Geth'n awoke the next morning feeling more rested, but more restless than he could remember ever being.

A strange sensation.

He looked across the room at his friend Pet'r who was still sleeping but twitching occasionally.

Must be dreaming.

He rose quietly and walked to the window looking out over the street below. It was almost impossible to determine anything about the city. He looked up and down the street as far as he could without opening the window, pressing his face against the surface. After noting a few curious things about those who wandered, he saw nothing that impressed him.

He looked at the skies and northward toward the distant hills spread out beyond the city. He felt a strange and tense sensation. Something about the colors of the sky and the grayness of the vista before him wasn't right, but he couldn't decide what it was that disturbed him about the scene. But something made him feel uncomfortable.

He turned from the window and was startled. Pet'r was standing in the middle of the room gazing at him strangely.

"There is something wrong," Pet'r spoke to him but seemed to be looking beyond, beyond what Geth'n was watching.

He wasn't looking at Geth'n, but rather through him with the strangest look on his face. A look Geth'n could only remember having seen before during the fight with the thieves on the road from home.

What is wrong with him?

Geth'n said nothing. Pet'r walked past Geth'n to the window, hardly noticing him.

"There is more trouble for our world than we could ever have imagined," Pet'r said, still looking out of the window. "You and I, we started so innocently on our little adventure but things are changing. My dreams reveal this world is headed toward calamity unless something is done to stop it."

What is he talking about? Who is this, it just isn't Pet'r?

Geth'n couldn't believe what he was seeing and hearing.

"Pet'r, Pet'r, wake up. Wake up, my friend," he said, as he walked to his friend's side, reached to touch his arm, but jumped back when Pet'r whirled about suddenly.

"I am awake, my friend. Maybe for the first time in my life," Pet'r answered, looking deeply into his friend's eyes.

Geth'n turned away from the intensity of the gaze, but he suddenly felt he too knew something horrible was happening and there must be something done to stop this strangeness.

What is going to happen? Why do we know, when no one else seems to?

He realized he and Pet'r must be a part of whatever was evolving and they were never again going to be what they were. There is a difference. Only now is there a difference.

It's the girl; there is something about the girl, but what?

"You're right. I also think we are part of the answer. We must meet with the girl we saw yesterday. I was given that message, on the way here, stating we were to meet "the girl with flaming red hair" and she, at least, fits that description," Geth'n said very seriously and with deliberation.

"Pet'r, I believe you and I, in some way, have been chosen to do something; something that will change, not just our lives, but the lives of all."

He turned and saw his friend nodding agreement and looking more somber than Geth'n ever remembered. A morning of revelations.

What can we do, what do we need to do?

"Yes, we must do something -- and soon, I fear," Pet'r spoke, as though his friend's thoughts projected to him, "I believe the girl has some of the answers; but she too may be like us and not know what the questions are."

"Let's go then. We have little time to waste," Geth'n began dressing, not knowing why he suddenly felt an urgency where before there had only been restlessness.

They finished getting dressed and left the room in search of the girl. They found her on the floor above theirs, cleaning a room vacated by another guest. They had walked almost directly to her not knowing where she was. They didn't speak to each other but followed the same path unerringly, found her, and stood silently watching her move about the room.

Anisah was working diligently, each morning was the hardest because she had to make certain the rooms were completely cleaned after the guests had gone, as well as change the bedding in those rooms where the guests were staying longer. She was bustling around more rapidly this morning and she didn't know why.

Suddenly, she was aware of a sensation, a feeling of awareness of a presence and the presence of many things and many people.

But more importantly, she felt she was being called to do something.

The urge was more adamant than her decisions to leave her home ever was. She paused in her scurrying, looked out a window, sensed something was immediate, turned to see the two young men watching her.

"We've come to talk to you. It is important, I believe, we do so immediately," Geth'n spoke softly to her. She wasn't startled by their presence; it was as though it should happen.

"Yes, you're right. Very important," she answered, looking at each of them with a great certainty in her eyes. She knew when she met them last night these two were now part of her world.

Pet'r nodded solemnly to her as she caught his eye.

158

"Let's go to the stables out back. No one goes there this early and the stable boy doesn't care what we do there," she suggested.

She placed the linens on the bed, walked to the door, turned and closed it behind her. They walked together to the rear stairs, down and out into the stable where they found some hay bales in the corner to sit on.

"My name is Geth'n. This is Pet'r," Geth'n started by way of introduction, "We are from Peetle."

Anisah gasped.

Geth'n stopped what he was saying and waited.

"I was told in a dream I would meet with 'two young men from Peetle'," she looked at them in wonder, "how can a dream be so real it comes true." Her eyes were wide and she looked at each of them, then shook her head and placed her face into her hands, as though to cry.

"We too were told of you. The gods have a need for us to be together and we have no idea why. There is just this overwhelming sense of urgency Pet'r and I feel. And for some reason, Pet'r is now receiving part of what and why, in his thoughts, but I too am now noticing I am learning some of what we must know. What we are seeing we are seeing together without speaking about it. What we are seeing we are seeing together without speaking about it," Geth'n was talking quickly, but quietly.

Anisah listened quietly.

There was another world beyond the three of them. She sat straighter and something about her face was losing its' youthfulness and changing, as Geth'n explained more, into a more mature and thoughtful presence. She knew her youth was gone. There was to be more to her life than she could have ever imagined.

"I believe I understand," she said, politely waiting for Geth'n to pause, "and I believe you are correct when you say our destinies are linked."

She turned to Pet'r, "What do you see now?"

Pet'r paused for a moment as though composing his thoughts. "There is to be a great Darkness flow over the land and eventually the world. And, there is within that Darkness, a force that can destroy this land and bring us and all our peoples into despair and desolation, if we do nothing. The Darkness is, even now beginning to creep over the land. And, for whatever reason, we three will, and must be, a part of saving our world."

"So we each must have a contribution to the solution of this problem. And though we don't know what that is now, we do know it is something we alone must do." Geth'n spoke with deliberation, "We quickly need to determine the cause and each of us needs to understand what we are feeling now?"

They each looked at the other and nodded their agreement. There was, or seemed to be, an aura about them -- the beginning of a bond that permeated the air about them. Their presence with each other completed an essence of something greater than each one possessed. They were overwhelmed by the sense as they talked and, for them, the rest of the world disappeared.

Col'n, the young stable boy who had helped Anisah, came into the stable and never saw them.

Anisah only caught a glimpse of him, wondered briefly why he said nothing to her, but returned to the conversation.

It wasn't until many days later she realized the three of them, when they were together and in harmony with each other were actually invisible to the outside world.

They talked for hours, needing no other incentive than they work out the puzzle and find a solution to this insurmountable catastrophe.

"So if we are in agreement we must take some action, what do each of you think our plan is to be?" asked Anisah.

"I believe I should continue my journey to Tariny, there is something there drawing me. Some kind of knowledge I do not possess but which I feel is vital to us if we are to find the answers to what we seek," Geth'n began, certain there was no other answer.

"I also was going to Tariny, but I wished to learn the healing powers of the land. Now I believe, within the knowledge of what I shall learn about those things, I will also find a part of the answer relating to this new found horror," Anisah added,

160

feeling her bond with these two men would make her contribution stronger.

"I'm to continue what I thought I wanted to do for a lark, but now I believe there is some sort of destiny in my desire to travel into the northern mountains," Pet'r spoke with great deliberation. "There is something there that must be done and I have been chosen to do it."

Anisah watched Pet'r as he spoke; she suddenly knew his destiny had already been mapped somehow. She also knew somehow Pet'r was to go away from them and, in some way, their lives though now bonded would be less than it was at this moment. She wasn't certain why she felt that way but she knew and she hurt inside knowing.

"Then we must depart as soon as possible. But it's too late to go today. There are still dangers on the open roads," Geth'n offered, "Let's rest tonight and tomorrow we'll begin our new journey."

The other two nodded in agreement, they rose from the bales, and the world reappeared for them.

"I have to finish my work inside," Anisah said, looking about her as though surprised she was here with these men, "Mistress Farlen will be upset if I'm not finished soon."

As she hurried back to her task, she seemed no longer a part of what they were, but only a chambermaid. Then she stopped, turned to them, laughed lightly, turned back and ran into the hotel.

The two men looked at each other and Geth'n placed his hand on his old friend's shoulders.

"We never knew what this would lead to, my friend, but there is no greater conviction on my part than we must do whatever comes our way. I believe you are taking the first step and I fear for you, but I also believe whatever you find on your journeys is indeed a vital element in answering the puzzle we have been chosen to resolve,"

he hugged his friend quickly and stepped back, a grim look on his face.

"I must do what has to be done. I'm already different than I was. I don't know how just yet, but I have been bothered by these dreams for some time now, and it is impossible for me to ignore the directive I have been given. I only hoped we could have followed our adventure together, my friend," Pet'r spoke quietly,

"But we will come together again because it is our destiny to prevent what lies ahead. We have a bond between us now that exceeds what our friendship has ever been. We're a part of something we do not understand yet, but I believe, it is to be more than we can imagine."

He looked at his old friend somberly, then he smiled, "But we shall always be friends. And I believe this sense of danger will be resolved in the end." He returned his friend's hug and a slap on the back as he always did after one of their youthful adventures.

Geth'n laughed aloud. Pet'r joined him.

"We're becoming such grumpy drools, my friend," Geth'n said, still laughing, "We need to have a little fun along the way. Let's see what tomorrow brings." They turned and walked into the hotel and returned to their room.

Later that night Anisah came to their room. They sat and talked for many more hours about what they did know and how they should proceed. They decided they would leave at dawn.

Anisah had already told Mistress Farlen she was leaving, and she wanted to thank the young stable boy again for all he had done for her, but she was eager to leave now.

Geth'n decided they should meet in the stable, get Anisah's horse to carry their few things and leave before the city woke. The other two agreed and Anisah returned to her room.

PARTING

Geth'n awoke several times during the night, looked at the stars sprinkled across the sky and wondered what the gods had in store for them. Three young people with little experience chosen to stop, or hinder, the madness that might overwhelm them and their world.

What is there about us? Why us?

He couldn't guess, there were no answers now.

The next morning the trio left as planned, departing quietly. They bargained for another horse from a fellow who had probably stolen it during the night; he was quick to accept what they offered in exchange. Then he ran away.

Walking westward along the road, leading the horses, took most the day.

They decided to stop and camp near a busy junction. One of the roads led to Tariny from this intersection according to information Mr. Farlen had given them that morning.

He told them the road running southward led to the sea,. The other led into the mountains.

They camped in a secluded area behind a nearby hillock, concealed from the road, talked into the night sitting by the fire, but soon decided they needed more rest and rolled into their sleeping blankets and soon fell asleep. But they all woke early, busying themselves with minor preparations. Geth'n was aware the other two were also experiencing these awakenings and wondering what lay ahead. Everyone was edgy, excited to be back on the road.

When they awoke, the morning was chilled, mist hanging beneath the trees. They finished packing their belongings and moved slowly out near the road.

Anisah had previously told them about her misfortunes with Sumt'r, and the boys had, of course, their own contact with such men, so none of them desired to repeat those incidences.

They had decided to travel only during the day.

Pet'r went onto the open road first, looked both ways, and motioned to his friends it was safe to come out of the forest.

They stood silently for a while; not wanting to talk about what was going to happen.

Then Anisah, on an impulse, went to Pet'r and clasped him to her tightly. Tears stood in her eyes, but she refused to cry.

"I believe I know why you are doing this," she told him softly, looking up at him through her tousled red hair, "but somehow that doesn't make it any easier."

"It is something we must do," Geth'n mentioned, looking at the sun rising to deliberately avoiding looking into the faces of the other two.

The air seemed stilled by their apprehension. Anisah stepped away from Pet'r finally, touching his hand as she did. Then Geth'n and she stood back a bit, not happy knowing Pet'r actually was going to leave them.

"But, my friends, couldn't you wish me luck?" Pet'r asked, feeling torn between staying with his friends, for Anisah now was a part of them, and not being able to resist the urge he couldn't explain to go.

"I have been wanting to do this all my life and now is the time. And now we all know this is necessary. Besides, I can take care of myself," he added, for Anisah more than Geth'n.

"You take care, old friend," Geth'n said softly, shaking Pet'r's hand for a longer time than usual.

"Yes, you idiot, please take care," Anisah spoke, her irritation showing. Then she began to cry softly, wiping her eyes on her sleeve. "You come back to us or I'll . . ."

She couldn't finish what she wanted to say but instead grabbed Pet'r around his waist, reached and kissed him solidly on the mouth.

Pet'r taken by surprise, staggered backwards and they almost fell before he regained his balance, catching Anisah and holding her close so she wouldn't fall too.

"I will," Pet'r answered, "and it shouldn't be too long. If you two haven't heard from me before Asiphis rises full again, you

164

can come looking for me, " he laughed lightly , but he felt his request was wise and reasonable.

He had no idea what the next few weeks were going to bring, and he wanted to give them a time they all could anticipate.

Only then did Pet'r step back, releasing Anisah and raised his pack from the ground, swinging it over his shoulders. He smiled at the other two and turned away. He walked toward the north, leaving his companions to watch him go.

When he arrived at the top of the first rise, Pet'r turned and waved to his two friends. He knew he was going to miss Geth'n; they were together since their youth.

Anisah was another story. There was a sense of sadness when he sat and talked to her, a feeling he was uncertain of. She seemed distressed and saddened by his urge to travel by himself and he thought there was more.

He turned back to the long road stretching into some low hills in the distance, shifted the pack on his back, and strode along the road.

****

Pet'r couldn't see the great mountains as yet. But he had read volumes of information about them and heard stories during his short stay in Varspree; stories of great cliffs, of glaciers, of canyons with crashing streams, of great trees growing near the water clinging to their hold on the soil, despite the overwhelming force of the water's rush, and more told about the snow, either softly dusting everything it touched or sometimes flying so thickly one could see no further than a step ahead.

Now he had decided and finally taken those first steps, he could hardly wait to see these things and felt some need to hasten not knowing whether from his excitement, or his concerns.

The country through which he strolled was largely a patchwork of long, low pastures with an occasional stand of trees, often surrounded by cattle or horses. The land was greener than any Pet'r had ever seen.

His home was by the southern seas and had more tropical vegetation than here. So the green here was more vivid and pleasant, comforting.

He saw cottages near the road. Occasionally, he would stop at one to get more water. The people seemed friendly, inquiring about where he was going, advising him about travel conditions a little further along and warning him about some of the dangers of the mountains.

"It'd be best, I believe, if you steered a little to the east as you go, probably follow the Vranila valley. You should come to a pass that will keep you out of the snows already falling up high," the elder gentleman advised, nodding his head as he talked, as though to assure himself to trust his own memory.

"The valley, you can get to it about four days walk from here, will lead you to a river crossing. There's a ferry that'll take you across the Vranila River. Then you should take the road to the northeast, cause the road splits there.

The other road takes you in the direction of Voravia's land. That witch is someone you don't want to mess with, boy. Yep, you should stay away from there; she'll make a ghoul out of you quicker'n you can blink. Nope, you go northeast, that's the best."

Pet'r chuckled to himself about the old man's direction, but he appreciated the gentle hospitality and kindness of the him and his wife.

This trip's going to be perfect. What can happen?

For four more days, the trip was perfect. He rose in the mornings, cooked a small meal and a boiled a pot of clarfine to warm his insides. He took quick baths in the cold streams he walked beside, climbed into his clothes and sat by the fire until he was dry and ready to go. Pet'r couldn't believe how perfect it was and wondered if he and his friends were wrong about what they had experienced before.

On the fourth day, things changed.

Great, black, clouds were blowing out of the northeast as Pet'r woke. There was no rain but the ground wind was whipping the limbs about, some of the weaker branches were snapping and falling.

Dust was flying with each gust, blocking a view of the area. Leaves and other loose debris were flying about dangerously. The cracking of the limbs, the leaves rattling like loose sails, told him a storm was upon him.

He sat and watched the display for a few moments then rose, packed his belongings, and walked along the road in search of shelter. He began to have difficulty seeing where he was going, looking only at his feet shuffling along in the old tracks in the road to guide him.

The dust blowing in his eyes blinded him. He occasionally turned his back to the wind and walked backwards to have some relief from the onslaught. The wind tore at his clothing, he held tightly to his pack, and pushed through the gale as best he could.

Suddenly, the rain came. The impact of the water was so hard it felt as though someone, or something, had dumped great tubs of water over his head. Even his experience with many storms at sea didn't prepare him for this unrelenting torrent of water. And the winds blew more fiercely than he had seen before.

Knowing he was wandering recklessly, he decided to not fight the obvious and turned to his left behind a great boulder near the road.

The wind stopped blowing him around immediately, but the rain still fell in great sheets around his new shelter, dumping ample water on him still. But now he could see beyond his nose.

Looking around, he saw a small cave between the boulder he was standing beside and another one, even greater in size, next to it. He must find better shelter from this incredible storm. He looked about briefly, decided, ducked his head against the deluge blowing between the boulders and leaped into the mouth of the cave.

He tumbled several feet before stopping and the darkness overwhelmed him; it seemed to eliminate all light. He turned and looked back and could only see the faintest light through the water falling over the opening of the cave. He saw no reason to go back up the tunnel for now, turned and looked down the tunnel. He thought he could see a faint light ahead.

Thinking he should determine whether the light was real rather than just wait for the storm to end, he decided to explore the cave further.

He knew, in this darkness, he needed some way to mark where he was before he descended in order to return along the same route. He dug a small hole with his hand in the side of the tunnel and placed a scrap of leather, used to mend his shoes, into it to mark where he changed directions.

He looked down the tunnel again and began to descend. The incline was not too steep but not tall enough for him to stand, so he scooted on his backside for some distance without difficulty when he came to a point where another tunnel intersected with the one he was in.

Being unable to see anything in any direction, not actually knowing why he was doing this at all, and wanting to have as little uncertainty as possible, he sat and pondered his situation.

Time to make a choice. Go ahead, go back, or take the right or the left.

He decided to go straight ahead, but before he moved further he placed another object from his pouch in the passage he was leaving.

He then moved forward for some time, without varying from his straightforward direction, more crossing passages intersected, and he marked each one with another object.

As he progressed, he began to smell odors which weren't too offensive, just dank and musty. He attributed these to the dampness, but, as he moved deeper, the odors became more offensive.

Suddenly, he heard noises ahead. He stopped to listen intently but wasn't successful enough to understand the source.

Maybe it's time for me to go back. But then what is happening? I need to discover the cause.

He was beginning to doubt his exploration was a wise one. His curiosity got the best of him despite a gnawing doubt about the wisdom of continuing. He then he smiled curiously and moved forward more cautiously. He shook his head in disbelief.

Now he could see a light ahead, wavering as though from fire.

And he could hear someone talking and grumbling, apparently in argument.

He crept up to the edge of the tunnel and peered cautiously into a small cavern. His tunnel came out at ground level and he could see across the floor of the cave.

Where I am must be an emergency exit of some sort, or a route to the other passages I saw.

Pet'r watched the activity in the room. Several men were wandering about busying themselves with chores. Two were standing near the fire, waving their arms and making some sort of guttural sounds Pet'r couldn't understand.

He ducked back into the darkness not believing what he saw. These beings were grotesque, with mangled bodies and twisted faces. The air was heavy with a repulsive odor even worse than the loads of fish Pet'r remembered from his youth.

Maybe these aren't men, if they are, there is certainly something wrong.

Suddenly one of the creatures growled loudly, then there was quiet. Pet'r slowly ventured a glance out of his passage to see what had changed and was roughly snatched into the room by several of the beings. They pushed, shoved and threw him across the cavern floor taking him to the fire. He decided not to fight.

As the capture took a few moments, he was able to determine there were a number of other entrances and exits from this cavern, an interlaced system of passages coming and going in many directions and probably all with purpose. He quickly noted where he had entered the cave in relation to several objects in the room. He intended to escape and wanted to return to the correct tunnel. The leader motioned for the others to bring Pet'r nearer the fire.

"Waf ish vou do heer?" he spoke, a guttural sound barely making sense. "Hows do vou git down blow?" He shuffled around the fire toward Pet'r, knocking aside those gathered to stare, and those holding Pet'r's arms. He threw his arm at Pet'r, striking him in his side and almost knocking him down.

"I came down the passage to get out of the storm," Pet'r wheezed, trying to catch his breathe, "who are you?"

169

"Shud uph!" The man shouted and smacked him again, much harder this time. Pet'r twisted around by the blows, but slowly raised himself upright each time.

His pulse was rising, his breath was coming more rapidly and his eyes were beginning to glaze at bit. He looked directly at the leader but didn't speak.

"We kil vou," the man grunted, walked behind Pet'r, snatched a weapon from one of the others, raised it above his head and was bringing it with great effort toward Pet'r's head.

Pet'r reached over his head and, without looking, grabbed and stopped the weapon abruptly. The man , his hand stung by the sudden halt of the blow, yelled loudly while dancing around holding his hand, shouting, "Kil hm, Kil hm," he shouted at the others.

Several of those closest to Pet'r reached for him, but he moved quickly to one side, grabbed two of them by their necks and threw them back into the others who were attacking. They all fell tumbling like discarded dolls, one rolling through the open fire.

Three more attacked Pet'r. One leaped on his back, the others grabbed him around his waist trying to pull him to the ground. Pet'r reached over his head, picked the man from his back and tossed him at the leader who was now trying to get back into the fray.

The man's head struck the leader squarely in the face, smashing it into an even more horrible visage than before. The leader roared his anger and pain; the other man fell unconscious. They became entangled and fell to the floor, twisting and rolling.

Meanwhile the other two jumped forward and shuffled rapidly around Pet'r, trying to knock him off balance. Again Pet'r stepped sideways but this time he swung his arm around violently, striking the men on their necks, knocking them backwards and slamming their heads to the floor. Then he turned to face the others still on their feet; they stopped immediately, looked at each other, turned and ran for several of the other entrances.

He let them go, shaking his head. He stood looking about the cave. His attackers were lying about moaning, or gone. He stood

170

for a moment with his eyes closed, trying to calm down. The leader and the one who smashed his face were still entangled on the floor. The leader was awake, moaning and trying to get free.

Pet'r was uncertain why he was free, and where all the beings had gone, but it seemed an opportune moment to escape. He turned, located his tunnel, ran to it and began to crawl as rapidly as he could up the steep climb. As he passed again into darkness he came to a passage. He checked for the mark he had left earlier, found it and proceeded up the long incline, repeating this as he scrambled through the dark. Soon he came to the top, pushed himself out into the open. It was a relief the storm had stopped.

He ran back to the road, turned northward, and jogged quickly along it until he spotted a small grove of trees away from the road. He stopped, looked back along the road, walked over and disappeared into the underbrush.

He found an open glade where the sun peeped through the leaves. He lay down in the wet grass, rolled over on his back and watched the great black clouds, still overhead, blow by for a moment while he rested.

I better go, those things may be coming out after me.

He jumped up, ran out to the road again, and jogged up the road for some distance stopping occasionally to look back to see if he was being followed.

After several miles, he stopped running. Breathing heavily, he looked around for a place to hide, walked into the woods on the right of the road, climbed to the top of a small knoll from which he could see back along the way he had come. He sat for a long time watching anxiously.

Nothing occurred, he was not being followed; it was quiet. Only the wind whistled through the trees overhead.

Pet'r sat, held his head in his hands, and tried to determine what happened down below. He could not remember anything after the leader had struck him in his side. He shook his head in bewilderment.

How did I escape, what happened? What's happening to me, am I becoming a freak like those beings?

He held his hands in front of him, turning them over, trying to notice if there were any changes in his appearance, but he saw none. He couldn't know yet about the streak of white hair beginning to appear just above his forehead; it was only a small band.

For now.

EVIL WAITS

If darkness brings forth the best in men of valor, it also brings forth the worst in those who savor it.

Men who have no will but to rule and control others are the first to explore the release of their bonds; destruction of the will of other men is the prevalent emotional prerogative for these.

Their sense of being is permeated with loathing for all others, and possibly themselves.

There are some among these who simply will rule, there is no concept of loathing, but rather one of indifference for others whom they consider only beings to enslave.

Power is an aphrodisiac, the virtue and reward for having accomplished yet another step in the conquest. It is to these the gods, who would defile, will turn for their lieutenants when the time is right.

Our tale continues with revelations of men of evil and those of strength . . .

Rab'k sat near the fire at his camp just north of Varspree. He had ridden hard to rejoin his troop and was sitting quietly enjoying drink and food. All the other men near the circle of warmth had departed except for Jond'r who sat, without speaking, while his commander finished his meal.

"Was the journey difficult?" Rab'k spoke, motioning with a wave at the camp.

"No, the wagons were heavily laden, but the road wasn't our enemy today," Jond'r answered, not looking at Rab'k.

"Are the men and horses fit for a hard ride tomorrow?" Rab'k asked. He took a last swallow from his cup and tossed the rest into the fire.

The steam rose, masking Jond'r's view of Rab'k as he turned to look at the man.

Though Rab'k had the solid, strong look of a man of power; he seemed to be weary from the ride from Varspree but not so

173

much that it affected his demeanor.

The horse Rab'k had ridden was still gasping near the watering trough rigged for the other animals; there was some danger of the animal foundering.

Jond'r instructed his herd master to allow the animal only small amounts until it cooled. Rab'k hadn't stopped to allow the animal rest, or water, until he entered the encampment.

Jond'r had no fondness for the mistreatment of the animals; this troubled him.

"We will probably do battle tomorrow," Rab'k said calmly, as though the statement had no importance to any one; it was just a statement of fact.

Jond'r was startled and glanced quickly at Rab'k.

"Battle? With whom?" Jond'r responded, not understanding why they should have to do battle with anyone.

Rab'k hadn't informed him there was to be any fighting on this journey and he couldn't think who Rab'k might consider an enemy.

"That isn't important now," Rab'k answered bluntly, but glared at Jond'r from under his eyebrows, as his eyes rose to look at the man, "will that be a problem?"

"Why? I don't see a reason," Jond'r answered, too quickly, knowing he was pushing the limits of his authority and right of command with Rab'k, "what fight could we have?"

"I have my reasons. Are you questioning me?" Rab'k answered quickly. He was watching Jond'r intently and his eyes seemed to pierce the darkness. Then, suddenly, he looked away toward the stars.

"No! But who are we to attack?" Jond'r knew he was proceeding beyond his right to ask such forward questions, but Rab'k had no reaction Jond'r could see. Rab'k continued to look at the darkness above.

"That isn't important either. I have chosen to pursue and fight a foe. It's simple really. They have something I want," Rab'k spoke firmly, still not looking at Jond'r but with an obviously intense tone in his voice.

Suddenly he whirled about standing and looking down at

Jond'r who was caught by surprise, "Do you have a problem with this plan!" Rab'k almost shouted. His intensity forced his words through clenched teeth, muffling the sound.

Jond'r sat back quickly, but straightened himself, composed his thoughts and said, "I see no problems, sire. When will we be leaving?" He did not move from his seat, nor did he look up at the huge man staring down at him.

"At dawn!" Rab'k choked out the words.

His fury was evident; he wasn't accustomed to having his commands questioned, and he certainly wasn't accustomed to someone openly defying him, "Be ready!"

"Yes, sire. My men and I will be awaiting your orders," Jond'r spoke quietly, stood slowly and faced the man, returning his glare. "And we will be ready to fight."

With that Jond'r threw his own drink into the fire, a cloud of steam billowed and sizzled, turned and walked away.

"Make certain you are!" Rab'k shouted after him, "there will be adequate punishment for those who disobey me!" He turned and strode away toward his tent, mumbling to himself as he went.

Jond'r's mind was boiling with anger and dismay, thinking of the thousands of things he might do to stop this insanity but shaking his head as he dismissed each one.

What can be happening? He must be talking about Garv'n. I am in-debted to Garv'n; he has been good to my family and me. How can I attack this man or his men? I must think of a way to stop this.

He looked across the camp, listening to the sounds of the night; he shook his head, uncertain what the morning might bring. Saddened, he walked slowly to his tent. He had to prepare his men for a battle; these were good men who hadn't been in one for years. The losses would be terrible. Garv'n's men, though they were a rowdy bunch with their bravado and gruff-ness, were good soldiers. Jond'r knew several of their leaders; they trained together as young men. He knew these men weren't prepared for actual battle either. The peace had lasted so many years the fury of battle was an unknown for many of them.

What sort of man is this Rab'k? How evil can he be?

175

DESTINY

Many good intentions never reach fruition. Much comes about by the process of natural selection. There is no precedence for discovering one's abilities in magic; the facts may be hidden beyond the imagination.

There are those things which one person is more suited than others to provide individual contributions pushing a culture along its promised route.

One person, or persons, seems to perform with much greater skill than others. A choice made by the strengths needed to survive and this should be no surprise.

We are often reminded of some particular, and often peculiar, talent of an individual who has an awareness not obvious nor measurable, until brought into play.

Now we will tell a tale of searching and discovery; a tale of two of our heroes who attempt to follow the normal path to such discovery, but find their destinies lead them there in a different way . . .

Anisah and Geth'n mounted their horses and turned back along the southern road after Pet'r disappeared from view. They didn't talk for a long while, walking the horses slowly, looking about without concern for what they saw.

"We probably need to stop soon. Thieves are about and we don't need to meet any of them during the day. It might be wiser for us to travel at night. The moons are out and we should have plenty of light to travel," Geth'n spoke first.

"It's a good plan. I've had enough of thieves. I would prefer to avoid them," Anisah answered, turned to look back one last time. Something inside made her worry about Pet'r. She didn't quite understand the feeling. Shaking her head, her thoughts returned to the road. She kicked the horse gently and trotted along beside Geth'n.

Their first few days progressed with no incident. On the fourth day, they saw a troop of men on horseback coming toward them with some speed.

176

Geth'n motioned to Anisah to follow him and they quickly galloped the horses into the forest edge out of sight, dismounted and stood quietly holding the animals' reins. The troops rode past them hurriedly, banners flying, not taking notice of them.

"Someone very important, I believe," Anisah spoke when she felt it safe to do so.

Geth'n turned to nod when his eyes opened wide as he noticed the man on horseback, with his sword drawn, sitting behind them, watching their actions.

"Anisah, maybe you should turn around. Slowly," Geth'n muttered.

Anisah turned around and found herself staring into eyes that pierced her heart.

The rider raised his empty hand. "Don't be afraid, you're safe. I had to make certain you meant his lordship, Garv'n, no harm. Be careful on your journey," he saluted them, crashed his sword back into his scabbard, turned his horse and trotted out of the trees, breaking into a gallop on the road to follow the others.

They both exhaled at the same time, then laughed.

"We seem to have our thoughts somewhere else. We can't afford to let something like that happen again. We've been on the road long enough to know better. We need to concentrate on our own journey and quit worrying about Pet'r," Geth'n said, looked at her and smiled, but had a stern look in his eyes.

"Yes, you're right. I learned the dangers on these roads and we can't afford to be less than vigilant at all times," Anisah added, glancing about her and out at the road as though expecting yet another surprise.

They rested for a while, still a bit shaky at their experience. As the moonlight became brighter they walked their horses to the road, mounted and began walking southward again. Each made an effort to survey the tree line and look down the route they followed. Geth'n, on numerous occasions, turned and viewed the road they had passed already. The rest of the night passed without incident.

At dawn, they withdrew again into the trees, scouted around

177

for a source of water and shelter away from the road, and set up a small camp. As the sun rose, they built a small fire and cooked a light meal.

Geth'n took the first watch as they had agreed and Anisah slept for most of the morning, then they changed places and Geth'n rested. They were not troubled by any more problems and, though a number of groups had ridden by them during the daylight hours, they were never discovered.

Following this pattern, traveling by night and resting by day, they reached the outlying villages of Tariny without incident. As they got closer to the city, the mixture of people became extreme and obvious. They had never seen so many different faces nor heard so many different languages in their lives.

Villages of various clans oozed along each side of the road. Those sitting near the road, talk would stop and the people would watch them suspiciously as they rode by, often breaking into laughter after they passed.

Anisah and Geth'n began to have more and more company along the way, bumping against other horsemen, dodging carts overflowing, wagons splashing mud over everything. And, in the distance and on each side of the road they were on, they could see yet other roads with masses of people moving toward the city gates.

They could now see towers rising above the rolling prairie. Geth'n pointed toward the glittering sea beyond the city. Sweeping the valley between them and flowing to the edge of the sea, the city was magnificent. Stopping the horses on top of the rise overlooking the plain leading to the city's great gate, they were awed by the spectacle.

Thousands of people, young and old; on foot; on animals; in carts; and riding wagons -- pushed to the gate and filed into the city. The gate seemed to swallow them.

A ponderous wall extended southward to the sea and seemed to slide into the mountains lying to the west like a great walrus resting in the sun. The low mountains flowed softly on the horizon, undulating higher toward the north as they disappeared into the distance.

The tops of the larger buildings inside the city glistened; some even twinkled, in the late afternoon sun. Anisah had never seen such a sight as this; she sat trying to take it all in at once, looking from one reach of the city to the other; disbelieving what she saw.

It is this beautiful place where I shall become what I want to be the most. It is here my dreams will be fulfilled.

Geth'n couldn't believe this amazing sight either. He felt almost overwhelmed at the immensity; he had expected the city to be large but had never anticipated the impact it was having on him.

Here I will find what I seek. There can be no doubt that such a place must have all of the knowledge one can ever achieve; the libraries must be immense. I must surely learn what and why I have pursued my dreams.

They didn't speak for a long while; sitting and watching as the sun moved slowly in the sky, turning the scene they watched into different surprises with each minute.

"Get out of the way, you idiots! I've got to move this wagon to the city today, not tomorrow!" A man sitting on his great wagon yelled impatiently as he approached them, "Do ya think this road belongs to ya!"

He glared at them as they moved their horses aside to let him pass, waking from their fixation on the city.

Geth'n looked back along the road from the direction they had come and noticed the traffic seemed to be moving faster than before. Those on foot were almost running, and the horses broke into trots as they came closer

"Why the hurry?" he yelled at a group of riders moving by.

"Tisn't safe outside the city at night. If you don't make the gate by sundown, they close it and won't let you inside 'til morning Can be hard on ya out here, lots of thieves about and no protection on the prairie," the back rider shouted and pointed toward the large encampments forming outside the walls as the others passed ahead of him.

Anisah looked over at Geth'n. "Maybe we should hurry ourselves," she said to him and punched her heels into the horse's flank and being to trot the horse behind the next group

179

passing.

Geth'n agreed, touched his horse, and caught her quickly.
They rode along not speaking, trying to absorb all they could
before night covered the land.

When they were midway across the plains, a great storm blew
in from the sea and practically drowned them. They had to pull
their capes tightly around them and hold their heads down to
avoid being blinded by the dense rain.

All they could see was the rain beating against them, their
horses and the muck sloshing about below and, only because
they could see the mire that was the road, did they know they
still were heading toward the gates.

Just before they reached the gates, the rain just as suddenly
stopped. The sky opened up, pouring its light over them. Then
the air became steamy in the afternoon heat and the road was
almost impossible to travel on; many of those walking pulled to
the side to get out of the mud, leaving a better path for those
on horseback. Were it not for their excitement, Geth'n and Anisah would probably have been miserable.

Anisah, though wringing wet, again had a chance to look
around and was even more astounded by the great mass and
variety of peoples passing through the gates.

Dark-skinned women covered in bright cloth from head to
toe, intricate beading over their head, covering their faces, and
adorning each like a crown; their men following along behind in
baggy pants and jackets with bead patterns woven into them as
well.

Women in another group wore gauzy veiled materials
wrapped around their bodies though the cloth was hardly thick
enough to conceal anything.

Tall dusky men dressed in animal skins, with long dark hair,
strong faces and bodies, arresting eyes that seemed to pierce the
air, walked toward them from a western road that joined this
one, and melded with the others.

Anisah became dizzy from the crush of this caravan of
people; she reached and held Geth'n's arm. Geth'n suggested
they dismount and walk the horses since sitting on them had be-

come tedious and the walkers were pushing ahead of them anyway.

They jumped off the horses and into the muck, moved to the side a bit and were able to move a little more quickly.

The press of the crowd carried them through the gate and into the open market inside. Stalls stretched down the street as far as they could see toward the center of the city. People milled about, pushing, shouting out prices and bargaining. No moment was the same as the last; the turmoil was endless.

Anisah tried to look above the crowd but could only see huge buildings, probably those they had noticed blinking in the sun. She thought she could see trees further down the street. They waited for an opportunity to escape from the mass, they were being pushed along without control.

Geth'n reached over an outstretched arm and grabbed her shoulder to get her attention. She turned to see who it was and noticed he wasn't looking so well.

"I never realized cities could smell so awful!" he shouted in her ear as he pulled himself closer to her. His face was wrinkled in disgust.

Anisah nodded. She too had noticed they had wandered into the area where all the livestock, chickens and ducks, horses, pigs, and every other sort of creature were corralled.

The smell was not affecting her as badly as it was Geth'n, but then she had grown up attending many of these animals back home.

Home? How long ago was that, only a few days, weeks, years? I can't remember how long. So much has happened since then. But now I'm here.

"It's probably not as bad once we're past these animals," she yelled back and pushed her way between two men arguing over the value of a piece of cloth they both were tugging on.

"We do need to find an inexpensive inn before it gets too late. At least for tonight," Geth'n said absently, dodging a chicken someone was trying to hold above the crowd. The bird was trying to free itself, its wings beating the air and everyone around it.

"I'd like to find the Healers College, perhaps I could persuade

181

them to let us stay there tonight," Anisah offered. Now she had finally arrived in Tariny, she wanted to start her studies as quickly as possible. Before whatever the three of them felt overcame them.

Geth'n was nice and kind to her, but the trip from Varspree was dull. It was a great improvement over the trip she had taken to get there. But Geth'n was distracted by his own odd dreams and his almost constant concern about the Ahar'n.

Anisah had also become more restless lately. She wasn't certain what this strange feeling was; it was more than just her desire to begin her studies but she wasn't able to put her finger on just what troubled her. Her memory of Pet'r seemed to linger and she desperately needed something to distract her.

"Well, since we don't know where we're going, I believe we should ask someone for directions. Trying to find your College is probably a good start; it's probably near the libraries anyway," Geth'n voice broke into her thoughts.

"Fine, but who?" she asked. The crowd had thinned a bit but still vibrated with life. Everyone was in a hurry to get somewhere else, pushing and shoving to get through.

There seemed to be no one to ask a simple question.

"One of these stall keepers would be a likely candidate and should know the city as well as anyone," Geth'n added, stepping toward a stall that obviously specialized in cheeses and great loaves of bread. "Sir, could you tell us how to get to the Healers College?"

The man raised his head and stopped shuffling his bread about on the table.

"You want to buy some of these nice loaves? Maybe some cheese?" he asked, raising one eyebrow in an arch above a deep-set eye.

There was a mock smile on his face now.

"I possibly could help," he said, "but then I must go home soon to my wife and children and tell them of my bad day. A day which will be even longer if I take the time to tell you these things," he added, and returned to sorting his wares without looking up again.

Geth'n looked at Anisah and shook his head. "Welcome to the great city," he said to her, reached into his small pouch and took out a small coin. "What will this buy?" he asked the man, holding the coin out to him.

"That, sir, will buy this loaf," he answered and scratching around, pulled out one of the smaller loaves and held it out, took the coin, bit it to test its integrity, placed it in his pocket and looked away to work on his sorting again.

"And about the College?" Geth'n asked, not quite realizing what had just transpired.

Anisah stepped forward and motioned to the man to lean toward her. The man sneered at her but leaned over. Anisah tiptoed and whispered something in his ear.

The man's head snapped around and he suddenly stared at Geth'n. The expression on his face changed dramatically and he began to turn pale. He lowered his head, reached for a large chunk of cheese, handed it to Geth'n and added another loaf of bread.

Then he began to explain how to get to the College, with a great deal of gesturing, while his voice kept rising a bit in volume with each utterance. Then he stopped, stared at Geth'n as though he expected a catastrophe to befall him and sighed a great breath when Anisah and Geth'n turned and walked away.

Geth'n, carrying the food carefully, leaned over to Anisah and asked, "What did you tell him?"

She looked up at him and grinned. "That you are a member of Sumt'r's gang and Sumt'r had sent you to find the College looking for some young tramp to wreak his revenge. And you would as soon kill him as not if he continued to treat you as he was.

That's all. After all, you do look very dangerous."

She laughed heartily when she finished, ran down the street backwards, leading her horse along behind, laughing even more. Geth'n was having trouble keeping up with her, but he too was laughing as they ran.

"Come on," Anisah cried over her shoulder as she darted down the narrow streets, "when we find an inn, we can ask about the Healers College."

All the inns looked the same as far as one could see along the street the stall keeper had told them about. The house fronts towered over them several stories; each one seemed to be a face staring at its neighbor across the way.

They tied their horses outside one of the first inns, which seemed clean enough, they came to -- *The Golden Angel* – and went inside. They entered through a door embellished with a heraldry ensign. There was a great room just inside with a number of people milling about talking. To their left was the bar and dining area, on the opposite side, was the registry desk with a young man standing and answering the questions of those who needed some assistance with baggage and other matters.

He looked up and noticed them. "Hello, may we help you?" he asked smiling, particularly at Anisah. She noticed.

"Yes, a room, I mean, two rooms for the night, please," Geth'n stammered his request, as protocol suddenly occurred to him.

He had traveled with Anisah for so long he felt a kinship with her, like a brother. It hadn't occurred to him, until that moment, others, and maybe she, might not agree.

Anisah turned and gave him an odd look. "Just one room will be fine. My brother is overly modest," she grinned and emphasized, gesturing dismissively, "We shared a room at home, so there's no reason to change that now."

Geth'n looked at her, sighed, smiled. He shook his head at his own foolishness. Not everything has changed; one's heritage often becomes a presence.

"Yes, Miss," the young man answered, "the room at the end of the hall is empty; the one on the right. Your horses, if you have any, you can take to the stable down the alley on the east side of the building and Nate'll take care of them for you." He pointed toward the corridor nearest to them and returned to his work on the desk.

Apparently he had decided any efforts to gain Anisah's attention would be fruitless.

Anisah, not noticing his dampened interest, turned and

walked into the hallway toward the room. Geth'n followed closely.

Neither had noticed any other people in the large room as they passed. But there was one, an older man who stood alone in the bar, who noticed them. He smiled at Anisah then turned to look out of a window as they passed close to him.

Anisah entered the room, looked around briefly, and threw her bags on the bed. Geth'n had followed closely, closing the door. "Thanks," he said.

She turned and smiled at him, "You worry too much, Geth'n. Let's take this, lead the horses around to the stables, come back in and we'll eat. I'm starving," she said and started out the door. Geth'n was still trailing behind, suddenly deep in thought, troubled by a feeling brushing across his mind.

They took care of the animals, returned, and went into the dining room to the bar. They ordered ale.

Anisah took a sip of her drink and asked the bartender, "Is there a Healers school in the city somewhere?"

"Sure. The Healers have a place near the low gate. Which way did you come from?" he asked

"We rode in from the north earlier, through the market place," Geth'n answered, waking from his reverie.

"Okay, you need to go to the west gate. The street behind the inn will take you most of the way, you can ask again when you get closer. I'm not certain exactly, but it's in that area," he finished, pointing his thumb over his shoulder.

"Thank you," Anisah said. She turned away from the bar and noticed the old man watching them. She pretended she didn't seen him, but nudged Geth'n and motioned in the old man's direction.

"I thought you wanted to eat? What are we going to do with the bread and cheese?" Geth'n asked, as he turned slowly in the direction of her nod.

He saw nothing of importance; there was a couple of swills talking loudly about the great sports match they were going to attend, another man, with ale in hand, trying his approach on a woman who gave the appearance of one who could care less

185

what happened, but nothing unusual.

"What? I don't see anything." He saw no one of interest. Anisah looked and there was indeed no one there. The old man had disappeared.

She looked puzzled, shrugged her shoulders. "Let's go find a table. I'm starving for a good meal." She answered, pointing her finger toward the corner where she had seen the old man. She wasn't going to give up that easily.

"I guess that means we'll need to throw away my hard-earned bread and cheese," he quipped, shaking his head as though in despair. Anisah punched his arm and left him standing.

They walked across the room, carrying their drinks with them, sat and waited for the serving girl to come take their order.

She came soon enough, though she had to deal with the drunks knocking her about as she pushed her way through the crowd. Anisah knew what she was going through, remembering Varspree.

"What'll ya have?"

"What's good?" Geth'n asked. The waitress looked at him as though he was stupid.

"We have the *special*," she answered almost sneering at him, "I ain't saying whether that's bad or good." She just stood looking at them unsmiling, waiting.

Geth'n looked at Anisah and grinned. "Well then, I believe we'll have that. And another drink each, please," Geth'n said.

The woman still had the blank look on her face as she turned away.

"I wonder if that's what we'll get," he added after she walked across the room, bumping aside a door on her way into the kitchen beyond.

Anisah giggled. "Leave her alone. Speaking from experience, she works hard and for little reward. We'll have whatever she brings and be glad for it. Besides, now I'm sitting down, I can feel the muscles stiffening from our ride today. I'll be glad to get back to the room and take a bath."

The meal came. They chuckled, for it was what they ordered. They sat and talked about their day, about the joke they played at the market place, and about the possibility Anisah might actually be able to enroll at the Healers College on the morrow.

They talked about Pet'r a bit, but that seemed to make both of them sadder than they wanted to be so they stopped and ate their meals in silence for a while.

Anisah didn't see the old man again though she kept glancing around the room. It seemed he had simply disappeared.

"Good enough," Geth'n broke the silence, pushed his plate away, swigged down the last part of his ale and rose to leave. Anisah had finished eating and was waiting for him. "Let's go take those baths. Tomorrow is another day for our adventure. We need to be ready for whatever comes."

They paid for their meals and walked out of the dining area toward their room.

The old man was there again with a cape pulled around his shoulders. Raising his head a little, he nodded as the two young people passed him, walked toward a wall, and disappeared.

No one noticed.

Geth'n and Anisah rushed to their room, took turns taking a bath, wrapped in their night clothes, and feeling much better, settled down and relaxed for a few moments.

But Anisah was too excited to lay down for too long.

"I have to go now," she said, rising off the bed, ran behind the modesty screen, gathering her clothes as she went. "Let's go find the College now. Please."

Geth'n rolled over, looked at her curiously. "Sure, let's go." he said, getting up. "As though we didn't walk all day through the city," he added, kidding her.

She laughed and acting as though she might punch him again, so he hurriedly jumped up, ran behind the panel, and put his clothes on. They were out the door in a moment.

It took them about an hour to reach the west gate area. Anisah stopped a friendly looking older woman toddling along and asked, "Please, madam, can you tell me where the Healers College is?"

The old woman was a bit startled at first, pulling her head back and looking up at the girl with surprise in her eyes, but

187

then she smiled, "Certainly, child, two more streets that way," she pointed in the direction from where they just walked, "then a right turn on Laurel. You can't miss it. It's a rather large white building and has a sign above the main door."

"Thank you so much," Anisah said. She grabbed Geth'n's arm. "I'm so nervous," she added, clenching her fingers into his arm.

"Ouch. Calm down. There's nothing to be nervous about. We're just going to take a look." he said, rubbing his arm.

"You're right. But it's been a long time coming and I'm more excited than I can ever remember being," she spoke with a small quiver in her voice and tears started rolling down her cheeks.

"Okay, okay. It's understandable. Let's go and see," he said softly, putting his arm around her shoulders and pulling her down the street beside him, "you need to take a look."

Anisah smiled up at him and let him lead her along. She couldn't help but remembered her dream about the children and herself.

Am I actually going to be a Healer?

"Here we are. Wow, the old woman was right," Geth'n interrupted her thoughts. "It's huge!"

Anisah turned and looked, suddenly feeling very small.

The building was quite large, made of stones lapped together. Large archways, larger than several inns together. There were several covered several openings along the face of the building.

She took a deep breath and held it, stared up at the walls as they walked through the first archway and entered. Her breath broke out in a great whoosh when she saw the massive wooden door before her.

Bracing herself, she marched up to the door, grabbed the great clapper hanging below a windowed opening above it, and bashed it down against the wood twice. Then she leaped back to stand by Geth'n who had watched all this with great amusement.

"You enjoyed that, did you?" he asked."I thought we weren't going to visit today."

She jumped, startled he had spoken, and turned to answer

when the door began to open.

"May I help you?" a woman smiled and asked.

Tall and elegant, she looked down at the two, waiting for a reply, "Perhaps, you are ill." She looked them up and down, appeared to be trying to decide what was wrong with these two young people.

"No! no. We aren't sick, my lady. We . . . I mean I . . . Well, I want . . . No, I have come a long way. . . Well, I was hoping that . . .", Anisah stammered, not able to say what she needed to.

"What she is trying to say is she's come a very long way talking constantly about this school and she desperately wants to be a student here," Geth'n blasted it all out for Anisah. He spoke calmly but with deliberation.

Anisah blushed, drew in her breath, clenched her fists and stood in awe. She couldn't speak. She stood mutely, nodding her head.

The woman turned, looked at Anisah and smiled.

"Anything is possible. Why don't you come in and have some tea, and we'll talk," the woman said, pulling the door open wider and beckoning them to come in.

"If you'll follow me," she said, shutting the door and turning back down a long hallway.

As they followed, Anisah gawked at everything. There were doors leading into rooms on one side of the hall and windows opening out into what seemed to be a courtyard on the other. They finally stopped at the end of the hall and stepped through the last door into an alcove.

The room was round, chairs and tables setting about casually. A window on the far side high on the wall allowed light to filter through, softly illuminating the room, This was obviously a gathering room, possibly a library, though Geth'n saw no books.

There was a young woman standing near another door on the left side of the room; she was wearing what appeared to be a light colored, clean and precise uniform. She smiled at them as they entered but said nothing.

"Oh, Mira, I'm glad to see you're here. This is . . . " the woman looked at Geth'n as she spoke the introduction. "I'm sorry,

189

but I don't believe I caught your names."

"Geth'n, m'am. My name's Geth'n. This is Anisah," Geth'n answered, with more humility than he had exhibited at the front door. "Please to meet you." Both women nodded toward him. He felt out of place somehow.

"Well, Mira. Would you please bring us some tea?" the woman continued, motioning toward a table indicating she would like for them to sit.

"Yes, m'am," the girl replied as she curtsied and pushed through the door.

"I must apologize to you, young lady. My name is Rianne Sanderol. I'm assistant to the head mistress, and what is your name again?" the woman asked Anisah.

"I'm Anisah," Anisah spoke softly, in complete awe. All she could do was look around the room and grin.

Rianne moved about the room with elegance and grace, listening to her talk, noticing her presence. Anisah had never met anyone so genteel in her life.

"Now, tell me about yourself," Rianne sat down at the largest table, motioned for them to join her. Anisah and Geth'n sat.

Mira brought the tea, set the tray on the table, curtsied again and left.

Anisah sat stunned, then slumped a bit because she now had to tell her story once again. Thinking about the arduous journey to get here though, she realized she had experienced more in the short time it took her to get here than she had in the first part of life. She had become more than she was when she left Caliste. She felt good about all that, so she perked up and began her story. This was a special occasion and she hoped somehow her dreams were coming true.

She told of her father's death, crying a bit at the retelling; about her Auntie Elspeth and what she had learned from her; about her long and difficult journey to Varspree; about her new friends, Geth'n and Pet'r, and how they had helped her.

She related her dreams and told of the magical orb that helped heal others. She did not mention however the strange invisibility phenomenon she had noticed in Varspree. It didn't

190

seem to be information to be repeated publicly.

Her tale was longer than Anisah thought it should be, but Rianne listened politely, showing considerable interest and even asking a question occasionally. Anisah finished the tale and waited.

"Well, that's quite a story. I can see you have a great interest in the healing arts simply as evidenced in your great struggle to get here. It seems you have received good teaching from your friend, your Aunt Elspeth, and, as for your magical orb, we could certainly use some magic in what we do."

"Unfortunately, all that we have is our skill, our herbs and our instruments to help others. But I can tell you this. Your story, and your desire, present strong evidence you could become a good healer."

"I will speak to the headmistress about you and let's see whether we might find a place for you here with us," Rianne informed her. "Can you come for another interview, maybe tomorrow?"

Anisah jumped up. "Oh, yes, yes. But I'm afraid I can't afford . . ." She sank back into her chair.

"Oh no, dear. If you're accepted, there is no tuition. All who are here work for their keep. We are very self-sufficient," Rianne's smiled warmly at Anisah.

She reached out and touched Anisah lightly on the head. Anisah felt a great sense of elation as though something magical had just happened to her. She looked quickly at Rianne, who smiled back at her.

Anisah looked at Geth'n who sat through the meeting without speaking; he returned her look and his face showed he too had experienced what she felt.

"Come, I will show you to the door," Rianne said, as she rose, proceeded out of the room, and back down the long hallway.

Geth'n followed closely behind Anisah who was still gazing all about her, not believing she was in this wonderful place.

"Tomorrow, why don't you come back a little after noon? I know the headmistress has a bit of time available for a meeting, and I'm certain she will be eager to meet you," Rianne told Anisah, looking deeply into her eyes. Anisah was almost dizzy with excitement.

"Bring your things with you. I have a good feeling about you and I believe it will all work out for the best." Rianne waved to them as they walked away and then shut the great door.

Anisah looked back, saw no one about, and let out a great whoop, and began running around the plaza. Geth'n stood and watched for a moment, smiling at his friend's good fortune.

About time.

He watched her slow down finally and come to him, smiling so hard he thought her face would surely be permanently creased.

"Can you believe this? Can you even know what I'm feeling right now?" Anisah told her friend, holding his arm tightly as they walked back to the inn. "Tomorrow! Did you hear that? Oh, wouldn't it be incredible if they want me. Oh, I can't wait!"

She began spinning around and around, almost toppling as she lost her balance and stumbled.

"See. Pet'r and I told you there was no reason to be afraid. Soon you'll be healing everyone and everything in sight," Geth'n teased her, but he was happy for her and was a little sad Pet'r wasn't there to see her so happy.

Anisah suddenly stopped, held out her had to stop him.

"Let's see if we can find the place full of books you need to visit," she said, hitting him on the arm and running down the street in a direction other than he had planned. "Come on, let's make a wonderful day of it!"

"You mean the library!" he shouted after her, trotting down the street behind her.

She soon stopped to wait and he caught her easily.

"Sure, why don't we? Things seem to be going our way for a change," she answered.

There was a young man passing by and Geth'n approached him. "Excuse me, would you happen to know where the library is?" he asked.

The young man looked at him curiously but pointed in the direction from which they had just come. "Go that way. Take the street just before the great gate and turn left. The library will be on your right about a hundred paces up the street."

"Thank you, sir," Geth'n offered, turned and grinned at Anisah. They started walking back along the avenue. Anisah was trying to imagine what the school was really going to be like -- hard work, joy in the learning, or both. She could hardly contain herself she was so excited.

"What exactly do you hope to find at this library?" Anisah asked after they walked for a few moments in silence.

"Hopefully, more information about the Ahar'n. Someone from long ago must have written something down somewhere in these great archives.

Our history is not without fable and myth concerning the stone but I was not able to find reliable sources in my previous research at the university at Larilla.

There were vague references to scrolls hidden in some far off place, but no location named; there were statements about the Ahar'n, its power, and about a guardian of the Ahar'n who became an all powerful human who stood with the gods.

But all of these things may only be part of the myths, so I wanted to come here to search for additional documentation," Geth'n explained, then with a sigh. "But I'm not convinced I'll have any success."

"Maybe the Ahar'n could help heal others? Do you think it possible? With such power, how could it not be used in a good way?" Anisah asked, now excited about the possibilities for the Ahar'n, she felt she could hope this amulet did indeed promise a better way to take care of others. Because of her dreams, she could envision a great deal. This Ahar'n Geth'n had described could be the orb she saw in those dreams.

"Well, I've not thought about the aspects of its potential powers, but, yes, I would assume such a thing could be possible. From what I have read, there seems to be few limits on its power. Any limits imposed are those possessed by the bearer of the Ahar'n and the one who makes use of its power, though I could be mistaken about the last."

Geth'n was enjoying discussing the Ahar'n. Pet'r had shown

193

only slight interest and usually had chided Geth'n about his crazy search; he and Anisah were so busy just getting to Tariny the subject had never come up before.

"I believe also the power of several people of like mind can be channeled and combined through the Ahar'n to increase its energy. Why are you asking all these questions now?" he asked, frowning a bit in curiosity.

"It's just you've come such a great distance just to read about a magical crystal, it just seems odd," she answered, "Is there some reason for this searching? Are you actually planning on finding this Ahar'n? I mean you've never shown any capability for magic I've noticed since we met. But then maybe you've been keeping that a secret?.Oh, my goodness!" she yelped, tripping over her own feet and almost bumping into one of the great stone lion in her path.

"You're right. No magic powers, just the ability to stay on my two feet which is more than I can say for someone else I know," Geth'n answered, laughing.

"Seems to be the place, certainly looks impressive. This place seems to be as huge as your Healers College. This town must thrive on building these monstrosities," He spoke quietly, almost in reverence despite evident disdain for the audacity, his eyes widened at this new sight.

This building was more ancient than it appeared. It, he knew, contained more writings in more forms than any other place on this planet. More, it was certain, than all the other libraries scattered across the other continents contained together.

Many scholars had archived their writings, and other discovered writings, throughout known history in this massive vault. The believers who tended this important storehouse of knowledge must have cared for them with love.

"Come on. I don't know what I expect but whatever I am searching for, I believe, ought to be here," Geth'n said, heading toward the huge vaulted doors that opened the way into this wonder.

They crossed a wide verandah as they approached the doors, so tall they had to look up to see the top. When they stood before one of these, they had no idea what to do next.

Geth'n reached out and pushed the door gently. It began to swing open slowly; he was surprised at how easily it moved. They stepped into a cool, dark interior, stopped for a moment to allow their eyes to adjust, and look around the chamber.

High above them were windows, only long narrow slits, allowing some meager natural light into the room. There were chandeliers, each with dozens of candles burning, hanging from vaulted ceilings in the center of each room they could see.

They also noticed there were smaller versions of the overhead lighting, though each one more bowl-shaped so they would rock, sitting on each of the study tables.

"Look," Geth'n said, pushing one of the table lamps, "these can't be tipped over. Much safer with the parchments lying about. I should remember this idea and take it back to the university with me. We still use open candles there, very dangerous indeed."

The tables seemed to extend beyond their view as though there was no end to them. The primary walls of the vaulted room where they were standing were relatively short in comparison with the great room ahead of them. But at the end of this entryway, the rooms on each side were as expansive as any other they could see.

Having grasped earlier the immensity of the library evidenced by the enormous outside of the building, they knew what they could see before them must be repeated over and over again on each succeeding floor above them.

They simply stood and stared, awestruck. Geth'n would never have imagined this even in his wildest dreams. The stacks they could see seemed to disappear in the hazy, sunlit air above them. Fine dust from some movements below swirled from one beam of light to another, creating mystical images only vaguely seen.

"May I help you young people?" a voice suddenly broke into their reverie. They both jumped in surprise then laughed sheepishly at themselves when they turned to see who had spoken.

A man dressed in cloistered robe smiled but patiently waited for them to regain their composure.

"Well, yes. I would like to know in what section the ancient myths and fables are kept," Geth'n answered. "I particularly wish to know about those concerning the ancient theologies."

"Yes, young man. Those documents, and most of very ancient ones, are on the third floor above. The stairs are around the corner to your right and behind the third door to your right. You should ask someone up there to direct you explicitly," the man offered.

"Strangely, you aren't the first to visit that section lately. For years, those readings were untouched, but recently there have been several visitors. Is there something, some news about, drawing this interest?" he asked, sincerely curious about the phenomenon.

"Not that I know of, I am simply satisfying my own curiosity," Geth'n answered, turned and motioned to Anisah they should go upstairs, "and thank you, sir, for your help."

Anisah and Geth'n walked toward the outlying room, turned and went down the corridor toward the door. They passed great stacks, reaching high above them.

One had to hold to something to keep from falling if they craned their necks to see the tops. There was more material here than any one person could ever conceive of reading.

"Strange. I wonder who else would have an interest?" Geth'n mumbled. "I wonder." Anisah only barely heard him and was too spell-bound by buildings' treasures to say answer.

They soon came to the door directed, went through, and trudged up the two flights of stairs, each step some two feet wide so extra steps were required to walk up the steep incline. Finally, they arrived.

Anisah looked back down. "It's a good thing we've been out on the road lately. How do some of these people who seem never to move away from these tables manage to climb those?" she asked, shaking her head, shrugging her shoulders at Geth'n.

"I'm not certain, but it appears they do," Geth'n answered, opening the door into yet another chamber which mocked the lower one with its grandeur. He stopped mouth agape, and stared. "I'm not certain I can get accustomed to this."

196

"Come on. You don't know what to expect, but I'd say if there is information about what you want to know, this is probably the place to look," Anisah said, strolling off to her left to look for someone to help. Geth'n, reviving himself, followed.

They soon discovered the robes the personnel wore distinguished each of the library workers into groups. They found another helper and asked him about the writings Geth'n wished to see.

"What exactly are you looking for, sir?" the helper asked. They later were to learn this was Alt'n, an apprentice; he and Geth'n would become close friends as the years went by. There would be a history of this friendship written by those who followed the legends and that archive would join all of the other volumes about this age.

"I'm looking for the history of magic," Geth'n answered, noticing the man's eyebrow rose just a bit, "specifically, there are legends relating to a certain magical orb. I've researched the item a great deal, but there are too many pieces of the puzzle missing. So, I have hopes of finding those pieces here."

"I believe I can help you. I too have some interest in the ancients, perhaps we can talk someday about my observations," the man, about Geth'n's age, said.

"But, come, I'll show you where I would suggest you start looking." He strode off swiftly between the stacks of manuscripts; huge, yellowed parchments filled the shelves.

Geth'n and, particularly Anisah, had to trot to keep pace with Alt'n. He was lanky, long limbed and strode along swiftly, his shock of dark hair flowing back over his shoulders.

Finally, they arrived at a small alcove near the farthest corner of the building. "This is the best section on magical things. I think you find many writings by those who saw and heard what happened long ago. If you wish to find information on a subject, you should learn to use these ledgers."

He reached and pulled a heft manual from the lower shelf. The book had a strange off-red color, and it became obvious, to Geth'n as he looked above him, each shelf had such a volume.

"These show a cross-index of all the writings on this shelf,"

Alt'n added, pointing along the distance of the shelves. "I hope you're able to find what you are looking for," he bowed his head, turned and disappeared down one of the rows perpendicular to the one they had followed.

Just before he disappeared, he looked back and told them, "By the by, we close at sunset. I'll come and check on you occasionally. Please don't be afraid to ask questions. My name is Alt'n – ask anyone," he added over his shoulder as he turned and walked away.

"Well, we found the library," Anisah broke the silence, "and we'll need some help, I imagine," she added, looking down the long aisle, and up at the shelves reaching to the ceiling on each side, "otherwise, we're not going to find anything."

Geth'n sat on the floor, still dumfounded by the sheer quantity of information surrounding him. Impatiently, Anisah reached, grabbed his hand, shook it, and led him out through the great hallway toward the stairs leading down.

"Thank you, sir, for all your help," she spoke to Alt'n who was sitting and reading near the doorway as she pushed it open, "We'll be back tomorrow."

"You're more than welcome. Come back anytime. If you are students, we open the doors a bit earlier so you can do some research without the general population intruding." Alt'n answered quickly, but he was certain they hadn't heard the last part

"Students indeed, a bit old I would say." Alt'n returned to his book.

Their exit was much faster than their entry. Stepping out onto the street, Geth'n gazed back at the building with a glazed look in his eyes. "What a wonderful place. I never thought it would be possible, this grandeur," he sighed.

"It is big," Anisah agreed. "I had no idea there could be so many writings."

She turned and laughed as she looked at Geth'n, standing there in the street with eyes only for the library. "You look like a lovesick cow! All for a bunch of manuscripts."

She began to walk away, but had to stop, go back and get

Geth'n.

"Come on, we need to get back to the inn. I'm starving and tired. All this walking has done me in." Anisah said as she led him along the street.

"Now you mention it, I'm hungry too," Geth'n added. "I wonder how early 'early' is?" he mumbled.

Anisah rolled her eyes.

"I doubt 'early' means the crack of dawn, if you're talking about what the steward said. Besides, if you wake me before the sun comes up, I'll be one angry woman. You'll have plenty of time to rummage through those old papers of yours after I'm off to school."

Just as the sun slipped behind the mountains, they arrived at the inn. The eating hall was crowded, but they found a table in a corner near the bar. A serving girl came and asked them what they wanted.

"A couple of ales and whatever you're serving for supper," Geth'n said wearily. Anisah just nodded; she couldn't remember being this tired not even when she had fled from Sumt'r.

The girl brought the food and drink, "I thought you two was goin' to fall asleep afore I could get these back to the table," she laughed.

"We were walking all day, it seems, and we are more tired than we realized," Anisah said, stifling a yawn.

The girl laughed, "Well, my name is Lena and if you need anythin', just raise your hand and I'll come a' runnin'," she giggled, winked at Geth'n who was too sleepy to notice.

"The nerve of that frog-eyed tart, winking at you, with me sitting right here," Anisah huffed.

"Oh, just eat. She's just trying to get a better tip by flirting a little. There's no harm done," Geth'n said stiffly, shaking his head. "Women."

They finished eating and Geth'n raised his hand to get Lena 's attention. She saw him and came over quickly. Anisah just sat and looked around the room with a frown on her face.

"Would you like a little somethin' else, sir?" Lena asked, smiling at Geth'n and largely ignoring Anisah.

"No, we just need to pay. Here, take these." Geth'n answered and handed the girl several coppers and a silver piece.

"Oh, sir. Thank you ever so much," she bubbled, looking at Geth'n, quickly looked at Anisah, stuffed the money in her pocket, turned and walked to another table. "Hello, my name is Lena and what could I get you this evening?"

Anisah rolled her eyes, stood up and quietly announced, "I'm going to bed. Would you like to come, or are you going to be spending a little time here? You know you overpaid her."

"No, it's past my bedtime, let's go," Geth'n, ignoring her sarcasm, headed out of the hall and into the lobby.

"Well, you come when you want, but give me a few minutes, because I'll be dressing for bed," she stormed off, leaving him standing and headed down the hallway. Geth'n watched her go, shaking his head in disbelief.

What caused that?

"Excuse me," a deep voice said, startling Geth'n, "I believe you dropped this."

Geth'n turned to face the man. He was older, with a salt and pepper beard and almost white hair. He was wearing a long teal cloak and was holding Geth'n's hat in his hand.

"Oh, thank you, sir. I didn't realize I had it with me," Geth'n said, reaching for the hat.

"You're most welcome, my son," the man said quietly. "Take care you are cautious for the next few days, there may be some trouble for you and the girl. Anisah is strong, but forces stirring around us are powerful and evil."

With that said, the old man smiled, turned and walked out the front entrance without looking back.

Geth'n frowned, in confusion, and backed away a few steps as he watched the old man leave.

He mentioned Anisah by name; how did he know her?

He shook his head, turned and hurried down the hall to the room.

He paused and knocked on the door softly, "Anisah, are you asleep?" He heard nothing from inside, pushed the door open gently and peered in. Anisah was an unrecognizable lump in the middle of the bed, hidden by a mound of covers.

He entered, closed and barred the door. Quickly, he shed his clothes, brushed his hands through his hair, stretched, climbed into bed and fell asleep in an instant.

Outside, the old man stood under a lamplight looking back at the hotel. "Soon, my young friends, you will learn of who you are and of what there is to come. Now, you must be made aware there is a need," he said, smiled, turned and disappeared into the night.

Geth'n woke with a start, sitting up in bed, his breath coming in gasps. He had seen Pet'r in his dream.

Or was it a dream?

Small misshapen creatures, neither human nor quite animal were attacking his friend. Geth'n knew he had cried out, "Pet'r, watch out behind you!"

His terror peaked as sheer numbers finally beat down his friend. One of the creatures had grasped a large rock, raising it high above Pet'r's head and smashing it down.

Geth'n knew he wanted to scream, "Pet'r, turn around!" but nothing came from his mouth; he was frozen in time yet knowing what time was showing him.

Anisah jerked awake startled, "Geth'n, what is wrong? You scared me to death," she said, trying to catch her breath.

"We've got to leave. We have to find Pet'r. He's in great danger. My dream seemed too real. I believe it was," Geth'n was babbling on, jumping from the bed, pulling on his clothes, gathering his belongings and ramming them into his pack.

Anisah sat on the bed trying to wake up enough to decide what to do. Then realizing Geth'n mentioned Pet'r, she too jumped up and dressed in a moment. She believed Geth'n and instantly became afraid for Pet'r; she wasn't certain why, but that didn't matter.

Her visit to the Healer's College all but forgotten, she gathered her things and filled her own bags, sat down on the edge of the bed and watch Geth'n pacing back and forth holding his hand on his forehead.

"Geth'n, you are the oddest man I know. You have dreams

201

about a magical Ahar'n drawing you to this city. Now, you are having dreams about rescuing Pet'r. How can we keep pace with your dreams?" Anisah asked, looking at him as though he had just fallen from the sky. "I don't doubt you, and I hope you are wrong about Pet'r. But did you're dream tell us where to find him?" she asked

"Not really, but I must find him. We are like brothers. I've known Pet'r all my life," Geth'n said, still pacing. "Somewhere in the north in the mountains; there was a great cavern with many smaller caves. Pet'r was being chased and was captured by what must be ghouls. I feel an overwhelming need to travel in a west-wardly direction. I don't know why these things have come to me, but I do know, I absolutely believe, they are true. Ready?" he asked suddenly, grabbed up his pack.

Anisah just nodded.

They left the inn as quietly as possible, went to the stable, saddled their horses tying their packs down tightly and soon were on their way.

They turned down the street they had traveled the day before to get to the Healers College, for it set near the west gate from the city, hailed the gate sentry who let them pass out into the night.

Near the old gate, an old man curled against the great city wall asleep. He opened one of his eyes, peered through the gate as it closed, watched the two young people ride into the darkness, and smiled, "Good travels, my young companions, there will be interesting days ahead."

The sun brought a quiet dawn in the east as they raced along the back road leading toward the mountains to the west.

CONCERNS

Garv'n's sergeant, Vil'n and his men found young Kyna'r lying in the alley, his neck broken.

"What sort of man would do a thing like this, Sarge?" asked one of his men, looking distressed, his faced screw into a deep frown.

Vil'n didn't answer but looked into the darkness of the alley, walked a short distance to assure himself no one was there then turned and walked back and out into the street, looked both ways from the walkway, then re-entered the alley to stand by the young soldier.

"How long do ya think he's been dead, sir?" another asked, as Vil'n returned. No one touched the boy; they shrank from the sight.

Vil'n glanced about again. He squatted near the body, reached and touched his hand to the boy's neck. "Probably two hours, maybe a little more. Not much earlier than Trines," he answered without looking up.

This boy was too young to have died like this. What sort of man did this? Indeed, evil only did this thing.

He stood.

"Pick him up and let's take him outside the city to bury him. This hell hole is no place to lay a man to rest," he ordered two of the men, pointing to them to gather the body to take it with them.

"You, Aron'l, you ride hard and return to Tariny and tell Lord Garv'n what has befallen us." The boy stood looking at the dead soldier.

"Go, ride quickly!" he said to the man by his side, pushing him by his shoulder toward the horses, "there is no time to waste. Let's leave this place. Come."

The boy ran quickly, leaped onto his horse, and rode out to the street then bolted through the crowd as he turned at the end

203

of the alley and galloped toward the southern road to Tariny. He disappeared quickly in the bustling street, many walking by grumbled about the horse pushing them aside as he charged down upon them. These grumblers simply melted back into the moving masses as though nothing disturbed the balance of things as they were.

"Let's go, men," Vil'n suddenly ordered, raised his hand, motioned to begin their ride. They mounted, turned at the street and headed northward. The crowd parted in waves before them.

Vil'n was not going to change his obedience to orders, but he was saddened by the young boy's death. He hadn't seen such a death since his youth when the last of the battles of the Samontha wars were fought. That was too many years ago and the tragedy of this death did not lose its significance on Vil'n.

Who indeed needed to kill this lad? What were they seeking? Could those papers Garv'n gave him be the cause?

Garv'n entrusted Vil'n with the papers; scribed from the original documents he found within those tomes searched through all these years.

Garv'n was ill now and weakened by the sickness upon him; this traveling, at such a pace, was not the kind of life he normally had and sleeping out of the safe environment of his home, all had taken their toll. He designated none of the papers be opened until Vil'n and his men were approaching the lands of the witch, Voravia, and only then must they be read and the instructions followed exactly.

As they rode from the gates of Varspree on their journey northward, Vil'n felt the papers against his chest, retrieved from his saddle packs.

They rode hard to leave Varspree, raising a cloud of dust that hovered above the street for only moments before it sank slowly back to the hot street.

A few miles from the city they paused, selecting a spot on a small knoll overlooking the shallow valley. The wind rose just as they left the city; now several trees swayed in the wind as they buried the young soldier, only a boy.

No one spoke as they worked; they stood quietly and shivered as the damp air blew coldly over the low hills, skies darkened even in midday.

A feeling of foreboding caused several of the men to look round at the open terrain near the graveside; their faces grave, showing their fear.

Vil'n decided to stay for a while to let his men calm themselves a bit. When he decided they needed to leave, Vil'n called Fan's, his page over and gave the hidden papers to him.

"Guard them well," he told the boy quietly, placing his hand on the young man's shoulder.

Then he walked to his horse and shouted, "Let's mount up. We have a long ride still."

They all walked slowly to their horses, pulled themselves into their saddles, and walked the horses back to the road. The horse of the young soldier was led by the last of them, a friend. His sword and scabbard were tied in place on the abandoned saddle. The boy died a soldier's death and they honored him as best they could.

They rode away slowly until Vil'n motioned for them to speed up. Vil'n was a man all in his group respected; he was strong in his will but honest and fair with his men in all dealings with them. He was not so demanding he didn't allow the men to enjoy the benefits of their travels; travels they endured in the service of Garv'n.

Garv'n, admired by his men, was considerate and though unbelievably wealthy, respected them and always genuinely showed his appreciation for their efforts. The men felt no malice toward either of their leaders; they would always serve them well because these were men they trusted.

"Sergeant, I see men riding hard towards us on the southeast road," the advance scout rode back to give the message.

"They should reach the forks of the road in those hills there about the same time we do," he added, pointing slightly toward the northwest where small hills were beginning to rise.

Vil'n's troop was approaching the first foothills of the great mountains and the land was beginning to undulate.

Probably just a small band of thieves.

Vil'n stood in his stirrups, turned on his horse and gave an order to his men. "Let's ride more slowly, men and ride in formation in case we meet a little trouble."

Behind his troop, he saw yet another cloud of dust rising above the road over which they had just traveled.

"Seems we're to have plenty of company today. Let's move to the trees on this rise. No need to leave ourselves unprepared for trouble."

He motioned to the scout. "Return to your post and report if anything else unusual occurs."

The scout turned his horse and galloped away to the north.

Moving off the road, the troops dismounted and walked into the trees, waiting for the formation following them until it came into view. The new group was flying Garv'n's banner.

Vil'n, recognizing it, moved a squad out of the trees to await the arrival; he was surprised to see the new troops, but even more so when he saw Garv'n with them.

"Afternoon, sire," Vil'n spoke to Garv'n, when the new troop halted, "are you to accompany us now." Garv'n looked worn and pale from his sickness and the hard ride they must have taken from Tariny, but his face showed great inner strength and determination.

"Yes, Sergeant," Garv'n answered, his breath coming in short burst as though the pain was almost too much to endure. I decided I felt better and was already coming to accompany you when the news of the young boy's death reached us on the road. So we came with greater haste."

Vil'n could tell Garv'n was not going to be able to travel much further without collapsing.

"Let's camp for the night, sire, so we can rest a bit. We think there's a band of thieves approaching from the east and we probably shouldn't expose ourselves to them today."

"You're right, Vil'n. My men need the rest too. We've been riding hard all day," he was breathing easier now and his speech was not so difficult for him, "please have your men take care of the horses."

Vil'n grinned to himself, but said nothing.

How curious this man of wealth and power should be tempted to tell me how to set camp but I'm not harmed and Garv'n obviously feels the need. So be it. He is a good master.

Vil'n motioned to Garv'n's troop leader and the new forces retreated into the stand of trees where Vil'n was hiding his men. Together they set up camp quickly. He and Garv'n sat near a central fire site.

"Sire, why did you come?" Vil'n asked the obvious question.

"I could not bear to miss the discovery I think these papers will lead us to," Garv'n said, after pausing a moment.

He pulled out the original scrolls, wrapped in leather and tied securely, from his own packs. He held them in his hands, and gazed at them as he talked.

"There are great mysteries in these scrolls, mysteries to stir the blood and inflame our thoughts with their majesty and message.

"I'm not certain I understand it all, but something about these writings speaks of the gods and our existence. I have no other explanation. I have been looking for these for over half my life and I still hardly believe the revelations written here are indeed true. If they are, the world will be changed forever by the discovery of what they reveal and what we are trying to find."

Vil'n was taken back by Garv'n's earnestness. This was beyond anything he imagined. He thought Garv'n wanted to engage in some sort of enterprise with Voravia and these papers he carried were to be the first correspondence with her.

That the papers led to something beyond hadn't occurred to him.

The forward scout sent to take measure of the band of men riding on the road from Varspree, returned and hailed the camp, rode quickly to Vil'n and dismounted.

"Sir, the band continued on to the north without stopping at the forks. I believe they aren't aware of us," he said, catching his breath from his quick ride back.

"May I be excused, sir." Vil'n nodded and waved his hand in dismissal.

"Good job, soldier. You need a rest.

"Corporal!" Vil'n shouted to a soldier passing by on an er-

207

rand.

"Get someone to replace the forward scout and send him to the post to watch the forward position," he shouted,

"If you'll excuse me, sire, I have a few things to attend to before nightfall," he turned back to Garv'n, asking permission to leave.

Garv'n waved his hand in consent.

The corporal stopped a man returning from the woods with an armload of firewood. There was a brief discussion then the soldier dropped his armload onto the pile near the center of the gathering, walked to corralled horses; selected his own, saddled it, then rode through the trees without hesitation.

"We shouldn't have a large fire tonight. Make several small ones around the perimeter and move around in the center of the camp, it'll makes us appear to be a larger party," Vil'n had called his corporal over and explained what he wanted done.

The corporal saluted, turned and trotted toward a few of the men. He told them to carry the wood to several points around the grounds. He followed and lit the fires with sparing use of the wood they gathered.

When Vil'n was satisfied the camp was secure, he returned to talk with Garv'n.

"I'm not certain, sire, but I believe young Kyna'r's attacker was looking for something; I don't think it was a random attack. Could anyone know about the scrolls?" he asked.

"I have determined, I believe, no one but you, myself, and the gods know about these writings and what they foretell. I know only one other person who might know."

"I sent Serl'n to Rab'k with a false message about a need in the south. Serl'n probably saw the scrolls when I was giving him his instructions. He had not returned when I left Tariny."

"You sent a false message to Lord Rab'k, sire? Why?" Vil'n responded, thinking it strange Garv'n might not trust Rab'k.

"I have suspected Rab'k is not providing me with just protection of my wealth; I believe he is forming a power base and intends to take some sort of political stance. He's a very ambitious man. Unfortunately, I believe he will use force to achieve

208

his ends," Garv'n frowned at the thought his handpicked lieutenant might, in fact, be deceiving him.

"I have a number of disturbing reports. I too have a few spies about. I'm supposed to receive daily reports from them -- even here."

Garv'n shook his head and lit a pipe. Vil'n glanced around the camp, pulled his pipe from his side pouch and did the same. The smoke curled around their head, they talked in low tones and finally stopped all together.

The night was quiet. Every one selected a spot to lay bedrolls and relaxed to talk and maybe smoke a pipe before turning in.

"Think I'll turn in, sir. You have a good rest."

"You, too, son. Tomorrow could be very exciting."

Vil'n walked the perimeter of his campsite again, stopping to talk to the outposts along the way. He found his own bedroll, lay down with his sword laying near him, and watched the stars.

Vil'n's men were getting a needed rest, especially those who escorted Garv'n. But he was restless; he had a gnawing feeling something wasn't right. The night gave no hint of any danger, but he paced most of it, checking on Garv'n and his men lying at the separate campfires.

All seemed well, but Vil'n was an old soldier. Something was happening; something that bode ill for them. He was disturbed he couldn't put his finger on the reason.

He slept little.

The next morning started with the arrival of a messenger for Garv'n. The rider was escorted to the camp by the scout Vil'n sent to watch the southern route.

Once the messenger was brought into the camp, the scout turned his horse and rode out through the trees and headed south to his post again.

"What messages today, young man?" Garv'n asked, looking up at the boy on the horse. "Jump down and rest. Vil'n, could we get the boy some food and drink?"

He sat down across from the boy, who jumped off his horse and sat on one of the rotting logs strewn about. Garv'n and Vil'n waited until the boy ate some of the food brought to him.

"Sire, the only message I bring is one of tragedy," the boy started.

Garv'n stared back at him expectantly. "Your spy in Lord Rab'k's castle reported. He saw Rab'k kill Serl'n, your servant. The spy said Serl'n told Lord Rab'k about some sort of magic orb, asked for money and just afterward his lordship killed Serl'n, accusing him of theft. His servants disposed of the body."

Garv'n sat stunned.

He would never have thought Rab'k would become an evil man; maybe he read the man's character incorrectly. He had given his complete trust to him. Rab'k seemed to work hard and perform his duties well. From what he was hearing lately, and this message was the most damning, his lordship Rab'k took his position and goals too seriously.

This is disastrous. I can't believe this -- but it must be, no, it is true. How could this man be so treacherous? How can he want power so much he would destroy what I have given him? How could he?"

Garv'n suddenly rose, stopping the boy in mid-sentence. He paled. His face was ashen. He turned quickly and walked toward the outskirts of the camp.

Vil'n gave orders the boy be given a place to rest and followed Garv'n.

"Are you all right, sire?" he asked as he approached Garv'n. He was concerned Garv'n's ill health would be effected by this news and be too much for him to bear. This shock could undermine the health of Garv'n even more.

"Yes, Vil'n, I'm fine. Well, maybe, old friend, I'm not fine, but I shall see yet another day completed. I wish to rid myself of this Rab'k."

"When we return, I will send for Jond'r. He and I must talk about what he knows and what must be done about this situation. But Jond'r may be in great danger now."

Vil'n thought for a moment. "All of us may be in great danger, sire. Lord Rab'k has great strength; his hand stretches far across the land. He will not relent to capture, or destruction of whatever he has built, without a fight, I fear."

"You could be right, Vil'n. We have no way of knowing just yet what his power must be. I'll not rest until it is finished; this man hasn't the power to fight the gods, and I believe they are with us." Garv'n spoke solemnly.

Vil'n looked at the lowering sky, gray still in midday, just as the previous day. If he looked to the north, he couldn't help noticing the skies were even darker than overhead. These things he'd noticed for several days; that disturbed him too.

"Tomorrow, we should continue our journey northward," Garv'n continued, breaking Vil'n from his reverie, "we shall see what the gods have in store for us."

I agree with you, Lord Garv'n. The gods will have something in store for us.

Vil'n was recalling some of the horror of the battles in the Varkanian wars; he shivered at the memory.

"The gods usually do have their way, sire. Maybe there will be good fortune for us."

We may need it.

PURSUIT

"There must be reason for your presence here. Out with it! What are you doing here?" Voravia shouted. The day had been a long and fruitless one; she was not interested in listening to the whining of these idiots.

The larger of the two stepped forward nervously.

"Ve haf sum trubbl, M'ladji. A mon come into th cavs, the outr ones on rood to mntns. Ve was vurkin. Ve catched he and vas to goin' kil him as you has ordrd. But he thrud us away vith gret strong, too strong for us. He thrud us around like ve was nutin. Ve ran away, he did not chase us, he runnd avay too, but I see hims go. He run to cave hole and onto rood. I not follow in light but get Ort and come tell you." He was down on his knees, cowering now, pushing backwards against the wall.

Voravia listened quietly, fists clenching ever tighter as the creature mumbled his story. She turned to look at the being, her eyes glittering in the candlelight. A malevolent hum filled the air. The men could feel the tension; they held their breaths, waiting.

"Describe this man," she asked calmly though clenching her teeth viciously. She turned away from the being, glanced out the window on the far side of the room and watched as the clouds blew violently from the sea across her land. She loved that sight and felt a rushing sensation, as though she was a part of the flight.

"Oh, yus, he be tall, great strung, hair be long with great white strek, but face be yung not old like hair," the fawning creature mumbled with his face now touching the floor.

She turned back to look at him.

"Get up, you fool. Get out of my sight! You are only spared your worthless life because I have no time to deal with you now. Be gone!" she shouted again, waving her hand toward the chamber door in dismissal.

She turned away from the little beings tumbling over each

other to escape her wrath; they fully realized their good fortune.

She looked out of the window again.

Who is this man of power? What does this mean, this stranger? I must investigate this. There may be a problem.

"Wait!" Voravia turned, her face ashen with creases of white forming around her mouth from the tension. "Find him," she hissed, "I want you to follow him, find out where he's headed and report back to me!"

Something jogged a memory, telling her she already knew where he was going even if he had no idea. She now remembered she had read about him in the scrolls. She recognized this man apparently was too powerful for a single group of her people.

No man would normally have the kind of strength her minions were describing. Could this man be a part of the sense of mystery lingering in the air? Baalsa'n is probably causing some — but other things obviously not from that source are randomly happening.

If this man is so powerful, could he be a part of the legendary elements of the Ahar'n? Could he be a real part of something that isn't only a legend? How could he have lived so long? If so, can he and these things be related to the Ahar'n? The stories of the Guardian are as old as Narhtrae. And what is this amulet and what power does it possess? Could this man actually be the Guardian of the Ahar'n? I can't believe that is true. There has to be another explanation.

But this is a part of the mystique of the Ahar'n and its strange magic. A human is chosen; someone destined to become a warrior. The Ahar'n reaches out and shapes the one selected, enhancing powers already possessed, shapes this person into something more powerful. That new "superman" is created to protect the Ahar'n from falling into wrong hands.

Strangely, the protector always ended by becoming the same man as those others from the past regardless of who he was before.

It was unknown whether a female ever held the position, by the time the protector became a warrior, it was always a man

Voravia, reviewing the information her people had given her, knew the only way to stop this man was to kill him. If this intruder was the Guardian to be, he had to be killed before he ac-

213

quired the Ahar'n. If he gained the Ahar'n before he could be killed, the powers from the Ahar'n would protect him, in turn, from any harm. He would be almost immortal.

Oh, this will be almost too easy. I shouldn't panic. I probably have plenty of time.

Her plan took shape quickly. She began to relax a bit and her anger left her as she prepared to leave the castle to execute this plan, gathering items needed to make a transformation of her own. Her guards would report soon enough on the whereabouts of this Guardian. She would come face to face with the problem.

Later, in the morning, her scout returned. He rushed to tell her what he had discovered.

"Mistress, Hes going to Vranila River Valley, to moutns," he huffed out breathlessly. "I follows for while but come backs to reports."

She was almost smiling as she strode down the hallway, shouting orders as she floated pass her servants.

"Ready my horse! Get me these herbs!" she railed, throwing her list at one of her people, flailing her arms about as she moved, "Stand extra guards at the gates!"

"I'll be gone a day or two. Keep yourselves out of trouble!" she said forcefully to Mord and Kesk who scrambled along just behind her as she flew along.

They stopped, of course, as she burst into her chambers. No one went there without her permission. She began tossing various things into a small bag, muttering to herself.

"Can't let him slip by me; must finish him before he becomes too powerful. "

The Ahar'n must be mine! Baalsa'n has no claim on it. I have my own plans for my world — this world. Why should I let him destroy it?

"Mord! Bring my horse around. I'm ready!" she shouted out at her servant still standing in front of the chamber door.

He scampered away and she walked to the window, noticing the great clouds gathering on the shoreline waiting to plow across the land.

Strange, that's the first time I've noticed them gathered so tightly. Is this

214

some sort of change? Who can be doing this? And why?

Mord knocked softly on her door. She ripped it open and he jumped back several feet, almost falling backwards in his retreat.

"Your horse is ready, my lady," he mumbled and bowed to the floor, crawling backwards.

She rushed past him, descended the back stairs, and broke through the entrance to the stables. The horse, her best, was indeed waiting. Grabbing the reins, she vaulted into the saddle.

"Remember, I'll be back in a few days. I want nothing to go wrong here or heads will roll."

She snatched the reins, wheeled the animal toward the great gate, and galloped off without looking back.

The servants, watching her disappear, could hear her laughing loudly as she rode furiously into the night.

TREACHERY

There have been battles and there have been wars, great wars. Gods have fought jealously among themselves for eons and nothing has been proven.

Men feel, for some vague reason, there was justification for taking other men's lives and for destroying entire civilization.

Unknown to our young friends, their entire world is one of a thousand such in this cycle of the universe, and they are unaware of what war is.

Now, there is yet again more anger among the gods and great sorrow will come from this new confrontation, for there is to be another Great War.

The fates are met and the issue is settled, but these three may be able to spare this civilization from utter chaos and despair.

But a war is inevitable; the forces are drawing the battle lines, evil against the good once again.

Battles are fought among those on each side; evil always seems victorious in the beginning.

The sorrow and plight of mankind seems beyond the capacity of such a frail entity to survive, but man has always endured.

For the thousands of civilizations fallen there has always been another.

So let us observe the beginning of this disruption of all things, let us go to the scene to begin the tales of the Guardian of the Ahar'n and reveal what malicious desire can do to men and gods . . .

Jond'r rode his horse into the encampment, dismounted near Rab'k's tent, and entered.

Rab'k sat on a large pile of camp gear near the corner of the tent. He was looking at the entrance of the tent with immense intensity.

Jond'r's entry did not disturb his gaze; Rab'k seemed to be staring into an unknown place. Jond'r stopped, came to attention and stood patiently waiting for recognition.

"What are they doing?" Rab'k asked without changing his stare, "Have they departed yet?"

"Yes, sire. They have broken camp and are headed our way," Jond'r answered, not breaking his stance, "For your information, sire, it seems Garv'n and his men caught Vil'n's group and have joined him."

Rab'k broke his gaze at that information. He looked around slowly at Jond'r. He knew Jond'r had long been a loyal soldier for Garv'n and probably had never changed his allegiance.

Rab'k wondered briefly if Jond'r was to be a problem, for what was about to occur was probably going against all such loyalty, but he said nothing.

"Are we prepared to break camp?" Rab'k asked, turning back to some documents he was holding when Jond'r walked in.

"Yes, sire. We should be on the road before Garv'n's group reaches us," Jond'r added, not changing his features, "do we ride to avoid confronting them, sire?"

Rab'k grinned slightly, turned back to look at Jond'r. "No, we should not make too much haste. Have the men begin preparing for our journey though; we shall be leaving within a few horas," Rab'k spoke slowly, pushing the forms on his field desk to one side then the other with his finger.

He was amused with this small game he was playing. "Oh yes, Jond'r. Have them battle ready in case we meet some of Voravia's forces along the way."

"Yes, sire. If you will excuse me then, I'll go see to the preparations and will report back to you when we're ready," Jond'r spoke deliberately, not surprised at all at Rab'k's orders, saluted, turned and left the tent.

Rab'k's gaze followed the soldier.

Your allegiance will be tested today, my young lieutenant. He smiled at about what he was intending to ask these men to do. *I can only assume you will indeed be an obedient soldier.*

Rab'k was aware all of these men knew each other; they was trained by Garv'n's officers and once held allegiance to Garv'n and his staff. They all helped Garv'n police the ever-widening territory his wealth, and Rab'k's pervasive persuasion tactics, had established.

These men had performed their tasks well; the land was well

secured and generally peaceful.

Places like Varspree were allowed to continue as small cells around the region so those foul elements existing could be controlled more easily than if they roamed freely about the country.

There, of course, could never be complete control of the bands of thieves riding the prairies, but then these were considered more a nuisance than a danger and were dealt with severely whenever there were signs any danger was real.

Several horas passed before Jond'r returned. Rab'k sat in his tent planning his strategy for not only the battle soon to be, but for any attack from Voravia and some of the wilder bands in the mountain passes.

The first would be a new experience for Rab'k; the latter he was thoroughly familiar with, so familiar he knew some of the leaders of those bands by name.

He had avoided Voravia's land when he first entered the lowlands largely because he had entered from the east. He was aware of those raving bands of ghouls and monsters and of the fanatic delirium with which they fought, if encountered.

He was attempting to estimate the number of his own band that would survive the attack against Garv'n and trying to ascertain his ability to fend off any attacks afterward.

"Sire, may I enter," Jond'r asked. He stood outside waiting for Rab'k to recognize him.

"Yes, come in," Rab'k answered, clearing his thoughts to concentrate on the moment.

"Are there any problems?" he questioned Jond'r, actually knowing from experience Jond'r prided himself on his abilities to organize and direct the men.

Jond'r's self-appreciation was warranted.

"No problems, sire. We are ready to depart at your command," Jond'r answered, standing at attention.

"What are the reports from scouts about Garv'n's troops?" Rab'k asked, making his questions seem nonchalant as though he was only curious.

"They have been on the move for a while, but they are yet two to three horas away." Jond'r answered, curious about whether

Rab'k was actually planning to attack Garv'n's band.

"I believe, sire, we won't been seen by them if we leave soon. I suspect their scouts, knowing we passed them by, were not too concerned with us once we went beyond the perimeter of their area."

"We have seen no evidence they followed us very far, nor are they aware we are still in the vicinity. I think they would believe, since we flew no banner, we were probably a band of thieves and no great cause for concern," Jond'r finished.

The bands of thieves who occasionally crossed paths with any of Garv'n's troops usually fled very quickly to avoid any contact, if possible. Garv'n's name was well known, and the fame of his police groups always preceded them.

"Then let's be on our way." Rab'k said, standing, "have someone break my tent down, if you will. I'll wait on the bluff overlooking the road. Come and inform me when we are ready to depart."

He strode out of the tent and headed for the overlook. He had personally chosen this high elevation so he could observe what was happening in both directions without exposing himself.

He was attempting to infuse some delaying tactics into his plan as things progressed, but he also needed personal assurance things were going as he hoped.

To the south, he could see the dust rising, revealing a group of men traveling. He could envision the movement up and down the lines of soldiers as they trotted along, and probably in formation because they were Vil'n's men.

Corporals rode up and down the lines reprimanding the men to maintain the pace and pushing ahead certain groups who lagged.

Rab'k could almost see Garv'n's banners flying above all this.

Jond'r walked up behind him, "We are ready, sire."

Rab'k turned to his lieutenant, looked into his face, smiled and walked toward the horses without comment. Jond'r followed closely behind.

They mounted and began their own march along a parallel

route to the road the Garv'n's men would soon be traveling.

Rab'k had decided on this maneuver at the last moment; he gave his reason as one of avoidance.

This path lay along a roadbed rarely traveled, as though long forgotten. More importantly, being grassy, it prevented entirely the clouds of dust Garv'n's troops were causing.

Rab'k intended to use stealth and cunning to place himself near enough to Garv'n and Vil'n without being detected until the moment he would call the attack. Great columns of trees on each side would shield them from view.

Rab'k was pleased with how well his plan was proceeding, employing an element of surprise would offset many discrepancies existing because of the hesitancy of his own men and the numbers of the contending troops.

His men were outnumbered but he suspected more involved in the process than Garv'n's would be. Garv'n made many assumptions inherent with complacency and self-assurance; the most significant -- he felt he was in control.

Vil'n, on the other hand, was dangerous and naturally suspicious; he would be a force to contend with when the time came.

CONFRONTATION WITH EVIL

The minds of men meld with the gods' thoughts to bring about greatness. Greatness in good, but greatness in evil is possible too. The gods do not care. These minds profit from that which men call their humanity, for better or worse.

That a man should doubt these instinctive forces is inexplicable; let man but look about his world and seek another form on which he might place the name of his own kind.

Evil is a diminishing of what a man might be had he no capacity to understand the difference between right and wrong. If he were not aware, then evil would be no more than a random act without foreknowledge of a thing being evil in itself.

Evil is defined through the cultural aspect of understanding what an evil thing is. To not be evil then must also encompass the element of decisions and choice.

To choose the path away from evil is a conscious capacity of men's minds to decide what is wrong and what is right and, in deciding, choosing what leads him throughout his, or her, life.

Evil is a capacity to forget one's humanity; good is the capacity to remembers. The good in man makes him a guardian of humanity, with all of its shades of black and white.

It is for the sake of being able to make a choice men achieve valor and are honored for what they have done.

We now follow one man who strives for the ends to preserve a place for the humanity in which he believes.

Our hero strives through and for his own choices . . .

Pet'r walked for days without incident. On one occasion, he took to the trees near the road to hide from a gang of men rushing southward. They didn't see him and he made certain they traveled far enough down the road before he continued walking.

He kept a steadier gait than when he first began. He carried a great staff to set his pace. A pace no ordinary man could achieve. His hair flowed back, reaching below his shoulder. It was streaked with gray and white, making him seem older. He needed clothing larger than those he began his journey with; he stopped by cabins along the way and purchased others.

Strong leather jerkins covered his body now, a belt hung with a short blade from his waist, and over it all, he wore a full cape reaching only to the top of his boots when he stopped. His face was stern, and yet alive, with an appearance so intense he seemed to look beyond what others might see;. Yet, on meeting others along the way, he smiled and nodded his head though he rarely spoke unless spoken to. He never noticed but other travelers would pause after passing him, turn and look back to study this man, this traveler.

Pet'r became, through his concentration to discover the source of his agitation, a warrior prince. His appearance drew respect from those who saw him striding along the road.

Stories were being told of his passage back along the path he traveled.

"You know he saved a woman and boy from the wolves in Litley," a man offered at the pub; others gave knowing whispers when they heard this.

"Yes, I heard old Jocr'l has no need for money any longer. This man beat off the tax collectors, took their money, chased them away and gave the lot to Jocr'l," told another in Alarne.

In this way, Pet'r became another man; a man who sought something and who knew where he should look to find it.

If asked his name, he would ponder the question for a moment, then usually answer, "Pet'r," , turn and walk away northward, always walking toward the mountains.

Some with courage, because a great fear of him grew along with the tales, would ask where he was going. "North".

It was known he harmed no one who left him alone, and on many occasions, showed kindness to others who were in need or offered him something he needed - such as water and food. He never took from others unless given freely, and most often, repaid the person generously.

No one knew exactly were he got his money, but then others noticed there seemed to be fewer and fewer thieves on the roads.

****

Several days before he arrived at the mountains, he paused when he noticed a small cabin nestled quietly at the edge of the trees. Something about the cabin wouldn't let him pass — his curiosity, and something else he couldn't determine, seemed to insist he stop.

He felt a need to discover what was drawing him to it. He walked warily to the door, knocked, waited for it to open and was surprised he was met by a frail and wrinkled old woman.

"What may I do for you, young man? I have very little to offer, if you are here to steal from me," the woman rasped.

"No, no, I am not here to steal, but to ask for a small meal for which I am willing to pay," Pet'r answered, bowing his head slightly as he spoke.

The woman looked at him, her head askew. She squinted against the sunlight lying across her face and craned her head to look up at the Pet'r's face.

"You are big one, you are," she croaked, pausing while survey the man, "and, if you think you might not eat me out of house and home, you are welcome."

"Thank you very much, ma'am," Pet'r said to her, ducked his head, and walked into the cozy front room. He surveyed the inside of the cabin with a quick, perceptive glance to verify there were no dangers here.

"What's your name? And where ya' goin'?" she asked, indicated Pet'r should sit at a small table in the dining area. She began shuffling back and forth from her cupboard, bringing more food each time.

"Pet'r," he answered slowly.

She looked at him with her head cocked to one side. "Doesn't seem like the right name for you," she spat out, leaned closer and peered into his eyes. It seemed she was trying to determine

223

whether he was bad or good by what she might see.

"Pet'r," he repeated, ignoring her. He seemed uninterested in the talking. He paused a moment waiting for the old woman to draw her head away and began to look around in the room.

It was rectangular with a fireplace, its great hearth taking most of the area on the inside wall. There were windows in each of the smaller walls, partly opened to allow the breezes to blow into the room.

Around each end of the hearth, a door passed into other rooms. Pet'r couldn't see from where he sat, but he could hear no unusual sounds from those rooms, and he also didn't sense any danger from those areas. So he assumed they were empty. He was thinking more about Geth'n and Anisah, wondering how they were doing. It had been a while since they were together on the road.

"So where did you say you were goin'?" she inquired again, not turning away from her preparations.

"North," he answered solemnly, largely ignoring her though trying to be polite. He was eating now and was enjoying the meal; the tastes were somewhat unusual but still delicious.

"Just wondered. Ya' know those mountains are hard to travel in, especially this time of the year" she turned, bringing more food, but he held up his hand, resisting her new offering.

She stopped and gazed at him intently.

"Do you plan to travel west at all?" she asked as she turned to shuffle the logs on the fire. The flames jumped into the chimney.

Pet'r thought he noticed a greenish burst from them as they leaped about, but the flames died down, and he decided he was mistaken.

"No, I plan to travel more toward the east. Try to avoid most of the high peaks."

"That way can be dangerous to. Will you go to the forbidden lands?" she asked, "I hear the passages by the sea are terrible and cold this time of year."

"No, I believe I can find a pass through the mountains," he said, finishing his meal and shoving the plate away from him, rising to go.

"No, no, you should spend the night here, my young friend, there is ample room and possibly you haven't had a good rest in a bed for a while," the old lady insisted, "there is no need for you to go out in this weather."

Pet'r hadn't noticed the change before, but the winds now howled outside the cottage. He looked at one of the open windows and noticed the curtains were whipping in the wind.

He was certain a moment before the sun was shining.

Curious? I've not seen storms come up so quickly as they do here, not even at sea.

"Maybe I will take your offer, but I can go to your stable, if you have one," he explained, not really wanting to take advantage of this old lady who was being overly kind to him.

Intuitively, he learned to be wary of others' kindness. Being offered and almost forced to take this hospitality seemed odd to him, "but I insist on paying for the meal and the lodging."

"Do what you will, young man, it isn't necessary to repay me, but you do as you will," she responded.

Pet'r, noticing a slight difference in her speech, it seemed he heard the sounds of a younger person, but he looked at her again and only shook his head at the error.

The winds became more intense outside; the woman shuffled over to one of the window and slammed it shut.

Pet'r aroused from pondering the memories of his friends, was startled by the windows shutting so violently.

Suddenly the storm ended.

How is it possible for a storm to end so quickly?

He looked around toward the windows and another woman, not the old woman, was standing there glaring at him.

"Surprise, my young friend, and I have many of those for you," the woman raised her arm, pointing in his direction with her finger, "many more than you would want."

She waved her extended arm and Pet'r was flung from his chair and almost fell into the fire.

"You are a nuisance. I have in mind to simply destroy you as my guards failed to do, but you have a undeniable strength so

225

we shall play a game," the woman spoke harshly, looking down
at him laying on the floor.

Tall and willowy, she was dressed totally in black; red-haired
flared framing her face; she was almost beautiful. She seemed
familiar to Pet'r but he couldn't quite decide why. Her stare was
evil and cruel.

She raised her hand and Pet'r rose from the floor, and though
he made no effort to get to his feet, he found he was standing.

He was at least a head taller than her, but he knew common
strength was not what she meant by her statement, And he
knew this was no common foe.

He stood and stared back at her without flinching, his appearance more intense. He simply stood and watched her. She, noticing the change, stepped backward out of his reach.

"And what are you really looking for -- 'Pet'r' is it?" she almost
spat the last out, "aren't you a little surprised by what is happening to you now."

Pet'r made no comment but turned to watch her movement as
she began to pace the room.

"Perhaps you are looking for magic!" she flung her arms
ahead of her violently and the side of the room opened with a
great whistling sound as it ripped away from the house and disappeared.

Pet'r did not turn away but kept her constantly in his gaze. He
seemed to be changing while she watched. His stature became
more erect, his face stronger, his hair flew away from his head as
though electric, the great streaks of white hair flashed in the
firelight.

Great bolts of lightning struck the trees nearby, but he never
flinched nor relinquished his constant grip on her eyes.

"I am Voravia. This land is mine. You are trespassing. I think
you are dangerous and here to take something that belongs to
me. I was going to poison you with the food, but I decided you
would know, or sense, that difference.

I plan to destroy you and dispose of the irritation you will become," she spoke calmly, holding her arms folded at her chest.

She made certain she kept him solidly in her sight, there was

226

something extraordinary about this man, but she couldn't quite put her finger on it.

"I am doing you no harm," Pet'r spoke slowly but with absolute intensity.

The walls crackled as though straining against some violent outburst expected.

"If this is your land then I will gladly leave. Your concerns about my intent are wrong, but I will not argue the point with you. I simply wish to leave -- now."

He seemed to become larger before her eyes with some manifestation of majesty and strength.

"I do not believe you, fool. You have come for the Ahar'n," she pushed her chin forward, chastising him as though he was one of her minion, "I will keep it because it is rightfully mine."

"I came for nothing." Pet'r spoke the words through clenched teeth. The air around him seemed to whirl in folding white mists with flashes of light swirling inside the clouds. This apparition began to fill the room, and Voravia felt her first sense of danger.

"You are going to die!" she screamed at him, raised her hands above her head to weave another spell over this insolent man.

It never occurred. She suddenly was flying through the air, tumbling end over end as she sailed out through the opening at the end of the room. She was taken by surprise. He hadn't raised an arm, nor seemed to even move at all, but she felt his power surge forth casting her aside like a limp doll.

Where did the strength come from?

She caught herself in flight and quickly returned to the building, but Pet'r was nowhere to be seen. She ran around the end of the hearth to check the passages in the back of the house, but he wasn't there.

"Come out, you idiot. You can't hide from me!" she hurled out as she turned to go back to the front room.

He was standing immediately behind her. She raised her hand again, but he clasped it and the other quickly, not allowing her to move them. She kicked at him with all her might, but missed as he simply stepped aside.

Raising her off the ground, he walked back into the front room, plopped her into a chair and wove an invisible field around her. She couldn't move, though she tried.

"I told you. I am looking for nothing," Pet'r spoke with some force, his face in hers.

"I am not concerned about your little treasures, nor about this Ahar'n. I have no use for either. I cannot allow you to bring me harm. There is a mission, but I am unaware of what lies in store for me. I want you to stop."

She tried to push him back; her surprise now concentrated into anger. He leaped backwards to avoid this attack, landing squarely on his feet but not wavering.

"I have more power than you, young man. I have long practiced the arts, and you are no match for me."

She flung one of the furniture pieces his way; he simply avoided it. She tried to throw him out into the forest as he had her, but he didn't move. He did nothing to attack her, obviously taking a defensive stance.

"You must go, do not come to the west," she scowled, realizing she had no great advantage and her efforts were futile.

I insist you leave. It is obvious I can't bring you harm, but I am more powerful and can bring harm to your world. So, you will leave. Now!"

He bowed while still watching her intently. "It would be my pleasure, madam," he spoke quietly, but the air around him was charged with energy. She could feel it rippling through around her and was now uncertain how this stalemate was to end.

He then simply turned and strode through the open wall and disappeared. She sat astounded when he disappeared and couldn't believe this experience.

A man of great danger. He will be trouble when the time comes. Baalsa'n will not be pleased, but then he never is.

She stomped out of the house and through the trees, to get her horse and the old house disappeared.

UNRELENTING

Garv'n, during the night, had pondered this strange twist of fate that placed him in a position of pursuing Rab'k.

Rab'k was his most favored lieutenant. Garv'n believed the man was loyal to him; it never occurred to him to think otherwise. Rab'k had obviously helped Garv'n gain a better portion of these great prairie lands. No one disputed Garv'n claim to these lands, no one contended with him about increasing these holdings while Rab'k was his liaison with the landowners.

Garv'n had often marveled at just how successful Rab'k was. That Rab'k might now be denying allegiance to him was a great surprise.

Why would Rab'k desire the Ahar'n? How could he have known that something like it existed?

It never occurred to him Rab'k knew about the Ahar'n, nor that Rab'k might be nearby waiting for him.

****

Rab'k and his group moved along slowly for about two hours. Jond'r stayed behind Rab'k a short distance as they walked their horses along the forest road, shadows flicking across the riders, changing them from horsemen to fairy riders flitting from dream to reality. They rode in silence, but very casually. There was no sense of urgency among the men.

Jond'r watched Rab'k riding stiffly in front, glancing in the direction of the road along which Jond'r knew Garv'n's group was traveling. Jond'r felt the strain of preparation for a battle he didn't want to happen and he was still searching to find a way to avoid it.

Suddenly Rab'k stopped and held up his hand. The group stopped. Rab'k turned his mount and walked it back to Jond'r's side.

229

"You aren't prepared for this, are you?" Rab'k looked at Jond'r with a wicked grin on his face.

"You aren't so foolhardy as to believe you can stop me, are you?" He spoke in low tones so the others couldn't hear.

Jond'r spoke through clenched teeth.

"Be forewarned, sire. I can't allow this attack. I will defend Garv'n and his men; it is my duty to them," Jond'r turned and looked the man in his eyes

Too late Jond'r saw the great sword swinging around to strike him. At the last moment, he threw his armored left arm up to defend himself, catching the blow just below his shoulder, feeling the pain shoot through his body. He shuddered from the blow. He pushed with his left hand to grab Rab'k's arm, to hold him while he drew his own sword, but already he felt the great flush pass over him as his body reacted.

Rab'k knocked his hand away with the hilt of his sword, reached across with his left hand and pushed Jond'r off his horse. Jond'r fell as though dead, thudding to the ground and rolling to the edge of the trail. His horse almost escaped, but Rab'k grabbed its reins and held it steady. He couldn't allow it to run wild.

The other soldiers sat stunned by what had just occurred. These men feared Rab'k but they had all been loyal to Jond'r for many years. They couldn't understand what had just happened. Rab'k had just attacked Jond'r and they were witnesses.

"What have you done, sire?" one of the men spun his horse about to face Rab'k, drawing his sword.

But he was much too slow. Rab'k thrust his sword through the man's neck, nearly decapitating him. There was a gurgle as the soldier's statements were cut off.

Rab'k ripped his sword loose and the man fell to the ground and rolled on top of Jond'r.

"Anyone else have a problem?" Rab'k growled at the rest of the men milling around, casting glances at the bodies on the ground, and grumbling to themselves about their predicament. Rab'k sat his horse easily. His great strength was never more evident to these men than now.

Then two of the men kicked their horses, bolting toward Rab'k in an attack. Rab'k waited, at ready.

When the men were just a stride away, Rab'k's own mount broke between the two, knocking their mounts aside. He hacked the man on his right, almost splitting him in half, withdrew his sword from the man's body with a quick flip, and twisting around in his saddle, sliced across the other's chest knocking him from his horse with a deadly wound. The man's sword flew through the air, stuck into the ground and swayed gently back and forth.

The rest stood their ground, afraid to move. Rab'k brought his horse around to face them.

"Anyone else want to discuss what just happened?" Rab'k scowled and opened his arms to the men, his sword red with the blood of those on the ground.

Strangely almost no sound disturbed the scene. The breezes blew the grass in billows on a small plateau nearby. The day was still, except for the wind which caressed the ground, small fluffy clouds passed overhead. The sky was almost perfect. No one moved nor answered.

"We are about to go into battle, ready yourselves," Rab'k had waited long enough and felt assured he would have no more mutinies.

The men jumped off their horses and began to quietly check their equipment, assuring themselves they were indeed ready. They all wondered why they were riding through this peaceful place in full armor; now they knew -- a battle. They had no idea who they were going to fight; what they did know was Rab'k could, with ease, dispatch any one of them. Each decided it would be wiser to face the unknown than Rab'k.

Rab'k had earlier decided he must ensure a minimal amount of loyalty from these men to do what he needed. His only choice, since he knew Jond'r would never cooperate, was to rid himself of that problem first so the danger of rebellion would lessen. His only recourse was the action he had taken, and now the rest of the troops would follow him into this battle because they were afraid of him.

231

*Not exactly what one might call loyalty, but at least I can concentrate on
the task at hand without concern for being attacked from behind.*

"Mount up!" Rab'k shouted to them. A few of the men were
looking at the wounded and wanted to help the men, "Now!"

The men hesitated, looked at each other, turned and climbed
back on the horses. They sat waiting, completely stunned by
what had just occurred.

Jond'r was lying before them dead; four of their companions
would not ride with them again.

Rab'k rode his horse back and forth in front of them, watching, daring another to attempt something against him. None
moved to attack.

"I will not permit insubordination. I'll allow you but one opportunity to leave and that happens now. If you do not go, I will
assume you are with me and you will follow my commands,"
Rab'k spoke deliberately, watching these men closely.

"Any one of you may leave now."

He pointed with his sword in the direction they had come.
The men looked at each other and at Rab'k. There were probably twenty men still on their horses and they had seen only a
few battles during their services to Garv'n and now Rab'k --
mostly against band of thieves.

Four of the men pulled their reins back, the horses backing
from the ranks slowly, hopping back and forth, trying to bolt
and run. These four saluted Rab'k, turned their horses to the
south, and slowly rode back along the old road.

Rab'k watched them ride away without much concern. He
only briefly considered these men might circle back to warn
Garv'n and his men, but he shrugged the idea away because
they would arrive too late to help or hinder his intentions.

The departing men disappeared around a bend in the road
and into the forest about a quarter of a league from Rab'k and
the rest.

"Gentlemen, we are going into battle in just a moment. I expect you to obey. There will be dire punishment for the man
who does not continue after this fight has begun. I will hunt you
down if you fail me now," Rab'k spoke solemnly, moving his

gaze from man to man.

Those remaining sat watching Rab'k as he talked; the horses flagged their tails against the insects and were stamping their hooves impatiently on the soft ground, agitated about standing for so long.

"On my command then. We will break over that low ridge just behind me and descend on the party traveling on the road beyond," Rab'k explained, "You may be surprised, but do not hesitate and your real rewards will come to you many fold; that is my promise which I vow to keep. Let us do this now!" He raised his sword, spun his mount about, and broke into a fast gallop toward the ridge.

The men hesitated for only a moment then charged after him.

Their rush caught Garv'n's soldiers off guard. Many were bowled over from the momentum of the horses hurling down the embankment. Some twenty of those men were killed instantly.

Once the fight was engaged, Rab'k's men thought no more of their doubts; they were now in battle for their lives and the surge of energy from the fear of death made them put all of their strength into their efforts.

They quickly turned, almost in unison, and crashed back across the remainder of the guard at the rear of the march, killing yet another fifteen or so.

Rab'k was in the thick of it, killing men with a single swipes of his blade, laughing loudly and relishing what he was doing. Vil'n called his personal guard to him and they surrounded Garv'n to protect him.

Rab'k hearing the commands above the din, spun his horse about and charged headlong into Vil'n's group before they were able to assemble and gain any order.

He bowled five of the horsemen off the embankment below the road; swiping his great sword and killing three more as he rode through the group, bashing against horses and men alike. He seemed possessed with what he was about; he wouldn't be stopped.

He ran his horse into Garv'n's, staggering the animal but not

233

knocking its rider off. Garv'n held on to his saddle, praying for his life.

Rab'k burst out on the other side of the group. His men had stopped; they sat watching this madman.

Vil'n, recognizing some of them, shouted out to them for help, but their fear of Rab'k held them and they refused to the aid these men they had known for so long. They sat stunned watching the slaughter.

Rab'k reined his animal about, kicked its flank viciously, and, once again, crashed into the group. He cut down five more men still trying to retain some sort of ragged order, smashing into Vil'n. The horses screamed with rage and fear, rearing high.

Vil'n was a better soldier than most of his men and ducked quickly below the sweep of Rab'k's sword; the clanging of Vil'n and Rab'k's swords rang through the forest. Rab'k smashed the heads of three more men as he passed, dropping them to the ground lifeless.

Vil'n's group was down to five men and Garv'n. They quickly huddled in a small circle around Garv'n and stood their ground waiting for another attack.

Rab'k had turned his horse about and halted about thirty feet from Vil'n, staring at the small clump of men around Garv'n. His men were backing their horses away from the melee, no longer participating. Rab'k noticed this movement, but didn't react. He had no time to waste with concern for them; these men had provided what he needed -- a surprise attack to help him take control. He didn't care what they did now and wasn't concerned they might attack him.

"Vil'n, must you all die today?" asked Rab'k casually, his bloodied sword lying across his animal's mane as he talked.

"Lord Rab'k, it is my duty to do what I must. If it means I must die doing this, then so be it. But protect Lord Garv'n, I will," Vil'n spoke with strong passion and strength.

He wouldn't surrender his position to anyone. He backed his animal closer to Garv'n and his men followed suit.

"You will serve no purpose talking, my lord. If you intend to destroy us then you'll have a fight on your hands. If not, I swear

234

I will hunt you down for what you have done today." Vil'n was not shouting, but his words thundered through the forest.

"Must you eulogize your own death? Sergeant. You are one of the bravest men I know. Come with me and I will give you great wealth and power. Or I must indeed take your life today." Rab'k spoke, sitting relaxed astride his horse.

This was not a game to him; it was pleasure.

"I'll not consider that statement worthy. You insult me by making it," Vil'n answered, bracing his back and sitting taller in the saddle.

"Then, Garv'n, dismiss these good men and come with me. I am here only for you, but these men may die to protect what they cannot. The blame for their deaths will follow you to your grave," Rab'k offered, sneering as he talked.

Garv'n was trying to recover his wits during this long lull. Rab'k, his protégé, was threatening his life.

Why is he doing this? I have never been anything but kind to this man? I don't understand.

"What do you want, Rab'k?" Garv'n asked feebly. He was frightened, but maybe there was a way to avoid this. He looked at the men dead, or dying, around himself and shook his head. "Why have you done this?"

Rab'k smiled. He knew the young lad, Farn's, sitting next to Vil'n was the current bearer of the map showing the possible whereabouts of the Ahar'n. He had attempted to strike down the boy during the initial attack, but Vil'n had moved into his path. He was pushed aside and missed the opportunity. Now he was watching the lad and where he sat in relation to Vil'n.

Vil'n was a man to deal with cautiously; there was strength and resolve in the man and that often would help the brave survive against overwhelming odds.

"I am doing this because I choose to. I have too long pretended to be loyal to you, and so you understand, I was never loyal to anyone but myself and my people," Rab'k answered solemnly.

He glanced around and noticed his own troops had all disappeared into the forest.

Good, there will be no surprises caused by a sudden surge of bravery and renewed loyalty from those.

"What do I have you would kill us all for?" Garv'n asked, his shock still evident in the tremor of his voice. This whole affair was beyond belief for him. "What is it you want?"

"Simple, old man. I want the Ahar'n," Rab'k snapped back, becoming more irritated with this conversation. He felt no need to answer these foolish questions, especially from someone he considered dead.

"Enough. There will be no more questions. It is time to take what I came for."

Suddenly, he kicked his horse into action, heading straight for Vil'n's lackey and sliced perfectly between the two.

Vil'n slashed at him as he passed and struck Rab'k across his shoulders with as strong a blow as he possessed. Rab'k swayed in the saddle from the blow but didn't fall.

Vil'n turned, but too late. Rab'k snapped the boy's neck and thrown him to the ground, charging into the back of the group, killing yet three more of the men.

He turned again, spinning his horse , and attacked Vil'n. Vil'n's thrust with a quick move that surprised Rab'k.

But Rab'k was able to block this as he slammed into Vil'n. Then he slashed at Vil'n and sliced through the man's shoulder to the middle of his chest as he tore by him.

Rab'k pulled his horse to a halt beyond and turned to wait.

Vil'n sat tall and strong in his saddle for a moment. He never uttered a sound nor slumped from his stance until he slowly began to lean to one side.

One of his men reached to stop him from falling, but to no avail. Vil'n's body turned slowly and gracefully as he fell to the ground. He had died quickly.

A brave man.

Rab'k was injured from Vil'n's blow, he shrugged his shoulder but refused to relent to the pain. He sat straight.

"You men, I release you. You may go," he held out his sword and pointed into the forest. There were but three remaining; he saw no need to kill them.

"We stay, sire," one of them spoke; none moved away from

Garv'n.

"I am truly sorry. You were brave men today," Rab'k said. He charged once again and passed closely in front of the group, slashing and killing one more. Another, at the rear, leaned forward to protect Garv'n and Rab'k disposed of him without pausing as he passed. The soldier, who had spoken so bravely, spun his horse about waiting for Rab'k's next attack.

As he turned, Rab'k threw his sword. It pierced the man's chest sending him flying from his horse, thudding to the ground. He didn't rise.

Garv'n sat hunched on his horse, waiting.

"So, my lord," Rab'k began with derision, "what have you wrought this day? All these good men have died for you. He spread his arm and slowly drew it across in front of him showing the bloody road and embankment.

"Why? I don't understand your hatred?" Garv'n looked at Rab'k, his eyes showing his sadness and disbelief.

"My people, for I am from beyond the mountains there," Rab'k said, pointing toward the north.

Garv'n noticed blood trickling off Rab'k's elbow from the wound Vil'n gave him. He stared at the drops falling and only vaguely heard what Rab'k was saying.

"We have always hated you southerners; it is such a part of what we are, we can't alter it. We don't understand ourselves why we hate you, but we know we do.

The Ahar'n is a part of what we know also. We knew it existed without knowing why; that too is a part of what we are.

We know within the Ahar'n lies the power to make this world, as we want it; we'll have the power to have domain over this planet and all the peoples who are spread across its face.

"I was the one chosen to pursue and search for it in this land; we feel certain it is here and we will possess it. And, in your own way, you have allowed me to reach my goal. For that I suppose I must thank you."

"But I don't know where this Ahar'n, as you call it, is," Garv'n refused to plead, but was trying to pursue a logical process of determination.

"I've only bits and pieces of information drawn together from certain hypotheses and other evidence of possibilities. You have killed all these men for nothing!"

Rab'k sat silently, his head canted to one side for just a moment, looking at Garv'n.

Suddenly, his free hand, the bloodied one, flashed to his belt, grabbed a dagger hanging there and plunged it into Garv'n's throat.

Garv'n sat, raised his hand to his wound, his eyes wide with wonder before they began to stare into nothingness. He slowly, as though transfixed in some slower time, slid from his horse and crashed on his back on the ground.

One foot still dangled in his stirrup and he lay there staring at the sky, the dagger sticking out of his neck, his blood oozing onto the ground beside his head. The horse didn't move.

Rab'k looked down at the old man; his face glowering with anger at the old man's impudence. He dismounted, flexing his shoulder where Vil'n's blade had struck him, feeling the tenderness of the wound. He walked around Garv'n's horse, snatched his dagger from the man's neck, wiping the blade on his victim's cloak.

He looked at Vil'n laying face down in the grass not far away and shook his head.

Rab'k found the young man he knew had the map hidden. Walking over to the lad laying limp and crumpled where he had fallen, ripped the boy's shirt away and found the small waist belt . Ripping the belt loose, he pulled the drawstring on the pouch, opened it and, reaching inside, found the map. He dropped the belt on the ground next to the boy, and slowly opened the map so as not to damage it in any way.

He peered over it slowly, frowned, put it in his own belt pouch, walked to his horse and mounted. He walked the horse a short distance away, turned and looked at the carnage.

Father will be proud of me for this day. Tomorrow, I hope I will be with him again.

He turned his horse northward and galloped away. He held his wounded arm out for a moment as he rode. Shaking his fist vigorously, he raised it above his head, trying to ignore the pain. Then he kicked the horse into a run toward the mountain pass he needed to reach before nightfall.

The forest glade was quiet with death. A leaf floated softly to the ground.

Over small ridge at the edge of the clearing, a small misshapen head rose slowly. The creature glanced about, looking at the carnage, turned and motioned for others to follow him.

ALLIES

Sometimes in the darkest hour, there comes a hero. One who cannot be matched for inherent valor and pugnacity in the face of certain disaster. He/she has the inner strength of the individual and the ultimate belief any problem can be transcended.

This belief drives such a person to accomplish feats normally beyond the capacity of a single individual, and exceeds the abilities of most during more ordinary times.

It is from these heroes the best of man's spirit comes. This spirit transcends the mock facade some of the gods suggest and will be the only source for the salvation of mankind.

Therefore let us follow still the adventures of one who would be a hero, a person with the strength of many men, a person who believes righting a wrong is the ultimate achievement of a life.

And so our young hero is beginning to realize there is more to his "adventure" than he had assumed when he first left his home in Peetle.

He sees himself in another light, and he is not at all certain he likes the transition . . .

Pet'r did not tarry long after his confrontation with the witch. He suspected the person he fought was Voravia,, based on what he was told by people along his way, but he wasn't interested in small talk nor becoming acquainted with the woman.

He recognized she possessed tremendous power, and he now knew he too possessed power as part of what he was becoming.

This new power could transcend his own mortal being, protect him, and also cause great destruction if directed toward those who would bring him harm, or attempted to stop him from accomplishing his own goal. Though he was still uncertain about what the goal was.

He recognized too he hadn't really bested Voravia, if that was his most recent attacker, but he did escape virtually unharmed.

And he realized he needed to hasten along. He needed to find his answers soon or there would be no need. Now he had a stronger sense of urgency driving him. So he left behind the struggle with Voravia and hurried up the road to the mountains.

Pet'r noticed during his travel northward the great clouds blowing from the southwest were making the sky seem more and more dismal. They rushed over the mountains, shoving upward against the open sky where the mountains met, rumbling as they escaped the hot desert air. The clouds twisted as they rose over the great wall of stone, tumbling over and downward at the peaks. The grinding together of these bodies of rushing dry heat created immense flashes of lightning with rumblings that shook the ground.

Freezing winds came rushing down the face of the mountains in waves, like great chinooks; racing at such high speeds the trees and boulders crashed against each other and lay strewn across the mountain meadows at lower altitudes. Winds strong enough to snap most of the smaller trees, and fling gravel, sand and dust ripping through the air; hail rattled violently against the larger trees and rocks.

Pet'r took shelter from these flying objects as he approached the pass. Stopping once behind a large boulder to rest, he felt it moving against his back as he rested.

He looked out across the plains just traveled only days before and saw the great clouds scudding just above the ground as they hastened away from him.

Something is strange. Some impending, and potentially disastrous, event is coming and I must be part of the what is to come. I must follow my purpose though I'm yet to understand.

He watched the skies overhead and wondered what he could possibly have to do with these changes. The elements were now dominating this entire environment. He wondered if these forces were affecting those areas through which he passed recently. It seemed likely they were, or were going to be, and it also seemed advisable the people below should prepare for the worst.

The people, with the exception of the witch, were good people, gracious and kind to him. They now believed he was a seeker of wisdom and power.

He didn't know but he thought the concept inaccurate, but there was no doubt he had changed.

It was often difficult now to remember his youth and his excitable spirit. Now he wondered why these changes were happening. He recognized his appearance alone might be shocking to others; his demeanor probably caused others to hesitate to accept him too openly.

Pet'r always gave as much as, and often more, than he received; he left no one, who showed some kindness toward him, without reward for having done so. Some he rescued from hardship or danger; for others, he performed some task too difficult for them but required no great effort for him. He always helped in some way. Those he met would probably remember his moment of passing through their lives and, with few exceptions, remember with fondness and appreciation.

I don't know what, or who, I will become. But I am becoming something I wasn't.

He shook his head, stepped out into the winds again, pressed on, dodging flying objects and finally reached the entrance to a valley leading into the pass above. There were landmarks he could identify from what the last farmer told him to look for. He trudged against the winds into the canyon. As he walked, the incline became steeper and steeper.

He noticed some snow patches on the hillsides above him and frowned, but he remembered the farmer assured him there would be a clear path through this pass, if Pet'r followed his directions.

The canyon became more narrow as he walked. As darkness approached, he began looking for a cave or shelter to stay the night and was ignoring the path in front of him. He walked around one boulder protruding into the path and bumped into a traveler coming from the other direction.

They both jumped back and took a fighting stance. Pet'r didn't attack and the other only stood his ground though he did draw a weapon from his belt.

"Sir, I have no desire to fight with you. I simply want to go through the mountains to the land beyond," Pet'r explained.

The other man listened, frowned for some reason, but made no attempt to move.

"Could I just pass without any problems?" Pet'r asked. The other man nodded his head once and began to lower his arms though warily watching Pet'r's reactions. Pet'r did the same.

"Can we talk?" Pet'r inquired, turning one of his hands palm outward as a sign of peace. The other man looked at his hand, again at Pet'r and held his hand out as Pet'r did.

"Yes," the man replied. There was an unusual accent, one Pet'r hadn't heard despite his recent travels.

"It's late and there's danger in the night in these places. Let's go back up the trail to a cave I just passed and we'll have shelter while we talk." The stranger said.

He stepped back, leaned against the narrow canyon's wall and indicated he would like Pet'r to precede him.

Pet'r sensed the other's concern and knowing one of them needed to show some trust, stepped around the other and walked up the path.

"Wait, flatlander," the man spoke roughly.

Pet'r spun around and prepared for an attack, but the man was standing, weapon at rest, pointing up a small, rough path leading toward the scree face of some ancient avalanche. Pet'r nodded his head and began the climb, following the path's torturous route and was soon able to see a darken area he thought must be the cave entrance. It was difficult in the dark to be certain but his guide persisted and only pointed up the path.

They climbed for another hour and finally reached the small plateau. There was a small cave tucked behind two large boulders leaning together. The men pushed their way through the small crease between the boulders by turning sideways. The cave was relatively small, but certainly large enough for the two of them. The boulders protected them from the elements.

The other man proceeded to pull some sort of material out of his rucksack and crumbled it into smaller pieces and piled them into a small mound on the floor.

Taking out two black stones he began to strike them together.

This produced a sharp clacking sound but, more importantly, sparks flew from the stones, some landing on the crumbled material. After several tries, one of the sparks rested on the material and began smoldering. A small stream of smoke rose curling toward the ceiling. The man lifted the mound and began to blow softly until the glow grew.

Soon a small flame broke free. He lowered the mass and placed it beneath some small twigs from a pile already bundled in the cave.

Pet'r noticed the twigs were already there and the man knew they were there. It was obviously the man's campsite; he was here before he met Pet'r on the path.

Soon there was a small fire. The light flickered along the cave walls and, though the material had a curious odor, Pet'r welcomed the pleasant warmth of the fire. There was no conversation during the climb. Pet'r, watching the other man complete his preparations, wasn't certain what sort of alliance he and the other one made, but was pleased no conflict arose.

The other certainly seemed to be a warrior. His clothing spoke of a man who lived in the wilds by his own means; ever alert with weapons not far from his hand, he peered at Pet'r occasionally and often walked to the cave entrance, looking out into the night then cocking his head to one side to listen to the sounds of the wind.

"What are you doing here, flatlander?" the warrior was looking directly at him now.

Pet'r had wandered into his own thoughts and wasn't thinking about his present circumstance. The question startled him.

"What? Oh, nothing, just on a journey," Pet'r answered without thinking. He had a stronger sense of needing to be on the move.

Is there something about this man that is making some difference?

"No one is 'just on a journey' going this way at this time of year," the man grunted, nodding his head toward the cave entrance.

He reached into his backpack and pulled out a small bag, pried open the top and poured out some of the contents into

244

his hand. He tossed them into his mouth and began to chew.

"Nope, someone from the flatland, going that way, is on a mission of some sort."

Pet'r was surprised by the forthrightness of the man and his obvious familiarity with his environs and this country.

It also occurred to Pet'r the accent Pet'r heard when they were on the trail was gone; this man had no accent at all.

Where's he from?

"Maybe, you should answer a few questions too, my friend," Pet'r said slowly, "What are you doing here?"

The other looked up from under his eyebrows, stopped chewing his food, and glared at Pet'r. He slowly began to reach for his weapon. "I'm not trying to create any problems. I believe we should maintain our peace but both of us are wary of this situation. We need to talk," Pet'r said slowly, raising his hand in front of him to ask for patience.

The other seemed to relax a bit. He pulled his hand away from his sword and began to eat again, not ignoring Pet'r entirely but obviously not wanting to talk either.

"Can you tell me where I am?" Pet'r started, realizing he would have to initiate whatever was to happen here. His hope was he hadn't fallen into the hands of another sorcerer.

"I am, as you guessed, new to these mountains, but I do have no more in mind than to explore. I'm from a small seacoast town, have always wanted to see this land, so I'm here."

The man stopped chewing, wiped his sleeve across his mouth, brushed his hands off on his trousers, and looked at Pet'r for a moment.

"You don't have the look of a man from the sea," he said, leaning back against the wall of the cave though still glancing at the cave opening periodically.

"I've been traveling a while," Pet'r admitted, "My name is Pet'r. It may be I'm on a mission but I am unaware of the goal, or its outcome. I'm just compelled to do this. Perhaps you could tell me about your reason for being here."

"I've been spying in the wastelands," the other said without concern, "Garv'n Anspar of Tariny feels some great change is

245

going to happen and needed to know how the nomad tribes in the desert were reacting to these changes." He motioned with his thumb.

"I've been there about three months and was returning when we met. That's why I am here.

"But I must add, your story does not ring true."

"I can thank you for your honesty. I too have noticed changes; the skies are darkening to the south. I agree most of the activity seems to be emanating from north of these hills, but I'm not knowingly here to investigate these things." Pet'r said, turning to gaze at the darkened opening of the cave.

The tension between the two slowly evaporated. The longer they talked the atmosphere of their meeting changed from suspicion to friendship.

"Arcon'n is my name," the hunter stated bluntly. He was a scout and was roaming the wastelands as a hunter, visiting small villages to spy as he traveled. He was eager to return with the information he had accumulated.

He was greatly concerned with what he discovered while visiting with the last village, Tynoc'l.

He found that a man from the south, Lord Rab'k, was actually a wastelander, not what he now seemed. Lord Rab'k was on a mission of his own and it wasn't one to improve Lord Garv'n fortune. The new discovery caused Arcon'n to hasten his return.

He admitted he was deep in thought about this news when he ran into Pet'r and wasn't being very cautious. His thoughts were of the danger to Lord Garv'n and to his own brother, Jond'r, who was now in service to Lord Rab'k.

Pet'r wasn't familiar with either of the men, but he vaguely recalled hearing about Rab'k.

Arcon'n also learned the desert people worshiped a man, Baalsa'n, who was an outcast from some powerful group. This Baalsa'n was gathering the desert people for some critical event. When Arcon'n asked in the village what the event was, no one actually knew.

Pet'r, in like turn, briefly told of his adventures. When he spoke of the incident with the witch, Arcon'n's face showed

246

curious astonishment.

"Has to be Voravia. No one ever escapes her if she decides you are in her way. How did you do it?" Arcon'n asked.

"I honestly don't know. It seemed I was able to escape each of her attempts by thinking I needed to. It just happened," Pet'r answered.

He truly wasn't able to determine how he escaped; it all seemed a blur to him.

Arcon'n looked at him a moment, glanced toward the cave door and added, "If you're determined to follow this path, my friend, you must be cautious. There are bandits all about, willing to slice your throat for your shoes.

I'll draw a small map on parchment for you before we leave this morning to show you the best and safest route; it is the one I used to get here."

After you cross the mountains and arrive on a short plain where an enormous and solitary boulder projects from the desert, you should turn west.

The village of Tynoc'l is but a half-day's walk from there. The open prairie holds few dangers but, if you hear the thunder of hooves, find a place to hide until they have passed.

There was a mysterious and ungodly occurrence in the desert recently and the natives are not certain of the cause. They rush about trying to discover the source and are potentially danger-ous." Arcon'n told him as he drew the map.

"Is there danger from the snows above?" Pet'r asked, remem-bering the patches he was the day before.

"Only on some of the narrow clefts. Here I'll give you my snowshoes," Arcon'n answered, reaching into his pack once again and dragging out two webbed paddles, bent limbs with leather plaited across to hold the whole together. "You can walk across the snow instead of through it."

"Thank you. You honor me with these gifts, and I hope we'll meet again when we have more time to talk," Pet'r said, clasping his new friend's hand and shaking it several times.

They talked for a while longer than decided to get some rest. The next morning, they went their separate ways.

247

Pet'r looked back once just before rounding a bend in the path but couldn't see Arcon'n, turned and continued his walk. He ran into a few large patches of snow, but no other trouble found him. He used Arcon'n's snowshoes to traverse these and was amazed at how simple they made the passage. Later, he stayed the night in another small cave, rose and continued upward.

When he crested the last pass he decided to rest and have a bite to eat. He looked back over the land he was leaving behind where the skies were cloudier, dark and foreboding moving sluggishly across the prairies.

He turned and looked northward. His view of the new land made him feel a greater need for haste. He finished his small meal, threw his knapsack over his shoulders and hurriedly walked down into the canyons below.

The air grew warmer as he walked down the path worn by the passage of thousands before him, but strangely there was less and less sunlight as he walked down one ravine after another.

At last he noticed the canyon walls were getting farther apart, but ahead, he could see no trees in the land before him, it was barren. And, in the distance, he saw the prairie disappeared into the blackness hovering above it.

This land is in turmoil too; what is the cause?

He quickly reached the edge of the plain and ventured away from the rocks carefully, watching for any movement. The heat shimmered like water above the land, but there was no water. No animals roamed these plains. Low growing sage spotted the landscape here and there; no trails crossed any of the low rolling hills though there was one well-traveled road passing just beyond the edge of the foothills.

The clouds were like smoke billowing from the parched earth, touching it, gray and black with high red undertones from the sun trying to break through. They scudded over the desert and seemed to gain speed as they neared the mountains as though attempting to race to the tops.

Pet'r could see, holding his hands flat above his eyes, the progress of the clouds was limited. The clouds became so cold as they got higher they simply rose until they dissipated high above the mountains. There wasn't enough energy to drive them over.

Yet. I wonder how long that will be true.

As Arcon'n instructed, he turned to the west when he saw the great boulder standing solidly against these ominous forces sweeping the plain. It seemed to have erupted from the ground alone, there were no other outcroppings of rock anywhere near it, as would be expected. It was as though this great monolith was a guardian placed at the foot of the mountains.

Is there a reason for that being there?

Pet'r couldn't help looking back at it as he traveled around and away from this monument. It finally disappeared slowly below the horizon.

He shook his head and plodded along in the heat, looking for any refuge. There was none away from the hills, and as he knew now, one had to travel back into the canyons to avoid the intensity of the burning land. But he continued despite the heat and began to trot with an easy pace.

After several hours, he saw objects rising from the horizon that appeared to be man made. A small, tented village became more and more obvious as he drew near. Pet'r was amazed at how simple this part of the trip was; there were no assaults, except the weather. He felt things were improving.

At dusk, he entered the village. Most of the people ignored him. Some didn't. Several women watched him closely as he walked slowly through the camp looking for food and drink. No one attempted to talk to him.

When he found a small marketplace, he asked a few questions of the man at the stall to get a sense of life in the camp. After talking for a short while, he obtained a flask of water and some flat native bread. Things were curiously out of phase in this encampment and he couldn't decide why.

"Are you here for the great arising?" the stall master asked him nonchalantly. Pet'r noticed however several heads turned their way, apparently wanting to hear his answer. Pet'r felt he should use care how he responded.

Arcon'n indicated these people worshiped in strange fashions;

he decided a certain amount of concealment might be wise.

"Yes. I've come a great distance to be here," Pet'r answered slowly, not interrupting as he sipped his drink, "what is the time now calculated for the event?"

"Within the fortnight, there will be a great sounding of beasts and demons. The world will be ours," the old man's voice was rising with his excitement. He began, as he worked, a soft but insistent chant.

"Baalsa'n be praised. He is the Lord of all; a god of magnificent power."

Those nearby looked up at the skies, continuing to roll and boil, and began nodding their heads in tempo to the recurring chant from the old man's lips.

Pet'r realizing he was the only one who wasn't nodding his head, corrected that and joined in unison nodding with the crowd. He also began to back slowly away, sipping at his drink and tearing chunks from the bread. He continued to nod as he turned and walked out of the marketplace plaza. Slipping quietly around the edge of one of the larger tents, he walked swiftly down through more, looking to each side as he crossed the paths between the tents he passed.

No one showed any aggression; no one spoke to him. Maybe it was the heat; maybe it was something else he still didn't understand. He decided he had obtained a sense of what was happening in this desert land and he had lingered long enough. He threw the flask and the bread away.

One of the things he noticed about the changes in himself was he had few needs now. He seldom ate or drank anything anymore; he wasn't certain why. It actually hadn't occurred to him to wonder why.

Suddenly, someone grabbed his arm and jerked him into a tent. A young woman stood before him, smiling, her hands still holding him tightly. The tent was elaborate, almost extravagant. Strong colors of green, yellow and red splashed about through large tapestries and luxurious rugs; the reds dominated and made the whole seem gaudy. There were several sleeping cots spread around the room but, since this was the middle of the morning, none were occupied.

"Are you a servant of our god, Baalsa'n?" The woman suddenly blurted out, still holding his arm.

"No, I've just traveled the desert and was looking for food, drink and a place to rest. Possibly this is the place," Pet'r answered, ignoring the question and attempting to engage the woman in light conversation. He hoped his accent wasn't obvious to her and realize he was from the south.

For some inexplicable reason, he felt that piece of information could be his undoing; he had little doubt these people had no love for the 'flatlanders'.

"Maybe you are one of Baalsa'n's servants. Maybe you are a mighty warrior. You have the look of a warrior; handsome, strong and intense," the woman said, acting stranger with each utterance.

"My name is Jasryn. Perhaps you can bring me what I most desire. Do you think you can?" Pet'r had no idea what the woman was talking about, or what her intent was. He didn't have to wait long for the answer.

"Have you come to sire children for His Holiness? Have you come, mighty warrior, to spread your seed through the land?" she was almost screaming as she attacked and clawed at him, trying to push him toward the rear of the tent, to one of the cots.

Pet'r, caught off guard by the attack, stumbled and almost fell. He staggered a few steps, regained his balance and grabbed the girl's arms to stop her.

"No! No. I've come for none of those reasons. I am a simple traveler. I am not the one you seek," Pet'r yelled at the girl, holding her away from himself.

Suddenly, Jasryn stopped, released his arm, shrugged away from him and stepped back a step.

"Are you not Lord Rab'k?" she asked simply.

"No. I'm not Rab'k," Pet'r answered.

Thinking quickly, he added, "I am but a scout for my Lord Rab'k. I came to learn about the preparations, to inform my liege about how well the encampment is being prepared for his arrival, and I believe he will be pleased. Certainly by the beauti-

251

ful women who await him."

He bowed toward her rather gallantly - he thought so anyway. The woman wandered away while he talked. He apparently was not part of her plan now.

"Tell his lordship I, Jasryn, await him for my heart and my body are his. Now leave me,"

Jasryn suddenly became haughty, not wanting anything to do with one as lowly as Pet'r. She waved her hand toward the opening and walked to the other end of the tent to avoid being near him. He smiled, turned and walked out of the tent, giving a great sigh of relief. He couldn't believe how irrational these people were.

He walked along one of the back paths and soon came to the western edge of the city of tents. He decided it would be wiser to remain concealed during the daylight hours, so he hid in an empty tent he discovered and quickly fell asleep.

Later, a great commotion from the south end of the encampment woke him; he knew Rab'k had arrived. Pet'r sensed his presence. He thought it odd he knew when Rab'k arrived, but felt no reason to concern himself with this unusual recognition. He did feel a heightened sense of urgency and knew he needed to leave without delay.

He peered between the tent flaps and could see a number of people running by; he watched cautiously until the pathway was empty. It was near dusk, a good time for his departure.

Checking each direction, he left the tent and passed between two other rows of dwellings before he reached the edge of the encampment; then he ran, staying low for the first hundred meters, slipped behind a low hummock, stopped and waited a while longer.

As darkness, closing with the great clouds roiling above, washed over him, he rose and began to trot toward the west following the edge of the mountains.

My reason for coming here is now clear. I must return home to warn the others.

He began to run. Pet'r ran, without rest, for half a day. Passing across a low valley, he noticed a distinct path, or road, etched in the prairie ahead of him leading into the mountains. The road was headed south; he decided this was his way back home.

His appearance was changed even more now. He was taller, larger through the chest and shoulders; his hair long, now almost entirely gray with great black streaks running its length, and flowing behind him as he moved. He trotted tirelessly for mile after mile; there seemed to him to be no reason to stop, nor rest.

DISCOVERY

Heroes, in the minds of the people, are those who have risked the one thing most precious to all -- their lives -- to fulfill a need to be more, and to mean more, to others than would be expected within a normal environment. An unusual circumstance and unusual factor humans may share with the gods.

We have followed our young saviors, for we now may call them this, from their naive beginnings. It now is the time of reckoning for these three, the time of the great cataclysmic disturbance I and all of the other immortals have feared would occur.

Our old enemy, Baalsa'n, is going to attempt yet another coup. We cannot allow him to have the success he had during the Varkanian situation. We must rely on children to accomplish the task at hand. This has come about because of our resistance to intrude, but no longer can we wait.

Blessed are the meek for they shall inherit the earth, an old adage we must rely on now. There were no more choices. The people have strayed from the teachings, but the bloodlines are still there. We use them and now must wait for the consequences.

So, returning to our story, what will happen next . . .

Rab'k entered the village, asked where Rena'x's tent was and trotted his horse through the place of his birth once again.

He was tired and his injury weren't quite healed. The riding kept his wound aggravated. Also, he had to fight off a band of thieves in the mountains earlier that day. But he was more than their equal, even injured. He killed a few and drove the rest back into the canyons and ridden on. The fight did reopened his wound, but his desire to deliver his small package kept him driving toward his goal both day and night.

He found the tent, marked with the standard of his family, jumped down, identified himself to the guards by showing the tattooed emblem on his forearm and entered the tent.

"Who goes there?" A shout came from the darkness where

the candlelight was low.

Rab'k recognized the voice. "Father, it's me," he answered, moving swiftly across the floor to embrace the only man he respected.

Rena'x was a large man like his son. Only age now was taking its toll and though stronger than most men, he was weaker than Rab'k remembered. Rab'k was gone for half his life now; much had changed.

"So, Father, I believe I have a map that will truly lead us to the Ahar'n," Rab'k started immediately telling the news he had ridden so far to reveal.

"Your decision to bring my life and Garv'n's together was accurate. He knew many things and was wise in his own way. I've brought a map he discovered over years of research showing the location. I believe we must ride immediately. The signs tell us the great scourge is at hand."

Smiling, Rena'x was always thrilled at his son's enthusiasm. He embraced his son again. Rab'k winced with pain; drawing back a bit from the great hug Rena'x was giving him.

"You're injured, son. Come, let's have something done about that wound before we do anything else. Then we'll talk," Rena'x helped his son lie down on a divan at one side of the tent.

"Woman, come take care of my son!" he shouted to his nearest concubine. She scurried to the bedside and began to remove Rab'k's tunic carefully, trying to not disturb the wound that was now very swollen, sore and seeping some blood. Vil'n's blade had cut deeply.

Rena'x, after making certain his son was being well cared for, stepped outside his tent and began to shout to those passing by.

"My son, Rab'k, has returned to us this day. He brings with him news for great rejoicing. Let us prepare a great feast to welcome him home!"

Several of those walking by stopped, listened to what Rena'x had to say, and gave a great shout. They scampered away in all directions to spread the news and gather the food and drink for a celebration.

Rena'x went back inside the tent, walked to his son's side,

leaned down to make certain all was being taken care of.

Rab'k reached into his waistcoat lying beside the couch and handed his father the small manual. Rena'x turned and walked with it to a small table, sat and began to study it closely.

After a moment, he raised his head, gave his son a generous smile, and said, "Yes, I too believe your friend, Garv'n, truly discovered the whereabouts of the Ahar'n. I often thought it was moved to such a location, and what more appropriate place for the Ahar'n to be than Voravia's land."

Rab'k was now sitting up on the couch; his wound now dressed.

"Voravia? The witch? Why is that appropriate? What does she have to do with all this?" he asked

Rab'k was surprised by the mention of her name though he did remember her from that long ago meeting in the great palace of Baalsa'n.

Living in the flat lands, he, like the rest of the population there, believed the best thing one could do with Voravia was to ignore her. Avoiding her avoided the trouble she created. He followed that simple rule and her form of trouble affected his work very little.

"Some secrets, my boy. You are not the only one who was sent from our land at the bequest of Baalsa'n. Voravia was sent to the western coast many years before you were. Now, it would seem she was sent there, though unknowing, as protector of the place where the Ahar'n is hidden," Rena'x explained.

"Another man was sent to the central part of the country, to report the feelings of the people, to report back whether these flatlanders would take up the standards of our god, Baalsa'n.

But I believe he died recently and we lost that source. Baalsa'n ended by cursing him. He took a family there and his devotion to his daughter became more important than our cause."

"Voravia, the other, and you, Rab'k, are half brother and sister, each born to a different woman, but the offspring of Baalsa'n himself," he stood solemnly watching Rab'k as he spoke these words.

Rab'k looked at his father with astonishment. He could not

believe what he was hearing.

Rena'x is not my father! How can this be possible! Why did Baalsa'n do these things? I am brother to Voravia, why was I not told this before?

Rena'x waited for his son to say something.

"If I am the son of Baalsa'n, why have these secrets been kept from me," Rab'k said, regaining his composure.

"Baalsa'n felt you should not know, but since he as returned, he watched over each of you," Rena'x explained, reluctant to continue because now he was losing his son.

"There were many things to be done. He wanted you to accumulate riches, he wanted the other to gain information, and he wanted Voravia to protect the place of the Ahar'n, it would seem.

Voravia and the other were the first to go into the flatlands; you were much too young."

"If he knows where the Ahar'n is, why doesn't he get it himself?" Rab'k asked, still angry and frustrated.

Rena'x explained.

"The Ahar'n cannot be taken by the gods from its resting place. One man, Areb'l, the first Guardian in our world, placed it in this secret place and the other gods sealed it with an ominous spell only another Guardian can release.

And there have been other Guardians, but the time was not at hand for Baalsa'n, so the Ahar'n has remained in its vault for these thousands of years, and all but forgotten. Even now there is probably a Guardian, but he or she is unaware of it.

The gods are no longer known by the people in the flat lands, they have foolishly dismissed them," Rena'x continued his story, revealing much Rab'k had never known.

"How would anyone know this Guardian?" Rab'k asked, realizing that if the foreseen event was to take place, a Guardian must be found who could possibly be forced to release the Ahar'n.

"There are some distinct factors, mostly in appearance, known about the Guardians. First, they are tremendously strong; secondly, they seem to possess even supernatural powers when drawn into a dangerous situation; thirdly, their faces seem to show a great wisdom and their hair becomes streaked, much like a sorcerer or sorceress, as they begin to become the one entrusted with the care of the Ahar'n.

They are not born with these traits, but when the need arises, the powers of the gods develop them. These are dangerous and ominous foes if you are their enemy.

The Ahar'n will be protected, but Baalsa'n has always felt that, by waiting long enough, all sorcerers and sorceresses would have stopped passing along their wisdom to others.

Should a Guardian begin to develop, it would be in ignorance and the potential for that person being deceived would exist. Baalsa'n feels this person could be tricked into submitting the Ahar'n without difficulty.

"Is this the great event? The Ahar'n could be handed to someone by this Guardian?" Rab'k asked, now pacing the floor of the tent, his wounds forgotten.

"Yes. You or Voravia must be there when that time comes." Rena'x answered, watching Rab'k, who had always been his son, walk back and forth sometimes holding his lip, as if in thought.

"Then this means I must return and go to Voravia. Does she know?" Rab'k asked.

"No, but it is soon to be revealed." Rena'x said, now knowing the mechanism for the great event had begun. Rab'k's full attention was now centered on pursuing the eventuality of the Event. One could almost see the plans being made.

Suddenly there was a commotion outside. The guards at the tent front stopped a small group of people. Several men were dragging a beautiful young woman to the tent and were clamoring to bring her before Rena'x.

Rab'k and his father walked out of the tent and confronted the crowd.

"Who is this woman?" Rena'x shouted, holding his hand high for quiet. The voices stopped.

"This woman had some stranger in her tent last night. She will not tell us who he was nor why he was there. He has disappeared now, but we thought you should punish this one for her wicked ways," a man who seemed to be the leader of the pack spoke up.

Rena'x looked at the girl. He noticed the attempt at petulant guile, but there was also fear in her eyes. He felt nothing for this woman and should have her stoned, but maybe there was something to be learned from her.

He was fairly certain another stranger, Arcon'n, wasn't from the wastelands though he wasn't sure. That one had disappeared only a fortnight ago.

He motioned for the crowd to release the woman and pointed toward the tent entrance indicating he wanted her to go inside. She bowed her head, ran into the tent and stopped. Rab'k and Rena'x followed.

The two men sat together while the girl stood in the center of the tent, shaking from fear, clasping and unclasping her hands.

"What is your name? What is your tale, woman?" Rena'x asked.

"My name is Jasryn, sire. I have no tale, my Lord," she answered with a quiver in her voice, looking first at one and then the other. "Something happened and I was afraid to tell."

"You can tell us without fear, my girl. Let us know what happened and we will not harm you." Rena'x insisted.

Rab'k sat without expression on his face, curious about how a stranger could have entered the encampment without being noticed. Some things were different; maybe his father was weakening in his old age.

But then Rena'x is not my father, but only human.

"I saw a man walking through the camp. He was a man of great strength as could be easily seen and his face was handsome. I thought it must be his lordship, Rab'k, whom I heard was returning.

I want Rab'k to sire my children, so I laid a trap for him and took him into my tent. But, sire, it was not Rab'k. He told me he was a scout for Lord Rab'k and I must wait for Lord Rab'k's arrival." She let the words roll from her, shaking constantly.

"How did you know Lord Rab'k was coming back?" Rab'k asked, amused by the fact this girl had no idea who he was.

"It was revealed to me in a dream, sire," she answered, trying

259

to conceal nothing. She felt she had done no wrong; her story was theirs to hear if they wanted. She now only feared for her life.

"In a dream? How stupid, girl. Dreams mean nothing . . ." Rab'k started demeaning her, but he noticed Rena'x shaking his head. He paused a moment then added, "But let us hear yours."

The girl told them about her dream.

"There was a great play for power that ripped the skies and tried to tear the world apart. Rab'k was to be one of those involved and would be one to help change the face of the world, as we now know it.

There were others, men and women, who come to face each other in the first battle. There would come many wars; wars such as this world has never known. Rab'k will be there." the girl told her story slowly.

She paused then added, "I-I wanted to be the mother of the children of such a man. That's all I wanted. The scout said Rab'k was to come soon, so I sent him away last night to tell his master of my desires."

She stopped and watched these two men who held her fate in their hands. They looked at each other for a moment, and then turned back to the girl. She felt extremely vulnerable, shaking so hard now she could hardly stand.

Rena'x paused a moment longer then said, "You may go, but do not tell anyone else this story, or you will die by stoning Now go!"

"I have not told a soul, my lord. I will never tell it. Oh, thank you, thank you," she was whimpering as she backed toward the entrance. As soon as she felt the flaps of the tent brush past her side, she spun around and disappeared into the encampment.

"The dream may be Baalsa'n's way of telling us of what is to come. I think the Ahar'n is not going to be taken easily, if this story comes true," Rena'x said, turning to Rab'k, "but it seems your way is clear. Besides, you have a volunteer."

Rena'x chuckled at the last but stopped when he saw the look on Rab'k's face. Rab'k was deep in thought and far away from the moment.

"Who was this 'scout'? Doesn't that description make you think? Could the Guardian have been here? Why? Is there some reason he wanted to know I came back? There are too many questions about this dream -- assuming the dream means anything at all." Rab'k said, malice showing in his face.

Rena'x didn't interrupt.

Rab'k continued, "Dreams aside, we know the man was here and only recently. There is only one explanation; he was here to determine where I was to be when the great cataclysm occurred. He was a spy to assure I wasn't where the great battle was to occur. But, I shall fool him. I leave at dawn to search out this man and kill him." Rab'k suddenly leaped to his feet. "Please have my things readied for I must rest awhile before I leave."

Rena'x only looked at his son with sadness, "Yes, my son. But you are weakened by your wounds, shouldn't you rest longer? The time is not yet at hand."

"We don't know when the time is? I think that is in Baalsa'n's hands, but there are others. If this Guardian has, or goes to the Ahar'n first, there will be little we can do to control him once he knows the power he has. He will no longer find it necessary to scurry away in the dark.

No, it is more likely he will come looking for us. And with help. We must act now." Rab'k was pacing again, punching about with his fists to emphasize the points he was trying to make.

Rena'x, without speaking, signaled to one of servants who came immediately and dropped to one of knees in salute and whispered, "Yes, master."

"Please see to it Lord Rab'k has everything he needs to travel and travel hard tomorrow," Rena'x spoke softly, so he would not interrupt Rab'k.

Today, I have lost my son. May he go with the god of our faith and may they together find a way to make our world a place we want to hold dear to our hearts. My time to die is near but my people should enjoy the blessings of the children of a god.

He watched Rab'k trudging back and forth across the tent floor and smiled to himself.

You did well, Rena'x, this man is a credit to you and to the god who claims him now. He will be known throughout the world.

Rab'k finally tired and lay down to rest, he too dreamed of great battles in magnificent wars. He was there and all knew who Rab'k and his father were.

The night passed calmly.

SEARCH FOR A FRIEND

In the Second Age, there were no mortal leaders who could summon magic. Only at the time of the greatest discontent, did there appear a woman.

From the innocence of youth to the mightiest of all people, she rose, through her own intellect and the fortunes of portentous chance, to become a savior of Aerolan, and of Narhtrae

She became a great leader and sorceress who would protect man from his own self-destruction and from the vagaries of the gods.

She had no need, when she first came to know what she possessed, to use these powers and hesitated more than once to bring forth even the least of what she could, for fear of becoming a destroyer herself.

Her moral code stood foremost in her mind. She, having been raised simply and honestly in a quiet village, did not consider a search for, or possession of, power something to seek after, simply because of her belief. Even had she known of the possibilities she would not have sought these things.

So it was, with ignorant simplicity, she came upon these possibilities and though she sought truth, she wouldn't have known had her friends, and the people, not needed her.

The story then is about the young Anisah and the great climactic moment when she discovered who she was and what she was to be . . .

"Geth'n, I'm tired. Can't we stop for the night?" Anisah said wearily; her companion was walking resolutely ahead of her into the dusky evening. She couldn't believe how taciturn Geth'n had become in the last few days of their travels in search for Pet'r.

She was anxious about Pet'r too; no, more than anxious, concerned for him, but she was having great difficulty keeping pace with Geth'n now. She wasn't certain what was happening to him nor herself, but something seemed different, she could feel it.

Something that went beyond the closeness she felt for Geth'n and for Pet'r who was far away, but somehow near; but this intense emotional sense from Geth'n was surprising even her.

Geth'n slowed, turned to look back at her, and frowned a bit.

263

"Yes, of course. I'm sorry I've been ignoring you today, but something isn't right somehow and I don't quite understand what I'm feeling."

He looked at her with a sadness in his eyes, then turned and looked to the north as though searching in the dark for what disturbed him.

She walked to his side, reached and held his arm in hers.

"Come, you need to rest. It should help you think more clearly," she gently pulled him toward the forest's edge; he resisted for only a moment.

As he turned from his searching gaze, back at her again, he smiled and said, "Once again, Anisah, you know what is needed. I might not agree with you but I don't doubt what you are saying is true.

We've been traveling quickly, I admit, but I'm greatly concerned about Pet'r. My biggest problem is I don't know why, nor how, I am feeling this."

They sat down in the shade of some large trees, on a small knoll overlooking the road. They didn't speak for several minutes; each lost in thought.

Anisah was looking about at the scene before her. The land here was beautiful as though untouched by gods and men for long ages. There was a small prairie stretching toward the mountains in the west; long rolling flower-dotted plains undulated toward those great hills as far as you could see both to the south and the north.

To the north though she noticed some perceptible change in the land, there seemed only stunted, grotesque images of plants, flowers were stunted and colorless for as far as she could see in that direction.

What she saw did not coincide with the rest of the land. She was wondering why when Geth'n interrupted her thoughts.

"What could have happened to Pet'r? This isn't like him at all. I have this terrible feeling something is wrong, and I can't seem to think clearly about what we should do," Geth'n was talking aloud, more to himself than to her.

She was feeling the same anxiety since they left Tariny and she too was beginning to think the worst. The opportunity to relax a bit she hoped would drive away some of the fear and some of the more fierce images that had come to her about Pet'r. She missed him, more now she thought he might be in danger; that impression alone gave her a strange sense of loneliness she couldn't account for.

Geth'n stood up as if to go, then sat down again, slumping to the ground as though exhausted.

"I don't know what to do. I believe we must continue on this road to Voravia's. I also sense there is a great danger for us to do so, but an equally strong imperative exists to arrive at her castle and find access to it as quickly as possible.

I now believe Pet'r has been captured and has been imprisoned there," Geth'n said, almost in entreaty, turning to look northward again, a wistful look of sadness on his face.

"Then I think we must go now," she answered, offering her own consent to the prospect of facing this danger.

Over the few weeks she had known Geth'n, she had learned to trust him implicitly. She felt there was a power within him not even he knew about; she sensed this as part of her desire to help him think these things through, a reaching out that seemed to come naturally to her.

Anisah had noticed, during the last days of their stay in Tariny, that she could feel what others were feeling both in their bodies, and more strangely, in their thoughts.

She was now beginning to realize she could touch the joys and, unfortunately, the pain of these others just by being near them. She wasn't certain why, but she knew this change was one she had expected since she left Caliste and she felt it enlarging her own soul as each day passed.

"Do you think there is something wrong here in this place?" Geth'n asked suddenly, not loudly but quietly and with searching eyes.

Anisah broke from her reverie and turned to him, looking in the direction he was.

Before she could answer, a horse whinnied loudly just over the rise behind them. Anisah stood quickly, turning in the direction from which the animal called out.

Then the pain overwhelmed her, sweeping over her in great waves, almost suffocating her as it passed through her thoughts. She turned and ran up the slope. Geth'n running by her side was shouting something she couldn't hear because of her sense of urgency.

She just ran.

Then Geth'n ran past her and reached the top of the embankment first; he searched the woods for some sign of the horse they had heard.

Anisah rushed by him quickly and was following her innate senses leading her toward the source of the pain.

Suddenly, she was grabbed from behind and gently pulled to her knees on the ground sloping into the trees just beyond where they now sat.

"Anisah," Geth'n was breathing hard and speaking in a hoarse whisper from near her left ear, "stay down. This might be a trap. Think. Have some common sense, this could be an ambush."

"Oh, the gods!" Anisah almost squeaked the pain was so intense. She held her hands over her ears to try to stop the screaming inside then she crumpled, sagging on her knees in the grass. Geth'n looked around again from his kneeling position and listened intently.

Both jumped when they heard the horse's snort come through the nearby trees. Anisah felt Geth'n pulling her down into a prone position. She sank softly into the tall grass without complaint, waiting.

She lay there quietly feeling the warmth of the earth beneath her and the smell of the grasses brushing against her face, but still feeling she felt the nausea and pain sweeping by her.

Someone needs my help. Someone is injured nearby.

"You have to be more careful, Anisah, this is dangerous country; you must remember to take fewer chances," Geth'n was hissing at her from behind, "but now, we need to get off this open ground. Run to those trees there."

Anisah looked to where Geth'n was pointing and shook her head.

266

"No. We have to go into the trees in front of us. Someone there is badly hurt. We have to help," she answered, jumped up and began running toward the trees she had chosen.

She didn't know whether Geth'n was following or not, but her own urgency pushed her toward her goal.

She burst into the shade of the trees, dodging through trees and bushes that tore at her clothing. As quickly as she could push through each obstruction, she ran on and finally out into a clearing on the other side.

An open stretch of land lay to the left and right where an old road passed through this part of the forest. Anisah stopped.

Geth'n ran into her, pushing her even further into the sun drenched path. Small dust clouds, caused by their scurrying feet, settled slowly around them.

"Well, I guess we aren't going to be ambushed," Geth'n spoke brusquely. Anisah looked around at him and frowned.

To their right, they saw several horses standing and grazing, their reins dropped to the ground. There were no riders to be seen.

"Maybe they've gone into the woods and don't want to be disturbed," Geth'n whispered in her ear, "maybe we should just leave."

"No, something is wrong. I know it. I can feel it, Geth'n," she spoke calmly, but forcefully. "We need to determine what has happened."

She began to walk toward the horses when she came upon the body of one of the soldiers; then she saw another.

"What has happened here? How terrible this is," Anisah gasped and began to run from one body to another wanting to help them, but she was too late.

"There seems to have been a battle between good and evil here," Geth'n offered. He stood leaning on a staff he now carried with him at all times. "I fear evil has won the day. But for what purpose?"

One of the fallen, lying down the embankment, moaned loudly. They both turned toward the sound, identified which body made the sound and rushed to his side.

"Lord, Lord . . ," he coughed blood from his shattered lungs, "Rab'k." He gasped with a gruesome gurgling sound and his head fell backward in death.

"Who is he talking about?" Anisah asked Geth'n, lowering the poor man to the ground and closing his eyes.

"Lord Rab'k. Pet'r and I met him once long ago on the road to Varspree. He did us no harm, but he exhibited no mercy toward a band of thieves who had attempted to kill us. He was a huge man and bold in his strength," Geth'n answered, "Could he be the one that did this?"

They both look around but saw no movement and sensed no danger here.

"What madness is this? We aren't at war. Why have these men been slaughtered? I sense this has much to do with the Ahar'n and is a warning to us of what is to become of the world if we can not find a way to save it," Geth'n spoke, as he looked at the bodies lying all about, "But I fear there are no answers here."

At that moment, they heard another muffled moan from beyond the underbrush on the far side of the road.

"There's someone still alive," Anisah gasped harshly, almost choking with anxiety.

Geth'n ran across the road, pushing ahead of Anisah, flailing at the undergrowth with his staff to clear the way better. She followed still scratched and pulled by the underbrush. They scrambled down the embankment looking for the source of moaning.

Anisah stopped.

"Oh," she drew in her breath.

Lying on the ground, grotesquely twisted by his fall and with no strength to straighten himself, was another soldier.

Someone had sliced his back open with a sword. His right side hung open; his blood dried and crusted in the wound though still oozing from the deep cuts.

She couldn't tell whether he still breathed or not. She knelt beside the dying man not knowing what to do.

"Geth'n, do you have the water with you?" Anisah looked up into the sun, squinted against the sudden light, but saw Geth'n handing her the water.

She began to wash the man's face; he moaned, opened his eyes and looked at her, smiled and fell unconscious again.

"Please get my bag for me," Anisah was pointing to her carryall bag she had dropped when they had fallen before. "I need my potions."

Geth'n turned, found the bag, walked to it and brought it back to Anisah who was holding the soldier's head in her lap. The man was mumbling, but Geth'n couldn't hear what he was saying.

"His name is Jond'r. He's actually mentioned the name Rab'k several times but no more. He's in terrible shape, Geth'n. I'm not at all certain he's going to live. I gave him a potion to help, I believe, but I won't know for a while.

He probably won't regain consciousness tonight, or maybe, never," Anisah talked quietly, watching the man's face contort from the pain and the dreams he was obviously having. Tears were streaming down her face when she looked up at Geth'n.

"Did he tell you anything else besides his name?" Geth'n asked, curious about this man and how he survived. Looking at the man from above, he couldn't see the wounds across the man's back, but he could tell from the victim's pallor he had lost great deal of blood. The ground where the man was lying was dark and the flies were already buzzing at the feast. This man was a strong man to have survived.

The attack had come from behind and must surely have slashed opened his back and maybe there were cuts across his neck and face; it was hard to tell.

"Not really. He just mumbles a few words now and then," Anisah answered. "We need to find him a place for shelter, if we can move him."

She cleaned the man's face. Then pulled him tightly to her and looked over as far as she could see, though afraid of what she might find.

She discovered there was a great cut across the right side of the man's head and that his ear was sliced but not cut off. Raising his head a bit more, she peered over the left shoulder and saw the deep gash cut upward across his back. She couldn't see any further down but she knew this man was near death and would not survive if they didn't get him to shelter as soon as possible.

"Geth'n, I can't help him here. We have to take him to a town, or someplace, to care for his wounds." Anisah almost implored Geth'n to do something, sitting there with her smock stained with this man's blood and more dribbling through her fingers and around her arms the longer she sat. "I can do nothing just sitting here holding him."

"Do we have time, Anisah? If he's going to die anyway, can we afford to take the time in trying?" Geth'n asked.

He wasn't trying to be cruel, but just practical. From what he could tell this man had no chance to live. The wounds had to be terribly deep and few ever survived that. "There are probably other men looking for these soldiers. I'm worried we're going to get too involved if we stay here much longer."

"We are involved, Geth'n. I, and I believe we, cannot leave this man to perish. I know I cannot. Maybe, if I do my job well, he will have gained consciousness by tomorrow. I will feel better and maybe we can learn something about what happened. But I just can't desert him -- he's alive," Anisah pleaded.

"I understand, but he's really in no condition to go anywhere. There's only you and me to try and move him, and I don't think we can do it." Geth'n added.

Anisah could tell Geth'n was having a hard time being so practical and stoical about all this, and she knew he was worried about Pet'r. She couldn't, however, bring herself to agree to just leave this man -- it was beyond imagining.

"We have to try. Please, Geth'n, we have to try," she answered.

"All right. Then let's see if we can get him to the next town. I admit I cannot, with good conscience, leave him to die out here. I believe you probably have the magic necessary to save his life, despite giving him some of that vile stuff you carry around. Let's try to do what we can. Our mission will just be delayed a day," Geth'n suggested, knowing Anisah was not going to leave the man and inwardly agreeing with her.

Anisah grinned at him.

"Thank you," she spoke softly.

"Now we need to turn him so I can look at his back. We probably need to get something to lie on the ground before we roll him. Could you get that blanket from the back of his horse and put it here?" she added, pointing to the area just in front of her.

Geth'n walked over and retrieved the blanket and spread it as she had asked. Geth'n held him while she slipped from under the man's head and moved the blanket into the spot where she was sitting.

He then positioned himself to hold the man steady as Anisah raised her arms and began to roll the man onto his stomach and straighten him so she could inspect the wound entirely.

Jond'r grunted with the pain of movement. But Geth'n was able to lower the man's left side and straightened the rest of his body.

Anisah gasped when she saw the gaping wound. It ran the length of Jond'r's back from his lower left side, across his back, and gashed deeply into his right shoulder. Blood oozed from the wound along its length.

"Oh, Geth'n. How are we going to move this poor man without killing him?" Anisah was crying but trying to maintain her composure.

She began to use the edge of her dress and the little water they had to wash the blood away so she could see the area more clearly. Each portion of the wound revealed a greater horror for her. She had never seen such as this and she was dizzied by it.

The man was no boy. He appeared, from several of the scars on his shoulders, to have been involved in fights before, a veteran perhaps of many battles. She stopped her cleaning for a moment; looked upward toward the sky with her eyes closed tightly, trying not to cry anymore. She didn't have the luxury.

"Can I help?" Geth'n asked, reaching and holding her shoulders gently. His touch help. Geth'n was a special person and helped her reassert her confidence.

"We do need more water. Maybe one of the other horses has a water bag strapped to it. Would you look?" Anisah asked, "or

271

if there isn't any, shouldn't there be a stream in this thicket here?" she nodded toward the woods with her head, not really raising it because she was concentrating on getting as much of the wound cleaned as possible.

She didn't notice when Geth'n trotted back toward the horses nor when he got back until he said something to her.

"Anisah?" he asked. She looked up at him; actually shocked he was there. "I found two more bags of water, but I'm going to need to go look for more. Will you be all right?"

"Yes. Thank you," she added as he sat the water bags next to her, took their empty one, and left. She only knew he was gone because his shadow no longer blocked the hot sun that bore down on her and her patient.

Her patient. A first and new beginning. I am going to save this man's life.

She used most of the water to clean the wound and was soon satisfied she was as thorough as she could be without causing the bleeding to start again. But she jumped nervously when Geth'n's shadow fell over her again.

"I did find some water down there. We have this one full now and I'll take these others and get more. I scouted around a bit. I don't think anyone will be coming by soon. It's nearly dark, and I doubt many travel this road anymore." Geth'n said. He gathered the two bags, turned down the hill and disappeared into the trees again.

Anisah stood, reached beneath her dress and took her under-skirt off. She spread it out on the ground and began to tear long strips from the cloth.

She then bandaged Jond'r's head trying to conserve the material she had for the larger wounds. Then she had to wait for Geth'n.

When he returned, he laid the bags to the side and walked to her. "You'll need to replace that somewhere," he said as he came to her side, pointing at the pile of cloth. "What do you want me to do now?"

Anisah ignored his statement about her clothing.

"You need to raise his body at the shoulders so I can run

these under and around," she answered, motioning with one of the strips in her left hand.

Geth'n slid his hand beneath the man's chest then gently raised him, trying to not bend or move the wounded area.

Anisah shoved her left hand, holding the lead edge of the wrapping, under as far as she could and, reaching across, grabbed the other end with her right. She brought the strip across and tugging on it, tried to close the wound some, and tied a knot with the longer piece.

She repeated this procedure, wrapping the strip around and around the body, each time pulling it as snug as she thought safe.

During the process, she applied herbs and ointments from her bag directly into the wound so it closed with the materials trapped inside. She had to tie several strips together as she continued, but when she had finished, Jond'r's torso was swathed in bandages that seemed to have help close the wound without causing any more bleeding.

Anisah was still on her knees beside her patient, watching him and wondering how well she did. Suddenly she felt exhausted and slumped back, sitting heavily onto the ground.

Geth'n was shaking from the strain of holding the man off the ground. He lowered Jond'r slowly, laid him evenly on the blanket and pulled another over the top to keep him warm.

"I have done what I can. I still believe we need to take him to better shelter," Anisah finally spoke though still numbed by what she had done.

"Well, not today. The shadows are too long; night will be on us within the hour. We have to stay here until tomorrow," Geth'n said.

"You did well, Anisah. If he doesn't make it, it will not be because of your effort. You do have a healing touch, maybe one of these days you can actually go back to Tariny and attend that College."

She smiled. "Thank you, Geth'n. I believe I will. But we shall see," she sighed.

"We can't build a fire; there is too much danger of it drawing

273

attention. The other horses had blankets and will be our only shelter for tonight," he informed her.

She took one of the blankets, wrapped up in it and lay down near her patient. Geth'n lay opposite her, rolled softly up next to her and they both were soon asleep.

The last thing Anisah remembered, as the stars peeped through the great treetops above, was the feeling of having done what she had always known she should be doing and knowing she had done well.

Jond'r woke her several times during the night moaning, but soon quieted each time. She made certain his blanket covered him, thankful the weather was good. And it was warm.

Then she would fall asleep again, dreaming about the girl in the meadow with the whirling globe. Each time she awoke, she marveled at how vivid the images seemed to be now and wondered why.

Once, Geth'n woke her, thrashing about. She moved back from him as best she could because he was flailing wildly. His blanket had wrapped around him and he was trying to break free, but his kicking only wrapped the blankets around him even tighter.

Finally Anisah was able to run to him without being kicked, "Geth'n, wake up. You're dreaming. You're caught in your blanket."

He stopped wrestling with the blanket, looked around in a stupor, caught a glimpse of her in the moonlight, and grinned so broadly she couldn't help laughing.

"Are you going to keep me up all night?" she asked. "Here, let me help you get unraveled. Neither of us is going to get any sleep if you continue this."

" Now lay back down and sleep; I'm going to check on Jond'r again and then I'll lay here with you," she told him as she helped him disentangle himself

"I feel I haven't slept at all," he said, his speech not quite clear, "maybe we can get an early start." He lay back down, moved a few times to adjust to the ground, and instantly fell asleep again.

Anisah smiled, shook her head in amusement, walked over to

274

Jond'r and gently inspected his bandages. She made certain he was covered, wrapped her own blanket around herself, lay down between the two men and quickly fell asleep herself.

She dreamed again the dream of old.

She saw herself sitting among the children, letting them play with the Ahar'n that touched each. As it touched them, there was healing, and the children danced and played.

Suddenly a dark force entered her dream. The children began to scream and run away. She looked everywhere for the source but couldn't find it; then the pain shot through her body and her soul.

She couldn't breathe; she struggled to find the Ahar'n but it was lost in the evil that was overwhelming her.

Anisah woke and bolted upright, looking from side to side in her dismay. She was wringing wet from the fear of her dream; she was frightened, reached and jostled Geth'n awake.

Geth'n woke quickly, jumped immediately to their defense holding his staff at ready, looked around the area and saw nothing. He turned to look at Anisah and saw the fear in her eyes even in the darkness.

"It's all right, Anisah. There's nothing," Geth'n said. He saw no reason to chastise his companion for her actions. He too was experiencing certain urgency in his own dreams. Dreams similar to the one he remembered from the days before he left Peetle.

The two sat for the rest of the night, warm air moving the forest about them as they talked, each telling the other of their dreams.

Jond'r occasionally moaned. Anisah would check on him, wash his face with water and return to talk to Geth'n.

They had no more rest that night, and the dawn met them with the first light creeping slowly over the forest and into their small nook.

"We have to move him today and take him to safety," Geth'n advised, pointing at Jond'r.

"Are you certain? I'm afraid he can't ride safely," Anisah said.

Geth'n could see her sense of concern for her patient, her brow wrinkling as she looked at him.

275

"You're right. We have to discover some other way to transport him to move him to safety. I sense there is great danger in this forest; there is something, or someone, here that unsettles me, and maybe you too. What about our dreams last night?" Geth'n responded, a worried look on his face as he once again nervously surveyed the area around them.

"I don't know how to answer your question. I know my dream was altered from all the other times it came to me. In this one there was death and destruction, something horrible was happening and I couldn't stop it by myself," Anisah answered.

She looked at Geth'n, sadness filling her face, and she knew somehow he sensed her fear. He looked away, scanning the area again. He too was beginning to feel, and his dream was confirming that feeling, he and Anisah were on a journey that was intended to not only save their friend, Pet'r, but to save something of even greater value. The consequence of loss for the latter could mean the doom of mankind.

He shook these images from his thoughts, looked around again, turned to Anisah, reached out and drawing her close, hugged her gently.

"We have come this far; we can but know now we have been chosen somehow to follow the paths we take. Only a fortnight ago, we were young and innocent, off on each our own journeys. Now we've strayed far from those original intents and don't understand fully why this is happening to us. Why did Pet'r go on his journey? Was it really curiosity, or was there another purpose? I don't know. Yet . . ," Geth'n spoke gently to her.

Anisah stood, and knowing their destinies now were intertwined, hugged and held tightly to her friend. She also knew what he was saying was true; she knew that absolutely.

"I think we should have a bite to eat before we go anywhere. We should discuss the wisest way to help our new companion," Geth'n added, "he certainly needs that and we should do what we can."

Anisah released her hug, without a word, turned to her bag of supplies and began to pull out some of the food. The bag was almost empty, but plentiful enough for what she thought they needed for the next few days.

After she spread the food out, Geth'n came and sat with her while they talked about their dilemma.

"We really must go on and find out what has happened to Pet'r. I believe something serious has happened to him, or he would have arrived in Tariny days ago," Geth'n started.

"I believe that too and my heart aches because he might be in danger, but we also have committed ourselves to helping this man now," Anisah added, pointing toward Jond'r lying peacefully in the shadows of the trees.

Jond'r's wounds seemed better though Anisah's inspection earlier had shown they were still very inflamed. The bleeding had stopped. And she felt the healing was going well.

"Maybe we should take him back to the town we came through yesterday. I've tried to recall whether I felt any apprehension about being there and I can't remember I did," Geth'n said.

"We weren't there long, but a number of those on the road nodded a friendly greeting to us. The only strange thing about the town was that, after we left, there were no more people traveling the road. Could there be some hidden boundary there?"

"Voravia?" Anisah added, knowing immediately her question answered the question, "but what about Pet'r, how can we not continue our search? We will lose another day if we go back."

"Yes, that ultimately is our biggest problem. We now have two who need our help," Geth'n said, looking at her.

As she started to comment, he interrupted.

"And no, I don't think we should go our separate ways. You are stronger now than ever before but as yet no match for any group who might attack you on the road, so I think you should not continue alone to find Pet'r. You are the one who needs to be with Jond'r, not me," Geth'n injected those thoughts quickly.

"So you think I should take Jond'r back to the village. And what then? Am I to follow where I think you are going, or do I have to find you and Pet'r alone?" Anisah asked.

"Nothing is easy for us now, we have come to that point

277

where we have to make a good decision."

"As much as I hate to say this, I believe both of us have to return Jond'r to the village," Geth'n said, after sitting for a while thinking through their dilemma.

"Let's assume Pet'r is not as yet in great danger. I have not felt anything from him that would indicate he feels he is, and I know he would want us to help this man," Anisah agreed. She ached to know the real answers about Pet'r, but she also felt she knew him well enough to make that statement about him.

"Oh, Geth'n. I miss Pet'r and am so afraid for him, but I too have not sensed he has come to any harm. This man, this stranger, is here, helpless, and we know he needs our help. As much as I am worried about Pet'r, I think you're right."

"Let's not waste any more time then. I believe we can transport Jond'r to safety without too much pain or harm to his wounds. There must be some way for us to arrange for his care until we return," Geth'n added, rising from his seat, "let's get ready as quickly as we can." He walked away toward the horses.

"I'll see to Jond'r and prepare him for the trip as best I can," Anisah added, as she began to gather her medicines and herbs into her bag.

She walked to Jond'r. She took more of the bands of cloth from the skirting material, wrapped them around his body, pulling tightly but not pressing too strongly.

She then wrapped his arms to his side for the extra support that afforded. She knew the move was going to be terribly hard on Jond'r and was making every effort to reduce any harm done.

She looked up and saw Geth'n walking back. She reached under Jond'r's head to wrap more bindings around his head where the wounds had crossed and cut through.

Geth'n bent down to help her.

"What ya doing there?" Someone shouted from behind them. Anisah almost dropped the soldier's head. Geth'n stood and spun around, his staff raised.

An old man with a great shock of hair and one eye that squinted through the afternoon haze at them, stood, bow drawn, the arrow pointed straight at Geth'n's heart.

"Are ya gonna rob that poor soldier? Is that what your about?" his voice crackled with age, but Geth'n could tell there was strength in the man and didn't move.

Anisah was the first to answer, still kneeling, holding the soldier closely. "No, we are trying to help him. Are you here to rob us?" She returned defiantly.

"No, I don't think so, Missy. I live just through those trees there, not far. I noticed the birds circling," he squinted and looked above the trees where several of the birds were flocking to feed. "So I came over to see what was about."

The old man lowered his bow slowly still watching Geth'n closely as he did.

"Missy, you two came bustin' through those bushes so quickly last night I thought you must be bandits robbing the bodies of these poor souls. And I wasn't gonna let that happen to this one, especially since I think he's still breathin'."

"He is. But we have to do something and soon," Anisah responded before the old man had finished, "we've talked long enough. Can you help us?"

Geth'n lowered his hand on his staff, the old man tensed a bit, but Geth'n moved the staff from one hand to the other and reached down to touch Anisah on the shoulder to let her know where he was.

"We must get him to more shelter. Will you help, sir?" Anisah pleaded.

The old man smiled a crooked smile and answered her softly, "I surely can, Missy. I was gonna do what I could myself, but you two scared me off before I could start. I was gonna take this one to my cabin. I'm afraid the others above," he motioned with his bow hand, waving it about now, relaxed, "are either dead or they're gonna be soon."

"So this one is the only one we can try to save. Have ya got the healing powers, Missy?" he cocked his head a little to one side; still squinting, his face twisted in a grimace from the effort.

"Yes, I do. We know those above indeed have died, so let's save this one, if we're able," she answered.

Geth'n turned to look into her eyes and gave her a reassuring

279

smile.

"I can help but we must get him to safety and more water so I can clean his wounds better," she added.

"We'll need the horses," Geth'n offered, silent until that moment. His attention was locked on the old man, trying to decide what he had to do to get them out of danger.

Now he felt the danger had passed, he began to relax.

"I'll get a couple from above" he added, nodded to the old man, turned and pushed his way back through the undergrowth, following the path he had plowed with his staff, and disappeared into the woods beyond.

"And who are you, sir?" Anisah asked, trying to turn the soldier so he could lay straight on the ground. She shaded his pale face from the sun and, using one of the rags, applied some water to his face. He moaned slightly from the gentle shock of the cooler water but remained unconscious.

"Borny'a, Missy. Name's Borny'a. And yours might be?" he asked now standing over them, providing shade so Anisah could attend to the cleaning without worrying about the sun.

"Anisah. And my companion is Geth'n. We've come here to find a friend and only chanced on this terrible thing," she answered while ministering gently. Geth'n arrived at that moment with the horses.

"We need to lift him onto the horse, but gently," Geth'n suggested, "but I think the movement will do more harm than good."

"I believe I got an answer," Borny'a suggested. He turned and walked toward the underbrush, "come on, boy. Let's cut some of these saplings and make a carriage."

Geth'n ran to help the old man who had picked up the soldier's sword as he walked toward the brush.

"This seems to be a good blade. Let's see." Borny'a took a swing and severed three or four saplings with ease.

"You take those and strip the branches. I'll bring a few more," he told Geth'n, raised the sword and sliced through the defenseless growth.

Geth'n did as instructed and was waiting for the old man to

arrive with the more saplings. "Glad to meet you young people today, this was goin' to be real hard for an old man like me. But come on, let's make a traveling bed for our wounded boy."

He began to shape the saplings and intertwine them into a narrow lattice form leaving the outer poles longer than the others. He pulled out a twist of leather hanging from his belt, tied the cross sections of the travois tightly. Finally he stood and admired his handiwork.

"Let's go get our fellow and take him to my cabin now. You grab the other end," Borny'a added, picking up one end, waited for Geth'n to follow. They strode over to the wounded man's side and placed the carriage beside him.

"Now, Missy. We should put this fellow on this as gentle as possible. Geth'n, you take the blanket off that horse, " he said, nodding his head in the direction of the horses," and spread it over this bed we've made."

Geth'n walked over to one the horses, removed the saddle and blanket, walked back and spread the blanket over the travois.

"So we've come to the hardest part, at least for this young fellow. We gotta move him." Borny'a added, "and, Missy, whilst Geth'n here and me hold this in the air you should lead that other horse up behind Geth'n there and run a tie down from pole to pole and tie it over the horse real tight."

Anisah lowered the man's head gently from her lap. She started to stand but her legs had stiffened from her cramped position, but she rose, with difficulty, and went to the horse.

Geth'n and Borny'a held the wounded man by his shoulders and by his knees, nodded to time their lift, raised the man from the ground and placed him as gently as they could on the carriage bed.

The man groaned loudly with the effort and his eyes opened briefly, staring into the sunlight, but he fell into unconsciousness again. Geth'n and Borny'a raised the travois onto their shoulders.

Anisah walked to one of the horses, led it between the poles and stopped just behind Borny'a. She took a length of rope that was tied to the saddle, laced it around one of the poles then threw the other end over the saddle, and walked around the horse.

Pulling on the rope from the other side she raised the opposite bar to the height she thought right, looped the line around the saddle horn several times, then around the pole several more and tied it tightly.

Borny'a stepped out from under his end of the travois, retrieved another of the horses, walked it to the front of the travois. With Borny'a and Geth'n holding each pole, Anisah coaxed the animal to back between the poles and tied that end off.

Geth'n stepped out from under the rig, stood back, and admired the handiwork of the other two.

"Well done," he said, "let's not tarry. We need to get him to a place where he can rest and heal."

Anisah busied herself collecting the injured man's belongings after the last lashing of the carriage, retrieved the water they had remaining, and trussed all into a great pack and heaved it over another horse and tied it in place.

All this reminded her of what seemed a long ago time when she had escaped Old Sumt'r, and she smiled thinking how strange that episode in her life was, and how much stranger it all was now.

They left the place of death behind. They decided burying the other men served no purpose and such an act might reveal their presence.

The danger they sensed was enough to justify not performing an act they felt in their hearts they should. But they left, pushing those thoughts from their minds.

SOLACE

Borny'a led the way through the forest into his valley over a narrow path that wasn't too steep.

Geth'n followed closely, leading the forward horse of the carriage assembly, and Anisah followed holding the rein of the horse packed with the baggage items.

They trekked for several miles without incident; only once did the rear horse of the travois move about roughly.

Anisah dropped the reins of her horse. It stopped immediately and she ran forward and held the animal's muzzle; stroking it until the animal quieted. Soon they broke from the wooded area and followed the path down the trail beside a quiet stream bubbling with clear water.

The horses wanted to stop for a drink, but both Geth'n and Anisah held tightly to the reins – there was still a need to finish this trip for Jond'r's sake. They continued to travel quietly and avoided any problems the rest of the trip. Finally they reached a small cabin nestled in the edge of the forest.

"Well, it ain't much, but its home," Borny'a said as he dismounted. Anisah was glad to see they had finally arrived. She had been looking of the countryside, relishing the beauty of the forest from the view coming down from the hills.

It's sad we have to accept we will need to fight to save our homeland. Why is there such a hate of one individual that our world has to suffer and be destroyed? And Anisah, why does that person have to be your grandfather?

They tied the horses and removed the travois gently from their backs. Geth'n and Borny'a took the wounded man, still on the carriage, into the cabin and set it gently onto the floor.

Anisah scurried about, grabbing some bedding materials Borny'a pointed out and made a small, but thick, pallet on a cot near the fireplace. Geth'n and Borny'a then gently raised the soldier from the travois and lowered him onto the bed.

Anisah began to cut away the clothing from Jond'r's upper body. Geth'n then helped her turned the Jond'r over onto his stomach so she could work with the wounds.

There was some bleeding caused by the trip down from the hills, but the herbal poultice compresses Anisah had concocted in haste and bound around the man's back on the trail were intact and had proven to be very effective.

It would take a while to cleanse the great gash across the man's back, but she could already tell none of the major blood vessels was severed. The healing process would probably be successful, but the man's muscles would take a miracle to heal properly. Massive muscle tissues were hacked and the damaged, possibly beyond repair.

Anisah sat and cried for Jond'r while she softly cleaned away the blood and dirt. She searched in her small medical pouch, trying to remember some of the advice that Mistress Elspeth had given her, and mixed some different herbs in a small bowl she found near to the fireplace.

Borny'a had stirred the coals, brought the small fire up with some small dry sticks of wood, and heated more water from the stream outside. Geth'n took the horses downstream to a large lake, covering most of the valley floor, and let them water.

He returned shortly. He and Borny'a sat and talked quietly. The air outside became a bit too cold so they soon went back inside and found Anisah had finished what she could and was cleaning the area around the Jond'r's wounds to make certain all would stay dry.

"I have done what I can. Borny'a. You are a good man. I thank you for what you've done today," she talked softly with tears running down her cheeks, held the old man's hands in hers and tiptoed to give him a kiss on the cheek.

"Well, Missy, I believe I was only the helper here. You seemed to have done the job up right, far as I can tell," Borny'a answered, his face a little flush with embarrassment, but he smiled broadly with the attention.

Anisah turned to Geth'n.

"Should we stay another day tomorrow, or should we go on?"

She was almost imploring him to agree to stay.

"I believe waiting another day probably would be the wisest thing to do. This man will survive this, but only by your hand, I believe. And Anisah, your own dreams are coming truer than you ever thought," Geth'n answered, realizing what she meant.

He smiled at his friend, put his arm around her shoulder, and squeezed her gently with affection. Borny'a agreed with them. So they stayed the night, both needing the rest themselves. They traveled at a rapid pace for several days previously and with excitement of finding Jond'r and the effort to rescue him, both were exhausted.

Geth'n lay down on another cot near the door and quickly fell into a deep sleep after only a moment.

But Anisah couldn't and rose frequently to minister to the wounded soldier. Once Jond'r awoke briefly, looked her in the eyes, searched the room for her, smiled at her , spoke only his name, "Jond'r", and softly returned to sleep. She felt much better afterward, feeling the man was healing properly and was able to rest more easily.

The next day and night proved uneventful. It was obvious the Jond'r's wounds would take a long time to heal.

On the third day, Geth'n mentioned to Anisah he thought they should be moving on. They still had Pet'r to worry about. Anisah stood over the soldier sleeping peacefully now, looked at Geth'n and nodded her head.

"Yes, we do need to go." She nodded her agreement.

"Borny'a, if you will, please give him a small spoon of this broth I prepared. Warm it a little so he can swallow without strangling and as often as he wants, once he's awake. Don't try to change the dressing until he tries to move. He shouldn't get up too quickly but let him decide." "You probably couldn't stop him anyway, but try to persuade him. You are a wonderful man for doing this for him, a complete stranger. And I believe he is also a good man so he should cooperate, if you admonish him as the gentleman I think you are," Anisah was giving some advice, some gratitude, and some admiration for Borny'a.

The old man, of course, blushed again at all the praise.

"I'll do just that, Missy. Don't you worry none. He'll be just fine. And I'll tell him about you two and what you did for him. But, if you're plannin' on continuing toward the north, be wary. You are about to enter Voravia's lands and she's not polite to strangers.

Her men, or creatures, or whatever they are, have never bothered me here though I don't know why. But those things are dangerous, be sure ya stay sheltered in the night," Borny'a advised.

"We've three horses here, Borny'a, and you should have them all, but Anisah and I have important business to for our friend. We need to borrow two of them to hasten our own journey."

"Take them all if need be, young fellow,"My small world provides for everything I need," Borny'a pointed toward the house as he spoke. "These animals are not of much use to me. But the soldier there. He probably will want to be on his way when he's able. So, I'll keep this one that was standing by him when he lay dying so he'll have a way to travel."

They rose early and prepared two of the horses for their journey. Borny'a shook Geth'n's hand and held Anisah's hand gently in his rough hands for a moment. Finally it was time for the search for Pet'r to continue.

"Come, Anisah. We need to go," Geth'n said, picked up his staff, walked to one of the horses and placed it through the loops on the saddle.

"By the way, don't fret over those two men on the road. If the animals haven't taken them away, rest their souls, I'll give them a decent burial."

"You are a good man, sir. I find you a most honorable man, a rare occurrence these days, and I'm pleased I met you," Geth'n added, reaching out and shaking the man's hand again. Anisah gave Borny'a another kiss on the cheek, and he blushed again.

"Maybe Jond'r can find and thank you some day. Who knows? Life has played stranger tricks," Borny'a called after Geth'n and Anisah as they led their horses back up the path they used to get to this peaceful place.

When they reached the edge of the forest, Anisah stopped,

286

turned and felt uneasy about leaving.

But she looked down at the kind old man and the little cabin with a light stream of smoke trailing from the chimney, smiled though she knew he couldn't see her, and waved her hand high in the air so he could see it.

She saw him return the wave, turned back to the path and followed Geth'n into the deep shadows of the trees.

GUARDIAN REBORN

Pet'r entered the canyon in the early morning, the sun hadn't reached this passage and darkness still ruled. He slowed now to only a fast walk as he slipped into the darkness and began to feel his way with his feet as he walked.

He didn't slow his pace because he couldn't see, the path seemed clear to him and he never faltered.

Once he came upon the site of what must have been a terrible fight, lying all around were men killed by a mighty sword, there may have been as many as dozen, or more.

Pet'r didn't delay his pace to observe the scene, he just noted someone, and he thought it was probably Rab'k, wrought the disaster there.

Pet'r knew Rab'k was to be an enemy. He didn't know why and when, but he knew it was to be, just as he knew Rab'k's whereabouts at that moment.

He sensed Rab'k leaving the encampment in the desert on horseback, traveling quickly in his direction. Pet'r didn't really concern himself with the information; something else was controlling his thoughts and actions. Something seemed to pulse with his heart and made him forge ahead more quickly.

He burst through the canyon narrows, but he was only aware of the urgency he felt. Strangely, he thought of his friends, Geth'n and Anisah, as he pushed himself into even greater haste and began running again. He knew they too were on a journey in search of him.

There was a moment when he felt he could talk to Geth'n over the miles, but he realized he had a more important object-ive today.

As he traveled, he began to feel somehow he recognized this place, it seemed he was here before. But more clearly, Pet'r knew he hadn't.

The sun rose above him now. He passed the great peaks at the summit and descended into the 'flatlands'. He was soon about halfway down the mountain and had traveled through the night at a relentless pace.

Suddenly he knew to turn to the west. He could see no clear passage in that direction, so he leaped on top of a large boulder, near the road, some six times the height of a man to see farther into the region; a leap no common man could have made so easily.

Through the gorges below him, he sensed a pattern. No, he knew there was pattern and he felt he'd traveled it before. Beyond the gorges, there was a small plateau shimmering with an aura rising above it as though, in time, something was to happen there but Pet'r didn't know what, nor cared at the moment.

Now obsessed with his journey, he jumped from the boulder and immediately into the gorges. He wasn't being cautious, nor making any attempt to conceal his passing. He plunged into the twisting and winding canyons, weaving his way without concern.

After pushing onward for about half of the journey, he felt another presence.

Voravia? Has she sensed me so quickly? Possibly our first meeting gave her impetus to always be aware of the signals I know I am projecting; perhaps she is receiving some help.

Geth'n, Geth'n, are you coming? Anisah, I have thought of you so often since we parted, you too?

He hadn't sensed Rab'k as yet but he was certain to be south of the mountains soon. Pet'r increased his pace dramatically. He traveled as quickly as any man could have and more. No mortal could have maintained this for so long, but, at this moment, Pet'r was something much more.

He suddenly stopped, checked about him for the familiar, saw what he needed, walked to a wall, spoke an incantation from a deeper memory, and stood quietly, waiting.

There was a loud creaking from the face of the bluff; the ground trembled as though stirred by some quake deep within the earth's bowels. Then almost quietly, the face of the bluff began to slide away as though it was silently disappearing.

Pet'r stepped through the opening, and the great wall closed noisily behind him. The outer face returned to its previous appearance, and there was no way for others to know there was a cavern behind.

The size of the chamber was overwhelming, the ceilings reached to cathedral pinnacles, a small sparkling stream ran across the center clearing, glowing stones provided a low light. There were no sounds but those from the stream trickling lightly as its waters passed.

Beyond the stream, there was a small alcove carved into the cavern wall. The recess seemed natural. On closer inspection, changes were evident. Its purpose seemed obvious. There was a glow emanating from the opening, shimmering as though light reflected from rippling water.

Pet'r had been here before with Kalbr'an. He waded through the stream slowly to disturb the stones as little as possible, stepped onto the far bank and walked slowly to the alcove.

He turned the corner and met a sudden surge of intense light only he, and the gods, could have endured.

Pet'r suddenly felt at home. Warmed by the glow surrounding him, he bathed in the luxuriant wonder he felt as the light tenderly embraced him. The hours passed and he wished to stay in this place forever. The old world was no longer with him. He found a oneness with the overwhelming sensations he felt, this wonderful embodiment of all that was good.

He couldn't sense who he was; he couldn't sense what there was. There was no then or now; there was no why nor how.

And there was only peace.

HIDDEN FOREVER

There often comes a time in the lives of those who are friends to determine where their allegiance lies.

There are often great surprises in the lives of each of these instances, but often the matter of friendship is ever more tightly wound through trust and concern for the other.

It is rare to find true friendship existing among men. We, of those who watch, have often seen such a function between men as shallow and pretentious.

Our story follows two young friends who have become more adventurous than possibly they should be, but for such a cause as there now is, these great and dangerous efforts are inevitable.

These two have seen the results of evil. They wish for nothing more, nor less, than to stop what they each foresee, even if only in their dreams, shall come to pass if nothing is done.

So they followed the allusive path to find their friend and the Ahar'n and hope it can bring to an end this thing they both now fear.

Let us see what they've discovered as we watch . . .

It took them only a short time to reach the old road though they came out at a different place than the one from which Borny'a led them . They dismounted to rest the horses after the long climb up from the valley. Geth'n, deciding they should protect both of the men in the valley below, scouted toward the north a short way and found an alternate route to the top of the ridge.

"Just over that ridge," he said quietly as he pointed above them, "was where we were two days ago. I think if we follow this old road, we'll probably make better time and should be a great deal safer than if we use the new road."

With that, he swung into the saddle and Anisah followed, mounting quickly after swinging her pouch up and hooking it over the horn. It felt good to be back in the saddle again. Geth'n looked around to see if she was ready, she nodded to him and they began their journey toward the north again.

They had traveled for several hours not talking, unless they needed to choose a direction, when they noticed an increase in bird activity overhead.

Remembering Borny'a's comments about that pattern, Geth'n raised his hand and Anisah halted. He eased himself to the ground and walked toward the small clearing ahead.

At the edge, he cautiously stepped forward and surveyed the area. It was quiet; too quiet. He motioned to Anisah to come closer. She walked to the edge of the clearing and almost cringed.

"There's something wrong here. I sense it. I can't see anything unusual but this is another place of death, you can almost taste it," she said, turning away.

"You're right. Something definitely is wrong. I get a sense men have died here too, just as those with our injured soldier. But, if this is true, where are the bodies, the weapons, the horses. Where is anything you'd expect?" Geth'n asked, thinking there was too much mystery.

He knitted his brow, still looking about for some signs to confirm their suspicions. They left the horses at the edge of the clearing while they walked about.

He walked slowly to the center of the area, carefully looking around, anticipating a surprise attack. Anisah, resisting an overwhelming urge to run, walked by his side, investigating the ground and their near surroundings.

Suddenly, she reached out her hand and touched Geth'n to stop him. On the ground, a few feet away, lay a human hand. A little further on, there was what appeared to be a helmet, again they saw an arrow protruding from the ground.

They circled slowly. Geth'n ever watchful while Anisah made a small inventory of the other small items. All this indicated some sort of massacre had occurred here. But there was nothing more substantial to prove anything, just those few things. And there was the sense of imminent danger.

After a moment, they looked at each other and nodding their

agreement of a need to leave began to back their way toward the edge of the clearing and the horses.

Anisah turned and scoured the path back for danger; Geth'n, backing toward her, watched the clearing.

They reached the horses, climbed into the saddles quietly, backed the horses into the shadows, turned quietly and walk back into the forest before they stopped.

"There was a horrible slaughter here," Anisah whispered to Geth'n, "many men may have lost their lives. But where are they? Where are the trappings of such a group? Where have all those things disappeared?" She looked all around her, her eyes wider in fear of this thing that had no explanation.

Geth'n answered quietly, as though he might disturb something he didn't understand. But he had an idea.

"I believe there was a battle here, but I also think Voravia's creatures, as Borny'a called them, have come and scavenged practically all the remains. We don't know what manner of beings these are though I suspect they're not quite human anymore.

They've taken it all away -- horses, men, clothing, weapons and anything else laying about. Undoubtedly, all of the people were slaughtered and there was no one to defend them. It's a horrible fate and I hope I'm wrong. Maybe there were some who survived and they have taken the others to safety and to secure their wounded. But I fear that isn't true."

Anisah, still looking about, turned to him, nodded and motioned she thought they should leave. Geth'n turned his horse back the way they had come to retrace some of their steps. Anisah followed without speaking.

They soon reached the old road and noticed it was bending more toward the northwest. They decided to continue follow the route and broke into a fast canter to cover ground more quickly.

They rode hard, resting the horses near streams they saw by the road, but continued with deliberation. They were beginning to worry more about Pet'r and their haste emphasized their concerns.

293

Soon Geth'n noticed the mountains rising above the trees and decided they should begin to use more caution. It was certain Voravia's men would be watching the land more closely near her castle; they assumed it wasn't too far away.

Anisah and Geth'n knew from their experiences they would need to be extremely careful about when and how they traveled. It was midday and they felt it would be folly to travel during the daylight hours now, so they decided to wait for nightfall.

They sat and talked about a plan, but they really didn't have one. So they mostly waited impatiently for the day to end.

Just after twilight, they noticed lights moving along the ridge of a nearby hillside. There were about ten torches wavering through the night and then, at one point, there was a brief stoppage in the movement and each light disappeared until all were gone.

Anisah and Geth'n made no movement toward the spot but each tried to remember dim landmarks to help find the entrance later.

They kept themselves hidden and waited quietly, making certain no other group of creatures was passing their way.

"There has to be a cave," Geth'n finally whispered to Anisah, "probably an entrance to caverns under the castle. Those may have been Voravia's people returning for the day. Maybe the ones who scavenged the scene of death we saw today. Come, let's go find this cave."

"I'm ready," Anisah said softly.

Geth'n rose from their hiding place, looked about the area, and walked slowly toward the place where the lights had disappeared. Anisah followed closely. They didn't want to get separated so she was keeping Geth'n's back clearly in sight especially as it got darker.

They crept along, avoiding open spaces, using the trees to hide, and carefully approached the spot where they thought the cave entrance was hidden. They stopped when they thought they had reached it, but could find nothing indicating there was an cave.

"Where is it?" Anisah whispered harshly, frustrated they

couldn't detect the entrance, "I know it's close. I can sense it almost, but I can't tell where it is."

"Me neither," Geth'n answered softly.

Just as he finished speaking, they heard sounds from down the path of others talking among themselves.

"Up here. Quickly!" Geth'n reached down, grabbed a rock from the ground and tossed it down the hill in the direction from which they had just come, grabbed Anisah's hand and pulled her up the hill.

Scrambling up several yards, they flattened themselves against the ground behind some low lying bushes, covering their faces to limit the contrast with their surroundings and the dark.

"Wha wuz dat noise?" one of the group shouted. The whole group scrambled toward the spot where Geth'n and Anisah had just been standing and, holding their torches high, began searching for the source of the noise.

The creatures were jostling and pushing each other trying to find something in the dark; it hadn't occurred to them there might be something, or someone, moving in any other direction. Finally they quieted and began to organize themselves again.

"Wuz nuthin. Wuz animal. We go. Now!"

The one talking walked to a boulder nestled into the hillside. He waved his torch in an arch over his head, struck the rock twice with a pole he was carrying in his other hand, stepped back several steps.

Geth'n raised his head enough to watch. The boulder slowly sank into the hillside; dust puffed about in the torchlight, soon the group of creatures began disappearing into the hole hidden by the boulder.

When they had all entered, the last threw the torch he was carrying to the ground; the torch threw sparks into the night air but then only smoldered, a stream of blue smoke rising into the moonlit night.

The boulder pushed outward into the night and came to rest, hiding the entrance. The air was still again, with only the night sounds from the forest below.

After a short wait, Geth'n whispered to Anisah, "I think it's safe now. Let's get back to the path." They rose, dusted themselves off as they worked their way back down onto the path. Geth'n motioned to Anisah to follow him and they walked over to the boulder where Geth'n had seen the creatures disappear.

"What now?" Anisah asked.

Geth'n looked around, spotted the torch the creature had dropped, picked it up and began to blow on the embers.

"What are you doing?" Anisah asked, thinking they needed to remain hidden yet Geth'n was trying to revive a flame that would expose them.

"We have to emulate the entrance procedure used to access the caves," Geth'n said then returned to blowing on the stake. The embers began to glow again and suddenly a small flame, then a larger one, grew from the end.

Geth'n quickly turned to the boulder, waved the flame high over his head twice and struck the boulder with the torch. The boulder began to rumble and move backward into the cave.

"Come, we have to hurry," he said. Grabbing Anisah's hand, he rushed into the opening, pulling her in with him.

As the boulder moved back into position, Geth'n held the torch, which he had wisely kept, over their heads so the light spread out ahead of them exposing the cave and the directions they might go.

"Do you think this will lead us to the passages taking us to Pet'r?" Anisah whispered. They both felt Pet'r was down one of these passages and had no need to discuss whether they should be in these caves, or not.

"I don't know but it seemed a wiser choice than walking up to the castle gate and asking," Geth'n answered her sarcastically, but smiled.

"Fine. Since you're now in charge, do you know the way?" Anisah swatted him lightly with her hand.

"Not really, but then there seems to be only one way offered at present. Let's follow that until we have to decide," Geth'n answered.

He took the lead and began to walk carefully down into the caverns. Anisah stayed close enough to reach out and touch his back, not wanting to get separated.

She occasionally took a quick look behind her to achieve some sense of security, but she couldn't help feeling apprehensive. The cave behind was too dark to see anything and that made her more nervous than if she had known there was something there.

They walked down on a long slope carrying them further into the mountain. Geth'n paused often, listening for other sounds. All they could hear was their own breathing and the sputtering of the flame. The light cast strange and unusual shadows on the cave walls, changing the shapes dramatically as it waved about.

These caves were dug through the hill; the marks of the tools remained vivid. Voravia had apparently ordered these passages built so her creatures could get to all points in her realm and not be exposed. A surprise attack on an enemy was one of the obvious attributes of such an underground system.

"Wait. We have to decide which way to go now."

Geth'n had stopped suddenly. Anisah bumped into him gently before she could stop.

Ahead of them, the cavern split into two passages. Anisah was perplexed by the possibilities. If they chose the wrong one, they could become lost and waste the torch they had and never find Pet'r.

Geth'n paused for a moment, bowed his head slightly, closing his eyes. Anisah realized he was trying to reach out to touch with his mind what he felt was real. He was searching for Pet'r; she could sense his mental probing. She too took up the search.

"This way," Geth'n said raising his head and pointed the torch to the left, "this way to the main caverns under the castle. Pet'r is there." Anisah looked down into the cave Geth'n had pointed out, looked into Geth'n's face, and nodded her head. They walked into the new opening with no doubts about their decision.

After making another similar decision some time later, they arrived at an opening to a larger cavern. They stopped and peered into the great room. No one else was about, so they stepped softly through the portal.

Looking about, they saw several large tables, all randomly covered with a large number of parchments; some opened and lying with their edges curled a bit on the corners; some rolled tightly and tied with leather thong; some flattened with a heavier object on the corner to hold them.

"Someone's been researching these scrolls, it appears," Geth'n spoke, not too loudly but not in a whisper, "I have to wonder for what?"

"What a horrible place. How could anyone choose to live here? It's so huge, cold, and hard. There's no warmth to it," Anisah was looking around the cave in wonder and pity.

"You're right, it certainly wouldn't be called charming unless maybe you were a bat," Geth'n agreed, looking over one of the scrolls lying open on the table.

"In fact I think there may be a few bats in here now." He peered upward into the darkness above them where no light could reach.

"Let's look around a bit and see if we can find anything more interesting than the inhabitants," Anisah turned away from the table with the scrolls. She searched the various chests and smaller hutches she saw sitting at various angles along the many rows of shelves covering the walls of the cave. Most were easily opened and there was very little of importance she could see.

"What exactly are we looking for?" Anisah said from across the cave where she was kneeling in front of an old trunk, raising her head to look in Geth'n's direction.

"A map hopefully, maybe, at the least some directions on how to get through these caverns with some knowledge of where we are going and what to expect," Geth'n answered, not really looking up from the scroll he had pulled into the light to read more thoroughly."

The Ahar'n is somewhere in these mountains. Everything I've ever read confirms that. Unfortunately, we don't have several lifetimes to search for it. More importantly, Pet'r is here somewhere and possibly in danger. We have to find him. We need a bit more help, something that will get us closer."

They shuffled about for a while longer, looking at various

pieces of information, when Geth'n growled, throwing his hands into the air in disgust, "Blast the gods! What we need could be anywhere here, or not at all."

Anisah stood. "It does seem rather hopeless," she said. Propping her hands akimbo, she looked around the enormous chamber. She wandered over to the large table in the center of the room. The table held half eaten bits of food, glasses of stale ale and wine, writing quills, ink pots, parchment, and more great books and scrolls.

Behind her there was a great shelf full of scrolls and other documents, covered in dust; the shelves hugged the wall of the cave and turned a corner into the shadows beyond.

Anisah moved into the new area, apprehensive because of the darkness, but searching for anything to help them find Pet'r.

She noticed, in the dim light, a scroll partly crushed beneath some loosely stacked books, pulled it out gently, unrolled it, and tried to press the corners down so she could read the bold strokes across its face.

"Geth'n! Look! This thing is huge. I haven't seen another one as large," Anisah yelled.

She rolled the canvas and lifted it, carrying to the table, grunting from the effort. Once there, she began straightening it, holding the scroll in place on the table with one hand, she swept some of the trash away with the other, finally spread it across the table and held each corner flat by placing books on them.

"Geth'n, you need to see this," she called out to him. He came around into the area and walked to the table to look at this new find and help position it to be read. In a moment, the scroll was spread out almost the entire length of the table. They had to move other scrolls, books and the remains of the food and drink off the table to have enough space.

They stood staring at the writings for a moment when Geth'n began to laugh.

"You'd think I would know better," he scolded himself.

Walking around to the opposite side of the table, he gazed only a moment more at the scroll.

"I think you've found something that provides us with many

299

of the answers we need." He looked up and grinned at her, "and it was just laying here all the time we, and others, have rooted around looking for these messages."

Anisah ran around to Geth'n's side of the table, stood back a bit from the giant scroll and realized she was looking at a map.

"It must be a map of these caverns. You can see here are the mountains," he added as he pointed to a ripple drawing, with a name they couldn't read written above it, "and this must be the great mountain range cutting across the whole continent just north of here."

"And these," he reached and touched different spots on the map, "must be the entrances to various caves permeating these mountains all along its base. This is all very simple, but the caverns and tunnels are defined in much greater detail than the other smaller maps."

He ran his hand along one of the passages. The line crossed through the dark indicators for openings into the caverns and weaved its way in a singular direction though it crossed many other lines slicing their way back and forth across the map.

"Is this going to help us find Pet'r, or your Ahar'n?" Anisah had turned away, leaning on the table out of Geth'n's way, looking at all the openings leading into this room alone. "There are so many passages. Can you understand the map, or what is written on it?"

"Yes, I can. Or, at least, most of it. Here, see here, is a passage referring to a crystal cave inside these mountains," Geth'n explained, tapping the map to show what he saw, "and here there is another reference to an even greater cavern buried far beneath the great desert to the west beyond the mountains."

"And it's noted a gathering of immortals met to form this world," he reached, pulling the map around so he might touch another portion. "And over here is a cave, the 'Cave of Areb'l', it has a magically sealed entrance no one but the Guardian of the Ahar'n and the Esfer'n can access. It must be where the Ahar'n is.

"And here then," he pointed to another area, "all these passages lead to the west and seem to converge and then seem to

300

be sealed."

"Who are the Esfer'n? And who is the Guardian?" Anisah asked, turning as she watched Geth'n's hand sweeping across the map as he explained the important elements to her.

"I don't know. But here it talks about the Crystal Cave -- meeting place of the immortals," he pointed to an enormous cavern near the bottom of the map.

Geth'n's hand was sliding quickly over the map now, searching for distinguishing marks, stopping on another mark.

"I think we are here. This entrance we just came down goes to here," he moved his hand quickly to what was definitely a portal to the outside, "and if I move my hand laterally, I see by going through this passage," he stopped, looked around one portion of the room and pointed, "we should be able to gain access to Voravia's castle without much trouble.

There are many references to the Ahar'n and to another stone, but no answer to what, or where, they are. Did the wizards, or the Esfer'n, or the Guardian find these stones and divine their uses; did they make it for some magical purpose; or is there some other hidden meaning yet to be discovered about the Ahar'n and the other stone?

I haven't read about the other stone in any documents I have researched, but it must have similar presence in our myths and legends. Now there is more I don't know about these stones and their purpose," Geth'n continued, puzzling over these new mysteries.

"Quite a lot of questions, young man. Do you think the answers will help you at all?" Geth'n and Anisah both jumped in surprise, whirled about looking for the source of the deep voice disturbing the quiet.

"Thank you for finding something I need. You've been a great help," a tall man stepped from the shadows near the entrance they used.

"Well, hello again, I believe we've met before. You and your friend on the road to Varspree, I think. It's a pity I don't see your friend here with you; he and I have a few things to discuss. It might be you won't recognize him now. I venture he isn't the same as he was," he added as he walked slowly toward them, a contemptuous smile on his face.

Geth'n and Anisah instinctively backed away from the intruder and away from the table. Geth'n casually picked up an old knife lying with the refuse and slid it inside his sleeve.

The man walked over, touched the map without picking it up, turned back to look at them, "However, despite your helpfulness, I fear you two are more nuisance than I need, so I must tell you I must be rid of you."

"Who are you?" Anisah asked, standing very close to Geth'n. Geth'n had, behind her back, slid the knife from his sleeve and was clasping the grip tightly.

The man looked at Anisah, eyelids drooping as he peered from under heavy eyebrows, dropped his eyes to look at the map again, without answering.

"Kings, queens, and learned men have been searching for this map for centuries and yet it took two innocents to stumble across it. Quite remarkable, I must give you credit. It's the least I can do, literally. By the way, I think you would be wise, young man, to put down the knife. You will certainly have no chance to use it," he talked to them quietly, as though they should not be alarmed their lives were being threatened.

"Rab'k," the man said suddenly, looking up from his investigation of the map, "that's my name. Executor to, and of, Lord Garv'n – rest his soul.

But I'm no longer interested in talking. I think we'll just be done with you, and I'll be on my way."

Rab'k began to move around the end of the table toward them. Geth'n pushed Anisah behind him and brandished the knife though uncertain what good it was going to do.

"Anisah, run. Run, Anisah!" Geth'n suddenly shouted and threw the knife at Rab'k. Rab'k raised one of his arms, covered in armor, and the knife glanced away harmlessly.

With his other hand he grabbed Anisah by her arm, as she tried to run by him. But Anisah was able to twist out of Rab'k's grasp and started running across the cavern. Geth'n turned, saw what direction Anisah was running, started to follow, but was grabbed harshly by his shoulder, pulled back, his arms clamped to his side, and lifted from the ground.

Meanwhile Anisah, running as quickly as she could across the floor, turned to look back for Geth'n, saw he was captured. She hesitated, turning back with intent to help him. Abruptly, she was knocked backwards as she walked into one of the creatures just stepping from the mouth of another cave. She screamed, stumbled back trying to regain her balance, and screamed even more loudly when the creature reached and grabbed her about her shoulders and lifted her off her feet.

Several more creatures rushed around their companion into the cave, but came to a halt at the sight of Rab'k. There was a sullen stillness in the cave; the sound of breathing could be heard in hushed tones echoing from the lost ceiling above.

The creatures were rocking back and forth. Some were lurching forward then scampering back to a former stance unwillingly to risk any attack. Some just stood and stared and seemed to be waiting for something to happen.

Suddenly pandemonium erupted, Anisah began screaming and kicking; she was striking her captor as hard as she could. The creature turned his head a bit to avoid being struck in the face but largely ignored his captive. Geth'n yelled at the creature to leave Anisah alone, trying to jerk free of Rab'k's grip. Rab'k bellowed for him to keep still.

All the creatures began to scream and jumped about, banging the cave floor with their clubs, throwing dust into the air, frothing at the mouth in their anticipation of a fight. From out of the cave mouth, another creature appeared and screeched loudly as he pushed his way through the group. The other creatures instantly stopped their aggression but continued to shout and cower, rocking back and forth on their feet again, waiting.

This new one walked boldly toward Rab'k, stopping only a few feet from him.

"You!" he shouted at Rab'k, seemingly with great courage but obviously cowering as he spoke. He shook his staff at Rab'k, menacing, but all at a safe distance.

"My mistress, she say wez not kil vou," he hissed through his twisted mouth, "she wants talk at you." The little leader strutted about, haughty and cocky.

Rab'k lowered Geth'n to the floor. "Don't move," he told Geth'n.

"Little man, I am not afraid of you nor your motley crew here," he waved his hand to indicate the group of creatures. The little leader flinched when Rab'k's hand came near him. Rab'k smiled but showed no other sign he noticed.

"But I am here to meet with your mistress, so if you wish to lead then I am willing to follow. These two we will take with us; they were rummaging through these papers. It seems they made a discovery she might be interested in. Tie them and we'll leave."

The leader shrugged, glared at Rab'k, turned slowly toward his group watching Rab'k closely as he did.

"You!" he pointed at one of the other creatures. Brings rope. Tie he and she," he shouted, indicating Geth'n and Anisah.

They were quickly bound with their hands in front of them; a line wrapped around their necks and knotted with the line being held by one of the creatures.

"You hold tight," the little leader warned the holder. Turning back to face Rab'k, he shouted, "Wez go!" He marched away toward one of the exits without looking back.

Rab'k watched the procession leave the cave, looked around the cavern noting all the documents lying about, thinking about what he was taught and wondering what these young people had uncovered. He smiled to himself as he left the cavern.

Wonder what I might do to catch Voravia's attention?

They traveled through the darkened caves with only the light from the torches wavering along the cave walls.

Anisah and Geth'n, the rope about their necks chaffing them, were yanked along, stumbling and bumping against the walls and trying not to fall for fear of being dragged. Rab'k came along behind walking quietly, knowing this meeting with Voravia was to be an important step in his future.

Soon they arrived below the castle and climbed the long stairs up into the chambers above. Geth'n tried to make certain Anisah was safe, following as closely behind her as he could, in case she fell.

When they finally stopped, the little leader pointed down a long hallway below vaulted ceilings. Anisah and Geth'n stumbled to keep afoot, stumbling into Voravia's large private chambers. Rab'k followed them.

The chamber was empty when they entered. Rab'k motioned for the creatures to take Geth'n and Anisah near the windowed side of the room.

"Tie them to the table there," Rab'k commanded quietly, pointing.

The little leader stopped, frowning at Rab'k and at his people who were going to follow Rab'k's order, walked quickly to the edge of the table holding a length of rope and shouted.

"Bring they here. Yous vill hang from win'ow by rope. Mistress will be pleased."

Suddenly Rab'k moved swiftly and without hesitation.

Rab'k was at the little leader's side before the other could turn to look at him. He grabbed him about his neck with his massive hand. There was only small sound, a brief squeak, from the being. Rab'k opened the window with his other hand and threw the creature into the air. Its screams could be heard for some time, but then were silenced.

Rab'k turned back to the couple tied, waiting.

"Put them up on the table," he ordered. Some of the creatures moved quickly, with fear in their eyes, and did what they were told. Anisah and Geth'n were hoisted into the air and now stood on top of the table, afraid to move. Rab'k looked up toward the ceiling, sighted a great beam traversing the space above.

"Throw a line over that beam. For each one. Tie up their hands and lift them over their heads," he commanded, pointing upward to the beam.

The creatures, with their leader's fate still fresh in their feeble minds, were moving more quickly than before and soon completed Rab'k's orders. Geth'n and Anisah soon stood with their toes barely touching the table; the ropes held their arms stretched above their heads.

"This should be an interesting surprise for your mistress," Rab'k chuckled. He looked around at the beings standing about, waiting.

"Now leave before I throw all of you away." He pointed at the window and laughed. The creatures began to back quickly toward the door, pushing each other and then panicked and rushed the door, shoving the weaker aside as they scrambled for safety. The room quickly emptied.

Rab'k sat and waited.

Geth'n managed to turn about and face Rab'k.

"What are doing to us? You are not acting like the man I met on the road, the one who help my friend and I escape from the thieves," Geth'n was shouting at Rab'k, who was barely attentive or offered any recognition Geth'n was speaking. "There is no need to treat us like this, we've done nothing wrong."

Rab'k looked around at Geth'n. "I have no need to explain myself to you. But it is all quite simple. I am the same man but I now have a different quest since I have dealt with the first. But now I also know what you are, whether you do or not."

"What are talking about? Who do you think we are?" Geth'n couldn't believe this man was acting in such a cruel manner. "We are looking for a friend? We thought he might be here," he offered.

"You search for the Ahar'n. It does exist, my young friend, despite your limited knowledge of it. I also believe you would have become much different than you are had you found it, or your friend had brought it to you. Then you would have become a formidable foe."

Rab'k answered deliberately, "It is therefore necessary you be destroyed, and the girl faces the same fate."

BORNY'A

Borny'a noticed the movement on the hill beyond the lake early that morning.

Probably just the herd moving down for water.

He watched for a while, then went back to his chores. Later, he stood, stretching his back from bending over his work for so long, and again saw the movement. Much closer now and more rhythmic than he would expect from a herd of wilants.

"Could be a hunting party," he grunted, left his work laying on the ground and moved to the cabin. He paused by the door but moved quietly inside. He looked out of the window on the lake side and watched, standing back in the shadows.

"Nope, movement is too direct. They're not chasing anything." He reached for his bow, a sturdy and unusually formed weapon. Borny'a had traveled in his youth; this weapon came from far across the Southern Welnon Sea.

He moved to the side of the man lying on one of his cots; reached down and pressing his hand to man's forehead, checked the warmth.

"Still runnin' a fever. I'll be back shortly," he mumbled, as though the man could understand.

He positioned the bow on one of its tips, placed his leg over the bow, bent the bow over his knee, stringing it quickly. He reached and clutched several arrows from a back quiver hanging near the door. Walking out of the cabin, he moved to the edge of the forest just above the lake shore, and slid into a position where he could see the approaching group when they cleared the trees. He determined the group had to be human, or, at least, human-like.

He was always aware of his circumstance. He realized he lived in a dangerous zone; there were unusual man-like creatures all about, If he saw one, or many, coming from the direction of Voravia's vast district, he was always caution and watchful.

As the group walked out onto the bank of the lake with the leader cautiously looking about for danger and for anyone coming from the cabin, he recognized them as Voravia's creatures. But strangely they didn't seem to be assuming any warlike stance, but rather only took precautions to avoid being surprised if they were attacked. The front scout, not noticing Borny'a standing nearby, motioned for the others to step forward. They crept around the lake, obviously headed for the cabin.

Two of them were carrying something in a large sling. With the human-like arm sticking out the end, it was obviously a body hung beneath the poles on the two beings' shoulders.

They hesitated a moment; the scout motioned for them to lower the sling. They did so without thought, merely dropping the poles and body. There was a groan from the canvas. Borny'a waited a moment to see what they planned next. The scout motioned and mumbled something to the rest, turned and begin to walk slowly toward the cabin.

Borny'a drew back the arrow he'd retrieved earlier and stepped out of the trees for a clearer path to the intruders. He yelled loudly for them to stop. The scout turned, bringing up his crude weapon as he did and threw it at Borny'a. Borny'a easily dodged the feeble effort and released his arrow; the man dropped where he stood. While the rest ran over to the dead scout, Borny'a reloaded, holding another arrow in his teeth, assuming another would be needed. But another of the band suddenly became the new leader of the motley group; he threw up both hands and the others followed his example. They bunched together, shaking their heads and motioning violently with their hands outstretched, trying, he thought, to discourage any battle. He relaxed his draw and waited a moment.

The new leader pointed to the body they were carrying. "Wes not be fightin'. Wes want trad' with old mens." He said pointing at Borny'a.

What do they think I have to trade? Or why would I want that body?

"Who is that?" Borny'a asked, nodding at the body laying on the ground.

"Wes not knows. Bigs fight at two valleys away." answered the spokesman, pointing toward the north area.

That's close to where we found Jond'r. Wonder if there's a connection.

Borny'a only stared at the speaker. He hadn't lowered his bow. The pause lasted longer than Borny'a expected. He was getting tired of being cautious; these men, or whatever they were, didn't seem inclined to attack him.

"What do you want – in trade?" he yelled at the new leader.

"Wes wants – needs – foods?" He gestured toward the others who stood staring at Borny'a, nodding their heads and looking between him and the leader slowly.

The leader waved his arms about while mumbling a few other things Borny'a couldn't understand, though the name Voravia was evident. Then the speaker's hands dropped to his side. He waited and dumbly stared at Borny'a. Borny'a relaxed a bit more, allowing the tension to ease from his arms and shoulders. He let the arrow slide forward but held everything at ready.

"Who is this?"

"Wes not know. Wuz battle with soljers, all die, 'cept him. Man moved when to take stuff." He pointed toward the sling, another moan eased from the bundle.

Borny'a knew the sound, pain.

"What do you want?" he asked again.

"Foods!" the leader shouted. He looked at Borny'a as though he'd made himself clear earlier.

"Okay, Okay. Name?" Borny'a raised the bow slightly, but not enough to arouse the being.

It took a moment but the other responded, "Is Gratz." He pointed at his chest, then as before, dropped his hand and stared vacantly at Borny'a.

"Let's look at what I have." Borny'a nodded then pointed, with the up cleat of his bow, toward the outbuilding where he kept his stores.

It was well hidden, buried in the side of the hill, beneath an overhanging Funelis tree.

"But caution." Borny'a warned.

Gratz bowed his head in submission. Borny'a walked sideways keeping the group in sight and watched them very closely. He was willing to try this exchange, more out of curiosity then need, but there was no reason to be stupid. The pack followed him. Gratz made a special attempt to avoid the dead scout, grunting and speaking to the body with disgust.

"Whas is yous tinkng, ful?" He flung his arm about, pointedly toward the body, as he passed, irritated.

Borny'a noted this but said nothing. He kept a safe distance between himself and the group, watching them as they mutely followed. He had positioned himself so the he was almost backing toward his storage area now.

When they reached the area, Borny'a pulled the tree limbs back and pointed at Gratz to open the door, using the point of the arrow to indicate what he wanted.

The being looked toward where he pointed, back at Borny'a once, then walked toward the door, snatching it open as he grasped the handle.

Gratz eyes widened. He saw more food than he could have imagined. He reached for the closest haunch of a wilant buck.

Borny'a reached and stopped him, "No! No. Not yet."

"I'll have to inspect your trade," he said, pointing toward the bundle and started walking toward the place the travois was dropped.

Gratz's face wrinkled and he looked back at the food locker as they walked away, but he followed. When Borny'a reached the bundle on the ground, he moved the poles aside but tried to move them slowly. He was a veteran of many battles and felt certain he was going to see a reminder of those times when he opened the blanket folded around the body.

He grasped a corner and raised it enough to determine the man inside was still alive. He noticed the wound cutting across the shoulder and the side of the man's neck, but more surprisingly, he was surprised by the clothing.

Refined landowner. What's he doing in this forest? I've not seen someone this fancy up here in too many years. And how did he get this knife slash across his shoulder? Who would have the nerve to do something like that?

He lowered the cloth and turned to Gratz who was standing quietly behind him. He stood to talk to the being.

"Where'd you find him?" he asked. Gratz looked at him a moment without moving then began to talk rapidly.

"Likes I say, the two valley. Wes searching bodies for good tings and draggin' away. Hez cry outs when pick hims up." Gratz stood motionless, only looking at the sling with blank eyes.

"Gursz thinks good thought to bring here. Now he deads." He looked over where the scout lay.

Borny'a just nodded. Looked back at the sling covering the body.

"Deal done. Let's get your food." He starting walking toward his locker. "But, I'll not have you coming back for more, nor to steal from me." he added, as he approached the opened door. "Take one man's supply each, no more." He motioned to them to enter the shed and stood back.

Voravia's beings shuffled into the locker, grabbed what they wanted, or could carry, and quickly left the small building. Then gathered in a small group and stood waiting.

Borny'a, after waiting for the last, shut the door and placed his lock back.

"We have traded fairly. I trust you to honor our bargain. If not, you each will pay for your mistake." He held the bow higher.

The group gazed at the bow a moment, turned away toward the forest, then back to look at Borny'a with just a glance, turned and walked away carrying their goods with them, then slowly disappear into the forest.

Probably have to move the rest. Can't trust them.

He turned and went to the sling on the ground. Squatting down he began to remove the material covering the man.

"Lot of blood lost. Big man, suppose I'll have to drag him," He grabbed the corners of the material and began pulling the man toward the cottage.

"Let me help," a voice spoke from behind Borny'a. He dropped the blanket, jumped across the wounded man, snatched the knife from its scabbard, turned in the air and landed facing the source of the voice.

It was Jond'r. Standing weakly, but standing, looking at

311

Borny'a, who lowered his knife and reseated it into his scabbard.

"What're ya doing out of bed, boy?" Borny'a blurted out. He ran around to the Jond'r's side, putting his arm around the younger man's waist to steady him, said. "Ya might open your wounds being out here. What possessed ya to come out."

Jond'r held his arm out; his sword was held firmly. "Seems you needed a little backup." He pointed toward the exit where Voravia's beings had disappeared. "I'll admit I only have a little to give, but here I am." He slumped a bit against Borny'a.

"Let's just get ya back to bed, young fellow. Then we can talk," Borny'a added, tilting his head back toward the cabin.

"I know this man," Jond'r said, with surprise. "It's Garv'n Anspar of Tariny. He was my master." He slumped a little more. "All right, but you need to lie down. Missy will skim me alive if ya get hurt again."

Borny'a began to lead the younger man back inside the cabin and helped him back into his bed.

"I'll take care of this," he nodded toward the man on the ground. "Later, you and me can talk. Just sleep right now."

"Right," Jond'r wearily answered and almost instantly fell to sleep.

Garv'n? Borny'a shook his head. "Things just got more and more mysterious."

He walked back outside to drag the other man into the cabin and with some effort managed it, laying the body on the floor to clean the wounds. He removed the clothing, disposing of them, cleaned the wound area and decided he would need to stitch it, or it wouldn't heal. After finally getting the wounds taken care of, he lifted the man onto the other bed, covered him and stood looking at him for a few minutes longer.

"You are a surprise, sir," He shook his head, turned and walked across the cabin, grabbing some blankets as he found an empty place on the floor by the door.

"Guess ya bumped me outa my bed, too."

He threw the blankets down and pulled out his pipe.

"Have to think on this for a while." Settling down in his favorite chair, he packed the tobacco and lit his pipe. The smoke curled lazily about his head.

"Yep, gotta a lot of thinking to do."

CAPTURED

Abruptly, something changed around him. Something shattered the quiet.

Voravia!

Pet'r reached gently for the Ahar'n, raised it from the pedestal one of his ancestors had carved so lovingly and placed it in a pouch inside his vest. He turned sharply and rushed out of the alcove and into another opening dug long ago for just such an emergency.

Once, he stopped and forged his way through a tumbledown, eroded by time, that allowed flooding of a small cave. He pushed aside the refuge and rushed on.

It was to no avail. Voravia's people had long ago dug larger tunnels through these mountains in search of treasures, great and small, and for traveling throughout her kingdom without being discovered. It was only because of the power of the Ahar'n others never entered the cavern from which Pet'r now fled. Without thinking about it, he had divulged its location. At each turn, Pet'r sensed the men ahead of him and turned down yet another path.

Violently he crashed into groups of these creatures whose only intent was to capture him, he slayed, or disabled, many and still ran more quickly than all others. But, in the end there were too many. For all his new found strengths and his urgency to save the Ahar'n from capture, he could not escape.

Finally overwhelmed by numbers, he stopped fighting. They put him in strong chains and started the journey back to Voravia's castle.

The trip took several hours and when they arrived, he was taken to the depths of the caverns and his chains connected to the wall of one of the cells.

Some time passed before his expected visitor arrived. "Good afternoon, Guardian," Voravia spoke slyly, as she walked to his cell door, "Are you comfortable?"

"As well as could be expected," Pet'r answered, not concerned with the title bestowed, "why have you done this?" He knew the answer but he wanted to hear it from one he must now also consider his enemy.

"You, my friend, are a great mystery. Though the scrolls I have studied stories of your kind, there have been no writings for thousands of years. Where did you come from?" Voravia asked, ignoring his question. "What do you intend to do with your bauble?" She held one of the scrolls in her hand.

Pet'r looked at her askance. "If you've actually read that, I suspect you know what this *bauble* can do. And I can assure you I'll not give it up easily."

Somehow he understood the Ahar'n could not be taken from him; the Ahar'n was protected but it also protected those who wore it. No mortal could kill him to obtain the Ahar'n.

"Perhaps there are some things beyond the value of the Ahar'n with meaning more to you than what you protect so closely. What is the Ahar'n to you anyway?" Voravia retorted, she was watching Pet'r suspiciously.

She witnessed his powers, at their first meeting, when he wasn't aware of them. He possessed more than enough to avoid her attacks then. This man was one to be very wary of and she chose not to take any chances.

The chains holding Pet'r to the wall of the cavern were triply strong. It was believed no man, or beast, could break them and maybe not even the gods. But she was uncertain. The Guardian seemed to be waiting; she was unsure for what and could not perceive the reasons with her strongest sorceress' powers. And, she discovered, she apparently couldn't conceal her thoughts from him. She felt vulnerable. She captured her prisoner as she planned but could do nothing to use him.

"Perhaps, you might let me go, if you are considering anything," Pet'r offered, realizing he was anticipating her thoughts. "The Ahar'n is not in harm's way here, and I need to exercise no effort unless that becomes true. We have something of a stalemate, I believe."

"I'll not let you go until I have the Ahar'n," Voravia spoke through clenched teeth, her own exasperation causing her anger to seethe. "I will have the Ahar'n."

"Then you will have to take it," Pet'r said, so matter-of-factually, it made her even angrier.

She knew it would be fruitless to attack the man; the Ahar'n would protect him. The Ahar'n wasn't going to be handed to her unless there was some other more important reason than existed at this moment for this Guardian to do so. She knew nothing about him except what he had become. She possessed no information about this man nor any of his personal history. It was as though he appeared out of thin air.

Mord came loping up to her and stood without speaking. She was glaring through the great bars of the dungeon cell at Pet'r but caught a glimpse of her servant.

"What! What do you want?" Voravia snapped at Mord, who cowered but didn't flee.

"My mistress, please. Lord Rab'k has arrived and he brought others wif him," Mord answered her. Now she was totally confused.

Rab'k? Rena'x's whelp? What sort of knavery is about now? Damn, this whole business is turning into a nightmare!

"Go away! Why did he say he was here?" Voravia whirled to face her servant now, her eyes glowering at him for interrupting her thoughts and for bringing this stupid news. "What does he want?"

"He say, my lady, he has news frum Baalsa'n, or Ballsu'n, or something liks dat. I did not know who was that, but that his only message," Mord stammered, trying not to forget anything Voravia might conceive as important but not knowing whether he was successful or not.

"He said the name was Baalsa'*n*," *she asked quickly, her eyes suddenly different.* They seem to show shock and alarm. Mord wasn't bright enough to know why the change, but he was glad the angry look was gone,

"Let's go now! You, Guardian. I'll be back and I will have the Ahar'n!" She turned and stomped through the cavern toward the stairs to her chambers.

"I'll wait anxiously for your return, *my lady*," Pet'r shouted after her, unable to contain his sarcasm.

Voravia halted; her shoulders hunched from anger. She stood a moment, staring at the floor, fists clenched, body shuddering. The she threw back her head, hair tossing wildly and strode deliberately to the steps and disappeared. She could hear the man below chuckling to himself and her anger soared.

This Rab'k news had better be incredibly important, or I shall be less yet another idiot manservant.

REVELATION

From the great hallway, an uproar announced the arrival of the castle's mistress. With her entourage, Voravia burst into the room; her underlings following her back into the room.

"Who are you? What are you doing here? Who are these two?" she was shouting at Rab'k. A number of her creatures, heavily armed, entered the room behind her.

"Rab'k, at your service," he gave a terse bow, only lowering his head slightly. He stood and smirked at Voravia.

"The great Lord Rab'k. So you have come at last. Where have you been?" she shouted, walking up to him and staring at him eye to eye. She obviously wasn't afraid of him.

"And what are you doing here?" she snapped, tired of waiting for his answer, "Why do I have to repeat myself?"

"I can tell you're pleased to see me," he laughed, backing away just a bit at the audacity of this woman, sorceress or not.

"I brought you a surprise. Some young captives from your caverns who seem disposed to take a bit of information they thought valuable. Also, I pursued another until I lost him near here. But I came because Rena'x told me I should."

"You idiot. Of course, he told you to come to me. As you probably know, I am technically your sister," she huffed at him, turned sharply and walked to look out her window, still open.

"Who opened this?" she reached and slammed it shut, turning back to attack Rab'k again.

"You fool, we are now near the time when we must began our great war. Where have you been? Chasing some other idiot across the desert and mountains? Why are you wasting so much time?"

Rab'k straightened but casually approached her.

"Because, dear sister -- if that is what you are -- I suspect this person possesses some powers we do not need in our lives. And I was intent on killing him before he could bring us harm," he

318

growled at her.

He pushed his face close to hers, a burning anger showing from his eyes. She reached up her hand, pushed against his chest and walked around him.

"Get out of my face! You have wasted precious time. I have your quarry imprisoned below. I knew he was near. He is dangerous. Also, you haven't performed the task Rena'x told you to – you still don't possess the Ahar'n," she said arrogantly, "and, I repeat, who are these two?"

Anisah, swinging herself about slowly, turned to look at Voravia. Voravia was walking back across the room fuming, but suddenly she stopped and stared at the girl.

"Well, what do we have here?" she said with very subdued tones, turning away from Rab'k for lack of interest and walked to the edge of the table on which Anisah and Geth'n stood.

Anisah's eyes widened at the sight of Voravia; a gasp escaped her.

The dream.

She stared, open mouthed. Voravia circled the table, staring back at her. Voravia begin to smile, then sneered.

Spinning about, Voravia snapped at Rab'k, "Are you so busy being important you have failed to notice who you have as a captive? It seems obvious the girl has noticed something you haven't."

Rab'k turned casually to look at Anisah who couldn't take her eyes off Voravia. He looked back at Voravia, then back at the girl. The resemblance was remarkable; he looked at each again.

"This girl looks like you," Rab'k responded.

"Very good," Voravia hissed at him. "And to what do we owe this visit, young lady?" she turned and spoke to Anisah in a syrupy voice. "It is very gratifying to have family visit occasionally."

"I am not part of your family," Anisah retorted in defiance.

"I believe you are wrong, my dear," Voravia almost shouted. She was becoming irritated with this new turn of events.

She glanced at Geth'n, frowned, "Who is this? Never mind. Kill him."

She flipped her hand in Geth'n's direction and turned to look out the window. Two of her creatures quickly jumped onto the table and, taking the rope from Geth'n's wrist, made a loop in it, dropped it over his head, and tightened it.

"Wait! What are you doing? This is my friend." Anisah shouted at Voravia.

Her voice was suddenly so strong Voravia's men hesitated and loosened the rope a bit. Geth'n gasped for breath.

"I forbid you to do this thing."

Voravia turned slowly, her eyes gleaming with ferocity. "Listen to me, my young niece! You do not command here! You would be dying too were it not for who you are."

"Just who do you think I am?" Anisah quickly responded. She suddenly realized she was not afraid of these people.

"What is your name?" Voravia asked, almost ignoring Anisah's question.

"Anisah!" Anisah shouted again.

"Anisah, how enchanting and lovely a name that is. Be not too dubious, young one, for I believe I know your history very well. Obviously better than you," Voravia spoke sharply, almost hissing. "You see, I believe you are the daughter of our," she explained, pointing at Rab'k, "brother, Mano'n, in fact, our long-lost brother."

"I know nothing of this Mano'n. My father was a good man, a trusted man who could never have been related to the likes of you." Anisah said icily, able now to control her first reactions and openly defy this woman who was making such ludicrous statements.

Geth'n stood on his toes, his neck twisted and his head pushed to one side by the rope. He was trying desperately to snatch breaths, but also to listen to this unbelievable argument between the two women.

Rab'k, his arms folded, stood across the room watching the banter with amusement. He hadn't noticed the girl resembled his family before, partly because he had only seen Voravia once before she came bursting into the room earlier.

He hadn't suddenly acquired any reason to like his sister, especially considering her rude and obnoxious entry into the room --

they shared a common goal, and a father, but at the moment there was no love lost between them -- he found this whole proceeding enlightening as well as humorous.

"That fool could not have been your father. You shall see," Voravia smoldered. Had it not been for the girl's heritage she would have executed her already. "You then, if this is your friend, must stand by him while he dies. Let her down immediately!"

The creatures both released the line holding Anisah aloft; she fell to the table. They bumped against Geth'n while he gasped for breath, reached the line above Anisah, and cut it free. Her arms, still tied at the wrist, dropped in front of her. The two creatures stood looking at her as though expecting her to command them. The resemblance of the two women seemed much too strong to ignore the possibility they were in trouble from either, or both.

"You idiots. Kill him!" Voravia shouted, pointing at Geth'n. They almost leaped across the table they jumped so vigorously, but turned and fought each other for the rope to swing Geth'n over the table. Geth'n's face reddened as he gasped for breath; he grimaced.

"No! No! You can't do this!" Anisah screamed, reaching past the creatures and trying to hold Geth'n up to relieve the pressure.

"I believe we can, my dear," Voravia answered, looking at Rab'k and smiling, "possibly this will be your first lesson of obedience."

She laughed.

FIRST BATTLE

So let us have this first great battle between good and evil. A conflict that will change the face of man, the face of this world, and the face of the universal truths most often no man understands.

More battles must be fought; wars must be won before there can be peace.

The task is long and we gods cannot interfere, at least not directly, until man knows we exist again and until we can assure ourselves we have been cleansed of the evil that weakens our own union.

The young will now have their day. Their first day of pain and salvation can no longer be avoided.

Let us see where we must go next . . .

Pet'r could feel the Ahar'n bouncing gently against his chest as he ran up the stairs and could sense what he was doing was a necessity. He needed to rescue his friends and provide safety for the Ahar'n. His escape was a requirement to do both.

Releasing himself from his bondage required no effort particularly; he simply broke the chains, tore open the cell door and went looking for his friends.

He raced up the staircase he saw Voravia taking earlier, came to a large closed door, threw it open and found his friends being held captive in Voravia's chambers. Geth'n's legs were bound tightly. He was dangling from the rafters by his neck, no longer able to keep contact with the table beneath. Anisah was holding Geth'n's legs trying to lift him and relieve the pressure on his throat.

All in the room turned, except Anisah and Geth'n, when Pet'r burst through the door.

Several of the creatures instinctively attacked him. He rid himself of those pests quickly, throwing them in different directions across the great room.

Voravia expelled a great gasp as he crashed in and she quickly ran to the far corner of the room. At first she felt fear, but during what ensued it was apparent she was regaining her composure and trying to devise some sort of spell to bring this man under control. She shook her head, as though deciding against one of those ideas, trying yet another.

More of the creatures attacked. Rab'k, having recovered from his surprise, joined the fracas. Bodies were flying through the air, not all of which were dead, but certainly not without some damage.

Rab'k came from behind, took a great swing with his sword and was astounded by what happened next.

Pet'r sensed the sword coming at him, paused, raised his arm out of the melee and caught the sword in his outstretched hand.

Rab'k stood for a moment, staring at Pet'r's hand. There was no damage; there was no blood. The sword simply stopped.

Then Rab'k was pulled forward violently. Thinking quickly, he released the sword and flew through the air, landed solidly on his shoulder, rolled and sprang to his feet.

He shook his head roughly from side to side. He could not believe what just happened. He had never experienced being tossed away from a battle like a limp doll. Anger rose in him; he charged back into the fracas, flinging Voravia's creatures aside to get to this man.

Pet'r immediately began to work toward his friends, one of who still hung helplessly. He finally came close enough to them to do something, but he had to rid himself, at least briefly, of this turmoil stirring about him.

He snatched a great curtain from a window nearby, flinging it, encircled the creatures around him and tugging with his great strength threw the entire bundle across to the other side of the room, smashing Rab'k against the wall with it.

He turned then, reached and snapped the rope holding Geth'n aloft. Anisah was staring at him with total disbelief.

Who is this man?

"Pet'r?" she stuttered. Geth'n fell to the floor coughing and sputtering, trying to get his breath. Pet'r turned back to Anisah and tore the bonds from her wrists. Spinning around again, he raised Geth'n from the floor and did the same for her. Anisah

323

reached and held Geth'n while he gasped, holding him up as he struggled.

The creatures meanwhile disentangled themselves, and with fumbling effort, were on the attack again. Others began to arrive from the other areas of the castle.

Pet'r glanced over at Voravia whose smirk told him there were plenty of these beings to expend. He looked toward the door from the stairs, realized there were too many of the monsters streaming from there, turned and saw turrets just outside the great windows.

He pushed his friends to the window, glanced again to assure himself this was to be their escape route, turned and met the next assault.

Rab'k, stunned by the impact of the bundle of creatures smashing into him, was only now recovered enough to join the fray. He was hampered, in many ways, by the swarming bodies. Because of the jumble of beings, he wasn't able to obtain a clear path to the man.

He decided this man was the very one he saw at the thieves' encampment long ago, but much more dangerous. He pushed against the pack, tossing some of the creatures out himself. He couldn't believe the strength of the man. He never knew anyone else who could fight this way, no one had ever bested him so easily.

Pet'r suddenly became aware of Voravia again. She was doing something, he wasn't certain what, hindering his efforts in some way. He couldn't understand but knew he had to change the situation.

Turning sharply despite the constant attacks at his back, he smashed the great window. It exploded outward and rained shards of glass down the castle wall, flying pieces fell to the crevices and porticoes below, and some reached the ground.

The hillside the castle was built on was not far below. The fortress itself was built into the great bluff rising high above the building. This wouldn't normally have been a safe measure, if the castle was intended for warfare. That problem occurred to the designer but was constructed and built on the whims of its new owner, Voravia

Pet'r, once again, threw his attackers off. He grabbed the lines previously holding his friends aloft, threw most of them out the window and tied them safely.

"Leave! Now!" he shouted to Geth'n. Geth'n stood for a moment, not knowing what to do.

"Go! I will follow!" Pet'r shouted at him again. Geth'n jumped into action. He grabbed Anisah, still staring at Pet'r. She looked again at Voravia who presented her earlier with the greatest shock of her young life.

Anisah's world was changing too rapidly for her mind to catch up; she seemed to be sleepwalking through this whole scene.

"Come, Anisah!" Geth'n was yelling at her, pulling her arm. Anisah shook her head to clear her thoughts, jumped up, reached out, grabbed the rope, and slid down it to the ground below while Geth'n watched.

When he knew she was safe, Geth'n ducked back into the room. He spotted the scrolls, reached and snatched them from under the feet of those fighting around him. Anisah stood below waiting and held the rope while Geth'n slid to safety.

It was impractical to try to circle the castle to run toward the south so they headed eastward along the foothills of the mountains towering above them on the left. They didn't know where they were, but they found a narrow path and began to run down it.

Geth'n followed Anisah trying to help her as she stumbled along. He looked back several times, wondering where Pet'r was.

Pet'r occasionally glanced at his friends as they escaped out the window; he was busy holding back this screaming and maniacal horde though throwing them about quite easily.

He became more aware of Voravia's efforts. Voravia was able to conjure a spell she knew instantly was effecting this Guardian. She was intent on destroying him and reaching the Ahar'n, but she wasn't quite able to bring her powers to the concentration needed to do great harm because of the commotion in the room.

Pet'r was weakening somehow and he needed to escape before

the deterioration in his strength became too serious.

Suddenly, a sword crashed down on his shoulder. He staggered from the blow, turned and saw Rab'k raising it to strike again. Pet'r grabbed the closest creature and pulled him between himself and Rab'k as a shield. Rab'k's blow practically severed the being's body completely.

Pet'r threw the lifeless form at Rab'k who flinched, raised his own powerful arm and flipped the carcass away. Pet'r, however, had leaped out of the window and disappeared.

Rab'k ran to the window, saw Pet'r land safely below and begin running after his friends.

"Come, we must catch them!" he shouted to the beings in the room still standing. He ran into the outer hall, raced down the long stairs at the end and out the great front gate with the creatures following him closely.

Voravia went to the window and looked down the path at the young people running away. Rab'k and his band came into view, running after them.

She paused for a moment, looked eastward, and saw what Pet'r noticed the day before.

A plateau, only short miles away, seemed to glow even in the smothered glare of the day. The clouds from the sea raced above the land, darkening but still light-filled.

Strangely the day was bright, though there was no direct sunlight. She knew she must reach the plateau before Pet'r. She wound a spell around herself and disappeared.

"Run! Run!" Pet'r was shouting to his companions scrambling through the rocky paths ahead of him. He looked back and could see Rab'k leading Voravia's creatures. He couldn't determine where Voravia was but sensed she was somewhere near; his decided she was ahead of them.

He halted for a moment, measured the widths and sharp angles of the path just covered, walked behind one of the larger boulders, heaved against it mightily. It began to roll ponderously down the hillside and into the path of those following, effectively blocking the way to the top.

He could hear shouting and cursing from beyond the great

stone as he turned and ran along the path to catch his friends.

"Where are we going?" Anisah gasped as she ran. She was feeling sensations strange to her. She couldn't understand them. Though she was running now, she felt no great fear. There was a different kind of urgency in what they were doing than simple fear. There seemed to be a purpose.

"I don't know. Keep running!" Geth'n answered from behind her. He looked back and saw Pet'r was quickly, catching them.

And Geth'n could feel something changing within him. He sensed a strength he hadn't known before. He knew his movements were becoming smoother, his leaps across the rocks longer, his pace faster and faster.

Ahead, Anisah too was increasing her pace. They were exceeding what was humanly possible. Yet when he looked back, he could see Rab'k also keeping pace though the creatures of Voravia were falling far behind.

More surprisingly, Geth'n could also see Pet'r was quickly catching him.

Where did Pet'r get these powers? This is all beyond belief. What is happening to us all?

He kept running, following Anisah.

They suddenly broke through the boulders, and ran onto a great plateau. The surface was astonishingly smooth, glass-like, glistening in the waning light. Strangely no flashes came from small glints of light striking the surface. The surface seemed indeed to absorb the light, drawing it into somewhere below.

In the center of the plateau stood a column rising from the plateau to the height of two men. On top of it set a small elongated black stone with six evenly cut sides. The whole glowed, as if by its own light, and seemed to draw great energy from the surface on which it sat.

Energy spikes crackled from the crystal and rippled across the mountains, flashing a dark light across the plains spreading southward, thunder reverberated through the canyons beyond.

Geth'n jumped through the last gap between the boulders and stumbled as he stepped onto the deceptive surface below him. Righting himself, he turned, looking for Anisah. She was standing to the left of a column, staring beyond it toward Geth'n's right.

He turned to look and saw Voravia standing, glowering at him and speaking in low tones some incantation he couldn't hear, moving her arms in an arc. A form, or wavering substance, gathered in the air above her. The same aura emanated from the column and surrounded Voravia. Suddenly, Voravia's arms stopped moving. She pointed both of her hands in his direction and he could feel something surging toward him, saw the light slowly traveling across the plateau directly at him. He couldn't move. He was stunned by the beauty of the light, oblivious of what was happening.

"Geth'n, Move away. You're in danger!!" Anisah shouted at him.

Her shout was too late. The full force of the charge of light struck him in the chest. He felt himself being lifted into the air, flying backward faster and faster. He could hear Anisah screaming as he floated away. He could see all of the area below him; it moved away in slow motion.

Anisah ran toward Voravia to tackle her; she could see Pet'r had almost reached the plateau.

Hurry, Pet'r. Anisah's in danger.

His mind beckoned. Geth'n flew away several miles then realized he was falling. Looking down he knew his fall was taking a long time and realized he was slowing as he fell.

How is this possible?

He raised his arms, extending them; his fall began to slow even more and he floated gently to the ground. He stood looking around for a moment, astonished at what just happened.

Did I stop my own fall? I must have; there is no other explanation.

He felt no pain from the attack; he looked at his clothing and realized no harm had come to him. He turned and looked back toward the plateau.

I need to return. I must save Anisah.

Once he completed the thought, he began to rise rapidly into the air, turned and flew back toward the plateau more quickly than he left it.

Pet'r bolted through the boulders, leaping into the air and tumbling on the hard surface. He couldn't see Geth'n, but Anisah was standing to his left, staring at Voravia. Voravia was glowing with an evil light.

Pet'r landed on his feet, grabbed Anisah and dashed into the boulders on the other side of the plateau. Voravia either wasn't able to react, or missed an attack against them, for he felt no sense of anything happening.

"Are you all right? Anisah, answer me. Please," Pet'r held Anisah close to him and whispered in her ear. Her eyes were staring wildly about; she seemed to be in some sort of stupor. Suddenly, her eyes cleared; she turned toward him and smiled.

"I'm fine. She has done nothing to me. I think she won't. But, you and Geth'n are in great danger," Anisah answered him, now looking with a soft tenderness.

He was surprised at the feelings rising inside him when he looked at her face.

"Why wouldn't she harm you as well as Geth'n and I?" he asked her, looking around him. It was too quiet now; he wondered what was happening on the plateau.

"Later. I'll explain later. I think you should go help Geth'n. She threw him into the air, in that direction," Anisah explained, pointing in the direction she saw Geth'n fly away.

Anisah placed her hand on Pet'r's chest, gently pushed him back. A look of surprise crossed her face. Pet'r turned to see what had happened.

Geth'n suddenly rose above the rock parapet, his robes rippling around him. He softly landed on the plateau.

"Woman! Dare you use the powers?" Geth'n shouted at Voravia. You cannot be so stupid to think you can eliminate us. You and the others have plans for this world, but they cannot be allowed to come true. This evil will be stopped now."

Pet'r could hear but couldn't understand. Anisah looked at him with alarm and puzzlement on her face. Geth'n was challenging Voravia.

But how?

Pet'r move to the edge of the plateau though still behind the boulders hiding Anisah and raised his head enough to see over the boulders.

Geth'n, to Pet'r's right, was standing solidly in place; his arms folded across his chest. From this stance, he was looking across and talking to Voravia on the other side. Geth'n was unprotected, was obviously angry, angrier than Pet'r could remember, and was obviously unafraid.

Suddenly a great bolt of the black light rippled from Voravia's direction, striking Geth'n squarely. But just before it reached him, a flash of white shimmering light surrounded Geth'n and the black bolt glanced away harmlessly.

Pet'r looked at his old friend in astonishment.

Have we all become something beyond ourselves? What are we now, who are we?

He turned and looked back at Anisah who jumped up and ran to his side. "What is happening?" she asked him breathlessly, as she peered over his shoulder.

"Geth'n. Geth'n has magical power I never knew," he answered, looking again, planning when he could bolt out and help Geth'n.

At that moment, Rab'k broke through the boulders on the far side and ran onto the plateau, almost bowling Geth'n over as he ran by.

Geth'n didn't step, but drifted backward, avoiding the charge of the other man with only a glance as he passed. Rab'k spun around and prepared to attack again.

Pet'r leaped through the air, struck the man with his own body, sending him flailing and falling to the ground.

Jumping up quickly, Rab'k turned to meet his attacker. Pet'r was already too near for him to do more than try to ward him away. Pet'r smashed Rab'k's head as he passed, dizzying him and causing him to stagger even more.

"No, Voravia. You can't do this!!" Anisah ran out of hiding and was shouting at this woman who claimed to be her aunt. Now though, she was running at her to stop her from harming so many.

There has to be something I can do to stop this.

330

Geth'n saw Anisah coming between himself and Voravia. He glided, floating laterally to his right, passing the column between himself and Voravia and diverted her attention from Anisah's approach.

He raised one arms, hand extended, and released a surge of white light. Voravia turned her attention to this attack and blocked the light away. Her face openly showed her surprise at Geth'n's new abilities, this man had power beyond any she had ever encounter. He may be as strong as Mano'n.

She jumped softly from the ledge, gliding to the surface below, watching Geth'n intently as she moved. He made no attempt to attack her again.

Suddenly Anisah interrupted the scene, knocking Voravia sideways. Anisah had boldly attacked when Voravia's attention turned to Geth'n. Voravia staggered and slammed against a boulder, reached down to clasp the girl by her shoulders. She threw her backwards through the air and back onto the gleaming surface of the plateau.

Anisah slid for several feet before slamming into a wall of boulders. She lay limp.

Voravia turned her attention back to Geth'n but discovered he had disappeared. Rab'k jumped up, shaking his head to clear away the dizziness and saw Pet'r attacking again. This time he stepped backward slightly, knelt on one knee and struck the other man solidly in his stomach. Pet'r seemed to hang there in suspension for a moment before spinning away, staggering backwards across the plateau.

Rab'k, thinking he now had an advantage, rushed to the advantage. But Pet'r straightened, stepped sideways and continuing to turn, slammed his elbow and forearm into Rab'k's back. Rab'k fell forward, catching his fall by reaching out and grabbing the column.

He felt a violent surge pass through his body. He instantly realized he had more strength than before.

"Come, boy. Let's engage and stop this dallying," Rab'k snarled at Pet'r, beckoning him to attack.

"There may be many more days we must do this. I am in no

hurry," Pet'r answered, his eyes flaring and a white aura circling around him.

"Let us see!" Rab'k blared out, rushing the other with blurring speed; a black shimmer surrounded him as though a shadow passed around the man. They smashed together. The new magic shields protecting them, sliding away from each and quickly turned to the attack again.

Geth'n floated down from above Voravia and just behind her. She was moving slowly toward the column, trying to find Geth'n but avoiding the great brawl Rab'k and Pet'r were having.

Anisah still lay where she had fallen.

Voravia turned to look at her there and noticed movement behind her. She whirled about and came face to face with this new and imposing adversary.

He's only a boy, only a boy!

Geth'n bowed to her, a mocking expression on his face. "It seems some things have changed," he spoke to her almost slyly, reached out his hand slowly, so slowly it seemed to Voravia she could move away, but she couldn't. He touched her almost gently and she dropped to her knees with the pain surging through her body.

"You must not continue this. You will destroy our world," Geth'n spoke to her, staring directly into her eyes. "I cannot allow that to happen."

"You can't stop it now, fool!" she spat back at him, jerked herself upright, stood and backed away several paces.

She felt her energy returning and prepared to destroy this idiot when Anisah stepped between them.

"No, please. This must stop. We need to try to heal the wounds of the land, not create them. Please, both of you stop!" Anisah pleaded, looking from one to the other, separating them with her supplications.

"There is no resolution, only death to this world!" Voravia stepped further back, bumping against the column as she did.

She reacted to the touch; her face began to glow with the changes in her power. She raised her face to the sky as though in passion, closing her eyes in her sense of power. She dropped

332

her gaze back to the girl.

"And, you, my niece, shall be a means to the destruction!"

She leaped sideways swiftly, clearing a way to attack Geth'n without harming the girl, flashed a bolt toward him. Anisah stepped into the path of the flash, staggered from the impact, stood stunned for a moment, then shook her head, and smiled.

"Maybe, aunt, I will be able to make my own choices about the outcome of this whole affair," she retorted, defiance in her eyes as she glared at the other woman.

"When the time comes, young lady, you will not be able to resist the strength of our obsession!" Voravia shouted back at her, but was truly surprised the girl withstood the attack.

"And I say I will not!" Anisah shouted back.

Geth'n stepped forward, pushing Anisah behind him. "There will be an end, an end for the good. You and yours will not be able to overcome," he spoke to Voravia.

He had no desire to destroy this woman though he knew instinctively he might be making a mistake. Pet'r grabbed Rab'k, whirled quickly, sending the man twirling across the floor and into the column again. He followed with a great rush to end the fight. Rab'k stood until the last moment, and then stepped aside suddenly. Pet'r was unprepared for the movement, rushed headlong, and crashed into the column.

Suddenly, the clouds above stilled; suffocation of sound and movement enveloped the space surrounding the column. A great plume reached downward from the sky toward the black crystal resting atop the column, as though drawn into a fissure. A great rushing sound hummed through the stillness; a sound increasing to a crescendo heard around the globe. As the skies folded inward, a vast shudder passed through the column. Then a flash of light — both dark and white — spread outward and into the sky above them.

Then nothing. With a silent departure, the plateau emptied.

The black crystal and all of those who participated in the first battle in a long war, only now declared, vanished.

The End

NEXT INSTALLMENT

THE YOUNG SHALL ENDURE
The Aerolan Saga: Book 2

(Coming Soon – Mid-2012)

Anisah, Geth'n and Pet'r begin to sense, and use, their own powers as more and more problems occur around them.

Geth'n discovers a new friend. Anisah and Pet'r still worry about their relationship.

The town of Roahan becomes the focal area for the young defenders, and their allies.

Sadness enters the fray with early, and serious losses, for them. Pet'r is injured, some questions about immortality answered.

THE AUTHORS

Both authors have tried to work and become authors, but then a great number of people have done that. And, of course, we now know how difficult that is. It's taken us over 10 years to get this all together and time has indeed marched along during those years.

Larry is a transplanted Floridian having lived here for about 25 years. He owned a bookstore in the 1980's and then traveled around the country as a computer (Unix) software consultant.- still calling Florida "home".

He got to see a lot of this beautiful country, but always thought of Florida as his home.

Jennifer is "native born" Floridian having lived here almost all her life. Well, there are some minor exceptions, but mostly she loves her home and long ago decided she'd just as soon stay here.

I asked her – "over 10 years ago" - if she'd like to help with "growing this book", and she jumped right in.

Both of us did a bit then, and put in another effort later, until it all came together. The typing was the worst – it takes a heck of a long time to type a 300-400 page book.

We're proud of our efforts and hope you enjoy the result.

Thanks for coming by.